CASSIE EDWARDS

THE SAVAGE
S E R I E S

**Winner Of The *Romantic Times*
Lifetime Achievement Award For Best Indian Series!**

**"Cassie Edwards writes action-packed sexy reads!
Romance fans will be more than satisfied!"**
—*Romantic Times*

SURRENDERING HEART

"Have you not longed to be with Silver Arrow as I have longed to be with you? Is it not my presence that you are enjoying over all else that you have spoken aloud?"

Silver Arrow leaned closer to Yvonne's lips. "Speak to me of that which has not breathed across your lips," he said. "Tell me what is in your heart that makes your eyes look so dreamily into mine. Tell me what has caused your pulse to race so."

He cuddled her closer to his powerful chest. "Did you not know that I could tell the rate of your heartbeat by the way your pulse beats in the vein of your beautiful neck?" he asked softly. "White Swan, it beats even faster as I hold you this close in my arms."

SAVAGE PASSIONS

CASSIE EDWARDS

LEISURE BOOKS **NEW YORK CITY**

A LEISURE BOOK®

February 1996

Published by

Dorchester Publishing Co., Inc.
276 Fifth Avenue
New York, NY 10001

Printed in the United States of America.

With love, I warmly dedicate *Savage Passions* to my friend Darla Jo LeBaron; also to my big brother Fred Cline and his wife Sally; also to my dear friends Lee and Bill Bell and the cast and crew of their shows *The Young And The Restless* and *The Bold And The Beautiful.*

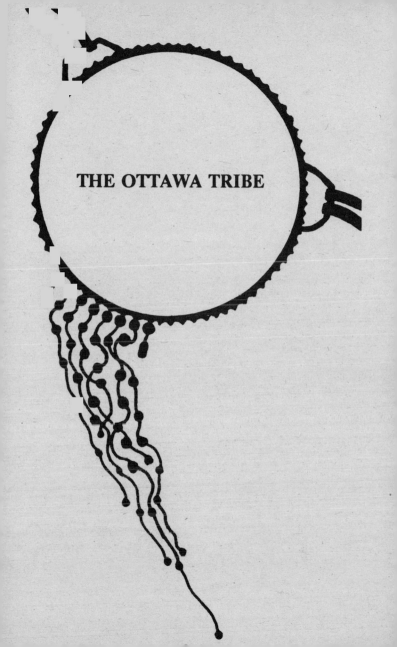

THE OTTAWA TRIBE

Chapter One

Michigan—1840
June—The Month of the Strawberry Moon

Dense stands of trees blanketed the country in lush, green foliage. Wild cherries glowed carmine in the woods. Surrounded by this beauty, a log cabin stood nestled within a thick growth of willows. The *Mi-zhe-gam*, Grand River, flowed like a silver band across the land only a short distance away.

Her face pink from the heat of the wood-burning cookstove, Yvonne Armistead patiently pitted a bowl of fresh-picked cherries. Her pie dough was rolled out and spread neatly in two pie pans for the cherry pies she was making for her family.

11

She was anxious to be outside today, in touch with nature. She always enjoyed feeling the warmth of the sun. She always loved watching the ever-changing face of the landscape where the waters ran, winds blew, trees waved, and clouds moved.

Yvonne's thoughts were wrenched elsewhere when she heard the sound of gunfire ricocheting through the forest outside the cabin. The muscles in her jaw clenched and her lips pursed in a hard, thin line.

"No, not again," she groaned.

She looked angrily toward the open door when the gunfire spattered again like firecrackers popping on the Fourth of July.

Wiping her hands on her apron, Yvonne rushed out the door and across the shaded yard. She knew she would not have to go far to find her stepbrother. She never would understand why he found such pleasure in shooting at the crow that frequented their cabin. The bird intrigued Yvonne. It was so friendly it seemed almost human.

But because it was a crow, which her stepbrother saw as a pest, he was determined to kill it.

Remembering the times when the crow had suddenly turned on Jake, Yvonne smiled smugly. As though the crow had the human ability to think and weigh out in its mind who was and who was not its enemy, it had begun to purposely taunt Jake. Yvonne had seen it fly low over her stepbrother, flap its wings close to his face, then

12

fly out of range just in time not to get shot.

Yvonne's smile faded. One day the crow might not be quick enough. Jake would take delight in killing the lovely bird whose eyes seemed always to be watching Yvonne, as though it *were* a person.

Hearing more gunfire now only a few yards away, Yvonne grimaced. Lifting the hem of her dress, she ran onward until she stood face-to-face with her stepbrother.

Her eyes sparkling with anger, Yvonne knocked Jake's rifle from his hand, then slapped him across the face. "You are wicked as sin!" she declared. "Why can't you leave the bird alone? It's wrong to be shooting at *any* bird just for the fun of it."

She took an unsteady step back from Jake when she saw his nasty glower. His eyes were two points of fire as he slowly ran a hand over his cheek.

When Yvonne heard a fluttering of wings at her side, she turned her eyes toward the crow. It landed on the low limb of a tree a short distance away. Again her eyes locked with the bird's. A tremor ran across her flesh when she saw how it peered at her, as though it were trying to communicate something to her.

A moment later she watched its wings spread as it flew away, high into the trees.

"You dumb wench," Jake growled, grabbing her by the wrist. "Don't you ever lay a hand on me again. And don't fuss at me no more over shooting at that crow. It's only a damn bird,

Yvonne. I'm using it as target practice."

"Why can't you listen to reason?" she said, wrenching her wrist free. "What possesses you to be so cruel, Jake? Your father is such a holy man. How can you be so different?"

She stared at him. He had been a mystery to her ever since the day she became a part of his family when her mother married Rev. Anthony Stockton, Jake's father.

How *could* Jake be so different from his Methodist preacher father? she wondered. Even Jake's appearance was undesirable. He never cared about what he wore. Today, as usual, he was attired in a ragged deerskin jacket worn over a shirt he refused to let her wash. His breeches were soiled and torn from living more in the forest, amidst the briars, than at home where he belonged.

His brown eyes always seemed filled with the devil. He had not shaved for many weeks now, and his scraggly blond beard covered his face.

When Jake bent to pick up his rifle, Yvonne's eyes followed his movements, then shifted to his boots. His hand-tooled Mexican boots, a gift from his father last Christmas, were now scuffed and worn.

"Yvonne, your place is in the kitchen, not out here bossing me around," Jake said.

He rested his rifle in the crook of his arm as he straightened to his six-foot height. He gazed down at her. Even in her plain cotton frock, and with flour smudges on her cheeks, he found her beautiful. Her chestnut hair was long and flowing, her cheeks round and dimpled, and her hazel eyes were tantalizingly large. She was petite, yet she had filled out quite well at her bosom.

But what he did not like about her was her feistiness. As far as Jake was concerned, she was always too quick to speak her mind.

Yes, at eighteen, she was a willful thing; a handful for any man who might come along and take her as a wife. Her stubborn, outspoken ways made her hard to handle even as a sister.

"Jake . . ." Yvonne said when she saw a softer look in his eyes. She was beginning to feel guilty for having slapped him. Although her stepfather had told her many times what had changed Jake, she still tried hard to understand what drove him; what made him so different from his father.

"Don't *Jake* me," he spat out. "And, by God, Yvonne, hear me well when I tell you not to slap me again." He flailed his free hand in the air, showing his frustration. "Just stay out of my way," he said thickly. "Stop interfering in my life."

At that moment Anthony Stockton hurried out of the cabin in his preacher-black suit and tie, his gold-rimmed eyeglasses perched on his hawk nose. He looked uneasily from Yvonne to Jake, then grabbed Jake's rifle. "I don't need to ask what happened here," he said, his voice and his dark eyes showing his disappointment in his son. "I heard the gunfire I heard the heated words "

Anthony watched the crow as it swept down from the upper limbs of the tree, flew past, and then disappeared into the thickness of the forest.

Anthony looked slowly at Jake again. "You just

can't leave it be, can you?" he said, his voice tense. "Why are you determined to take that crow's life? Why?"

"What good does that bird do anybody?" Jake said, eyeing his rifle. He started to reach for it, then hesitated when his father glared at him. "Father, I need target practice. The bird makes a perfect target."

"Tin cans would suffice," Anthony said, sighing heavily. He nodded toward the cabin. "Son, go to your room. Stay there and think about what you are doing with your life. Think about the way you are treating your sister. She has more than earned your respect, son. Why, Jake, she does everything for you a mother should do. You should be ashamed at how you treat her. Do you hear? Ashamed."

Yvonne stood by, listening to Anthony scolding Jake, and feeling uncomfortable being there. Although everything Anthony said to Jake was true, she did not want to fuel the fire of Jake's resentment toward her. She was well aware that Anthony treated her as if she were a princess.

Since her mother's death, Anthony had acted as though he had a debt to pay Yvonne . . . as though he blamed himself for the death.

In truth, no one was to blame.

Not even the child who was born to Yvonne's mother on the very day she died.

Yes, Yvonne had another brother, a half brother whom she adored. Stanley was another reason for Jake to resent life.

Yet Yvonne felt that Jake carried a chip on his

shoulder for no good reason at all. He was not treated with less respect and love than Yvonne or her half brother Stanley. It was Jake who took no pride in himself. He always ignored his father's orders about finding his niche in life. His father had always hoped that Jake would go into the ministry. Instead, Jake schemed to find the gold that an Ottawa chief had buried long ago. He always bragged that once he found it, he would live a life of luxury, alone.

He also enjoyed trapping. He often bragged to Yvonne about the many pelts he sold at the local trading post. Yvonne knew that Jake spoke hardly at all to his father about the traps that were used to catch the animals. Jake hid them well from his father, saying that he had heard enough of his father's sermons against the use of traps to last him a lifetime.

More than once, Anthony had tried to explain Jake's behavior to Yvonne. He had told her that Jake's personality had changed when his mother died. As Anthony had explained to Yvonne, a bear had mauled Jake's mother to death right before the boy's eyes when he was only six.

Jake had held himself responsible, even though he had not even been old enough to carry or know how to use a firearm. All that Jake knew was that he had not been able to save his mother's life. He lived with that knowledge day and night. He carried the weight of his mother's death on his shoulders and found life cruel for having taken his mother from him.

Yvonne was drawn from her thoughts when

Jake leaned down into her face, glowered, then stormed away.

"I'm sorry, Yvonne," Anthony said. He took her gently by an elbow and steered her back toward the cabin. "I can't seem to talk or pray the devil out of my son. I had so badly wanted to start our lives fresh here in our new home in Michigan."

"Please don't let Jake spoil things for you," Yvonne said. "You are working miracles here. The children in the school you started are so blessed to have you."

And she felt equally blessed. Every day she saw why her mother had married this gentle, sweet man, after having lived the life of a widow for too long.

Yvonne missed her mother, but she had never resented young Stanley, her half brother. In fact, she had become her younger brother's mother in virtually every sense of the word.

As they stepped up on the porch, six-year-old Stanley came out of the cabin, sobbing. "Jake called me a four-eyed sissy," he cried, flinging himself against Yvonne's legs and hugging her.

Yvonne knelt and returned her younger brother's hug. "Sweetie, please pay no attention to what Jake says," she murmured. She stroked her fingers through his shoulder-length blond hair, brushing it away from his small face and thick-lensed glasses. "He carries much anger inside his heart. He just seems to have to release that anger from time to time on someone. You must not take it personally. You see, just moments ago, Jake and I had words. He took his anger at me out on you."

"He's not nice," Stanley sobbed. "He's *mean*."

"You mustn't cry," Yvonne said, gently gripping Stanley's frail shoulders. She held him away from her so that their eyes could meet.

With a thumb, she smoothed his tears away, noting the pallor of his cheeks. "Now, now," she murmured. "Isn't that better? You don't want the other boys at school seeing your eyes all red and swollen from crying."

Everyone had eaten breakfast at daybreak. Stanley had gone to his room to dress for school while Yvonne had begun making the pies.

Because of the time she'd lost arguing with Jake, she would have to hurry now. She knew that she would have to finish the pies later if she was going to get Stanley to school on time.

"We'd better leave for school now, Stanley," Yvonne said. "I'll get your books. You go and get the horse and buggy for me."

She stopped at the door and smiled at her younger brother. "Your first year of school," she said, sighing. "And it's one week into the school session. Stanley, your whole life lies ahead of you. What a future you will have! I doubt I have ever met such a smart child as you."

She made it a point to encourage Stanley as often as possible; she knew that most children poked fun at him for his frailties. As usual, her words of encouragement made him beam.

"I won't be long," he said, turning to run toward the barn.

Anthony followed Yvonne into the house. He stood with his back to the roaring fire in the fireplace as he watched her gather up Stanley's books. "You are so good for the child," he said, clasping his hands behind him. "You have missed your calling. You should be a teacher."

Yvonne grimaced at the words. As she placed Stanley's books on the kitchen table, she gave Anthony a weak smile. She realized by the stricken look on his face that he was suddenly aware of having said something to remind her of an affliction she usually tried to forget. She had never been able to learn to read.

She had given up long ago trying to make sense of letters that often seemed reversed to her. The problem was something left unspoken between herself and her father, the only other person who was aware of her affliction.

"I'm sorry, hon," Anthony murmured, gathering her into his arms. "I never meant to—"

"I know," she murmured, clinging.

She slipped from his arms and untied her apron. Blowing a loose strand of hair back from her eyes, she laid the apron across the back of a chair.

"Anyhow, I much prefer being a homemaker," she said, laughing softly. "I don't think I would much like standing before a classroom of children all day, hoping that I was reaching them with my teachings. When I make pies and bread, I only have a few to please. Not many."

"And one day you shall be using those skills on someone other than brothers and a father," he said, wiping the smudges of flour from her cheeks with his fingers. "There will be a certain man that will sweep you off your feet. And I imagine it will happen soon. You have developed into a beautiful woman, Yvonne."

Yvonne's thoughts filled with images of a certain man, the handsome Ottawa Indian chief with whom her father had made a fast alliance. Unfortunately, she had only seen him from a distance.

Thus far, her father had not included her in his journeys to the Ottawa Indian village where he met often with Chief Silver Arrow, to strengthen his agreement with the chief about the Ottawa children attending school. It had been a struggle, but now, thanks to her father, the Indian children went to school side by side with the white children.

She had wanted to accompany her father to the Indian village, and had tried to think of ways to convince him to allow it. But he had said that it was best that she not interfere. This was a man's business.

"Yes, I'm sure a certain man will come along soon," she said, knowing that at least she could dream that it might be the young chief, who had not yet taken a wife.

She yanked on a coat, which had a .36 caliber revolver tucked in its left pocket. Although her stepfather was a God-fearing man who preached against violence, he had not only taught Yvonne the use of firearms, he had also told her to carry the revolver to protect herself from the riffraff that frequented the nearby trading post. It was a hotbed of crime. If any of those men came upon her suddenly on her trips to and from the school, she would have a surefire way of persuading them to pass on by.

She grabbed up the books, and Anthony followed her outside to the buggy, where Stanley sat on the seat, with reins in hand.

"I'll be going to the church later to work on my Sunday sermon," Anthony said. "But first I've got to talk some more with Jake. So often I feel I am wasting my breath on that boy."

"He will come around one day," Yvonne said, settling down comfortably on the cushioned seat beside Stanley. She gave him his books as he handed her the reins. "Just be patient, Father. Down deep you know there is much goodness in Jake. How could there not be? You are his father."

She turned back to smile at him, then slapped the reins and rode away into the shadows of the forest. They were traveling down a lane that had been carved through the woods from the many trips to and from the church and school that sat side by side only a half mile away. Her father had supervised each and every log and nail that had gone into the building of those two establishments. He had chosen the schoolbooks and hymnals.

From the very beginning, the building of the school had been a labor of love, and it had become a successful venture.

Yvonne was as proud of her stepfather as she could be. He had planned it all from scratch, back in their lovely home in Saint Louis, before they had ventured to this wilderness to bring the word of God, and knowledge of book learning.

Smiling and at peace with herself, Yvonne traveled onward. She always enjoyed her outings in her new home. The flowers were always beautiful to see: the arbutus, daisy, goldenrod, iris, lady's slipper, tiger lily and all the rest. Ah, how Yvonne loved flowers, especially those she planted in her own charming, circular flower garden. It pleased her to stand back and gaze at her "Eden."

Although the garden was small, Yvonne had made it into a few glorious feet of pure fantasy. Her garden was like a play with acts, each flower having its time on center stage.

In early spring, when frost still painted the land with glistening white, the urge to enter the garden, to plant or just to sit, was almost irresistible. When the jonquils made their triumphant appearance, Yvonne loved the instant gratification of making a bouquet. She felt that when flowers were available, dinner must always be served with a bouquet taking pride of place on the table.

A doe bounding quickly out of the way of the buggy made Yvonne jump. Then she smiled as she watched the doe leap into the shadows of the forest.

Yes, she thought to herself, there were animals aplenty in the forest. Almost any time of the day she could see squirrels, woodchucks, chipmunks and rabbits. There were also snowshoe hares, porcupines, black bears and bobcats, moose and timber wolves.

And there were always birds overhead in the

trees. The songbirds were her favorites: robins, thrushes, meadowlarks, wrens, bluebirds, orioles, bobolinks and chickadees.

"I hope to find a good friend soon at school," Stanley said, giving Yvonne a quick glance.

Yvonne nodded as she drew her reins tight and stopped the horse and buggy. She watched two wagons of Ottawa Indian children as they appeared from the forest and crossed in front of her where the paths intersected.

Over the dull, weathered wood of the wagon sideboards, Yvonne could see the many dark eyes, the raven-black hair, and the beautifully smooth copper skin of the Indian children. On their laps were the schoolbooks that Yvonne's father had taken to the Ottawa village.

As part of the treaty with the Ottawa, the United States government had offered the use of wagons to transport the Indian children to and from school, just as they had supplied a good portion of the money to purchase their schoolbooks.

Yvonne's father had been hired by the government to see that everything was handled with kid gloves in these parts, so as not to stir up trouble with the Ottawa, who had made peace with the government some years ago.

Her father had taken the opportunity to build his church next door to the school, in the hope that this would bring the Ottawa into contact with the Bible as well as schoolbooks.

Thus far, the Ottawa had agreed to everything but allowing their children to enter the church. They had their own God, they had said time and again to Yvonne's father. They did not need the white man's.

Yvonne's eyes were drawn elsewhere and her heart leapt when a horse came up beside her wagon. On it sat Silver Arrow. He was the very man who sent her heart into a tailspin every time she saw him. He rode a gorgeous spotted pinto stallion, with zigzags of lightning painted on the steed's cheeks. Yvonne marveled at how the young chief sat so straight-backed and square-shouldered, ah, so *masterful*, in the saddle.

Yvonne's eyes shifted. On the saddle before Silver Arrow sat his six-year-old sister, Rustling Leaves, a cornhusk doll clutched to her chest.

Silver Arrow held Rustling Leaves protectively against him with an arm around her tiny waist, his eyes patiently watching the wagons clatter past.

Yvonne's heartbeat sounded loud as thunder in her excitement at being so close to this wonderfully handsome, buckskin-clad figure.

She knew something about Silver Arrow, since her father had spoken about his visits to the village. She knew that he was from the Grand River Band of Ottawa. They spoke English well because of their many earlier contacts with white settlers, and with priests who had come to Michigan long ago to befriend the Ottawa as they tried to Christianize them.

Yvonne had learned from her father that Silver Arrow was twenty-nine and was not married.

Yvonne swallowed back a tight, anxious feeling, for up this close she could see so much more about Silver Arrow than she had seen only from a distance. He was very stately, with the manners of a great chief. His sleek, carefully groomed black hair hung neatly to his waist. His face was sculpted. He was dressed in a tight, fringed buckskin outfit that revealed the play of his muscles. He also wore high-topped moccasins. His medicine bag hung by a braided sinew cord around his neck.

His eyes were dark and penetrating as he suddenly looked at Yvonne, catching her staring at him.

A sensual shock swept through Yvonne as Silver Arrow's eyes locked with hers.

The way he looked at her!

It was as though he was seeing clear into her soul.

What was it she saw in his eyes, she wondered, as he continued to stare at her.

Did he find her attractive?

Or did he see her as just another white woman, nothing to him but an intrusion in his life?

And how strange it was that as she looked into his eyes, she felt as though she might be looking into the crow's!

There was the same penetration, the same interest, the same . . .

She shook her head to clear her mind of such foolish thoughts.

Yet, for the moment, she was speechless, which was out of character for her. She always knew what to say, and when. Hardly ever did anyone cause her to be this awkward, or to feel this . . . this . . . strange!

But when she did finally find the courage to say something to Silver Arrow, he turned his eyes away from her, slapped his reins, and rode onward up the narrow path.

Totally taken by the man, Yvonne watched him for a moment longer. But when Stanley tugged at her coat sleeve, bringing her back to reality, she smiled awkwardly at him, then faced straight ahead and traveled onward.

With a throbbing heart and flushed cheeks, Yvonne looked anxiously ahead of her, through the cottonwoods and willows, disappointed when she no longer could see Silver Arrow.

When she reached the school, she saw that Silver Arrow had already dropped his sister off and was gone.

As Yvonne drew a tight rein, she looked through the crowd of children for Silver Arrow's sister. She gasped and paled when she saw several white children surrounding her and the other Indian children, mocking them. They were calling the boys filthy Injuns, the young girls ugly, copper-faced squaws.

"I don't want to stay here," Stanley said. His eyes revealed the fear and uneasiness he felt as he watched the taunting of the Indian children.

"You must," Yvonne softly encouraged. "Father has worked hard to establish this school where Indian and white children can learn together. It will take a while, Stanley, for the white children to accept those who are Indian. You must go and be a part of them. Show them your strength and convictions about what is right and what is wrong."

Stanley gave her a forlorn stare, swallowed hard, then slipped from the buggy.

"Go on, honey," Yvonne said. "Things will be all right."

Stanley gave Yvonne another unsteady look, then moved onward and stood with the white children.

Yvonne's heart grew cold when she saw that her brother quickly became a target of ridicule after the white children left the Indian children alone. They turned and began poking fun at him for wearing glasses and for being so frail and puny.

She had started to climb down from the wagon to scold the children for their poor behavior when the school bell rang and the children quickly disappeared inside the small, one-room log cabin.

Her pulse racing, anger still fanning her temper, Yvonne stared at the school building for a while longer. She hated to envision what might happen inside. Her only hope was that her father had hired a stern schoolmarm, one who could take any situation and turn it into something positive and right.

She turned her gaze over her shoulder when she heard the approach of a horse and buggy. She smiled with relief when her father pulled his buggy alongside hers.

"You are troubled by something," Anthony said, pushing his glasses farther back on the bridge of his nose. "What happened, Yvonne, to cause you to look so worried?"

Yvonne blurted out what had happened between the children. When she spoke of Stanley's humiliation, her voice broke.

"We must be patient and let things work out on their own," Anthony said, reaching over to pat Yvonne's knee. "If we interfere in Stanley's problems, that will only make them worse. We can't be there every minute of the day to protect him. He must learn to look after himself."

He looked toward the school, then over at Yvonne. "I'll be in the church right next door to the school. Alice, the schoolmarm, knows to come and get me if things get out of hand," he said. He suddenly laughed. "You haven't seen her, Yvonne. In height, she makes two of me. I dare not think any child will stand up against her."

"I hope not," Yvonne said, glancing at the school again.

"Back home, those cherries are waiting for someone to make a pie," Anthony said, his eyes dancing. "I can already taste them. Don't disappoint this preacher who can never get enough of a daughter's pies."

"I shall make the best ever," Yvonne said, laughing. She gave the school another lingering look. She then wheeled the horse and buggy around and rode away as her father left his buggy and sauntered toward the church.

When Yvonne arrived home, she was glad that Jake was gone, probably hunting. She secured her horse and buggy for the journey back to the school to get Stanley later in the day, then grabbed up a bucket and strolled leisurely to the river.

As she knelt down on the riverbank and sank the bucket into the water, she saw a reflection in the water and gasped.

Yvonne almost fell into the river when she looked up and saw the crow soaring overhead, its eyes on her. Her heart pounding, she scrambled to her feet.

Shivers ran up and down her spine as her eyes and the crow's met and held. When it landed on a tree limb overhead, she felt a presence, as though something . . . someone . . . were there, watching her.

Frightened by her feelings, and the way her imagination was playing tricks on her, Yvonne grabbed the bucket and ran back inside the cabin.

She set the bucket down beside the table, then crept back to the door and peeked out just as the crow flew closer and landed on a fence post, watching the cabin, ever watching.

Chapter Two

Morning had broken. The glorious sun slowly wheeled from the east, shedding its lustrous light on great, undulating hills above the Grand River that flowed eastward through the picturesque valley. In this country covered with virgin forest, the trees had been cleared from the top of a low hill, on which sat Chief Silver Arrow's Ottawa village.

Silver Arrow had scarcely slept all night. His thoughts had returned time and again to the white woman and the way she had revealed her feelings for him the prior day. Since he had first caught a glimpse of the woman at the trading post with her father, Silver Arrow had watched her many times during these past weeks. He knew now that he would have her as his wife, especially since she had shown her interest in him through the language of her eyes.

But presently, with the Ottawa children gone again to the school, where they would learn book reading and numbers, Silver Arrow knew that he must focus on other things besides the woman.

He was chief. He was there to guide his people, especially when some of them still questioned the wisdom of sending Ottawa children to attend school alongside white children.

For the most part, the parents wanted this for their children. Yet there were those few parents who still worried about their children being away from the village, where they were in charge of them, not a white schoolmarm.

Even Silver Arrow's sister feared attending the school. Until today, he had taken her, to give her the moral support that she needed.

But from now on, she would travel with the other children, especially since Silver Arrow's best friend, Four Horns, had suggested to him that it might look as though he was showing favoritism toward his sister.

Believing that his friend Four Horns was wise in the ways of this world, Silver Arrow always listened well to his suggestions.

Besides, it was best that his sister learn not to depend on him so much. In time, Rustling Leaves would be a woman who would join the others in their daily duties. In the Ottawa culture it was believed that the women possessed and controlled the faculty of reproduction, so it was they who had the sole care of the planting, cultivating, harvesting, and milling of the crops.

The women of the village had gone to their fields early that morning, while the men were arriving to have council with Silver Arrow in the large council house, where he now sat waiting before a great roaring fire in a fire pit in the center. The longhouse was a dome-shaped structure covered with bark. A smoke vent was open in the roof, where the smoke now spiraled lazily upward.

Outside, his village was made up of several longhouses and wigwams. For some distance, reaching away from the village, were fields of various crops. Maize and squash were the Ottawa's staple foods. Tobacco was also raised in small plots of land close by.

Now that all of the warriors had arrived and were sitting on blankets around the fire, Silver Arrow sprinkled a handful of sweetgrass in the lodge fire to purify the air. He watched and waited as the yellow flames licked up the sweetgrass, the black smoke churning skyward.

Silver Arrow then lifted his long pipe and lit the tobacco with a twig from the fire, puffing on the pipe until the tobacco was glowing red in its calumet bowl.

After making the tobacco offering to the earth, sky, and the four directions, Silver Arrow passed the pipe around to the rest of the men, until finally it came back to him.

Silver Arrow bowed his head. "Oh, *Gitchimanitou*, Great Spirit, who created us and created all things for the good of his creatures, kindly look down upon us in council today," he murmured.

He then settled back in his rabbit-skin robe and relaxed. Smoking soothed him, and as he pulled meditatingly at his pipe stem, the others began the long deliberation about their feelings on the issue of the day—schooling for their children.

"It is good medicine that our children attend the school," one man said. "If our children learn the ways of the *wa-me-to-go-zhe-wog*, then they will learn how to keep the white people from digesting more Indian land."

Four Horns sat at Silver Arrow's right side. "*Ae*, yes, I, too, see the importance of the children having the same knowledge as the white children," he said. "I see it as good medicine, yet when I take a wife and have children, I will not want my children to become Christians."

He gave Silver Arrow a concerned stare. "Chief Silver Arrow, what dangers are there in our Ottawa children being coerced into becoming Christians?" he asked softly. "The very man who built the school has also built a church beside it. He is a Methodist preacher. Surely he will try to pull our children to his church and teach them the words of his Bible."

Seeing his friend's concern, understanding it, Silver Arrow laid his pipe aside and reached a comforting hand to Four Horns's shoulder. "My brother, this man, who is called Brother Stockton by those of us who know him, does not speak with a forked tongue," he reassured. "*Ae*, he wears the black clothes of a preacher, and he would enjoy seeing us attend his church, but he has promised me that he will never force his religion on us. His sole interest is in seeing that the children learn the ways of the white people, for he, too, has seen the injustices done to our people. He sympathizes with us. That is why he does not call his school a white man's school, but sees it as one that was built for both the white *and* Ottawa children."

Silver Arrow paused, then said, "All white men know that we Ottawa are not infidels or idolaters. Brother Stockton knows that we believe there is a supreme ruler of the universe, the Creator of All Things, the Great Spirit, to whom we offer worship. As I have told you all before, this man will not push his religion on us."

There was an interval of silence during which no sound but the crackling of the fire could be heard.

And then another warrior spoke of his concerns. "And so you do trust Brother Stockton this much, that you speak in his behalf, as though he is a friend who occupies the right side of your heart?" he asked, his eyes questioning Silver Arrow.

Silver Arrow eased his hand from Four Horns' shoulder and gave the other warrior a reassuring smile. "*Ae*, I trust this preacher man as much as I trust that night will always turn to day," he said, nodding. He looked slowly around the circle of men. "But, my friends, concentrate only on our children now, and the importance of their having the knowledge of the white people. We must *want* them to learn the basic reading and writing skills. We must *want* them to learn how to recognize various denominations of money. We must *want* them to learn how to count."

He paused and gazed into the dancing flames of the fire. "*Ae*, at first, when it was suggested that the Ottawa children join the whites at the schoolhouse, even *I* did not understand, or truly know, what the word 'education' meant," he said softly.

He looked around at each of his men. Their faces were looking trustingly at him, all except for one. Silver Arrow tried his best to keep the bitterness he felt for his cousin, Antelope Skin, hidden inside his heart, yet knew that most who knew them both, knew that the feelings that flowed between them were *motchi-manitou*, bad.

Silver Arrow quickly skipped over Antelope Skin's brooding face and looked at the man next to him. "I thought education was a trick of the white man, used to steal our children away from us," he said. "But I patiently listened to Brother Stockton's explanation. I soon learned that it was an honest, kind thing that he did, and that he *does* care for our children, as though they are his very own blood kin."

"Yes, I can see that doubting this man was wrong," another warrior said with conviction. "Even we, our warriors, our wives, our entire families, will benefit from what our children will learn. Have we not already benefited? We, the adults, knew English well enough before this white man preacher arrived to have many conferences with us. But do we now not know it even better? I can converse freely and knowledgeably with the white man now. When our children bring their teachings home to us, I am excited to see how it will affect our lives so positively."

"*Ae*, it is as important for our young Ottawa children to learn good business skills as it was for us to learn to hunt and fish when we were children," another warrior offered.

"*Ho-wah!* Every Ottawa parent is a preacher to his children at every feast and council. You all are fools to depend on the teachings of white people," Antelope Skin blurted out. "It is *motchi-manitou!*"

All eyes shifted to him. Most of the men considered him a loudmouthed troublemaker who always found a way to interrupt the ease and rapport of their councils.

Antelope Skin gave Silver Arrow a malevolent glare. "You, who knows where there is enough gold buried to make your people rich, are wrong to encourage our people to depend too much on white people!" he said, his hands doubled into fists on his lap.

"Gold?" Silver Arrow said in a tight hiss. "You speak of gold when you were taught even as a child that to the Ottawa, earthly happiness is not in money, houses, and land? You know that personal power is the one thing to be most desired! Not the evils of gold!"

Then, as though Antelope Skin were not there, Silver Arrow turned away from him. He ignored the way Antelope Skin's swarthy face darkened in his anger at having been reprimanded publicly again.

Silver Arrow knew this man was dangerous, for he was always forcing his chief's hand in one way or another, trying to make Silver Arrow look ridiculous in the eyes of his warriors.

The best way to handle this sort of man was to ignore him, and Silver Arrow now wished that he had not even responded to Antelope Skin this morning.

He was learning how to treat this man of disrespect. And one day soon if Antelope Skin spoke out of turn one time too often, Silver Arrow would find a way to quiet him, forever!

"It is good, my friends, that the school our children attend is associated with Methodism instead of Catholicism," Silver Arrow said calmly. "Brother Stockton has not demanded that the students stay and take room and board in order to attend his school, as the Catholic priests and nuns have required at their schools in nearby towns. The children who attend the Catholic schools up the river, close to Grand Rapids, are required to live there, as well as attend classes. Each child is assigned a daily job. Girls assist in household chores. They clean the nuns' dwellings. Boys work in the priests' gardens and orchards, and are required to sweep the floors. Those who attend the Catholic schools are also forced to attend church services."

Silver Arrow paused, uneasy, when he felt the cold stare that Antelope Skin sent his way. Then he continued, trying his best to ignore this man, his own cousin.

"My friends, the only thing required of our children by the Methodist school is to learn," Silver Arrow said. "And the Ottawa children say they are teaching the white schoolmarm their Indian language while she is strengthening our children's English. It is a fair exchange, would you not say?"

"Schooling is foolish!" Antelope Skin said, laughing sarcastically. "I say again to you, Silver Arrow, if you would reveal where your grandfather's gold is buried, the Ottawa people could dig it up. Our lives would be enriched, far more than foolish schools will ever enrich our children's. We would not need the white man then. We, the Ottawa, would be wealthy."

Silver Arrow's eyes blazed as he turned to Antelope Skin. "Had my powerful, great chieftain grandfather seen the need to use the gold to enrich the lives of his people, *he* would have used it instead of burying it in the ground as though it were something unholy," he said in a slow, deliberate fashion.

As Silver Arrow talked about the gold, he was remembering the times in his youth that he had spent with his grandfather cleaning and shining the pieces of gold. Over and over again, while polishing the gold with a soft piece of buckskin, his grandfather had told him the story of how he had acquired it.

The story was that several warriors from various Ottawa villages had given the gold they received from trading to his grandfather for safekeeping, since none of them felt the need to spend it. They were self-sufficient people with their spacious gardens and animals, with their pelts and *wampum*.

When Silver Arrow was a child, every once in a while his grandfather would dig the gold up and clean it; then he would dig a new hiding place. His grandfather hid it many times during his lifetime. And he had told Silver Arrow never to tell anyone where it was.

He had warned Silver Arrow that owls would get him if he told!

Silver Arrow had loved his grandfather more than life itself, and when his grandfather died he had left Silver Arrow his greatest inheritance, his *magic*. Silver Arrow's bow was even strung with his grandfather's silver hair.

Like his grandfather, Silver Arrow was *Na-na-bo-jo*, a great chieftain with supernatural powers.

"Our Ottawa children must learn to make their own way in the world without the lure of gold to blind them," Silver Arrow said. "They must learn the ways of counting and reading and writing, to enable them to compete in the white man's world. All of the gold in the world will not bring them such knowledge. It must be taught to them, and the teaching costs them nothing. It is by treaty with the white man's government that our children have the privilege of learning."

Antelope Skin dared to speak then even more boldly to his chief. "*Uk-say!* Are you being truthful in explaining the reasons why you do not share the gold with your people?" he asked, his eyes gleaming into Silver Arrow's. "Is it not because you wish the Iroquois chief, Chief Old Elk, to have it? It has been rumored that Chief Old Elk is planning to offer his daughter Searching Heart to you in marriage. Would he then not demand a great bride price for her? Would he not demand the gold in exchange for his precious daughter? Is Searching Heart not the bewitching daughter of the great chief who rules the destiny of his Iroquois people?"

Silver Arrow's thoughts went to the white woman whose name was Yvonne. It was *she* who entered his heart night and day. His heart was open at last to loving a woman! And the woman was not Searching Heart. His heart had been opened by the white woman. The first time Silver Arrow had seen her, desire had leapt like a fountain within him.

His White Swan, he called her. Ah, her skin was as pure and white as a swan's feathers! Her neck was as long and as sublime!

But Silver Arrow had told only one person about the woman and the plans he had for her. Only his best friend, Four Horns, knew that he was considering eventually approaching the pale-skinned woman with an offer of marriage.

"Cousin Antelope Skin, you go too far in your disrespect to your chief," Silver Arrow growled. "You are wrong to speak so boldly about whom this chief does or does not wish to marry, or about what he might use for a bride price, for everyone who knows me well knows that I would never use my grandfather's gold in such a way. And never should you forget that my word among our people is final in all things."

He paused, his teeth grinding, then resumed. "Today I tell you to leave this council," he said smoothly, unemotionally. "You who are a jealous cousin, who wishes more than anything to be

41

chief, are a disturbance to our council, instead of a contributor. You try too hard, too openly, to discredit me in front of our people. It works against you, *witaw-wis-e-maw*, cousin. Do you remember the meaning of the word 'banishment'?"

A startled look entered Antelope Skin's eyes. He scurried to his feet and, cowering, backed away from Silver Arrow, then turned and stumbled from the lodge.

Silver Arrow laughed. "Did you see how quickly Antelope Skin left our council when I mentioned the word 'banishment'?" he said, his eyes dancing. "He knows that he is tempting his chief too often with words that are unwise. He is frightened of his chief's words, as rabbits are frightened in the presence of a wildcat."

A ripple of quiet laughter went around the circle of warriors.

"But, my chief, do you not see the good that might come from having a close alliance with the Iroquois?" one of his warriors dared to say. "Old enemies could join hands and hearts, as friends. This could make a force for the whites to reckon with, the Ottawa and Iroquois joined as one in deeds and strength."

"*Ka-ge-ti*, truly so, Chief Old Elk is not that much of an enemy to us now," Silver Arrow said, his voice tight. "But I am as close as I wish to be in alliance and friendship with him and his people. Do you all forget so easily the blood of the Ottawa people which was spilled in the past at the hands of the Iroquois? How can any of you forget that the Iroquois killed my very own parents? My grandfather died then because of the death of his son. His heart could never accept what was done to his family by the Iroquois. And Antelope Skin wished to have me marry an Iroquois woman? It is something that can never be! *Ho-wah! Te-way! Never!*"

Silver Arrow rose quickly to his feet. He looked each man in the eye, glaring. "I gave my word in council that our children would attend the white man's school, and they will attend!" he said, his voice flat. "The Ottawa's word of promise is as good as a white man's promissory note, even better, as these notes sometimes are neglected and not performed according to their promises. Ottawa promises are very sure and punctual. We have no timepieces. We measure our time by the sun!"

He moved his eyes from man to man again, then left in a huff.

After he was outside, beneath the loveliness of the blue sky and in the sweet scent of the air, only then could he breathe more easily and allow his anger to wane.

All of this confusion! he thought to himself, inhaling a frustrated breath of air. All of the suspicions and questions! They were always brought on by Antelope Skin's presence!

As the warriors left the lodge, one by one they came to Silver Arrow and embraced him, offering soft apologies and words of support.

And when they were all past him and Four Horns was there, with his hug of reassurance, Silver Arrow laughed softly as he eased from his friend's embrace.

"He did it to me again," Silver Arrow said, falling into step beside Four Horns as they walked slowly toward Silver Arrow's longhouse. "When will I ever learn not to allow my cousin to embarrass me in front of my warriors? Such simple questions about the Iroquois would have been treated more gently by me had they not been caused by Antelope Skin's prodding into my private life during council."

"My friend, you must learn to ignore him," Four Horns offered. "Antelope Skin is succeeding too well at stirring up the feelings of the council. Banish him now, Silver Arrow. Banish him before it is too late. You are a chief with a considerable reputation to maintain."

"*Ae*, that is true, I could banish him only for what he says in council," Silver Arrow said solemnly. "But that would make me look little in the eyes of our people, as though I am not strong enough to stand up to criticism. What I need is proof of other underhanded deeds he has done which harm the stability of our people. Then everyone, not only myself and you, will understand and demand his banishment."

"When he brought up the question of whom you will marry, I saw something enter your eyes that I have seen before when you talk about the beautiful white woman you call White Swan," Four Horns said. He smiled devilishly at Silver Arrow. "Am I right? When Antelope Skin spoke the name Searching Heart, was it not White Swan who entered your thoughts and stirred the sensual side of your imagination?"

"You are astute," Silver Arrow said, nodding and smiling at Four Horns. "*Ae*, I thought of White Swan today. More than once I have thought of her."

"Did you *see* her today?"

Silver Arrow exhaled a tight, inaudible sigh of hope and longing. "*Ae*, more than once."

"In the early morning, Silver Arrow, just after the sun rose in the heavens?"

"*Ae*, when she was washing her hair in the river before she went inside her lodge to prepare the morning meal for her family."

"When are you going to share your feelings for her?" Four Horns asked as they reached Silver Arrow's longhouse and stood outside the door. "When will you marry her?"

"*Wau-e-baw*," Silver Arrow said. "She will know my feelings soon. She will be my wife soon after. I cannot wait much longer to have her in my arms, to hold her."

"You feel you have watched her enough to know that she will make a good wife?" Four Horns asked, keenly aware of how often Silver Arrow observed the white woman.

"*Ae*, and each day brings closer the day she will be in my lodge each morning and will be washing her hair in the river that shines close to my door," Silver Arrow said, envisioning her even now as she would look, standing there with him in the shadows of his longhouse, his woman, his wife, his lover. . . .

Chapter Three

The sun shone bright over the Iroquois village, a short way downriver from Silver Arrow's village.

Searching Heart, Chief Old Elk's daughter, laughed and played with other women her age in a cornfield. They had already plucked many ears of corn and thrown them into heaps on the ground, and were now braiding them into bunches of twenty to be hung up and dried. Teasingly, they gaily tossed ears of corn back and forth to one another.

Searching Heart let out a squeal of excitement. "Look what I found!" she cried. "A bright red ear of corn!"

"Oh, Searching Heart," her friend Pink Rose said as she gazed at Searching Heart's exquisite copper face, her waist-length raven black hair drawn back into one long braid down her back. "How wonderful. How lucky you are. A bright red ear of corn is the sign of a secret admirer! Do you think the admirer is Chief Silver Arrow? You have spoken to him often. Will you marry him?"

Searching Heart held the red ear of corn to her breast as though it were a precious keepsake. "I have never seen anyone as handsome as Silver Arrow," she said, sighing. The tail end of her fringed buckskin dress whipped around her long, lean legs in the brisk breeze. "I do so wish he would be the one who pined for me, as I do for him. How wonderful it would be if he would come to our village and lavish me and my father with gifts and ask me to be his wife."

"Make it happen, Searching Heart," Pink Rose said, clasping her hands excitedly before her. "You are the most beautiful woman in the world. Who could not love you?"

"He cares not for me," Searching Heart said sullenly as she held the ear of corn before her and stared at it. "No matter what I do, I cannot seem to draw his attention to me. Whenever I am around him, his thoughts and eyes are elsewhere. There has to be another woman. But who? Where?"

"Do not give up on him," Pink Rose said, gasping when Searching Heart suddenly and angrily tossed the ear of corn away from her. "Do you not know that every maiden has fond hopes that sooner or later her charms will attract a young man's attention? Even when he has been heedless to all such allurements? For each woman who is in love, sooner or later the nymph of love makes an appearance. That will happen to you. Then Silver Arrow will be yours, Searching Heart."

"There is also another warrior who makes my heart skip a nervous beat from time to time," Searching Heart said, her eyes dancing.

"You have feelings for two men at once?" Pink Rose gasped, her eyes wide.

"Perhaps, perhaps," Searching Heart said, giggling as she pictured the handsome Ottawa warrior Four Horns in her mind's eye.

Then her lips curved into a pout. "But he too is Ottawa, and the Ottawa men seem always to shy away from us Iroquois women," she said sullenly. "I wonder if there might be another man out there who is not Ottawa who would appreciate me."

Pink Rose grinned at Searching Heart. "You are wicked," she teased. "So very, very wicked."

"I know," Searching Heart said, her eyes flashing.

Chapter Four

The sleeves of her white cotton blouse rolled up to her elbows, Yvonne stretched her stepfather's white shirt across the ironing board, then placed the iron on the cooking stove and waited for it to get hot.

Just as she started to take it from the stove, she stiffened. Her gaze moved quickly to the open door as she listened to the sound of an approaching horse outside the cabin.

She wasn't expecting anyone. Her stepfather was at the church, her younger brother was in school, and Jake was hunting. Neither Jake nor her father was expected back until much later.

Always cautious, Yvonne hurried to grab a rifle that she always left leaning against the wall beside the door.

As she stepped up to the door and peered outside, the horseman reached the hitching rail and dismounted.

"Lordy, lordy, what does *he* want?" she whispered in exasperation.

Her eyes burned with disgust as she watched a man she despised lumber toward the cabin. Knowing that Rod Sanders was no true threat to her, Yvonne leaned the rifle against the wall again and stepped outside onto the small porch.

She shivered as her gaze moved over him. He was a large man with carrot-colored hair and unruly whiskers. His bulbous nose was mottled by broken veins. And as usual, he wore blood-stained buckskins that she knew stank like death itself from the many animals he killed and cleaned each day.

Most people called him by his nickname, River Rat, because he did his trapping along the riverbanks where large, fine-furred muskrats made their homes. He was also known to trap rats and sell them for ten cents apiece.

Because of this man, Yvonne didn't want anyone to even mention muskrat soup in front of her. To tease her, knowing that she despised anything that reminded her of River Rat, Jake often uttered the Ottawa word for muskrat soup in her presence. He had learned how to speak some words in the Ottawa tongue from men at the trading post where Ottawa warriors also did their trading.

She could hear Jake even now saying *zush-ka-*

boo-bish, Ottawa for muskrat soup, over and over again in front of her.

"Howdy, ma'am," River Rat said, his pale gray eyes squinting at her. One cheek was filled with chewing tobacco. "How's things?"

"River Rat, until you arrived, things were just fine," Yvonne said, repulsed by his very presence. "What do you want? You have disturbed my morning chores."

"You know why I'm here," River Rat said, his eyes gleaming into hers. He spat a stream of tobacco over his shoulder.

"Now, how on earth would I know why you do anything?" Yvonne said, folding her arms across her chest. "To me you are nothing but a pest."

"I wouldn't be so hasty with such nastiness as that," River Rat said, wiping a dribble of tobacco from the corner of his mouth with the back of a hand. He then gestured toward his horse. "Take a look yonder at my catch for the day, and it ain't hardly midmornin' yet. If I wanted to, by evenin' I could more than triple those pelts you see on my horse. In my lifetime, I've accumulated enough money from the sale of my pelts to make any woman comfortable."

Yvonne paled at the thought of what he was implying. He was going to persist in trying to get her to marry him, even after having been told countless times that if he were the last man on the earth, she wouldn't marry him.

"River Rat, get on out of here," she said, turning to walk away. But what he said next caused her to stop in midstep and turn slowly to face him again.

"I plan to get my hands on the Ottawa chief's gold," he said, chuckling when he saw how his words had suddenly piqued Yvonne's interest. "I could build you a mansion, Yvonne. You could be my queen."

Yvonne had heard Jake and her father talk about Chief Silver Arrow's gold enough times to know exactly what River Rat was referring to. She knew that many men had searched for it. But only Silver Arrow knew where it was buried.

"You'd best forget about that gold," she said guardedly. "You are messing with something out of your realm. From what I've heard, Chief Silver Arrow won't allow anyone to get near the gold." She smiled smugly. "I even hear that it's protected by Indian spirits."

Stroking his jaw, River Rat retreated a step. "Spirits?" he said, frowning at her. "I ain't never heard tell of any Injun spirits guarding the gold."

He took another step toward her. "Why, pretty lady, you just made that up, didn't you?" he said, chuckling. "There ain't no such things as spirits anywhere. When Injuns speak of their spirits, it's only a lot of hocus-pocus. It's damn hogwash."

He stepped up on the porch, now only inches from Yvonne.

He edged himself closer.

Her eyes locked with his, Yvonne took an unsteady step away from him.

"Whether or not I find the gold, I could make you a good husband," River Rat said, his eyes squinting into hers. "I'd provide well for you. Wouldn't you rather sew and cook for a husband than a stepfather and two brothers? Don't you realize you're bein' used?"

"I do what I do because I love my family," Yvonne said, feeling suddenly threatened. He was more persistent today than ever before.

And suddenly she realized how alone she was, how vulnerable.

Her pulse racing, she took another step away from him. She gave the rifle a quick look out of the corner of her eye.

River Rat balled his fists and planted them on his hips. He rocked on the heels of his soiled boots. "Ah, now, pretty lady, are you saying that you love *Jake*?" he said in a low rumble of a voice. "That you love him in a sexual way?"

Yvonne blanched and gasped. No man had ever spoken so openly to her about sex.

And to imply that there was something sexual between herself and her . . . her . . . stepbrother was shocking.

"You filthy-mouthed man, get out of here this instant," she hissed. Hoping that he wouldn't notice, she slowly reached her right hand out for the rifle.

River Rat noticed all right. His gaze moved like lightning to the rifle, and back to Yvonne. Just as her hand reached the firearm, he grabbed her by one wrist in a pawlike grip and pulled her roughly from the door, and against him.

Repulsed to be touched by him, Yvonne yanked her wrist free and gave him a shove. Before he fell, he grabbed her by the wrist again and dragged her from the porch onto the ground with him.

"You beast!" Yvonne cried. "You bastard!"

She pummeled his chest with her free hand when he rolled over on top of her, trapping her beneath him.

"Get off me, you filthy, horrible man!" Yvonne screamed.

Pinning her to the ground with his full weight, River Rat held her by one wrist. He laughed throatily as Yvonne continued hitting his chest, the blows only firing his sexual urge more.

"I like a woman with spirit!" he said, his eyes dark with evil passion.

His free hand sneaked up her fully gathered skirt. He smothered her cry of alarm with a wet kiss.

Yvonne's eyes were wild as she lay defenseless beneath the vile man. Her lips stung from his teeth cutting into them as he continued kissing her. She groaned and shoved at him without avail.

Then her heart seemed to stop when she heard the unexpected beat of wings drawing close overhead.

Her eyes widened and her breath caught in her throat when the whir of wings swept down over River Rat's head.

And the eyes!

The eyes of the crow met hers and seemed to read the alarm she felt.

The crow banked away upon the wind, and then came again in a flurry of wings and pecked River

Rat on the head, once, twice, and then three times.

River Rat scurried to his feet. He grabbed his rifle. Yelping and waving the rifle over his head, he frantically tried to keep the bird away from him.

Yvonne stared disbelievingly at the trickle of blood that flowed through River Rat's thick red hair from the wounds the bird had inflicted on his scalp.

She moved slowly to her feet and watched unbelievingly as the crow swept round and round River Rat's head, screeching, the man ducking and cursing as he ran toward his horse.

"This is a crazy place!" River Rat screamed as he swung himself into his saddle. He glared at Yvonne. "*You're* crazy! I don't want no more part of you!"

He stared up at the crow as it sailed away, flew down over the crest of a knoll by the river and then was gone from sight into the dark depths of the forest.

Almost paralyzed by what she had witnessed, Yvonne watched River Rat ride away. When he was out of sight, she turned and looked slowly around her for the crow, seeing it nowhere.

Then, shaken by the experience, by her near rape and by the crow's attack on River Rat, as though it knew that it was saving her from terrible degradation at the hands of the filthy man, Yvonne ran inside her cabin and slammed and bolted the door.

Panting, ashen, she leaned against the door.

The crow!

What could it mean?

Chapter Five

The trading post smelled of whisky, smoke, and leather. Animal pelts pressed tight in packs for transportation lay along the floor and on a counter.

A tall, buckskin-clad clerk stood behind the counter, transacting business with several trappers, white and Indian alike.

A bar stood along the wall opposite the counter. Jake leaned back against the bar, his arms folded across his chest as he watched River Rat whittle off a slice of black chewing tobacco.

Jake chuckled when River Rat stuffed one cheek until it bulged like a gopher's.

"That stuff or the damn cigarettes you smoke are going to be the death of you," Jake said, turning to face the bar as River Rat stepped up beside him.

"Barkeep, give me a whisky," Jake said as he slammed a coin down on the bar. "And give one to my pal River Rat; my compliments."

Jake looked over his shoulder at the pile of pelts he had just brought in. His pockets now jingled with coins, yet he still could not get his mind off the Ottawa's gold. Somehow, some way, that gold would be his escape from living with his preacher father.

The thought of his father still urging him into the ministry made a shiver ride up and down his spine. He had discovered long ago that religion was a fake. If it were worth anything, his mother would still be alive. All of the prayers he had uttered to Christ had not kept his mother alive!

"I just had the damnedest experience at your place," River Rat said, nodding a thank-you to Jake when the shot glass of whisky was placed before him on the bar.

"Oh?" Jake said, lifting an eyebrow. "What? And what were you doing there? You knew that we'd planned to meet here."

"You know why I was there," River Rat grumbled. He emptied the glass of whisky in one swallow, then glowered at Jake. "Your stepsister. *She's* the reason."

"You're going to get shot if you don't stop pestering Yvonne," Jake said. He smiled crookedly at River Rat. "And I'm not talking about my father doing the shooting. My sister knows how to fire a rifle. Father saw to that. She'll shoot you in the seat of the breeches, River Rat, if you don't stop going there, asking for her hand in marriage." He curled up his nose and gave River Rat a slow looking-over. "Just look at you. Take a whiff of yourself. No decent woman would want you."

"You'd best watch your mouth," River Rat said, slamming the empty glass down on the bar. "If that damn crow hadn't come and interfered, I'd have showed your sister what I had to offer." He chuckled. "And I ain't speakin' of pelts, neither."

"What crow?" Jake asked, turning to face River Rat. "And what about it? Yvonne told me that you tried to kiss her one other time. River Rat, don't tell me you tried something more aggressive than a kiss."

"Yep, and I got a good feel of her thighs. I would have poked her good if that damn crow hadn't come and attacked me," he spat out angrily. He leaned his head down so that Jake could see the dried blood. "See my head? That damn bird pecked me. Not once, but several damn times."

Jake only half heard what River Rat was saying about the crow. What he had said about coming close to poking Yvonne meant only one thing to Jake. He had come near to raping her!

The thought made a sick feeling churn inside his stomach. He reached over and grabbed River Rat by the collar and yanked him close. "Stay away from Yvonne," he hissed out. "If you had succeeded in raping her, I'd have cut your heart out."

River Rat's eyes were wild. "Not only is your damn *sister* crazy, so are *you*," he said, struggling to get free. "Jake, let go. We're friends. Friends don't threaten one another!"

"They do where sisters are concerned," Jake said between clenched teeth. "Promise me, River Rat, that you won't go near her again, or to hell with friendship."

"I don't even *want* to go near her again," River Rat said somberly. "There's somethin' about her and that crow that's eerie. Jake, you can have her, however you want her. As a lover. Or as a sister. I don't care. I'm keepin' my distance from her *and* your damn cabin."

"I have only the deepest respect for Yvonne," Jake said, dropping his hands away from River Rat's collar. "Sure, she's pretty and desirable. But she's my sister. I won't ever forget that."

"She's no true blood kin to you," River Rat said, straightening his shirt collar as he took a step away from Jake. He spat tobacco over his shoulder. It pooled in a dark brown glob on the wooden floor close to the spittoon. "You could do anything you damn well please with her and it wouldn't be incestuous."

"Like I said, I have the deepest respect for Yvonne," Jake reiterated, nodding to the bartender to pour him another whisky. "I'll never approach her in any other way. She's going to find herself a fine husband someday." He glowered at River Rat. "And by all that is holy, it won't be you."

River Rat slapped a coin on the counter. "Give me another whisky," he said to the bartender, his voice flat. "The crow, Jake. What's with that crow

that seemed almost human? He came out of nowhere and protected your sister as though it was
a man protecting his woman."

"The crow, huh? I've been trying like hell to kill
that damn thing," Jake said. He lifted the glass to
his lips and swallowed the whisky in one fast
gulp, then slid the empty glass back onto the bar.
"It *does* seem almost human." He frowned at
River Rat. "I'll get him. I'm going to kill that damn
bird if it's the last thing I do."

"Let's talk about something profitable," River
Rat said, chuckling devilishly. "Like the Ottawa's
gold. Jake, we've got to find a way to get our hands
on that gold. We'll split it fair and square and still
have enough to live comfortably on for the rest of
our lives."

"Yeah, I've been doin' a lot of thinking about
that gold, myself. I want it. And I've concluded
that I can't get my hands on the gold without
help," Jake grumbled. "I'll gladly share it with
you, River Rat, if you can help come up with a
plan that will get it in our pockets."

"I think I might have it figured out," River Rat
said, turning to gaze out the open door. Horses
were browsing in a crude corral of buffalo-hair
rope. Standing beside the corral, beneath a tree,
was someone River Rat knew and despised, yet
used.

"How?" Jake asked, raising an eyebrow.
"What's on your mind?"

"Not how, or what," River Rat said, spitting a
long string of tobacco on the floor. "*Who*, Jake.
Who."

Jake turned and followed River Rat's line of vision. His gaze stopped on the swarthy Indian who leaned against the tree outside the trading post.

"See that Injun?" River Rat said, motioning toward Antelope Skin.

"Yeah, that's Antelope Skin," Jake said, folding his arms across his chest. "What about him? All I know about him is that he's worthless, and that he'll do anything to get a drink of firewater in his gut."

"Yeah, anything, Jake," River Rat said, chuckling. "Like maybe lead us to the Ottawa gold?"

Jake took a step away from the bar. "Why, River Rat, I think you've got something there," he said, laughing softly. "Surely since Antelope Skin is an Ottawa, he knows something about the gold."

"Or how to find out, eh?" River Rat said, turning mischievous eyes on Jake.

"It's worth a try," Jake said, lumbering toward the door. He reached inside his front breeches pocket and took out two coins. He turned to River Rat and flipped the coins one at a time toward him. "Go and get us a jug of whisky. I'll meet you outside. I'm going to say a few words to our friend Antelope Skin, the *Addowa*, as I've been told by Indians the word 'Ottawa' should be pronounced."

River Rat sidled back to the bar.

Jake wandered on outside and walked up to Antelope Skin. "Mornin'," he said, stopping and folding his arms across his chest. "Have you brought skins to the trading post for tradin', or goodwill?"

"I don't have skins," Antelope Skin said. "What

do you mean by 'goodwill'?"

"You don't know what goodwill means?" Jake said, laughing. "Why, Injun, I think you should be in school with the rest of the dumb redskins. How else will you ever know the true meaning of that English word?"

Antelope Skin glared at Jake and turned to walk away, but the sight of River Rat approaching with a jug of whisky made him stop. He licked his lips when River Rat thrust the jug into his hands.

Then he turned slowly and looked suspiciously from River Rat to Jake.

"It's yours if you give us some information this morning," River Rat said, smiling at Jake as he came and stood beside him. "Ain't it his firewater, free and clear, Jake, if he gives us the right answers?"

Smiling, Jake nodded.

"What answers do you want?" Antelope Skin asked warily. He shook the jug close to his ear, to see how full it was. Excitement entered his eyes when he realized that the jug was brimful of firewater.

And it could be his.

"We want to know where the Ottawa gold is buried," Jake said, placing a hand on Antelope Skin's shoulder. "You know, don't you? You'll tell us, won't you, Antelope Skin?"

His heart hammering, Antelope Skin hugged the jug to his chest. "The gold belongs to my chief," he said, his voice drawn. "I do not know where it is hidden. Only Chief Silver Arrow knows."

"Ah, now, you know that ain't so," Jake said, pretending friendship as he placed an arm around Antelope Skin's shoulder and started walking him toward the forest. "But no need in worrying about it. Come on. Let's go and sit down somewhere private, where we can share the jug of whisky."

Understanding Jake's ploy, River Rat chuckled beneath his breath and followed Jake and Antelope Skin until they reached the river. He stood back and whittled several pieces of chewing tobacco from his plug. After thrusting the pieces into the corner of his mouth, he slipped his knife back in his pants pocket and sat down with Jake and Antelope Skin.

"Drink, enjoy," Jake said, watching Antelope Skin eagerly swallow the whisky in long, quick gulps. He gave River Rat a sly look, then watched Antelope Skin again.

When Antelope Skin offered the jug to Jake, Jake shook his head. "Naw, it's yours," he said, hoping to get him drunk quickly. "Drink up, friend. It's . . . all . . . yours."

He exchanged a wicked smile with River Rat, then leaned back on an elbow, patiently waiting for Antelope Skin to finish off the whisky.

When the jug was lying beside Antelope Skin, empty, and he was groaning drunkenly as he hung his head over the river, retching, Jake gave River Rat a knowing smile.

Then Jake took Antelope Skin by an elbow and led him down on the grassy slope. "You need to lie down, my friend," he slyly suggested. "That way your insides won't churn so much from the firewater."

Jake rubbed his whiskers as Antelope Skin stretched out, his eyes hazed over drunkenly.

"Now as I was saying earlier," Jake said as he sat down beside Antelope Skin, "River Rat and I would like to know where the Ottawa gold is buried. We gave you the whisky. Now you give us the information."

"Only . . . Chief Silver Arrow . . . know," Antelope Skin said thickly.

"Perhaps so," Jake said, nodding. "Then, Antelope Skin, it's up to you to find out from your chief. Surely you are his friend. Don't friends share secrets?"

"He is my cousin and chief, but I am not sure if he would call me a friend," Antelope Skin stammered out.

"A cousin?" Jake said, his eyebrows raising. "Why, my friend, cousins should stick together. You've got to go to him and ask him about the gold. If you do, and you get us the answers we seek, I'll give you a lifetime of whisky."

Antelope Skin licked his lips and stared at Jake.

"Doesn't the firewater give you a sense of power?" Jake taunted, leaning into Antelope Skin's swarthy face. "Doesn't firewater give you better insight on things? With a lifetime of whisky at your disposal, you could have the power to eventually unseat your cousin. You could be chief!"

When Antelope Skin said nothing more, but only closed his eyes and fell asleep, Jake took several more coins from his pocket and thrust them into River Rat's hand. "Go and get some more damn whisky," he growled.

"His brain is already too soaked with firewater to drink any more," River Rat grumbled. "*Or* think."

"This jug ain't for him," Jake said sourly. "It's for *us*."

River Rat scrambled to his feet and left.

Jake glared down at Antelope Skin.

Antelope Skin feigned sleep. Although he was quite drunk, his thoughts of his cousin Silver Arrow were clear enough. Silver Arrow was an admired young chieftain who possessed supernatural powers. Silver Arrow's grandfather had been blessed with magical powers, too. They were now Silver Arrow's, not only because Silver Arrow had inherited his grandfather's magical coat made from the white bear of mystery and magic, but also because Silver Arrow's bow was strung with his grandfather's hair.

The Ottawa believed in spirits, both good and evil. Sometimes Antelope Skin believed that an evil-minded magician had cast a sorcerer's spell on him, for nothing good ever happened to him. All he could think about was ways to harm others.

But Antelope Skin knew that Silver Arrow's powers were far stronger than his ever could be. Antelope Skin feared that power. He feared the magical coat that his cousin had in his possession.

Often Antelope Skin had tried to make people believe that Silver Arrow was an evil sorcerer, but no one listened. Those who did listen warned him to watch what he said about their beloved chief!

Antelope Skin had wanted to go inside Silver Arrow's lodge to steal his magical coat, to burn it, to take away his power. But Silver Arrow's elderly grandmother was always in the lodge. And she was a beloved Ottawa princess. Antelope Skin loved and respected her too much to harm her while trying to steal the magical coat.

River Rat came back with the jug of firewater. He sat down beside Antelope Skin and gave him a slight shake of the shoulder. "Antelope Skin, wake up," he said, frowning at Jake as he yanked the jug of whisky from his hand and began guzzling it down in great swallows.

Antelope Skin rose shakily to a sitting position. He eyed the jug of whisky. He wiped his mouth with the back of a hand as he watched Jake drinking it.

"Antelope Skin, we have more whisky," River Rat said. He gave Jake a frown, then looked at Antelope Skin again. "Wouldn't just a wee bit more whisky make you glad?"

Antelope Skin reached over and grabbed the jug from Jake. He took several swallows, then hugged it possessively to him. "*Ae*, I will do what I can to find out where the gold is buried," he said thickly, sheepishly looking from Jake to River Rat. "If you promise that I will always have firewater when I want it."

"Yes, as much as you want," River Rat and Jake chimed in together. "Always."

"Somehow I will get the answer you seek," Antelope Skin said, rising shakily to his feet. He stumbled away, then looked at them over his shoulder. "Give me time. My cousin is more powerful than you can ever know."

Antelope Skin staggered away. He trembled at the thought of Silver Arrow's special powers. He had to make sure that his cousin Chief Silver Arrow didn't know that he had aligned himself with the white men.

It was certain that Antelope Skin must find the location of the gold in a clever way, a way that did not include his having to come face-to-face with Silver Arrow!

Jake watched Antelope Skin mount his horse and ride away. "The gold? It's as good as in our hands," he boasted, his eyes dancing.

"Yeah, ours," River Rat said, nodding.

Chapter Six

Needing to work off her frustration and anger at River Rat, Yvonne had finished her ironing, then had jumped right into other chores which had to be done. She stood back and gazed proudly at the two loaves of bread and two apple pies she had made.

She had also weeded her vegetable and flower gardens. Her flower garden, her "Eden," was a breathtaking symphony of hues. Yes, she had created an enchanted world overflowing with blooms, the sun-ray yellow California poppies basking in the sunniest spots, the columbines preferring a more shady, moist glade.

She closed her eyes and saw her garden in her mind's eye . . . the marigolds, chrysanthemums, the patch of brilliant geraniums. There were

many more, but her favorites were the divinely
scented pale-violet tangles of pansies, and her beloved lilies of the valley.

She looked slowly around the cabin. It too had
profited by her need to keep busy today. Everything was spotless and in order, from the botan-
ical print curtains and large chair pillows that lay
on the sofa and two matching chairs, to the
needlepoint floral rug on the floor before the huge
stone fireplace. Where the floor lay bare, it shone
from a fresh scrubbing.

Yvonne had dusted the row after row of shelves
along the far wall, which held many books. She
had also straightened her father's oak desk with
its stacks of journals and papers.

Two doors off the living room led into two bed-
rooms. One was Yvonne's, the other her stepfather's. A ladder led to a loft overhead, where two
rooms had been partitioned off for Jake and Stanley.

She had dusted them all until not one dust ball
could be found beneath a bed.

Yvonne slipped her apron off and hung it on a
peg, then went to her bedroom and brushed her
hair. She gazed into the mirror, her thoughts
once again on Silver Arrow. She wondered what
he had thought of her during those brief moments
when he had stared at her while waiting for the
Ottawa wagon of children to pass.

After her dreadful encounter with River Rat,
she had changed into a dress made of gingham,
a fabric that was forever fresh and crisp. She had
always loved the innocent allure of the fabric.

While living in Saint Louis, where there were so many fancy shops, she had enjoyed going through the many bolts of fresh-smelling gingham prints to choose one for her next dress. She was almost as fond of sewing as of gardening.

She laid the brush aside and smoothed her hands down the front of her dress, across her hips, then her waist.

She couldn't help wondering what Silver Arrow would have thought of her if she had not been wearing her coat when they met. Would he have admired her tiny waist? The slight curve of her hips? The . . . swell of her bosom?

She laughed softly and blushed when she allowed her eyes to travel to her breasts, where she could just see the hint of cleavage above the low-swept neckline of her bodice.

She was glad that she had not been wearing this somewhat revealing dress earlier in the day, when River Rat had come to the cabin.

She shivered at the memory of his vile hands sneaking up the insides of her thighs! After he had left, she had not been able to remove her clothes fast enough to bathe away his stench.

The clatter of a buggy's wheels and the clip-clop of a horse's hooves approaching drew Yvonne away from the mirror. She had cause for alarm, for it was not yet time for her father to return home. Although she had worked at a frenetic pace since River Rat's departure, it was still only mid-afternoon. At this hour, her father should still be at his study in the church, and Stanley should still be in school.

Yvonne rushed to the bedroom window and swept the sheer curtains aside. Her eyebrows lifted. It *was* her father, and not only he, but also young Stanley.

Her eyes widened when she saw that Stanley wasn't wearing his eyeglasses. She gasped when she saw that his eyes were red and swollen from crying. Even now, as he saw her standing in the window, new tears flowed from his eyes.

Yvonne stiffened. "What now?" she whispered to herself.

She left her bedroom and hurried outside to stand on the porch as the horse and buggy drew to a stop. Yvonne flew down the steps.

Stanley climbed from the buggy and rushed to her, flinging himself into her arms as she knelt down on her knees to receive him.

"A mean boy at school broke my glasses," Stanley cried, clinging to Yvonne.

She hugged him tightly and looked over his shoulder at her father. He stepped down from the buggy and held out the broken glasses for Yvonne to see.

"Please stop crying," Yvonne crooned, stroking Stanley's tiny back. "Shh. It'll be all right, Stanley. It'll be all right."

"The boy responsible for this has been punished," Anthony said thickly. He eyed the broken glasses, then looked down at Yvonne. "The teacher whipped the boy's bare legs with twigs from a birch tree. Each day for a week, during school hours, he will stand in the corner of the schoolroom, facing the wall."

"I hope that not only teaches that boy not to be cruel," Yvonne murmured, "but the other children, as well."

Yvonne leaned away from Stanley and wiped his face with the hem of her dress.

"Not only was Stanley mistreated today," Anthony said, his voice drawn, "but also Chief Silver Arrow's sister."

"Oh, no," Yvonne said, her eyes wide as she gazed up at her father. "What happened to her?"

"A boy dipped one of her pigtails in an inkwell and soaked it with ink," Anthony said, sighing heavily. "Not only that, when she cried and left her desk, the boy stuck his foot out and tripped her."

"Was she hurt?" Yvonne asked, rising slowly to her feet.

"She has a slight bump on her head from falling against a desk," Anthony said solemnly. "Rustling Leaves is going to be all right. But this incident might be all it takes for the Indians to take their children from the school."

"Where is Rustling Leaves now?" Yvonne asked softly.

"School was dismissed," Anthony said, pushing his eyeglasses further back on his nose. "Alice took it upon herself to take Rustling Leaves to her village. I offered to go with her, but she insisted on going alone. She said that she was doing a poor job, it seemed, of earning her pay. She said that she could at least do this to make amends for not having full charge of her schoolroom."

"Do you think she was well received when she

arrived at the village?" Yvonne asked. "Don't you think you should go and see if things went all right for her?"

Her heart skipped a beat as inspiration struck. She, herself, wanted badly to go to the Indian village. Just possibly, if her father approved of her plan, she might finally get to meet Silver Arrow!

"Father, let me go with you," Yvonne said. "I have made fresh bread and pies today. Let's take them to Silver Arrow as a peace offering. Just perhaps that might persuade Silver Arrow not to take the children from the school. Didn't you once tell me, Father, that kindness works miracles?"

Anthony kneaded his smoothly shaved chin.

"I will bake more tomorrow for our family," Yvonne quickly offered. "Please, Father. Let me go with you. Let us all three take the peace offerings to Silver Arrow and his people."

Anthony thought for a moment longer; then he smiled at Yvonne. "Yes, let's give it a try," he said. He took Stanley's hand and walked him up the steps beside Yvonne. "Yvonne, get the pies and bread ready. I'll get Stanley's spare eyeglasses from the desk."

"Then I am going with you?" Stanley asked, his eyes filled with excitement.

"Yes, it's time I introduce not only my daughter to Silver Arrow, but also my youngest son," Anthony said, stepping aside at the door so that Yvonne and Stanley could enter the cabin ahead of him.

"I like Rustling Leaves a lot," Stanley said, beaming, having already forgotten the torment he had experienced at the school. "She's become my best friend."

Her lips parted, her eyes wide, Yvonne turned to Stanley. "Your best friend?" she asked softly. "How wonderful, Stanley. She appears to be a sweet young lady."

Yvonne could not believe her luck. Although she hated the circumstances that would bring her and Silver Arrow together, there was no getting around the fact that she was glad to have the opportunity.

And for her brother to have singled out Rustling Leaves to be his best friend was the icing on the cake! That would make it much easier to become closer to Silver Arrow. A younger brother and sister could be the best means possible for them to find an excuse to meet . . . and to talk . . . and . . .

Her face flushed hot with a blush at where her mind had taken her. In her mind's eye she could not help but envision herself in Silver Arrow's arms.

It was not even hard to imagine how his lips might feel on hers if he should kiss her!

"Yvonne, have you got the pies and bread ready?" Anthony said, interrupting her thoughts. "Are *you* ready?"

She had, without conscious thought, wrapped the bread and pies with soft, blue linen napkins while she had been thinking about Silver Arrow. She laughed softly, knowing now how easy it was to drift off into another world while doing things mechanically.

Ah, how wonderful it was to immerse herself in thoughts of Silver Arrow. She only hoped that soon there would be more than imagining for her. She hoped to draw him into loving her.

"Yes, both the food and I are ready," Yvonne said.

She grabbed a shawl from a peg. She was certainly not going to wear an ugly coat. While in the presence of Silver Arrow, she wanted to look feminine.

Her heart raced at the thought of being near him; of actually talking with him!

"Son, here are your spare glasses," Anthony said, handing them to Stanley.

Stanley put the glasses on, then looked questioningly at his father as Anthony also handed the broken spectacles to him.

"Take the broken eyeglasses with you to the Indian village," Anthony said flatly.

"Why, Father?" Stanley asked.

"I have a good reason," Anthony said dryly. "Just please place them in your pants pocket."

"Yes, sir," Stanley said, thrusting the glasses into his right front breeches pocket. He turned and walked quickly toward the loft ladder. "Wait for me. I've something to do."

When he came back down the ladder from his bedroom, he held something behind him. He smiled broadly from Yvonne to his father.

"Stanley, what do you have behind your back?" Yvonne asked, a wrapped pie held between her hands.

"You are taking *your* gifts to the chief; I am taking mine to Rustling Leaves," Stanley said, bringing his hands out in front. In them he held a tiny carved horse. "You know that my hobby is carving wood. I recently carved this pony. I want Rustling Leaves to have it."

"That's so sweet," Yvonne said, her heart melting with love for her brother. "I'm sure Rustling Leaves will adore it."

They placed the bread and pies in the back of the buggy, then climbed aboard, Stanley sitting in the middle.

Before they could leave, Jake suddenly rode up. "Where are you going?" he asked, his gaze shifting to the back of the buggy when he got a whiff of the pies and bread. "Where are you taking the food?"

Anthony gently explained to Jake what had happened at the school, and about the gift of food they were taking to the Ottawa village.

"What about *our* supper?" Jake asked, his voice loud with complaint.

"I don't think you'll starve," Yvonne said sarcastically.

"Come along with us, Jake," Anthony quietly encouraged. "It might do you some good to have this chance to make friends with the Ottawa."

Jake's insides lurched at the suggestion. Perhaps meeting the Ottawa chief and befriending him *might* be to his advantage. But on second thought, it might be too risky. There had to be other ways to learn about the gold. He hadn't returned home for long. He was going to meet River Rat in the forest. Ironically, they also planned to go to the Indian village and spy on it.

"Naw, I think I'll pass on that one," Jake said.

"I thought you might," Anthony said sadly. "Jake, I feel as though I'm losing you. Don't you even want to try to prove that I'm wrong?"

"This ain't the time," Jake said, lowering his eyes.

"*Isn't* the time, Jake, *isn't*," Anthony corrected. "Would you listen to yourself? You sound as though you have had no education whatsoever, and, son, you couldn't have had any better than what you received in the fine schools of Saint Louis."

"Father, surely there are more things to worry about than me," Jake said, his voice breaking. "Please, *please*, let me be my own person!"

Jake gave Yvonne a quick, silent stare, then rode off in a huff.

"It gets worse each day," Anthony said. He snapped the reins and rested them on his lap as the horse moved onto the narrow path that led through the thick trees.

Uneasy and dispirited from Jake's strange behavior, Yvonne wrapped herself more closely into the folds of her shawl. She was so troubled over Jake, it was even hard to focus her thoughts on Silver Arrow.

She rode with her father and brother in silence, noting how the trail to the Indian village wound like a tattered ribbon through the trees, never far from the river.

A tremor shook Yvonne at the slightest sound, the unexpected beat of a wing, the tap of a woodpecker, an uneasy shifting among the leaves, or the whir of a startled grouse.

Suddenly her heart skipped a beat when she saw the crow as it swept down low over the buggy. Her eyes locked with the crow's. She felt strangely warm all over. The crow again looked so knowingly at her, so penetratingly.

Then it suddenly spread its wings and flew away. Breathlessly, Yvonne watched it until it was no longer in sight. It had flown in the direction of the Ottawa village.

Yvonne couldn't help feeling that there was something magical about the crow. Indeed, she felt a bond with it.

"Did you see that crow?" Anthony said, looking around Stanley at Yvonne. "I've never seen a bird act like that." He laughed. "It certainly seems fascinated with you, Yvonne."

Yvonne smiled awkwardly at her father. "Yes, it seems so," she murmured, surprised that even her father had noticed the crow's mysterious behavior.

"Father, tell me more about the Ottawa," she blurted out, to change the subject, to get her mind off so many things.

"Let me see," Anthony said, kneading his chin. "What's there to say that I haven't told you already?"

"I don't mind hearing it all again if you don't mind telling it," Yvonne offered. "I just want to know everything about them. They are our neighbors, you know."

"Yes, and it is good that you are interested in

their culture," Anthony said. "It might come in handy much sooner than you think."

"Tell me, Father," Yvonne softly encouraged.

"The Ottawa were raised to speak the Algonquian language, yet they now speak English as well as white men," Anthony said. "They raise many of the same crops we grow in our own little patch of garden, such as corn, beans, squash, peas, and melons. One interesting custom that we might adopt ourselves is that when their crops are poor, they make flour from beech nuts."

He paused, then continued. "The fur trade has flourished among the Ottawa ever since the French traders made their first appearance on the shores of Michigan. Many French traders married Indian women, mainly to establish kinship networks that were beneficial to them."

Yvonne looked quickly over at her father. "Then the Ottawa do marry out of their culture," she said, her voice guarded. "They see nothing wrong in marrying someone with white skin?"

Anthony gazed at Yvonne. He smiled slowly. "Why, daughter, do I sense too keen an interest in the subject of marriage?" he teased.

Her face hot with a blush, Yvonne looked quickly away from him. She felt dizzy from the rapid beat of her heart.

Perhaps it *was* possible for her and Silver Arrow to pursue a relationship!

Anthony turned his eyes back to the path. "It is going to be difficult for the Indian children to conform to the rigid discipline of a classroom," he said solemnly. "The Ottawa prefer the openness of nature and the woods. And they are taught not to destroy any part of nature unless it is necessary to do so for their survival."

"Perhaps it would be best if you try again to encourage the Ottawa to attend your church services," Yvonne said. "Wouldn't that give them even more opportunities to learn our language? The hymnals are all printed in English."

"Yes, that is so, but I have given my word to Silver Arrow that I won't press the issue of them attending my church," Anthony said. "And I have been with the Ottawa enough to know that the precepts . . . the moral commandments by which the Ottawa nation is governed . . . are almost the same as the Ten Commandments which God Almighty delivered to Moses on Mount Sinai."

"Yes, you explained to me earlier that very few of these divine precepts are not found in the religion of the Ottawa, except with regard to the Sabbath day," Yvonne said softly.

When they came to a clearing, Yvonne looked out over the hills toward the village, which was strategically located on a hill above the Grand River.

She looked farther still, marveling to herself at the maize fields that were visible against the darkness of the forest, beyond.

As they grew closer, Yvonne saw many bent, brown figures scattered among the yellow of the maize. She realized they were all women.

Shadows were long on the ground, and dark clouds lay low on the horizon. The air was cool and heavy with moisture when they reached the outskirts of the village.

Yvonne scarcely breathed as she looked slowly around her, at the longhouses with their barrel-shaped roofs, and at the wigwams scattered among them. Men dressed in breechcloths and moccasins, and women dressed in skirts and blouses and dresses went on about their business. Some stopped and stared, since this was the first time that Anthony had brought someone besides himself for council with their chief.

When Yvonne noticed some of the people glaring at the newcomers, she wondered if she and her family might now be considered enemies because of what had happened to Rustling Leaves today. She held her breath as they rode on toward one of the largest longhouses in the village, which she concluded must be Silver Arrow's.

Jake and River Rat sat on their horses on a butte that overlooked the Ottawa village. "Do you think we can trust Antelope Skin?" Jake asked, stiffening as he watched his family enter the village. "Do you think he can worm the information about the gold out of his cousin?"

"Time will tell," River Rat said, glowering as his eyes went to Yvonne, remembering how soft her thighs were to the tips of his fingers. "Yes, Jake, only time will tell."

Chapter Seven

Silver Arrow stiffened and gave the closed door of his lodge a searing stare. For the second time in one day a horse and buggy was approaching his lodge. He was not in the mood to talk with anyone. Not today. Perhaps not even tomorrow. He wanted peace in his and his sister's lives, not heartache brought on by whites!

Grumbling to himself, he went to the door and edged it open enough to see who was coming to disturb him this time. He relaxed slightly when he recognized Brother Stockton's buggy.

It did not take much thought to know why the Methodist preacher would be coming for council. Still angry at what the white boy had done to Rustling Leaves at the school, Silver Arrow turned away from the door and went to stand before the fireplace. Troubled, he gazed down at the fire. This was the first time he did not look forward to council with the white holy man.

What could the white man say to make things right for Rustling Leaves? The schoolmarm's apologies had been coolly received, and he had seen that she was escorted safely back to her home. That was the end of it as far as he was concerned. He wished not to discuss the incident ever again!

He sighed heavily. He had no choice in how he should receive Brother Stockton. Having formed a solid friendship with the Methodist preacher, which had grown each time they had met and talked, he had no choice but to bury any resentment he felt toward him for what had happened today. This man with the generous, loving heart was not at fault. The parents of the child who had done this dishonorable thing to Rustling Leaves were the ones at fault. They had obviously not spoken against prejudice in the presence of their son.

Rustling Leaves ran up to Silver Arrow and clung to his leg. "Someone is here," she said, her eyes wide as she gazed at the door. "I'm afraid."

Silver Arrow placed his hands on his sister's waist and lifted her into his arms. She straddled him with her tiny legs and rested a cheek against his chest as he stroked her long, unbraided, raven-black hair.

"*Wish-ko-bun o-mi-say-i-maw*, sweet sister, it is only Brother Stockton," Silver Arrow said softly. "He has always brought sunshine into our lodge.

Not fear. Do not fear him now."

"Where was he today when the ugly boy ruined my braids?" Rustling Leaves asked, her voice filled with sadness. "Where was he when the boy tripped me?"

"It is not Brother Stockton's duty to be at the school," Silver Arrow tried to explain. He lifted her chin and gazed at the bruise on her forehead. It was only slightly raised and yellow. "That is why he pays money to the schoolmarm. *She* is supposed to be there for you, should you need her."

A knock on the door made Silver Arrow's insides tighten. *Ae*, he always welcomed the white man in his lodge, but today he still felt too much resentment to enjoy small talk and laughter with the holy man.

Then again, perhaps Silver Arrow *could* make this council worth his while. In his mind's eye he could not forget the loveliness of the preacher's daughter, or how he ached to have her in his arms.

Ae, he could bring talk of *her* into the council.

Ae, it was time for him to bring his feelings for her to the forefront. And it was always best to approach the father first, the woman second.

That way, the road to the woman's heart would be easier.

Slipping Rustling Leaves from his arms and placing her moccasined feet firmly on the floor, Silver Arrow smiled reassuringly at her as she gazed up at him. "Remember always the goodness of Brother Stockton," he said softly. "There is no reason ever to be afraid of him."

"*Ae*, I know," Rustling Leaves said, nodding.

She ran to a chair and grabbed up her corn-husk doll and held it behind her, then went and stood directly behind Silver Arrow at the opened door.

When Silver Arrow saw Yvonne standing there with her father and her young brother, Stanley, standing beside her, his heart did a strange flip-flop. She was so close he could smell the sweet fragrance of her hair as the breeze lifted the wavy tendrils from her shoulders.

Yvonne's breath caught in her throat when she found herself eye to eye with the man of her dreams. Her knees grew weak and her stomach churned as their eyes held.

Yvonne could not believe that Silver Arrow could be even more handsome up close than he was at a distance. Yet it was true! Even in the dimming light of early evening she was able to see how sculpted his features were. And his eyes! They were so midnight dark! She swallowed hard at seeing how tall and majestic he was.

Silver Arrow stared at Yvonne, his pulse racing as he realized that she was even more beautiful each time he saw her. The live-coal glow in her hazel eyes. The gentle slope of her jaw, her dimpled cheeks, the perfect curve of her lips.

Slowly he shifted his eyes downward. His breath caught when her shawl slipped down from her shoulders and he saw, as he had many times before, how perfectly rounded her breasts were beneath the smooth fabric of her dress.

And her waist. How perfectly tiny it was. If ever he had the opportunity, he knew that he could place his hands around her waist and touch his fingertips together.

Seeing the exchange of silent admiration between Yvonne and Silver Arrow, Anthony cleared his throat. "Silver Arrow, I hope we aren't intruding on things you may have planned for this early evening," he said. When his words did not break the spell between his daughter and his Ottawa friend, he slid his eyes slowly from Silver Arrow to Yvonne, and then back again to Silver Arrow.

Then Silver Arrow's eyes leapt quickly to Anthony. "*Koo-koo-skoos*, I am sorry," he said thickly. "I did not hear what you said."

A thrill coursed through Yvonne's veins to know that this wonderful man was as taken with her as she was with him! Her soft eyes lit with joy as she watched him with Anthony. She was delighted that she was the cause of his not having heard what her father had said to him. He had been too absorbed in her!

Oh, dear Lord, perhaps her dreams would come true, she thought to herself. She knew now for certain that she loved him. Without even exchanging conversation, kisses, or embraces, she knew how she felt about him.

"I said I hope we aren't intruding on your privacy at this time of evening," Anthony said, gazing up at Silver Arrow. "I normally send advance word of my wish to have council with you. But today there was no time. I wanted to come and offer my apologies for what happened to your sister at the school."

"*Kau*, no, you are not an intrusion," Silver Arrow said. "But you did not have to come with apologies. The schoolmarm's explanation was adequate."

"I felt that it was my place to come and personally offer my own explanations and apologies," Anthony said, his gaze shifting when he caught Rustling Leaves peeking out from behind her brother to give Stanley a shy smile.

Anthony looked up again and saw Princess Pretty Hawk, Silver Arrow's elderly grandmother, standing in the shadows of the lodge behind them. She stood ever so still, watching and listening, her eyes scarcely blinking.

"You are welcome to my lodge anytime," Silver Arrow said.

"Thank you, Silver Arrow," Anthony said. "I appreciate your kindness." He looked over at Yvonne and Stanley. "My young son and my daughter have come with me today. Silver Arrow, I would like for you to meet Yvonne and Stanley," he said proudly as he gestured toward them.

"It is good to know you both," Silver Arrow said, first extending a hand to Yvonne.

Yvonne's pulse raced at the thought of actually touching him. She could not control the tremor in her fingers as she fit her hand in his. "It is a pleasure to know you," she murmured, hoping that her voice did not reveal the anxiousness she felt.

Silver Arrow held her hand for a moment

Cassie Edwards

longer and gazed down at her with his warm eyes, then eased his hand away and shook Stanley's.

"It is nice to know you, young brave," he said.

"And I am glad to finally meet you, sir," Stanley said, looking proud to be treated like an adult by this powerful Indian chief.

Silver Arrow dropped his hands to his sides. "Do come in," he said, stepping aside.

Rustling Leaves moved with him, her doll still held behind her. Her eyes held Stanley's as he walked past her with his father and sister.

As Yvonne moved past Silver Arrow, her heart accelerated. Her cheeks flamed with a blush, for she was quite aware of his eyes on her, following her every move.

She took a deep breath and willed herself to take control of her emotions so she could get through these next moments without looking like an utter fool in the eyes of this wonderful man. She wanted to impress him so much that he could never forget her! She wanted him to want her as much as she wanted him!

Silver Arrow could not take his eyes off the white woman, his White Swan. Everything about her betokened energy and strength. Her firm, steady step, the determined curve of her lips, the sparkle in her eyes.

And he was not blind to the way her cheeks were suddenly flooded with color. He understood well what caused it: his study of her, his obvious interest in her!

He smiled slowly. *Ae*, soon he would be holding her. He would be kissing her.

But first he must get the formalities between her father and himself behind him.

Today had not been the best of days for his sister, his people, or himself.

When even one of his people was ridiculed openly by white people, they all felt it as though it were a personal insult.

As Yvonne stepped further into the longhouse, the light of the fire from the great stone fireplace gave her the opportunity to see how Silver Arrow lived. She was surprised to see that his home was not much different from her family's cabin, except for the wall and floor decorations.

She was quite impressed. The longhouse was spacious, with more than one room on the lower floor. As in her own family's cabin, this longhouse had a loft overhead which offered more sleeping area.

Bearskin rugs were spread neatly across the floor where rush mats were not strewn. Rich furs of elk and beaver, and bright blankets and wampum belts, beads, and embroidery hung over the walls and rafters. The furniture was no less comfortable than the pieces in Yvonne's cabin, with overstuffed chairs positioned close to the fire.

At the far side of this outer room was the kitchen area. Yvonne was amazed to see a cast-iron cooking stove. There was even a comfortable-looking table and chairs. And shelves along the walls displayed an assortment of dishes and pots and pans.

Her gaze shifted. Baskets of wampum beads, to be strung into belts, sat in the corner. Skins lay over shelves along one wall. Bark boxes decorated with dyed porcupine quills in appliqué work sat beneath a window. The flickering candles around the room were homemade, like those she made for her family.

Her eyes drawn by a movement in the shadows, she saw an elderly woman coming from one of the back rooms, walking slowly toward a rocking chair in a corner away from the other seating.

Yvonne had heard her father speak of Silver Arrow's grandmother. This must be Princess Pretty Hawk.

Yvonne became uneasy under the close scrutiny of the elderly lady as she rocked slowly back and forth, her eyes never leaving her, as though she knew Yvonne's deep desire to be loved by her chieftain grandson.

For a while there were no sounds but the crackling fire and the squeaking of the rocking chair. Yvonne was glad when Silver Arrow's voice broke the silence. She looked quickly at him as he bent to one knee and began talking with Stanley and Rustling Leaves. The children's eyes lit up as he suggested they join the youngsters outside to play.

Stanley looked up at Anthony for permission.

"First, Stanley, we have something to show Silver Arrow," Anthony said, going to stand over his son. He nodded toward Stanley's pants pocket. "Son, show Silver Arrow your broken eyeglasses."

Stanley reached inside his pocket and pulled out his glasses.

"Give them to Silver Arrow," Anthony softly suggested.

Yvonne scarcely breathed as she watched Silver Arrow take the glasses.

She then looked questioningly at her step-father, wondering why he would have Stanley give the glasses to the Ottawa chief. Then she smiled slowly when she listened to her father's explanation.

Silver Arrow rose to his full height and turned the broken glasses over and over in his hands, then looked down at Anthony. "And so these were also broken today at the school?" he said, arching an eyebrow.

"Yes, and they are proof that not only was your sister ridiculed but also my son," Anthony said, his voice drawn. "The same child that was cruel to your sister was also cruel to my son. He took the glasses off Stanley's nose and stomped on them. Do you not see then, Silver Arrow, that your sister was not singled out for ridicule?"

"*Motchi-manitou*, that is bad," Silver Arrow grumbled. He gazed down at Stanley. "Young brave, I am sorry."

"Thank you, sir," Stanley said, lowering his eyes bashfully.

Rustling Leaves, who until now had held her doll behind her, suddenly drew it around for everyone to see. "See my doll?" she cried. "That same mean boy yanked the doll from me and tore its head off as I walked past him to leave the school."

"I was not told that he also did that," Anthony said, frowning.

"But he did," Rustling Leaves said, tears falling from her eyes. "My pretty doll no longer has a head."

Stanley gently took the doll from Rustling Leaves. He examined it, then smiled at her. "I can make you another doll," he said. "Would you like that, Rustling Leaves?"

"That would please me so," Rustling Leaves said, looking at him as though he were a king. "Can you? Can you make me another doll?"

"Yes, and I shall do so today if you wish," Stanley said, beaming.

"*Ae*, please do, Stanley," Rustling Leaves said, looking adoringly up at him.

Stanley turned to his father. "Father, may I be excused so that I can go with Rustling Leaves to the garden and gather more cornhusks for a doll?"

"It will be dark soon, son," Anthony said, glancing toward the door, seeing the waning light. Then he patted Stanley on the shoulder. "But go on." He looked up at Silver Arrow. "That is, if Silver Arrow doesn't mind."

"Your son has a good heart," Silver Arrow said, smiling down at Stanley. "Go, young brave, with my sister. She has found a good friend in you. I think it is a good thing for you both."

"Thank you, sir," Stanley said in his usual courteous manner. Then his eyes widened as he looked over at Rustling Leaves again. "But first, Rustling Leaves, I have something to give you."

He slipped his hand in his left breeches pocket and took out the carved pony. "I have brought this gift to you." He placed it in her small hands. "Do you like it?"

Rustling Leaves gasped with delight as she looked down at the carved figure. She smiled at Stanley. "Why, it is more beautiful than anything I have ever seen," she said in the perfect English her brother had taught her. "Thank you, Stanley. You are such a dear friend!"

Stanley blushed and lowered his eyes, then looked at Rustling Leaves again. He placed the headless doll on a chair, then reached a hand out for Rustling Leaves.

She placed her free hand in his and left the lodge with him, giggling.

Princess Pretty Hawk still sat in her rocker, slowly rocking back and forth, offering no conversation, only watching and listening.

"My daughter and I have also brought gifts this evening," Anthony murmured, giving Yvonne a smile. "Yvonne, shall we go out and get what we have brought Silver Arrow and his family?"

Silver Arrow's gaze shifted to Yvonne.

As her eyes locked with his, she was again taken by his handsomeness, by his majestic presence.

Anthony moved closer to her and cleared his throat. "Yvonne, the pies . . . the bread . . . ?" he said, his voice hardly more than a whisper.

"Oh, yes, the pies . . . the bread . . ." Yvonne said, laughing awkwardly.

Silver Arrow went outside with them and helped them carry the gifts from Yvonne's kitchen inside. His eyes danced and a smile tugged at his lips as he gazed from Yvonne to her offerings, pleased by both.

Yvonne and Anthony followed Silver Arrow to his kitchen and placed the pies and bread on his table. They then returned to the sitting room. Silver Arrow gestured toward the chairs that sat before the fire. "Please sit and talk," he said.

Yvonne's heart raced to know that she was going to get to stay longer with Silver Arrow. She smiled politely at him, her insides stirring passionately when again he gave her more than a look of mere acquaintance. She shivered as she recalled the crow and how it always looked as probingly as this at her.

But this was not the crow. This was the man of her fascination!

"Thank you, I would enjoy resting before we head back for home," Yvonne said. As though on a cloud, she moved in a glide to a chair and sat down.

She sat with her back straight and her hands folded on her lap as her father sat down, and then Silver Arrow.

She watched as Silver Arrow lifted a long-stemmed calumet pipe from the hearth and filled it with tobacco. He started to offer it to her father, then withdrew the offer.

She smiled to herself, knowing that Silver Arrow understood, through his many councils with her father, that Anthony did not smoke, drink, or curse.

Yvonne watched Silver Arrow rest against the

back of the chair and take several long draws from his pipe. Out of the corner of her eye she saw Princess Pretty Hawk rise from the rocking chair and go to the kitchen. Yvonne turned and watched the elderly woman who was so heavy that her every step seemed to pain her.

When Yvonne saw Princess Pretty Hawk reach for three cups, then pour something from a kettle into them, she started to go and offer her assistance.

But she chose not to when her father reached over and patted her knee as a message to sit still and let things happen as the Ottawa wished it to happen.

Soon Princess Pretty Hawk came to them with the cups on a wooden platter. She said nothing when she offered mint tea and berry cakes to each of them.

"Thank you," Yvonne said, smiling up at Princess Pretty Hawk, scarcely able to see the woman's eyes for the deep folds of wrinkles that crisscrossed her face. She took a cup, then a cake, and waited until everyone else was served.

Then she nibbled on the cake and sipped on the tea as her father and Silver Arrow engaged in quiet conversation.

Yvonne relaxed as they discussed what had happened today to the children, her eyes roaming again around the longhouse.

She gasped at the richness of a beautiful coat hanging on a peg on the far wall. It was made of a bear's snow white pelt, with all sorts of symbols sewn on it with beautiful beads. It looked like some sort of ceremonial coat.

"I wish I could promise that it will never happen again," Anthony said, drawing Yvonne's attention back to him. "But one never knows when children will get mischievous ideas inside their head."

"*Ae*, yes, I understand that, and the Ottawa children will continue to attend your school," Silver Arrow said. "It has been proven to me today that prejudices are not only acted out against redskins, but also against whites. You were wise to bring your son's broken eyeglasses today to me, to show proof of this prejudice and injustice."

The more her stepfather and Silver Arrow laughed and talked, the more Yvonne fell hopelessly in love with the Ottawa chief.

Chapter Eight

Antelope Skin had seen River Rat and Jake watching the village. He went to them. He was hazy from drinking. He listened to what they were saying, offering no conversation himself.

"River Rat, I have a plan that might get our hands on the gold," Jake said. "As I watched Silver Arrow and Yvonne get the baked goods from the wagon, I saw how their eyes would suddenly lock and hold. I think they have feelings for one another. If Yvonne married Silver Arrow, she might be able to find out from him where the gold is buried. If she hesitates, I will force answers from her. She *will* tell me."

Disillusioned about Yvonne, although he would never get over hungering for her, River Rat laughed throatily. "Yeah, I think you've got something there," he said. He spat a stream of tobacco over his shoulder. "Encourage it, Jake. Send your sister into the arms of the chief."

Antelope Skin frowned at the idea. He did not see how such an alliance between his chief and the white woman could help his plans of one day being chief.

He stumbled away.

Jake and River Rat laughed at his awkwardness. They hurried after him.

"Where you goin', huh?" Jake prodded. "Aren't you ready for some more firewater?"

Antelope Skin fell over a log. His face flamed hot with humiliation as the two white men stood over him, ridiculing and laughing at him. He was beginning to dislike them, yet he needed them to further his own plans. He couldn't do this alone. One man against a whole village of Ottawa, especially a chieftain cousin who had magical powers, was a man who would be doomed.

And without Jake and River Rat he would not have the firewater!

He hung his head as Jake gave him a shove when he tried to get up from the ground.

"You no 'count Injun," River Rat said, laughing boisterously.

Antelope Skin glowered up at him, hate building in his heart.

Chapter Nine

The morning was fresh and new. Alone, Yvonne was finding it hard to get her mind on her morning chores. All she could think about was her time at Silver Arrow's village. Although she had not been alone with Silver Arrow, just finally becoming acquainted with him was wonderful.

Recalling how often his eyes shifted her way as they had talked before the roaring fire at his longhouse made Yvonne's heart sing.

And the touch of his hand against hers when they had made their acquaintance had been a moment of pure magic.

Still deep in thought, Yvonne spread a comforter across her bed, the morning sun spilling through the window in golden threads across the floral-designed, embroidered fabric.

How could she ever forget being so close to Silver Arrow that she had smelled his manly, woodsy scent? she thought, sighing dreamily as she closed her eyes in continued sensual thought of him.

It was not hard to imagine how his lips would taste, and how masterfully his hands could bring her alive with each touch, each caress.

Suddenly Yvonne's eyes flew open when she heard gunfire coming from the woods a short distance away.

Flinging an angry glance at the window, she tightened her hands into fists at her sides as the gunfire continued.

Jake.

He had said he was going hunting, but she knew better. Never did he hunt this close to their cabin. He was surely shooting at the crow again!

Her hands slowly unclenched when she heard no more gunfire. Perhaps Jake had gone on his way. Just perhaps, he had decided not to shoot at the crow anymore.

Or somehow realizing the danger, perhaps the crow had flown away.

Jake was laughing as he entered the cabin and headed for Yvonne's bedroom door.

When he came and stood just inside her room, his eyes were filled with the devil as he smiled smugly at her. Yvonne was afraid to ask what had suddenly become so humorous.

Then a thought gripped her heart with an icy fear. Had he finally succeeded in shooting the crow? What else could make him so jolly this early in the morning, while earlier he had been moody and distant?

"I finally winged that damn crow," Jake said, laughing throatily.

Yvonne's confirmed suspicions aroused her anger, yet she kept her ground, for she knew that if she got anywhere near Jake, she might do worse than slap him!

"You say you winged the crow," she said tightly. "Does that mean it is only wounded? Or did you kill it? Is it dead?"

"I'm not sure," Jake said, shrugging nonchalantly. "I lost sight of it when it fell from the sky. I hope the wolves find it and eat it. It'd be good riddance of that pesky thing."

"How could you be so . . . so . . . heartless?" Yvonne cried, stunned to know just how unfeeling Jake was toward the forest creatures.

"Hey, sis, how'd your visit go at the Indian village yesterday?" Jake asked, purposely ignoring her building anger. He absently ran his hand up and down the barrel of his rifle. "When are you going to marry up with the chief? You'd make a damn pretty squaw. I think you *should* marry him. His gold would then be, in part, yours. You'd be rich, Yvonne. Rich! Rich enough to share some of the gold with your brother. You would, wouldn't you, Yvonne? You'd share it with your brother?"

Wondering if Jake somehow knew of her feelings for Silver Arrow, Yvonne paled. She listened as he continued talking about how the gold would be partly hers if she married Silver Arrow, wondering why Jake was pursuing the subject so intensely.

But, too concerned about the crow to worry about anything else, Yvonne stamped up to Jake and leaned into his face. "Get out of my way," she hissed.

When he didn't budge, she raised a hand to slap him, then had second thoughts when she saw the warning that leapt into his eyes.

She lowered her arm to her side, her fingers clenched into a tight fist.

"I'd watch it if I were you," Jake said, moving away from her. "I told you never to slap me again."

"I should do worse," Yvonne said, inching toward him as he still slowly backed away from her. "And as for my marrying Silver Arrow? If I am ever lucky enough for him to have me, I won't be marrying him for his gold." She laughed sarcastically. "And, big brother, forget about thinking I would share anything with you, *ever*. You are lazy, shiftless, worthless. . . ."

Jake glowered at her, then stormed out of the cabin.

Yvonne waited until she heard him leave on his horse, then ran outside and began a frantic search for the crow, for it had become more than a crow to her.

When she couldn't find the crow, tears filled her eyes. It was hard to envision it dying somewhere out there, helpless. And Jake had been right to think that it might be eaten by wolves, or anything else that stalked the forest.

That thought sent her on another lengthy search, this time closer to the house than in the forest. Something told her that the crow would know to seek her help. If it was alive, perhaps it had managed to find its way out of the thick forest.

Now moving more slowly, her eyes darting around her, Yvonne walked beneath a tentlike arbor of birch saplings where annual vines of sweet peas, canary creeper, morning glories, and ancient wisteria climbed and tangled in the boughs.

She moved through her vegetable garden where radishes were fat and red in the ground, and where the corn was already knee high. Zucchini was just emerging from the stub of their blossoms, spiraling and twining up the tall, slender poles she had placed there for them.

She walked around the piece of land where peanuts had been planted, then entered another garden which displayed an assortment of beautiful flowers, the seeds having been carefully preserved and brought from her flower garden in Saint Louis.

Slowly she made her way through the zinnias, snapdragons, and marigolds, and then entered another part of the garden where hollyhocks stood sentinel over the other flowers.

Then she stopped. Her breath caught in her throat when she saw the crow lying on its side amidst the tall-stalked flowers, a spattering of blood on its wing.

When the bird did not move at the sound of her

103

approach but lay there so lifelessly, Yvonne covered her mouth with a hand and stifled a sob, for surely the bird was dead.

"Damn you, Jake," she whispered as tears crept from her eyes.

She moved softly onward, then fell to her knees beside the crow. As she leaned lower over it, her heart leapt with joy when she could tell that it was breathing.

Her fingers trembling, she slipped a hand beneath the crow. Placing her other hand softly over the injured wing to steady the bird, she gathered it into the palm of her left hand.

The heat of the bird's body blended into the palm of her hand. She could even feel its steady, strong heartbeat, which proved that it was not all that badly injured. She studied the wound, and could tell that it was not very deep. The bullet had only grazed the wing.

Her gaze shifted to the bird's eyes. Until now they had been closed, but suddenly they were open and looking up at her. What were usually vibrant eyes were now hazed over with pain.

Yvonne gasped at how the bird seemed to momentarily plead with her, and then closed its eyes again.

"I so badly want to help you," she whispered. "But what can I do? If I take you inside the house, Jake will find you. He'll kill you this time for certain."

But recalling Jake's words about wolves eating the bird, Yvonne knew she could not leave the crow there, to die. The bird must be kept from predators until it could fly again!

A thought sprang to her mind that made her smile down at the crow. "I will take you to my bedroom, see to your wound, then hide you under my bed until you are well enough to fly again," she murmured.

Before standing up, she looked slowly all around her. Although she had not heard anyone arrive, she wanted to be sure that she was not observed, for what she was about to do would seem strange to most people.

How could she explain her attachment to this bird, and its to her?

Even she didn't understand what was happening between them. All she knew was that she wanted to protect it, make it well, then release it to nature again and hope that Jake would forget his obsession to kill it if he saw it again.

Yvonne covered the bird with her apron and rose to her feet. Her pulse racing, she rushed to the cabin and into her bedroom. Gently placing the bird on the floor, she grabbed a blanket from the foot of the bed and folded it in fours, then arranged it neatly on the floor beside the bird.

Scarcely breathing, she lifted the crow onto the blanket. For a moment she stared down at the bird, wishing it would open its eyes again or do anything to show that it was going to be all right.

When it still just lay there, lifeless, Yvonne rose and went to the kitchen and pumped some water into a small wooden basin, grabbed a dishcloth, then hurried back to the bedroom.

"Don't be afraid," she whispered as she carefully washed the blood from the bird's wing. "I am here to make you well again."

She was glad to see that once the blood was removed, the wound was not as bad as she had at first believed. There were only a few feathers missing. The flesh of the wing was exposed only where the wound still seeped blood.

"Dear bird, you will fly again," Yvonne whispered, dropping the cloth into the water. "And I hope *soon*. I'm going to have a terrible time keeping you a secret."

Lovingly Yvonne stroked the bird's wing below the wound. "You are so pretty," she whispered. "Your wings are so sleek and black. How could Jake hate you so much?"

As though the bird heard what she said, its eyes fluttered open and stared up at her.

Touched deeply by the way the bird was gazing at her, Yvonne felt hypnotized. Although its eyes were still somewhat hazed over with pain, it was as though the crow were looking into her very soul.

Yvonne swallowed hard as she came out of her trance, knowing that she must return to her household duties. "I wish I understood what has transpired between us," she whispered. "Will I ever know?"

The crow closed its eyes again.

"Sleep, sweet thing," Yvonne whispered, slowly sliding the blanket and crow beneath her bed. "I shall return later to check on you."

As she backed out of the room, her eyes on the bed, Yvonne's insides trembled. At all costs, she had to keep Jake out of this room, as well as Stanley and her father. No one would understand her obsession with the bird.

How could they, when even *she* didn't?

Chapter Ten

The terrifying dreams came one after the other, tumbling through Princess Pretty Hawk's mind so quickly she shook and quivered in her sleep.

She cried out when the dreams worsened, waking her up in a start.

Sweating, her eyes wild, she gazed slowly around her dark bedroom. The savage light of the dancing shadows made from the low-burning embers of the fireplace beyond, in the living room, made the night seem even more mysterious and frightening.

She swallowed hard as she slowly sat up and drew a blanket around her thick shoulders. Although her grandson, Silver Arrow, owned her late husband's coat of magic, which his grandfather had made from the white bear of mystery and magic, the dreams she kept having tonight of white bears were frightening to her.

The bears in her dreams were enormous and white, nothing like anyone had ever seen. And they had not brought goodness to her in her dreams! They had brought mayhem, mystery, and despair to her people as the bears had suddenly turned into Iroquois warriors, who murdered and maimed many of her beloved Ottawa people.

Princess Pretty Hawk recalled her father telling her, so very, very long ago, that he received all of his luck of every kind from his dreams.

He had told her that *she* could have such dreams. Any man or woman could. She wanted to believe in her dreams. But tonight's was not the sort to thank the Great Spirit for. They were too terrifying. The horrors of the dreams were . . . too . . . real.

As she placed her bare feet on the cold wooden floor of the longhouse, she again looked cautiously around her. Her fingers trembled as they clutched the blanket more snugly to her.

"*Uk-say*, oh, horrors! What could the dreams mean?" she whispered to herself. "Was this message sent to me as a warning from *Gitchimanitou*, the Great Spirit?"

She shuddered. "I must go and share my dreams with Silver Arrow," she said aloud, her jaw firming determinedly. "He will know what to do. As were his grandfather and father before him, who now ride their spirit horses in the sky, Silver Arrow is the wisest of all men."

She lumbered toward the door, her heavy weight causing the boards to creak beneath her feet. Now that she was fully awake and knew that her grandson was only a room away, she was no longer filled with so much fear and apprehension. As her husband and son had protected her when they were alive, her grandson now cared for her with dignity, respect, and undying love.

Yes, she was proud to have such a grandson. He was everything to her.

As sparks suddenly sent a spray upward from the dying embers of the fire, filling the living room with a strange trembling glow, Princess Pretty Hawk jumped with alarm.

She glanced at the fire's glowing ashes, then shuffled her feet onward until she came to Silver Arrow's room.

As usual, the door was ajar so that Silver Arrow could hear the sounds from the outer rooms. Princess Pretty Hawk shoved the door all the way open and gazed into the room. She squinted her eyes as she peered at the bed. But it was too dark to see Silver Arrow.

She tapped lightly on the door, so as not to awaken her grandson too quickly and frighten him. A slight tap was usually enough to awaken him, for it seemed that he slept with one eye open, his ears always alert to all movements around him, both day and night.

When Princess Pretty Hawk got no response, her shaggy gray brows forked quizzically. She had expected Silver Arrow to speak quickly in response to her knock, but instead there was a muted, ghostly silence in his room.

"Silver Arrow, it is I, your grandmother," Princess Pretty Hawk said, taking a step inside his room.

Again there was a showering of sparks behind her in the fireplace, sending off enough orange glow for her to see more clearly around her in the bedroom.

Princess Pretty Hawk's knees weakened when she discovered that Silver Arrow was not in his bed, nor had his blankets been disturbed since she, herself, had lovingly straightened them earlier in the day for him.

Her shoulders tightened and her throat went dry as she stepped into the room, then turned and looked behind her.

Her heart thumped wildly in her chest. She suddenly feared for not only herself, but also for her grandson. This was not like him. Never did he stay overnight anywhere unless he sent word to her.

Kau, no, never would he worry and frighten her like this, not unless he was somewhere, harmed, or . . .

She wanted to not think any further about what might have happened to him, about why he was not there, peacefully sleeping in his bed.

The dream!

Now it frightened her more than before!

Perhaps the dream was an omen of what had happened to her grandson!

It could have been a warning!

Tears flowed down Princess Pretty Hawk's

cheeks. Weakened by her fear for her grandson, she found it hard to put one foot ahead of the other as she left the bedroom and walked toward the front door, to go and seek help, and hopefully positive answers from Silver Arrow's best friend, Four Horns. Four Horns knew everything about Silver Arrow . . . about his magic, his thoughts, his wishes, and his desires.

If Four Horns did not accompany his best friend and chief as Silver Arrow went from place to place, at least he knew where he could be found.

"Surely he knows where Silver Arrow is," Princess Pretty Hawk whispered as she stepped out into the moonlight. A sob lodged in her throat. "Four Horns *has* to know. If not, who is to say where my grandson is, or what may have happened to him?"

Four Horns lived in a lodge quite different from Silver Arrow's. He had chosen the smaller, simpler lodge of his ancestors, a wigwam covered with birchbark mats, where inside there was only one small room with a fire pit centered in the floor.

Four Horns had said that until he took a wife, this lodge would suffice. He did not have that much to keep clean. And his personal possessions were few.

Winded from her long walk across the village to Four Horns' lodge, and worried about the commotion she had stirred up by disturbing the village dogs into yapping, Princess Pretty Hawk was relieved when she finally reached her destination.

She stopped and took a deep breath. She wiped perspiration from her brow. Then she stepped up close to the gently swaying buckskin fabric that served as Four Horns' door. Quietly she spoke Four Horns' name.

She was glad when he came quickly outside, his hands fumbling as he tied the leather thongs at the waist of his buckskin breeches.

"What is it, Princess Pretty Hawk?" Four Horns asked, his dark eyes imploring her as the moon's glow revealed her troubled expression. "Why are you here at this time of night?"

He bent low beside her and brushed a sniffing dog away from her, sending it off in a hard run, yapping, its tail tucked between its legs.

"I dreamed of the bear *Maiyun*, but it was not of normal size, and there were many," she cried. "In my dream the bears turned into Iroquois warriors! They came to our village! They slaughtered so many!"

Four Horns placed a gentle, comforting hand on Pretty Hawk's shoulder. "Princess, do not be frightened of your dreams," he said softly. "Most times they mean nothing."

Then a thought came to him that sent a cold spiral of fear through his veins. "Why do you come and tell *me* of such dreams, when your grandson is there in your lodge for you, to comfort you, to make you less afraid during the midnight hours?" he said, his voice thin with wariness.

"I came to you not only to tell you of my dreams, but to also tell you that my grandson is

113

not in his bed as he usually is," Princess Pretty Hawk said. "Please tell me that you know where Silver Arrow is. Please tell me that he only forgot to tell me that he would be elsewhere tonight. I do not want to hear that you, too, do not know where he is. That would only mean that harm might have come to him!"

She covered her mouth and stifled a sob behind her hand. "He . . . might . . . even be dead!" she cried. "My dream might have been sent to me to tell me who killed him! The Iroquois! Did they not also kill my son? Are they not to blame for my dear husband's death?"

Knowing that Pretty Hawk would not have come to him with her dreams if Silver Arrow had been there, Four Horns sighed with despair and apprehension.

How could he tell this aged woman that he had no idea where Silver Arrow was?

All he knew was that Silver Arrow had left sometime in the afternoon to watch the lovely white woman another time, to know her better before taking a bride price to her father.

"Tell me what you know about my grandson," Princess Pretty Hawk pleaded, her voice breaking. "I can see that you know something you are not saying aloud. Tell me. It is not fair that I do not also know."

Four Horns swallowed hard. His eyes wavered as he dropped his hand down from her shoulder. "There is a woman," he said thickly.

"My grandson is with a woman tonight?" Princess Pretty Hawk said, her heartbeats slowing somewhat at the thought of him being safe with a woman, instead of lying dead on the ground somewhere.

Yet that, too, was not usual for her grandson. He had never slept overnight with a woman before. He had not yet found that perfect woman with whom he wished to share his life. Surely he would have told his own grandmother of such a thing!

"I did not say that," Four Horns said, not sure how to tell Princess Pretty Hawk about Silver Arrow's recent actions, unsure of whether or not Princess Pretty Hawk knew the true depths of her grandson's mysterious powers.

"Then he is not with a woman?" Princess Pretty Hawk said, getting more confused by the minute. The pain of fear of something having possibly happened to her grandson again grabbed the pit of her stomach.

"He has not been with a woman, but only *watching* her," Four Horns said. He immediately saw how that explanation puzzled the princess even more. "He has found a woman he wishes to bring into his life. He will soon offer a bride price to her father."

"Who is this woman?" Pretty Hawk asked, yet in her mind thinking she might guess her identity. Had she not seen the fascination between her grandson and the white woman whose father was a holy man?

She was not sure how she felt about her grandson's fascination with a white woman. Yet Princess Pretty Hawk had seen the gentleness and sweetness of Yvonne Armistead. Those qualities would make it easier for Princess Pretty Hawk to look past the color of her skin.

"Her father is one who has made a close alliance with your grandson, and now with our people as a whole," Four Horns said.

"*Ae*, I know her," Princess Pretty Hawk said softly. "I observed her closely when she accompanied her father to our village recently. She is *mi-no-e-zhi-wa-bawt*, kind. She is *wish-ko-bun*, sweet. She appears to be a kindhearted, gentle woman."

Then she reached out a hand and grabbed Four Horns' arm. "You said that Silver Arrow is not with the woman, that he only watches her," she said, her voice trembling. "He cannot be watching her now. The night is black. It is time for everyone to be asleep. He could not watch her sleeping. She would be in her lodge. If he does not watch her, then . . . where is he, Four Horns? Where is my grandson?"

Four Horns knew that Princess Pretty Hawk had an old, tired heart, weak from many years of living, and from the many heartaches she had been forced to endure, which made it hard now to tell her of his true concerns about her grandson.

But he could not stand there with small talk any longer. He had to round up many warriors into a search party. They would go and search for Silver Arrow.

And time was their enemy. The longer Silver Arrow was gone, perhaps lying injured in the forest, the greater the chances of his not surviving.

"Again, *ni-wob*, I see a fear and concern in your eyes that you are not speaking aloud to me," Princess Pretty Hawk said, her voice again breaking. "Tell me what you are thinking. Tell me what you are going to do."

"I am going to gather together many of our warriors and we will leave on horseback and find Silver Arrow," Four Horns said, his voice drawn. He drew her into his arms. "Princess Pretty Hawk, I will not stop until I find him. His heartbeats and mine are as one. I . . . will . . . find him."

"I know you will," Princess Pretty Hawk said, taking comfort in his muscled arms.

She then stepped back from him and clutched the blanket around her shoulders. "Go, my grandson's best friend," she said, tears streaming from her eyes. "I shall go to my lodge and pray to *Gitchi-manitou* that you will bring my grandson home safe. Without Silver Arrow, our people will be only half alive. He breathes life and love into each of our lives. Without him, we will be only half a people!"

"*Ae*, I know, and I *will* bring him back to you and our people," Four Horns reassured. He placed a soft kiss on her brow, then turned and went back inside his lodge to finish dressing and grab his rifle.

Princess Pretty Hawk went to her longhouse. Before entering to begin her prayers, she stood at the door and watched the warriors gathering, the barrels of their rifles gleaming in the moonlight, their proud steeds snorting and pawing at the packed earth.

She stiffened when one warrior whom she despised stepped up to Four Horns, a look of defiance in his eyes.

She cringed when she heard what he had to say as the others guardedly and silently watched and listened.

"In my cousin's absence I will be acting chief," Antelope Skin boasted, boldly lifting his chin. "It is only right that I do this. Our people should never be without the guidance of a chief. It is I who should take over these duties. Besides Silver Arrow's elderly grandmother and sister, I am his only next of kin."

A hush fell over everyone as they stared disbelievingly at Antelope Skin, then turned slow eyes to Four Horns as he leaned angrily into Antelope Skin's face.

"Do not act so anxious to be chief," Four Horns said from between clenched teeth. "Or, Antelope Skin, it will look as though you have had a hand in your cousin's strange disappearance tonight." Four Horns laughed sarcastically. "You fool yourself by thinking you can ever be chief," he said. "You are not worthy of the title, not only because your heart is filled with suspicion and hatred, but because your belly is filled too often with firewater."

Four Horns sniffed. "Even now you reek of the white man's devil drink," he hissed. "You have lost your reasoning and your ability to think clearly. Do you not know that your brain shrivels up more and more each time you take firewater into your body? Antelope Skin, because of your misguided use of firewater, you have lost the respect of your people. How ignorant you are to not know that intoxicating liquor is the great destroyer of mankind."

Antelope Skin glared at Four Horns for a moment, then cowered away from him. He stood in the shadows of the lodges as the warriors rode off.

Princess Pretty Hawk stepped out of the shadows.

Antelope Skin turned with a start and stared at her.

"You shame me so," she said, her voice drawn. "You shame our family name."

Antelope Skin gasped, then hung his head and walked away.

Her thoughts again on her grandson instead of Antelope Skin, Princess Pretty Hawk went inside her longhouse. She took a small buckskin parfleche bag from a shelf and went and knelt down before the fire.

As she sprinkled sweetgrass from the bag onto the glowing embers of the fire, she lifted her eyes heavenward and began her soft prayers for her grandson.

"*Gitchi-manitou*, please . . . please . . ." she whispered.

Tears streamed down her cheeks and across her lips. "Silver Arrow is all that is good on this earth. Why would you take *him* away from his people? Why? Was it not enough that you took my beloved son? And . . . then . . . my husband? If you must take anyone, why not take me? I am old. I am worthless. Can you not hear me? I . . . am . . . worthless!"

The mournful cry of a loon wafting across the river outside her lodge sent shivers up and down Princess Pretty Hawk's spine. She now knew that her prayers had been heard, but what did this response from the Great Spirit mean?

What was his answer?

Was her grandson alive . . . or dead?

Chapter Eleven

The night was a clear blue-gray with stars scattered between black clouds. Overhead the moon hung in the sky like a great luminous rock. Its rays streamed in through Yvonne's bedroom window. They touched the room's corners, bounced off its walls, and radiated an almost heavenly light on Yvonne's face as she stood at the window in her cotton nightgown, gazing outside.

Anxiously she watched the path that led from the woods. It was way past midnight. She wished that Jake would come home and go to bed so she could do what she wished to do without him catching her.

Yvonne was anxious to sneak into the kitchen and get some food for the crow without anyone being the wiser.

She gazed down at the skirt of the bed, where the crow still lay on a bed of blankets. It concerned her that the bird had hardly budged the entire day or evening. And it had only opened its eyes for short intervals.

Yvonne had to believe that its lethargy was from hunger, for she knew the crow had not been badly wounded.

She hoped that by morning it might be able to fly again, at least enough to get safely to its nest where it could recuperate in its own natural way, without the presence of humans.

The sound of an approaching horse drew Yvonne's eyes back to the window. She watched Jake dismount and lead his horse to the corral.

Then Yvonne watched him lumber in his lazy, slouchy walk toward the cabin.

She flinched when he let the door slam, as though he did not care whether or not his father had lain awake, listening for his arrival. Jake was getting more and more out of hand, seemingly unfeeling of anything or anyone but himself and his selfish needs.

Sighing, Yvonne paced the floor as she waited for enough time to elapse for Jake to get into bed and fall asleep. If he caught her taking food to her room, and found the cause, who was to say what he might do?

He might even grab the crow and wring its neck as he so casually twisted a chicken's neck from its body when fried chicken was the preferred meal of the day. Yvonne always volunteered to fry the chicken, but had trouble eating it while thinking of what it was, and how it had died. She had never even gotten used to eating wild fowl that Jake brought home for the dinner table. If she had her way about it, she would make a meal only out of vegetables!

When the sound of snoring wafted beneath Yvonne's door, she smiled. Jake was the only member of the family who snored. Finally he was asleep. Finally she could feed the crow.

As she opened the door and crept from her room, she thought about how her stepfather had noticed how edgy she had been the whole evening. He had remarked how anxious she had been to get to bed. In truth, she had not wanted to go to bed, but to be in the privacy of her room with the crow.

Her stepfather had also puzzled over how little she had eaten at the dinner table. She had even rushed Stanley through his schoolwork.

She and Anthony had discussed Jake's absence when he hadn't arrived home before bedtime. Jake had even missed the evening meal, which was quite unusual. He always looked forward to Yvonne's cooking.

Her father had said that the devil had a firm grip on Jake's soul. Anthony had further stated that he feared God could never be the victor in Jake's life, now that Jake had lost his religion.

Yvonne felt that she had spent too much time, herself, worrying about Jake. She grew tired of it, *and* Jake.

And tonight she had something else on her

mind, something that for now was the center of her attention. The crow.

"Well, Jake," she whispered to herself. "The crow isn't out in the woods, dinner for some four-legged critter. The crow is right here, sharing the same roof that you are sleeping beneath."

She laughed softly as she went on her way, wishing she could boast out loud to Jake about what she was doing. She would love to tell him that the bird was alive to pester him some more once it was able to fly again. She hoped that if Jake ever tried to shoot the crow again, the bird would inflict the same sort of pain on his skull as it had on River Rat's head.

"Sweet bird, I owe you a lot, more than I can ever repay," she whispered, wishing again that she could understand this crow, and what made it know that River Rat had been attempting to rape her.

The moon's glow and the slow-burning embers in the fireplace gave off enough light for her to make her way around the kitchen without stumbling over the furniture. Soundlessly, she plucked chunks of meat from the turkey she had baked for her family's meal tonight. Piece by piece she placed the bits of meat on a saucer. She then placed several blueberries and strawberries on the saucer with the meat. Knowing that the bird must be thirsty, Yvonne poured water from a pitcher into another saucer. Feeling that this was enough food and water for the crow to feast upon, Yvonne clutched the saucers in her hands and tiptoed from the kitchen.

When Jake's snoring suddenly ceased, Yvonne paled, stopped, and stood frozen to the floor. She turned slow eyes up the ladder that led to the loft. If Jake was there staring down at her, she was not sure what she would do. Even now her knees were trembling to think that he might catch her with the food.

She was not a skilled liar. If she said she was taking the food to her room for a midnight snack, he would hear the lie in the tone of her voice. What then could she do?

One thing was certain; she would not let Jake lay one hand on that crow, not if it meant placing the barrel of a shotgun in her brother's ribs to stop him!

She gazed in silence at the loft, waiting for the boards to creak; waiting for the menacing eyes of Jake to peer down at her. When she heard snoring again, and realized that Jake was still asleep, Yvonne breathed more easily and her knees became strong enough to carry her on to her room.

When her bedroom door was closed behind her, Yvonne stopped to lean against it, to take a few deep breaths. Then she rushed to the far side of the bed and sat down on the floor. After she placed the saucers of food and water on the floor beside her, she slowly lifted the bedskirt and gazed at the crow.

When she found it asleep, its head tucked beneath the wing that was not injured, she sighed. She almost hated to disturb it. But she knew that it needed nourishment to get its strength back.

Hoping that it would not become frightened by

being awakened, Yvonne gently, very slowly, pulled the blanket on which the crow was asleep out from beneath the bed. When its eyes opened and gazed up at her, the moon's glow silvering them with its light, Yvonne was shaken deeply. The crow seemed to be trying to communicate something to her. It opened its beak and let out some sort of garbled sounds, as though it were trying to say something.

"What are you?" she whispered back to it. An involuntary shudder raced across her flesh. "*Who* are you? Are you someone reincarnated? Or are you something even more? Will I ever know?"

She placed some turkey pieces in the palm of her hand and offered it to the crow. She watched it grab the meat with its beak and eat ravenously.

She then slid the water closer to the crow and watched as it drank thirstily from the saucer.

Then she placed the berries in her palm and watched the crow pluck them in its beak, one by one.

"I feel guilty for having made you wait so long to eat," Yvonne whispered when the crow seemed to have had its fill.

She dared to place a hand on its head, then softly stroked its sleek, bluish-black feathers. "You are so beautiful," she whispered. "You are so sweet and gentle. Damn Jake for shooting you. How can you even trust *me* after that? What is it, sweet crow, that has caused this bonding between us? Oh, how I wish you could truly talk, so that you could reveal the mystery of yourself to me."

The crow gazed at her as she continued to pet

it. Its eyes seemed to penetrate her clean to her soul, unnerving her.

Then it tucked its head beneath its wing again, trustingly asleep before her very eyes.

"Sleep, sweet crow," Yvonne whispered. "You are safe with me." She laughed softly. "But, of course, you know that, don't you, or you wouldn't have fallen asleep in my presence."

Yvonne looked down at the crow, then up at her bed. Although it was June, the nights were chilly. Even now the coldness of the board flooring was seeping through the thin cotton of her nightgown, giving her a chill. So then surely the crow would feel the same chill, she decided.

Gently she placed her hands beneath the blankets and lifted the crow up to her bed. "You can sleep with me tonight," she whispered. "Right next to me on my pillow. That way I know you will be warm, and absolutely safe. Jake doesn't dare enter my room when the door is shut, and he is the only one in this household that you have to fear."

Slipping into bed, Yvonne reached for her favorite patchwork quilt and pulled it over her, then carefully eased a corner of the quilt up over the bird, leaving only its head exposed. On the very edge of sleep herself, Yvonne snuggled down on her side and lay there awhile watching the crow sleep, the moonlight glimmering on its lovely black feathers.

The night noises outside, where the wolves howled at the moon, and where the loons echoed their mournful cries back and forth over the river to each other, seemed far distant to Yvonne. All that she was aware of was right there on the bed with her.

Suddenly thoughts of Silver Arrow filled her mind. Strange how it seemed that he was near her tonight. Was that because he lay in his bed at this very moment thinking of her? Was he recalling the way their eyes had locked when they had been together? Had he been aware of how his nearness had made her tremble with ecstasy; how his nearness had made her speechless with the passion she felt for him?

Smiling almost drunkenly from being so tired, and from her thoughts of Silver Arrow, Yvonne closed her eyes and drifted off to sleep.

In her dream, she found herself first lying beside the crow, and then beside Silver Arrow! The transformation was so quick, Silver Arrow and the crow seemed one and the same! Then she settled into a sensual and soul-arousing night of dreams about Silver Arrow. In her warm, pink dreams, she was with him in the curling shadows of the forest, her laughter bubbling as he drew her into his powerfully muscled arms, holding her.

She wore a beautiful lacy silk chemise, its bodice low and revealing.

He . . . wore . . . nothing!

When Silver Arrow cupped one of Yvonne's breasts through the thin fabric of her chemise, his mouth covering her lips with a frenzy of kisses, Yvonne's laughter changed to deep moans of heady pleasure. And when his mouth shifted and he placed his lips over the nipple, drawing it and the silken chemise between his teeth, nipping, softly and teasingly biting, Yvonne threw her head back in a guttural, sensual sigh.

Suddenly in her dream she no longer wore her chemise. She was lying on a soft bed of moss beneath a spill of moonlight. Smiling, she held her arms out for Silver Arrow as he stood over her, his powerful body revealing his need of her.

When he came and knelt low over her, his lips drugging her with fiery kisses, his hands molding her bare breasts, Yvonne was only vaguely aware of one of his knees parting her thighs. What followed came to her in heated flashes, causing her to cry out softly with rapture; how Silver Arrow plunged himself inside her and made love to her slowly and wonderfully; how kissing her long and deep made pleasure spread through her in a delicious, tingling heat.

His embrace powerful, yet sweet, Silver Arrow leaned away from Yvonne and spoke to her body with his tongue and lips, his large, masterful hands kneading her breasts. Filled with a drugged passion, Yvonne tossed her head from side to side. Again he entered her. Her hips moved and rocked with him, the passion building in heated leaps throughout her.

When Silver Arrow whispered a name against her parted lips, Yvonne's breath quickened.

"White Swan. You are my White Swan," Silver Arrow whispered in the dream that seemed so real and wonderful. When she occasionally found herself floating back to reality enough to realize that she was only on a bed with a crow, not the man of her wildest, midnight dreams, Yvonne tried to prolong the fantasy.

"White Swan?" she whispered, her words coming alive in the room, instead of only in her dream. The crow stirred at her side and emitted some soft chatter, drawing Yvonne quickly, fully awake.

Shaken by her dream, and by the way the crow was gazing into her eyes, Yvonne scooted slowly away from it.

"You heard me," she said, her voice wary. "You heard me say 'White Swan.' It is as though you know who said it in my dream. Oh, Lord, how could you? How . . . ?"

The crow remained quiet.

It stared at her for a moment longer, then once again tucked its head beneath its wing and was soon asleep.

"Am I going crazy?" Yvonne whispered, hugging herself to try to calm her nerves.

She closed her eyes and relived her dream about Silver Arrow. The dream had seemed so real. His lips and hands were so warm on her flesh. His . . . his . . . manhood had been so hot and wonderful inside her!

Yvonne smiled as she snuggled back down beneath the patchwork quilt, thinking that if all of this was what it was like to be crazy, well then, she would welcome it! Closing her eyes, she hoped to return to the dream. While in the arms of her phantom lover, there was much left to be done!

Chapter Twelve

Yvonne drifted easily, almost magically, into a continued dream of being with Silver Arrow. In her dream, she lay beside him. His powerful arms snuggled her close as he breathed sweet words of love against her parted lips.

"My White Swan," he whispered huskily. "I have longed for so long to be with you, to hold you, to make love to you. You are mine now for eternity."

"I, too, will love you for eternity," Yvonne whispered against his warm lips. "Hold me tighter. Please never let me go."

She fought against a distant sound that threatened to disturb the paradise of her dream. She clung to Silver Arrow. "No," she softly cried as the sound kept pulling at her consciousness, attempting to awaken her. "I don't want to go. Hold me, Silver Arrow. Something is trying to take me away from you."

"*Will* it away," Silver Arrow whispered harshly to her in his dream, his powerful arms holding her more tightly. "Will it away, and *stay. . . .*"

"I . . . can't. . . ." Yvonne cried. "The pull! It is too hard!"

She drifted from his arms, yet clutched desperately to one of his hands. "Oh, Silver Arrow, please keep hold of my hand," she cried. "Don't let it slip away!"

But no matter how hard he tried, the real world would not stop its beckoning. Yvonne was wrenched quickly awake, her heart pounding. The knocking on the front door persisted, and she was aware now that the sound was what had been calling for her in her dream.

Shaken by the intensity of her dreams, Yvonne felt that she had truly been with Silver Arrow. His lips had been there drugging her. His hands had been there, teaching her the magic of lovemaking.

She jumped when she felt eyes on her and looked quickly at the crow. It was fully awake, its eyes watching, again as though it were trying to communicate something to her.

"What are you thinking?" she whispered, reaching out a trembling hand to the crow, softly stroking its feathered head. "It is as though you were a part of my dream, as though you, too, shared the magic."

Her father's voice broke through the silence that fell in the cabin when the knocking ceased momentarily, only to start up again. Someone was adamant about rousing the household.

Fear rushed through her.

At this time of night there were never callers unless someone was dying and her father's prayers were needed.

Without thinking to grab a robe, or to put her feet into slippers, Yvonne rushed from her room and met her father just as he came from his room, buttoning his trousers.

"Who could it be?" Yvonne asked, hurrying beside him as they both walked toward the door. Her father lit a kerosene lamp. Her knees weak, she stepped up to the door with him.

"Who is there?" Anthony asked.

"It is I, Four Horns, from the Ottawa village," Four Horns said, his voice drawn. "I have come with many of my warriors. We are on a search party for our beloved chief, Silver Arrow."

Yvonne paled at the thought that something might have happened to the man with whom she had just been sharing such wonderful dreams. If anything happened to Silver Arrow, she would forever have only the dreams to sustain her when she hungered to be with him.

She realized now that the dream wasn't enough. She wanted to experience the true touch of his flesh against hers, the passion that came with his lips truly kissing her.

"You say you are searching for Silver Arrow?" Anthony said, gazing over Four Horns' shoulder at the many other Ottawa warriors on horseback. "What do you think has happened?"

"Our chief never stays overnight anywhere unless he tells someone that he will be gone from the village," Four Horns said. "He especially tells his grandmother, Princess Pretty Hawk. He would never do anything that would worry her. Have you seen Silver Arrow tonight?"

"No," Anthony said, raising an eyebrow. "I haven't seen him since my council with him."

"*Ae*, I know that you are the last man to have council with Silver Arrow," Four Horns said, his eyes shifting to Yvonne, yet still directing his words to Anthony. "That is why we have come to you. Did he happen to come to your lodge for another council?"

Yvonne was becoming unnerved under Four Horns' close scrutiny. After having momentarily locked his eyes with hers, he was now raking them slowly over her, making her keenly aware that she wore nothing but her nightgown.

She hugged herself in an effort to hide her breasts, sighing to herself when Four Horns looked away from her and focused his attention on Anthony.

"No, Silver Arrow did not come here for council," Anthony said. "While I was at your village, your chief and I seemed to have covered all that needed to be talked about."

Anthony's spine stiffened when once again he noticed how Four Horns looked at Yvonne. His eyes widened when Four Horns then directed questions toward her.

"White Swan, have you seen my chief tonight?" Four Horns asked.

Yvonne paled and felt faint at his use of the name White Swan, when only in her dreams had she ever heard it. And only while she dreamed of Silver Arrow.

He had called her that. How could Four Horns know? How could *she* have known to dream it?

An involuntary shiver raced across Yvonne's flesh. "Why do you call me White Swan?" she gulped out.

It was obvious that her question caused Four Horns sudden alarm. "White Swan?" he said, his voice guarded. "Did I call you that?"

"Yes, and I need to know why," Yvonne said, trembling at the implications. Too many things were happening that made no sense. First there was the crow, then the dreams that seemed so intensely real, and now Four Horns had spoken a name that she had only heard in a dream!

She had always heard that Indians had many mystical beliefs. Was she now a part of those beliefs? If so, where might they end?

All she wanted was to be loved by Silver Arrow. She wanted nothing to do with these things that threatened her sanity!

"It is not my place to explain the name White Swan to you," Four Horns said, his voice wary.

"But you must," Yvonne insisted. "Why did you call me that?"

Four Horns shifted his feet uneasily. "Because my chief calls you by that name when he speaks of you," he blurted out.

Yvonne gasped. His explanation sent shock

135

waves through her and she reached for the door frame to steady herself.

How could this be happening? she cried to herself.

How could she have dreamed of Silver Arrow calling her something that she knew nothing about before her dream?

Fear of the unknown flooded her. She was so taken aback, she was speechless.

"I must know, white woman, if you saw my chief tonight?" Four Horns asked, too worried about Silver Arrow to concern himself over using the special name his chief had given the white woman. He was not even going to wonder over her strange reaction to his words. His main goal was to find Silver Arrow and see that he was safely escorted home!

If he was alive, he despaired silently to himself.

Yvonne placed a hand on her throat. "Why would I have seen Silver Arrow tonight?" she asked, eyes wide.

"My chief has spoken more than once about you, and his need to speak privately with you," Four Horns said, realizing that he was speaking out of turn again, by telling this woman something that only Silver Arrow should have said to her.

But his concern for his chief overpowered his discretion. If Silver Arrow had come to this woman and told her his true feelings, and she had turned him away, that might be cause for his chief to act irrationally, and go into hiding to spend time with *Gitchi-manitou*, to pray for the healing of his damaged pride.

"Silver Arrow told you that he wishes to have a private council with me?" Yvonne asked, her heart suddenly thudding inside her chest.

"*Ae*, he has said that to me, his friend with whom he speaks his confidences," Four Horns said, nervously resting a hand on a knife sheathed at his right side. "Did he come tonight and speak with you?"

Yvonne's thoughts went quickly to her dreams, feeling that, yes, in a sense, Silver Arrow had been there.

But her mind came back to the present. Her anxiety that something might have happened to Silver Arrow made a slow ache circle her heart.

"No, he wasn't here," she murmured. "I have not seen him since my father's council with him."

"Then we must go elsewhere with our search and questions," Four Horns said, his voice full of renewed worry. "Thank you for your time, holy man, and daughter. I apologize for having disturbed you from your sleep."

"I hope with all my heart that you will find Silver Arrow, and that he is all right," Yvonne said.

She blushed when Four Horns gave her another lingering gaze, then was relieved when he quickly mounted his horse and rode away with the rest of the Ottawa warriors.

"Yvonne, your feelings came through tonight for Silver Arrow," Anthony said as he closed the door. He held the lantern out before him and gazed intensely at her. "You care for him a lot, don't you?"

"So very much," Yvonne said, stifling a sob behind a hand as she ran from him and rushed back to her room.

She closed the door and leaned against it, her heart sinking to think that she might never come face-to-face with Silver Arrow again.

For certain, the dreams would never be enough! She sorely wished to know the wondrous touch of his lips against hers, and the mystery of how his body could make hers come so much alive.

"I may never know," she sobbed, wiping tears from her eyes.

Her thoughts went in many directions as she tried to piece together in her mind what might have happened to Silver Arrow. Surely he had many jealous contenders for the title of chief. Yet she could not see how he could have any enemies. He was a gentle-speaking man who sought to keep his people free of war.

But there were such men as Jake who wished to have this powerful Ottawa chief's hidden gold!

Jake had been gone very late tonight. He had talked about Silver Arrow's gold even today.

What if he had abducted Silver Arrow tonight and forced him to take him to the burial spot of the gold?

What if Silver Arrow had turned on Jake and fought him, in order to keep the gold out of Jake's hands, and Jake . . . killed . . . him?

And why had Jake not come from his room tonight to see what the Indians wanted? Was it because he had been too bone-tired from his activities tonight to be awakened by the commotion? Or was it because he was guilty of something and was afraid to face the Indians?

Yvonne shivered and shook her head to clear her mind of such terrible thoughts.

No, Jake was not a killer.

Yes, he was mean sometimes through and through, and did not flinch when he killed animals. But never could he be a cold-blooded killer. Surely Jake was not *that* desperate to have gold.

And he would surely know the consequences of abducting a powerful Indian chief!

Sighing, too unnerved to sleep any more tonight, Yvonne went to the bed to at least lie there and rest.

As she reached the bed, she stopped with a start and gasped.

The crow was gone!

Fearing it had tried to fly in the small confines of this room, and might have injured itself even worse than it already was, she searched frantically around the room.

Her heart sank when the bird was nowhere to be found.

Then she felt light-headed and numbly cold inside when she noticed something else.

The window! It was open! She hadn't opened it!

She looked quickly toward the door, anger filling her.

Jake! He had surely come into the room and found the crow and let it out the window!

Her jaw clamped tightly, her pulse racing, she went to Jake's door. Her fingers trembled as she yanked the door open and stamped over to Jake's bed.

She glared down at him. "Don't pretend to be asleep," she said, yanking the blanket off him, too angry to even notice his nudity.

Jake awakened with a start. "What are you doing here?" he gasped. He grabbed the blanket from her and covered himself. "What do you think you're doing?"

"You went to my room tonight, didn't you, while I was with Father talking to Four Horns?" she said, placing her hands on her hips.

"I've been nowhere but here since I returned home from a night with the boys at the trading post," Jake said, leaning up on an elbow. "I played poker and lost. I stayed until I won it all back."

"Then you've been asleep ever since you came home tonight?" Yvonne asked, somehow believing him.

"Yes. And why would you think I was in your room?" he said, laughing. "God, Yvonne, I know better. I know what is and what isn't decent. You know how I respect you. No. I wasn't in your room tonight. I don't see why you would think so."

Now realizing that no one had been in her room tonight but herself and the crow, Yvonne again felt light-headed.

She hadn't opened the window.

Jake hadn't.

Her father had not gone into her room, nor had Stanley.

Then that only left the *crow*!

But that was impossible, she cried to herself.

It couldn't be!

"Yvonne, you look as though you've seen a ghost," Jake said as he peered up at her.

Yvonne swallowed hard and left the room in hasty, yet shaky steps. When she returned to her room, she went to the open window and leaned out of it.

She paled when, in the spill of the moonlight, she caught sight of a lone crow feather on the ground beneath the window.

Chapter Thirteen

Clutching his bare left shoulder, the pain from the flesh wound only enough to make him slightly uncomfortable, Silver Arrow ran stealthily through the forest. He had left his pinto stallion tethered far from White Swan's cabin, so that no one would discover it while he had gone this last time to watch her before taking the bold step of going to her lodge with gifts for her and her family.

He was glad now that he had left the horse where there was knee-high grass for grazing. He was relieved that he had used a long enough rope for tethering his steed. He had made sure that it was long enough so that his horse could go to the river when it needed to quench its thirst after feasting on the thick grass.

If Silver Arrow had not considered the comforts

of his horse, it would be suffering even now from hunger, thirst, and neglect, since Silver Arrow had been detained by unfortunate circumstances.

As he pushed his way onward through briars and low-hanging limbs of trees, Silver Arrow's thoughts went to his White Swan. He was well aware now that she was kindhearted and had intense feelings for things other than "self."

She was perhaps the sweetest and gentlest woman that he had ever met. He would never forget the softness of her fingers, or the caring in her voice as she had . . .

His thoughts were wrenched back to the present when he heard the sound of many horses approaching a short distance away.

Wildly, his eyes swept around him for a hiding place. He did not trust anyone who would be out at this time of night, unless it was . . .

His eyes brightened with a thought and he became more confident that those who approached would not harm him. He recalled how, only a short while ago, his warriors had been at his White Swan's cabin, making inquiries about their missing chief.

Surely Four Horns had now found the path made by Silver Arrow those many times he had come to view the white woman, his fascination with her like that of a small, awestruck child who watches the mystery of the stars in the dark heavens.

Confident that he was right, that these were his warriors who were still scouring the forest for him at this late-night hour, Silver Arrow stepped out into the path and waited.

When his warriors came into view, Four Horns at the lead, Silver Arrow ran out to meet them.

"My chief!" Four Horns cried as he spied Silver Arrow running toward him.

He brought his steed to a shimmying halt as Silver Arrow reached him, panting. His heart skipped a beat when, in the moonlight, he saw trickles of blood running through Silver Arrow's fingers as he clutched at his shoulder.

A quick anger leapt into Four Horns' eyes at the thought of anyone maiming his beloved chief!

"Four Horns, it is good to see you," Silver Arrow said, grabbing hold of Four Horns' horse to steady himself. He looked at his warriors who circled around him on their steeds. "My valiant, kind warriors, thank you for your devotion to me, for searching endlessly at this late hour for your chief."

Four Horns slid from his saddle. He reached a hand out for Silver Arrow and gently took him by an elbow. He looked at the shoulder wound as Silver Arrow slid his bloody fingers down from it.

"Who did this to you?" Four Horns growled out.

"It is only a flesh wound," Silver Arrow said, glancing down at it. It *was* only a flesh wound, he thought, but his activity in running through the forest had broken the wound open somewhat.

He smiled to himself as he thought of White Swan and what her reaction might be if she saw that his wound was bleeding.

She would be alarmed. She would softly wash the blood away. She would medicate it.

"It might be only a flesh wound, but it is something someone has inflicted on you," Four Horns said, his voice so drawn with concern it drew Silver Arrow's eyes to him.

"Silver Arrow, tell me who did this," Four Horns persisted after a few moments of strained silence when everyone waited anxiously to hear the answer from their chief.

Still Silver Arrow did not respond, for he felt somewhat trapped by circumstances, in that he felt safe to confide only in Four Horns, no one else.

Only Four Horns knew his most deeply hidden secrets. Silver Arrow did not wish for anyone else to know, for there were dangers in revealing too much to his warriors about himself.

The more knowledge he could keep to himself, the better.

Even Four Horns did not know everything about Silver Arrow.

His life, his secrets, were to be guarded, just as his grandfather had kept his powers mostly to himself when he was alive . . . powers that Silver Arrow had inherited.

"Silver Arrow, why do you not tell us who did this to you?" Four Horns prodded. "Your shoulder has been grazed by a bullet. Whose bullet?"

Silver Arrow gave his other warriors a troubled glance, then took Four Horns by an elbow and led him aside, out of the voice range of the others.

"Do not ask any more questions about what happened to me tonight," Silver Arrow said thickly. "*Ae*, a bullet grazed my shoulder, but the bullet was not meant for me. I will say no more as to who shot the firearm, or what the target was. Think, friend. Then you will come up with the answers without me saying them."

Four Horns' eyes narrowed and his jaw tightened as it came to him exactly what must have happened. Knowing the depths of Silver Arrow's powers, and how he used them in accordance with the white woman he wished to make his wife, made a fearful apprehension enter his heart.

"*Ae*, now I know," Four Horns murmured, casting a troubled glance over his shoulder at the waiting warriors, their eyes intensely watching him and Silver Arrow.

Four Horns edged closer to Silver Arrow. He leaned his lips close to his ear. "I have countless times warned you that perhaps you are misusing your special power," he whispered. "And I fear that it is a misuse of power if tonight you again used it to get even closer to the white woman than before, the one you call White Swan, to gaze upon her unique loveliness."

Four Horns would never confess to Silver Arrow that while talking to the woman, he had referred to her as White Swan. Yes, he expected the woman to eventually question Silver Arrow about that. But until she did, it would be a subject not spoken about between himself and his friend.

"Do not forget, ever, that what I do is done for the benefit of not only myself, but our people," Silver Arrow softly scolded. "When I chose to have this white woman as my wife, I had to watch her often to see if she would fit into the lives of our people. How I choose to watch her is my own affair. Do not speak of it again to me, and do not ever forget that it is I, Silver Arrow, who is chief."

Silver Arrow paused, then said, "If anyone else was disrespectful enough to chide me for what and how I do things, they would risk banishment from our tribe. But being it is you, and knowing that you worry about me because of your love for me, as though I were your brother, it is easy to forget these occasional slips of the tongue."

"And I will remember these warnings," Four Horns said, nodding. He smiled at Silver Arrow. "And I understand how you would risk so much to be near this woman, for tonight I, myself, saw her up close, and so near I could smell the perfume of her hair and her body."

"*Ae*, I know that you were at her lodge," Silver Arrow said, placing a gentle hand on his friend's shoulder. "And I know that you saw her in her nightclothes, her hair loose over her fair, pale shoulders."

"*Ae*, and I see now that she is worth taking risks over," Four Horns said, his eyes dancing as he brought her to his mind's eye. "She *is* as lovely and fragile as a white swan. The name suits her well, my chief."

Silver Arrow was taken aback by his friend's sudden interest in White Swan, troubled by it. "*Ae*, she is, but hear me well, Four Horns, when I say, as far as she is concerned, let there be no reason for there to be risks between friends."

After Silver Arrow lifted his hand from Four Horns' shoulder, Four Horns took an unsteady

147

step from him. "*Koo-koo-skoos*, I am sorry. I did not mean to imply that I am looking at her as I would look at a woman I wish to take as a bride," he said. "She is a woman spoken for. By *you*. I would not interfere in matters of the heart, Silver Arrow, especially yours. Never would I do that, for we have been friends for too long to ever allow a woman to interfere in such a friendship as ours."

"*Ae*, that is *ka-ge-ti*, truly so," Silver Arrow said. "If you remember that, then all will stay the same between us. But if I see you showing too much interest in White Swan, I shall assume that our friendship no longer means that much to you."

Swallowing hard, his eyes lowered humbly to the ground, Four Horns edged backward until he came to his horse.

"My pinto stallion is up the path a short distance," Silver Arrow said, watching Four Horns slip into his saddle. "Go on, my friend. Lead the warriors back to our village. In due time, I will follow."

Four Horns lifted his eyes and momentarily locked them with Silver Arrow's. Then he smiled warmly, made a gesture of friendship in sign language to Silver Arrow, then swung his horse around and rode away, the others following.

Silver Arrow watched the riders for a while, then broke into a slow run back toward his tethered steed, his mood troubled. He knew now that he must not delay any longer before voicing his feelings for White Swan to her and her father. He had been foolish to wait this long. This woman was the loveliest on the face of the earth. Many men could be hungering for her.

If a best friend could show such an interest, then might not many whom Silver Arrow did not know be having midnight dreams of her? There were many unwed men in these parts, both white and red skinned.

Ae, tomorrow he would go to her. He would hide the wound well beneath his shirt so that she would not see it and perhaps realize truths about him that might frighten her.

"*Ae*, tomorrow," he said, seeing his pinto stallion beneath the moonlight a short distance away. "White Swan shall know the depths of my feelings for her tomorrow!"

Chapter Fourteen

It was Saturday, the day before the white man's sabbath, Silver Arrow having learned that from Brother Stockton. Today Silver Arrow would begin giving gifts as his bride price to White Swan's family, preceding the day when he would soon offer his full bride price to her father.

Silver Arrow had watched their habits long enough to know what they did each day. And today was the best of days to meet with Brother Stockton with talk of marriage to his daughter. He knew they were normally all at home on Saturday.

The sun was halfway toward the noon hour as Silver Arrow placed the last of his gifts in his canoe. There were gifts for all of White Swan's family except for one . . . her brother Jake, for proper introductions had yet to be made between them.

And even if there had been, there would be no gifts for that arrogant, devious man who uselessly maimed and killed not only birds of the forest, but also many innocent animals in the jaws of his steel traps.

When Silver Arrow had come face-to-face with Jake at the trading post that first time many sun-rises ago, it had taken all the willpower that Silver Arrow could muster not to grab him by the throat and warn him against using the inhumane traps in this land where at one time, not that long ago, only the red men traveled and hunted.

From that point on, Silver Arrow had purposely kept his distance from Jake, for he had not wanted to risk doing anything that might cause his White Swan to choose loyalty to her family over Silver Arrow when he announced his inten-tions toward her.

"But one day I will get my say," he whispered to himself. "Jake will then know the wrath of this Ottawa chief."

He stood back from the canoe and assessed the number of gifts that he had placed there. A slow smile fluttered on his lips. "*Ae*, for a start, this will do," he said, nodding.

He turned his eyes quickly when he heard the dipping of a paddle in water. His insides stiffened when he saw someone approaching upriver for whom he did not have the best of feelings. He tolerated Chief Old Elk, but only to keep a meas-ure of peace between himself and the middle-aged Iroquois chief.

Silver Arrow saw Old Elk's daughter sitting at the back of the canoe, her eyes anxiously watching Silver Arrow.

As always, Silver Arrow was taken by Searching Heart's earthy loveliness, but that was as far as his feelings for her went. There had never been any desire aroused within himself for this young woman. His heart had not fluttered strangely in his chest when he looked at her, as it did when he gazed upon White Swan's beauty.

And now that he was certain that White Swan was gentle and sweet through and through, these traits that he wished to have in a wife, her loveliness was compounded in his eyes and heart.

He waited until the canoe was beached, then met the Iroquois chief and his daughter's approach. "Welcome," he said stiffly, shifting his gaze back and forth between Old Elk and Searching Heart. "If you have come for council, it would have been best had you sent ahead word that you requested it. I have only a moment. I have business elsewhere."

Searching Heart stood beside her father, her gaze locked on Silver Arrow. Her face was flushed from being there so close to him. She could hardly control her breathing. This man, oh, he was so handsome, so virile! Although she had her eye on more than one man as her choice for a husband, it was Silver Arrow who she truly wished to share her blankets at night.

When she noticed that Silver Arrow kept glancing down at his canoe, she followed his gaze, wondering about the various objects there. They did not seem the sort of thing he would take to the trading post. These things were more like what one might take as gifts to someone for whom he had affection.

Searching Heart could not help but admire the lovely rabbit-skin robe, the beautifully strung beads which would make a woman even more beautiful, and the dainty, intricately designed moccasins which would fit only a woman's feet.

She swallowed hard. Now she was almost certain that she had come with her father too late to talk of marriage, when surely Silver Arrow already had a woman whose heart he wished to have as his. Such gifts as these were not given to mere acquaintances.

She glanced at her father's canoe and the piles of plush pelts and colorful blankets that had been meant to be offered to Silver Arrow to stir his heart into wanting this Iroquois daughter. But even these gifts would surely not sway him from what he seemed destined to do today.

Searching Heart edged closer to her father and yanked on the sleeve of his fringed buckskin shirt. When he gave her a quizzical stare, she leaned close to his ear. "Do not speak of marriage to this man," she whispered. "Father, do you not see what is in his canoe? Gifts! See the moccasins? See the beads? The gifts are for a woman!"

He frowned down at her. "Be quiet, daughter," he whispered back. "I have brought you here for a purpose. When Silver Arrow realizes that he can have you, thoughts of all other women will leave his heart."

"Father, although this man is the one I told you I wanted, I do not need him for a husband after all," Searching Heart whispered back. "There are others as handsome."

Her gaze was on Silver Arrow as she spoke to her father. She could see that he was puzzled by this whispered deliberation between daughter and father. She was glad that he was confused. It angered her that he had never given her a chance to prove her worth to him!

"Handsomeness is not what you look for in a husband," her father scolded in a harsh whisper. "This man is a powerful chief!"

"Chief! Shaman! Warrior!" Searching Heart argued back. "I do not care!"

Old Elk stepped in front of his daughter, facing Silver Arrow, blocking her view of him, and Silver Arrow's of her. "Proud Ottawa chief, I ask you to take time from that which you had planned to do this morning to first give me council so that I can speak to you about my daughter's feelings for you," he said flatly. "Will you give this council? Will you smoke the pipe of peace with Chief Old Elk?" He gestured toward his canoe. "I have brought you many gifts to prove my seriousness in offering my daughter to you for marriage."

Searching Heart gasped behind him, then turned and ran to the canoe and climbed inside. Not wanting to be gawked at, already ashamed of her father for almost begging this man who did not want to marry her, she knelt down low in the canoe and covered herself with a blanket.

Silver Arrow stared at the blanket that covered

Searching Heart, finding her behavior odd, yet set aside the wonder of why she did this and gazed flatly down at the short, squat Iroquois chief. "I must refuse your offer," he said solemnly. "My eyes are on another woman. My heart is hers."

Chief Old Elk doubled a hand into a tight fist at his side. He moved his eyes slowly to Silver Arrow's canoe, assessing the fine objects which lay there so neatly.

Then he turned angry eyes up at Silver Arrow. "You have known for some time that my daughter wished to be your wife, yet you turn away from her as though she is worthless," he hissed out. "How will she live with the humiliation of being rejected?"

"*Ae*, I knew that Searching Heart cared, and had I wanted her, do you not think that I would have come to you with a bride price long ago, instead of waiting for you to come to me?" Silver Arrow said, folding his arms across his powerful chest. "*You* are the cause of your daughter's shame today, not I."

Old Elk glared up at Silver Arrow, then turned and stamped back to his canoe.

Silver Arrow watched Old Elk shove the canoe back into the water. He watched as the Iroquois chief boarded the canoe and angrily drew his paddle through the water, taking the canoe swiftly back down the avenue of the river.

"And so there might go any alliance that my people might wish for now, and in the future," Silver Arrow whispered to himself.

But that risk had to be taken. Silver Arrow was

not the sort to be coerced into anything, especially not when it came to women. He would marry only once in his lifetime, and that would be to the woman he wished to wake up to each day for the rest of his life!

"And that is White Swan," he whispered determinedly.

He gave his canoe a shove into the water and climbed aboard, then sent his vessel up the Grand River in the opposite direction from that which the Iroquois chief hastily and angrily traveled.

Silver Arrow's faint, swift dipping of his paddle barely broke the stillness of the hour as his canoe moved onward through the mighty river's silver-clear water. A bird stirred in the thicket. The whitefish, which the Ottawa called the deer of the water, were swimming swiftly upstream.

Those things only kept Silver Arrow's attention for a moment, for he could not stop thinking of what lay ahead of him—that he was finally going to face his White Swan with the depths of the emotion that he felt for her.

His destiny was hers!

They would grow old together!

They would have many children and grand-children together!

Just like his mother and father, Silver Arrow and his wife would not only be lovers, but also the best of friends!

Just the thought of the future he would have with his White Swan sent a shiver through him.

Silver Arrow's heart hammered wildly when he caught sight of White Swan's cabin on an embankment not far from the river. He turned his canoe in that direction and watched the cabin, hoping to get a glimpse of White Swan as she might come out to gather flowers in her garden. Or just to get a breath of air while admiring this lovely day of summer, where butterflies flitted by, birds sang, and even the river sang a song of peace and tranquility.

Silver Arrow had watched her enough times to know that she was one with nature, her very soul in touch with the loveliness that surrounded her.

He, too, felt the same bonding with nature. It was something for them to share, to marvel over as they embraced, touched, and kissed the rest of their lives.

Wau-e-baw, soon, he thought to himself, all of this would come true in reality, instead of just in the thousands of dreams he had dreamt of her these past weeks and months.

His canoe beached, Silver Arrow swung a child's bow over his shoulder and laid a small quiver of blunt-tipped arrows on top of the other gifts. His arms full, he walked with an eager heart toward the cabin.

Suddenly Yvonne was there, stepping from the door of the cabin with a basket of clothes. Silver Arrow knew, from having so often secretly observed her, that those clothes would be hung on a line strung from tree to tree at the side of the cabin.

Not having been noticed, Silver Arrow stood in the shadows and watched White Swan, and how the soft breeze fluttered her beautiful, long and flowing chestnut hair around her shoulders, and how the breeze lifted her skirt from around her ankles, revealing to him just how exquisitely tiny and tapered they were.

His gaze shifted to the gentle swell of her breasts pressing against her dress. He so longed to feel their softness. He so longed to taste the sweetness of her flesh.

Yvonne set the basket of clothes down on the ground, having washed them inside in the basin, one by one, instead of outside in a large tub over an outdoor fire, since they were only her light-weight undergarments and gowns.

The breeze brought Yvonne the sweet scent of wildflowers that grew along the forest floor. She placed her hands on her hips and lifted her chin, inhaling the fresh smells of this beautiful day of early summer. Then she ran her fingers through her hair and closed her eyes as she lifted her face toward the sun, enjoying it now before it reached the hotter peak at noon.

The only thing ruining this day was her worry over Silver Arrow. She had worried about him all night, whether or not his warriors had found him. And if so, had he been alive, or dead?

And then there was the crow, the mystery of how it had vanished through her bedroom window. Who had opened the window? Had she just possibly left the window open, thinking that she had closed it? She did like the fragrances of early evening in her room, to freshen her bedding and curtains.

Yet no matter how much she wanted that to be

the answer, she could not recall having opened the window the prior evening.

A shiver of apprehension soared across Yvonne's flesh, making her aware that she might not be alone while outside to hang her clothes. Too often she felt as though, besides the crow, someone were there watching her. As now, she felt as though she were on display!

Yvonne turned with a start and stared at Silver Arrow, only now discovering he was there, watching her.

Chapter Fifteen

Yvonne was stunned to see Silver Arrow approaching her, and not only because he was there for the first time ever, and not only because she now knew that he was all right, instead of lying somewhere dead in the forest.

But because his outstretched arms were filled with many beautiful things. It seemed as though he was bringing gifts to the family.

Her breath caught in her throat when she recalled reading novels about Indians in which it was the custom for a warrior to bring gifts when seeking the hand of a certain woman in marriage. The thought of Silver Arrow possibly coming this morning for that purpose made a thrill spread through Yvonne.

But surely she was foolish to believe that he

would do this without first becoming better acquainted with her.

It seemed that her dreams at night made her fantasize when she was awake!

She must get hold of herself and not show her feelings for this man on her face, or in her eyes. Thank goodness he could not see within her heart, or he might scoff at her foolishness for wishing for what surely could never be.

Yet the way he looked at *her!* It was the same as the other times he had gazed at her. It was with such compassion, such warmth, such . . .

She swallowed hard, thinking that, yes, he was gazing at her with the look of a man who desired a woman.

Willing her fingers not to tremble, Yvonne nervously ran her hands down the skirt of her dress, to smooth out any wrinkles that may have fallen there while leaning over the basin, washing her clothes.

Then she smiled and walked toward Silver Arrow, to welcome him.

Oh, Lord, she prayed to herself, do not let her voice betray her when she spoke to him. If it trembled, oh, then he would know that his very presence affected her, and *how!*

The last thing she wanted was to be embarrassed in front of him. She wanted him to admire her, to want her, to need her.

"Good morning, Chief Silver Arrow," Yvonne said as she met his approach. She reached a hand out for him, for a handshake of friendship, then laughed awkwardly and dropped her hand to her side when she realized that he could not accept it. His hands were otherwise occupied.

Silver Arrow stopped and smiled down at her. "*Ae*, it is a good morning, is it not?" he said, his eyes dancing into hers. He nodded toward his canoe. "It is the best of mornings for a ride down the river. Perhaps you would like to take a slow ride with me after I meet with your father?"

Yvonne was taken aback by the suddenness of Silver Arrow asking her to go with him. She glanced down at the things in his arms, wondering anew why he brought them. Then she smiled at him.

"Why, I would love to go canoeing with you this morning," she murmured. "It would be delightful. The flowers and trees that line the riverbanks are lovely at this time of year."

Stanley came to the door of the cabin. When he spied Silver Arrow standing with Yvonne, he looked over his shoulder at his father. "Chief Silver Arrow is here," he said excitedly. "Father, he has many things in his arms."

Stanley pushed his thick-lensed glasses more securely on the bridge of his nose, his gaze locking on the small bow slung across Silver Arrow's shoulder. He had seen bows of that size before. One day when he had wandered in the forest, he had seen several braves his same age with that type of bow. He wondered why Silver Arrow carried a bow like that, instead of one his own size.

Anthony went to the door. He smiled broadly when he saw Silver Arrow, and waved when Silver Arrow glanced up at him. "Silver Arrow, it is good to see you," he said. "Come inside my lodge. Your company is quite welcome."

Anthony, too, looked at Silver Arrow's heavy-laden arms. He scratched his brow in wonder at why the Ottawa chief had brought gifts, for surely that was what the pelts and other things were.

His eyebrows arched over the number of gifts, and the grandeur of those he could see. Could it be that Silver Arrow was bringing a bride price to make an offer for Yvonne's hand in marriage? While Anthony had been at Silver Arrow's village with Yvonne, he had noticed the chief's interest in her. Anthony knew Yvonne's feelings for Silver Arrow.

Was that one visit all it took for a powerful chief to make his mind up over a woman?

Or had he, unknowingly to Anthony and his family, been watching Yvonne for some time, assessing her, to see if she was worthy of marrying a chief?

Yes, surely Silver Arrow had seen her often at the trading post while she had been getting household supplies. Anthony had not seen Silver Arrow there when he had taken Yvonne for the supplies, but that did not mean that he was not close by, silently taking everything in.

"Brother Stockton, I have come with many gifts," Silver Arrow said, walking beside Yvonne the rest of the way to the cabin. "I wish that you would accept them and listen to my reason for bringing them to you and your family."

Yvonne's face flooded with color as Silver Arrow glanced down at her with a slow smile, now for certain knowing why he was there. Her knees grew weak with the knowing. Oh, but if she could only control the beat of her heart. It felt as though it were in her throat, ready to leap out!

"Brother Stockton, I have gifts for all members of your family but one," Silver Arrow said thickly. "I have not made your eldest son's acquaintance. I did not bring gifts for him."

Anthony again stared at what Silver Arrow held in his arms, then smiled and gestured toward the door. "Come on inside," he said softly. "Let us relax in the sitting room."

Silver Arrow nodded. He stepped aside so that Yvonne could go on up the steps, then followed her into the cabin.

Once inside he looked slowly around him. His eyes lit up when he saw the neatness of the place. A woman's touch was visible everywhere.

Ae, he had been right to see White Swan as an industrious woman, and one who took pride in her home. He looked forward to how she would change his lodge into a lodge befitting a woman such as she.

"Here, let me lessen your burden," Anthony said as he began taking items from Silver Arrow's outstretched arms.

"The quiver of arrows and the bow are for your son Stanley," Silver Arrow said, drawing a happy gasp from Stanley as his father handed him the quiver of arrows.

Stanley looked anxiously at the bow which still hung across Silver Arrow's shoulder, knowing that he would have to wait until everything else was removed from his arms before he could have it, also.

"Thank you, Silver Arrow, for what you brought me," Stanley said, beaming.

"Young brave, I have brought you a child's bow, and arrows with blunt tips, which all Ottawa children use for practice while shooting at crickets and grasshoppers," he said, smiling down at Stanley. "When you grow older I will give you an adult bow and a quiver of sharp-tipped arrows."

"I can hardly wait to try these," Stanley said, still anxiously looking at the bow. He was going to carve his initials into it. That would make it his forever!

As Stanley took the beautiful white robe from his arms, Silver Arrow gazed over at Yvonne. "The robe made of white rabbit is for your daughter, as well as the beaded necklace that my grandmother made with her own nimble fingers," Silver Arrow said. "And also moccasins."

"They are so lovely," Yvonne sighed as her father hung the robe across her arm and gently placed the necklace in her hand. She gasped softly at the loveliness of the moccasins which her father placed on the table.

In truth, she felt as though she were dreaming again, for how could any of this be real? That Silver Arrow was actually there with gifts! She knew why Indians brought gifts.

Her pulse raced to think of why this Indian had brought them.

And his eyes! They spoke to her in ways that thrilled her very soul. It was hard to keep her composure, for, Lord, how her insides were bubbling.

"Thank you, Silver Arrow," she murmured. "I shall proudly wear everything."

His only response was a lingering gaze; then he turned to her father again. "My preacher friend, the pelts and blankets are for you, as well as a pouch of Indian tobacco."

He smiled when the mention of tobacco drew Anthony's eyes quickly to his. "Yes, I know you do not share the Ottawa's love of smoking," he said, chuckling low. "The tobacco is for your offering to the Great Spirit when you lift your voice to him in your prayers."

Yvonne paled as she glanced quickly at her father, then up at Silver Arrow again. "My father prays to God, not the Great Spirit," she softly corrected, saving Anthony the awkwardness of having to do it.

"As I see it, your God and my Great Spirit are one and the same," Silver Arrow said, gesturing heavenward. "The one above who made the earth and men and women is there for all of us. You call him God. We call him *Gitchi-manitou*. When the prayers reach the heavens, the one above does not sort out which color of man and woman breathes them across their lips. He answers them as though we are all one and the same."

"That is a beautiful way to believe," Yvonne said, smiling sweetly up at Silver Arrow, his height towering over hers.

Moment by moment her love for him deepened. And she no longer cared if it showed on her face, or in her voice. She no longer cared who knew her feelings for this man. After waiting and wanting Silver Arrow for what seemed an eternity, it was now all happening so fast.

Again she gazed down at the beautiful fur robe, and the necklace, and the moccasins. She gently placed the robe over the back of a chair and ran her fingers across it. Never had she felt anything as soft.

She turned to Silver Arrow. "Thank you so much for the gifts," she murmured. She held the necklace out before her, then smiled as she slipped it over her head. She removed her shoes and slipped her feet into the heavenly soft moccasins. "I love this necklace. I love the robe. I love the moccasins. Again thank you, Silver Arrow."

Stanley watched Silver Arrow slip the bow from his shoulder.

"May your hunt be good," Silver Arrow said, chuckling as he handed the bow to Stanley.

"I shall always cherish this," Stanley said, clutching the bow proudly. He turned and left the cabin with the bow and arrows.

Anthony went to the door. "Son, do not wander far!" he said, then turned and gazed at Jake as he came down the ladder from the loft.

Silver Arrow turned toward Jake as he took the last rung and stood at the foot of the ladder.

Anthony went and took Jake by an elbow and led him over to Silver Arrow. "Silver Arrow, this is my son Jake," he said. "Jake, of course you know Silver Arrow."

"Yes, I know him," Jake grumbled, his eyes narrowing into Silver Arrow's.

"As I also know Jake," Silver Arrow said tightly. Hate stirred deeply within his soul for this evil-hearted son of a minister. Smiling mischievously, only now realizing that he did have a gift for Jake after all, he slipped a hand inside the front pocket of his buckskin breeches.

"What are you doing here?" Jake asked warily, seeing the many items that Silver Arrow had brought. His gaze locked on the beaded necklace around Yvonne's neck, then slid to the moccasins on her feet.

He smiled to himself, thinking that just perhaps he would not have to work so hard to get his sister and this Indian together. It was obvious that Silver Arrow had made the first move toward Yvonne. These gifts were the beginning of a courtship, that was for certain.

"I have come today to give gifts and to speak to your father," Silver Arrow said, his eyes twinkling mischievously when he pulled the bullet out of his pocket. "My gift today to you is this."

When Silver Arrow held the bullet out toward Jake, Jake paled and took an unsteady step away from him. The bullet was the very sort that Jake used in his rifle.

Jake swallowed hard when he realized that this was a spent bullet. It had been fired! It was among those fired yesterday when he had been shooting at the crow; when he had *shot* the crow!

"Are you not going to accept my gift?" Silver Arrow taunted as Yvonne and Anthony stared, perplexed by what was transpiring before them.

What could it mean they wondered. Why would Silver Arrow want to give Jake a spent bullet? Why was Silver Arrow acting so peculiarly about it, and Jake even more peculiarly? He seemed frightened to death at having seen the bullet.

Jake's hand trembled as he reached out for the bullet. Then he yanked it away from Silver Arrow, curled his fingers around it, and backed slowly away from him.

"Are you not going to thank me for the gift?" Silver Arrow asked, his face split with a wide grin.

Jake said nothing as he stepped into the shadows and watched and listened.

Silver Arrow turned toward Anthony again. "I have come today to talk, but that can wait until later," he said. "But it would greatly please me if you would allow your daughter to go canoeing with me. It is a fine summer day. The leaves of the trees are like canopies over the river which will shade your daughter's skin from the damaging rays of the sun."

Anthony was still somewhat unsettled by what had transpired between Silver Arrow and Jake, aware that Jake's presence had changed Silver Arrow's mind about wanting to have a council with him. There was no love between these two men, that was for certain.

But Anthony did trust Silver Arrow, and he did see how Yvonne felt about him, and saw no threat in her feelings. She was old enough to know her own mind about things, even men. If she was in love with a man of a different skin coloring, that made no difference to Anthony. In the eyes of God and himself, everyone was equal.

He turned to Yvonne. "Do you wish to go with Silver Arrow?" he asked softly.

Yvonne blushed and smiled from her father to Silver Arrow. "Yes, I would love to," she murmured. She glanced down at her apron, then reached a hand to her hair. "Please excuse me. I will go to my room and make myself more presentable."

"Make sure you get a sunbonnet," Anthony said as she walked toward her room. "And shawl! The breeze along the river is cool this time of day."

"Yes, Father," Yvonne said over her shoulder, then went breathlessly into her room. She placed her hands to her cheeks and laughed softly, her insides aflutter to know that she was going to finally be alone with the man she adored.

Could it truly be happening?

Her hand slid down and her fingers went over the necklace.

She wiggled her toes in the moccasins.

Yes, those things were absolute proof that he was there, and that he cared!

"Sis?"

Jake's voice behind her drew Yvonne around. She hadn't closed the door, which allowed him a too easy entrance.

"Jake, what do you want?" Yvonne said, untying her apron. "And what was all that fuss about out there with Silver Arrow and that bullet?"

Jake uncurled his fingers and stared at the bullet, then thrust it inside his breeches pocket. "To hell with the bullet," he grumbled. "I didn't come here to discuss that bullet."

"Why *are* you here?" Yvonne said, angrily folding her arms across her chest.

"It's obvious that the Ottawa chief has a thing for you, sis," Jake said, his eyes gleaming. "Take advantage of it. Encourage him. Marry him. The gold, sis. Think about the gold and what it can do for you."

"Jake, get out of here," Yvonne said, stamping up to him. She gave him a shove. "Keep your lousy schemes to yourself. I never want to hear anything about that gold again. Do you hear? Never!"

She closed the door in his face.

She took in several shaky, deep breaths, then went to her dresser and hurriedly ran a brush through her hair. She stood back and looked at herself in the mirror. She smiled at her reflection, then grabbed a straw bonnet and tied it beneath her chin. Then she lifted a shawl around her shoulders.

Again she took a deep, quavering breath, and said a soft prayer that she would say and do everything right from this moment on. If she didn't, she may never get another chance to be with Silver Arrow!

As she left the room, her knees scarcely held her up they were so weak with excitement. When she came face-to-face with Silver Arrow, and he smiled that familiar smile that she adored, she melted inside.

Stanley ran into the cabin, breathless. His face

was flushed from excitement. "I love this bow," he said, holding it out for Silver Arrow to see. "I carved my initials on it. See them, Silver Arrow?"

Silver Arrow gazed at the initials. "You are skilled at carving," he said, placing a gentle hand on Stanley's frail shoulder. "When I bring you the larger bow, you might want to carve all types of intricate designs on it. Mine is most elaborate."

Silver Arrow smiled and patted the child's head, then turned to Yvonne. "Shall we go?" he said.

"Yes," Yvonne said. As she gazed up at him, her pulse raced. This was the moment she had dreamed of, yet had felt would never happen. How could it be? This wonderful, gentle Indian chief showing affection toward her?

The one thing that disappointed Yvonne was that Jake had interfered in the magic of the morning, causing Silver Arrow to delay his talk with her father. But she didn't think that had changed his mind about what he was going to talk about. Her!

"Can I go with you?" Stanley begged, grabbing Yvonne's hand. "Please, Yvonne? Can I?"

Silver Arrow intervened. He placed a gentle hand on Stanley's shoulder. "Young brave, you can go another time," he said, tactfully adding, "I will choose a day just for you and myself to do something together. Does that suit you, young brave?"

Stanley thought for a while, then nodded. "Yes, that satisfies me," he said, then left the lodge again with his bow and arrow.

"That would be even better," Stanley said over his shoulder.

So excited that she could hardly stand it, Yvonne left with Silver Arrow. Her insides trembled with ecstasy when he lifted her into his powerful arms once they reached the river, and gently placed her in his canoe. Her heart was pounding so hard she felt as though her whole body was quaking from the thundering beats.

Silver Arrow settled down on the seat in front of Yvonne, his back to her, then paddled the canoe out to the center of the river. When the canoe was sliding through the pristine water, Yvonne stared at Silver Arrow's muscles as he manned the paddle. He was powerfully built. His long, jet-black hair fluttered in the wind over his shoulders and down his back. She was so absorbed in watching Silver Arrow, all thoughts of where he might be taking her were lost.

After a while, she noticed that the river was no longer broad and beautiful. It was much narrower as the canoe glided past great cliffs that, delicately veiled in a purplish gray haze, cast huge shadows over the water.

Yvonne grabbed the sides of the canoe when Silver Arrow made a sudden, wide turn in the river and headed toward the sandy shore. Her heart leapt when he beached the canoe, then stepped out and turned to her.

"Why did you stop?" she asked, somewhat anxious to be this far from home with a man who made her feel reckless. If he were to kiss her, she knew that she would follow wherever that kiss took them, even to paradise and back, if he wished that of her.

Shame filled her for thinking such thoughts. In dreams she had no control over what she did. In real life, and living with a preacher father, she should be able to control her feelings . . . her desires!

Yet when she was with Silver Arrow, she felt that she had no control over anything.

"We shall sit awhile before I return you home," he said, for the second time in one day sweeping her up into his arms. "Have you enjoyed your outing so far?"

The way he looked at her as he asked her that, with quiet amusement in the depths of his eyes, somewhat unnerved Yvonne. Surely he could feel her uneasiness. Surely he saw it! He had to know that only he could be the cause!

"Yes, I always enjoy the river," she murmured, slipping an arm around his neck as he carried her to the embankment.

"Is there anything else today that you enjoy?" Silver Arrow asked, his deep black eyes almost hypnotizing her as he looked at her with such intensity.

"Yes, I am enjoying the sunshine, the song of the birds, and . . ." Yvonne stammered out, stopping when he interrupted her.

"I was not referring to those things," he said huskily as he stood with her amidst knee-tall grass. "Have you not longed to be with Silver Arrow as I have longed to be with you? Is it not my presence that you are enjoying over all else that you have spoken of aloud?"

He leaned closer to her lips. "Speak to me of that which has not yet breathed across your lips," he said. "Tell me what is in your heart that makes your eyes look so dreamily into mine. Tell me what has caused your pulse to race so."

He cuddled her closer to his powerful chest. "Did you not know that I could tell the rate of your heartbeat by the way your pulse beats in the vein of your beautiful neck?" he said softly. "White Swan, it beats even faster as I hold you this close in my arms."

Yvonne blanched. She held her head away from his chest and gazed up at him with confusion. "What . . . did . . . you just call me?" she asked, her voice drawn, recalling the dream in which he had addressed her by that name.

Yet why should she be so shocked? she mused to herself. Had not Four Horns spoken that name when he had come searching for Silver Arrow? She had learned then that Silver Arrow had given her that name!

Still, it was shocking to hear him say it, himself! How could she have dreamed something that was so real? How?

"Often when I think of you, a white swan comes to mind, because your skin is as white . . , your neck is as sublime," he said huskily. "And how do you think of me?"

"How do you know that I do?" Yvonne asked, trembling inside when he placed her on her feet.

"Can you honestly say that you do not?" Silver Arrow prodded.

"I didn't say that," Yvonne said, flinching sensually when he slipped his arms slowly around her waist. "I . . . I . . ."

Her words were stolen away when he lowered his mouth to her lips and kissed her. Nothing could have prepared her for how his kiss in true life would affect her. In her dreams it had been wonderful. But now, as he swept his powerful arms around her and molded her close to the contours of his hard, lean body, his kiss caused an incredible sweetness to sweep through her.

The press of his lips was so warm, soft, yet demanding.

Her senses dazzled, Yvonne closed her eyes and twined her arms around his sinewed shoulders and passionately returned the kiss, suddenly realizing that her answering heat and excitement were dangerous.

A part of her warned her that this might go farther than it should.

Another part of her told her that should she protest, she might lose him.

She could feel the hunger in the press of his body against hers, and by his kiss. She could feel his strong thighs against her legs. And when he began to slowly gyrate himself against her, the magic between them was quickly broken.

Although she had thought she could travel down that road of paradise with him, she now knew that she could not give herself to him *this* easily.

She would not risk losing this man's respect, or her own.

She slid her lips from his and gently shoved his chest. "Please don't," she whispered, her face flushed hot.

He released his hold on her and their eyes locked. "I did not mean to go this far this soon, nor this quickly," Silver Arrow said, then took her hands. "But I have wanted you for so long. Now that I am alone with you, and know that we share the same feelings for one another, I could hardly resist you."

"And I, you," Yvonne said, her whole body encased with sensual shivers. She eased her hands from his and hugged herself, the shawl having fallen into the canoe when he had lifted her from the seat. "But I just can't. This is the first time we have been together. I . . . don't . . . want you to think that I am a loose woman."

Silver Arrow took her hands again. "I could never think anything bad about you," he said thickly. "I will be patient. We will meet again and again, and when you are ready to allow our passions to mingle as though we are one body and soul, only then will I kiss you again. There is much for us to share as only a man and woman in love know how to. We are that man and woman. And I promise that soon you will open your arms out for me and welcome not only my lips against yours, but also my body."

Yvonne's heart soared to the heavens to realize that he loved her this much. It took much willpower on her part not to fling herself into his arms again and tell him to make love to her.

"It's best that you take me home," Yvonne instead said, slipping her hands from his. "I only hope that I haven't spoiled the outing for you. I hope you aren't too disappointed."

"Disappointed?" Silver Arrow said, laughing throatily. He swept a lock of hair back from her eyes. "My woman, my beautiful White Swan, you could never spoil anything for me, and no, I am not disappointed. I admire your restraint. I should have practiced it more, myself."

He swept her into his arms and carried her to the canoe. Their lips so close, their breaths mingling, he fought against kissing her again.

"I so badly wish to be kissed," Yvonne murmured, stroking his cheek with her fingertips. "Please . . . please kiss me?"

Silver Arrow bent his lips to hers and kissed her again, his body yearning for that which must be denied him today. Nothing should be rushed with this woman of his heart. He wished for everything to be perfect between them. He did not want to frighten her away by forcing her to give up her virginity until she was ready to do so, herself, at her own discretion.

Yes, everything must be perfect between them, for theirs was a love of a lifetime!

Their lips parted. They gazed at one another for a moment, then Silver Arrow placed her in the canoe.

"Silver Arrow," Yvonne blurted out. "Tomorrow, after my family returns home from church, will you please come and have Sunday dinner with us? Sunday dinner is always the special meal of the week for my family. Please, please come and join us?"

It did not take Silver Arrow long to give her his answer, though he had never made it his habit to eat with white people in their dwellings. But she was not just any white person. She would soon be his wife.

"*Ae*, I will come to share your meal with you and your family," Silver Arrow said.

"I'm so glad," Yvonne murmured, her cheeks hot from her soaring, wondrous bliss.

Silver Arrow shoved the canoe out into deeper water, then climbed inside and sat on the seat in front of her. He grabbed up the paddles and sent the canoe back up the long avenue of the river, toward her home.

Yvonne smiled at him when he gave her a soft glance over his shoulder.

When he looked away, Yvonne picked up the shawl from the floor of the canoe and placed it around her shoulders. She was so happy, she could hardly wait until tomorrow.

A sudden thought came to her.

The crow!

She hadn't seen the crow all day today!

She became sad to think that it might not have made it safely to its nest last evening when it left her room.

She scanned the heavens, and then the trees on both sides of the river.

No, it was not near.

She doubted that she would ever see it again.

Chapter Sixteen

Candles flickered at both ends of the dining table. The oak table was laid with a gleaming white tablecloth, the best of china, and fine silver, all brought from the beautiful, two-story stone house in Saint Louis.

Yvonne sat down stiffly in her chair as the others shuffled into theirs. She smiled awkwardly from her father, who sat at one end of the table in his black Sunday suit which contrasted starkly against his stiff, white-collared shirt, to the other end, where Silver Arrow sat in his spanking new fringed buckskin outfit.

Then she gazed across the table, where Jake sat in a neat suit, the white shirt with its stiffly starched collar looking out of place on him since he usually wore his hunting clothes, which he refused to let her wash as often as she felt she should.

At her right side sat sweet Stanley in his Sunday suit and tie.

Yvonne had hurried home from church and had changed clothes long enough to prepare the noon meal. After the food was arranged on the table, and just before Silver Arrow arrived, Yvonne had changed quickly back to the dress she had worn to church. It was a fully gathered organdy dress of a luscious pale green, with lace spilling across its bodice.

Her hair was drawn back from her face with wooden combs, and just above both ears she wore small clusters of roses and lilies of the valley stuck in the locks of her hair.

"Shall we say grace?" Anthony said, breaking the silence.

Silver Arrow's eyebrows forked. "Grace?" he said, looking at Anthony's hands as he clasped them together before him and held them up close to his face. "What is grace?"

"It is a term used for praying," Anthony softly explained. "As you use tobacco as a blessing before your meals, in our house we give our blessing by speaking words to our Lord."

"I see," Silver Arrow said, glancing quickly at Yvonne. He had never seen her so pretty. He would gladly sit through these formalities with her and her family when, in the end, he would finally be alone with her.

She had agreed to go horseback riding with him once the meal was eaten. When he had asked her in the presence of her father, he had seen the slight blush and timid lowering of her eyes. He gathered from her shy behavior that she had been recalling yesterday and what they had shared. His loins burned even now at the thought of the kiss, and the sweet press of her body against his.

When Anthony began to pray, and Silver Arrow noticed that everyone's heads were bowed, he quickly lowered his eyes and listened to the words of the holy man. Brother Stockton's prayer did not seem so very different from his own when Silver Arrow prayed to his Great Spirit. They were words of gentleness and of thanksgiving.

This time, Silver Arrow would not sprinkle tobacco and say his own words of thanks, for this was a white man's house where white men's customs took precedent over his own.

He slightly opened his eyes and gazed down at the white cloth spread across the table. While no one watched, he ran his fingers over its smoothness, and then placed his fingertips on the silver fork beside his plate. He had learned the use of such implements yet still ate more comfortably with his fingers, except for such things as soup or stews.

Today, for Yvonne, he would show his skills at the table. He would prove that he had the same table manners that *wa-me-to-go-zhe-wog*, white people, boasted of having.

The aroma of the food wafted into his nose. He looked from platter to platter, smiling to himself when he realized that his White Swan had gone to so much trouble to prepare food that he would like.

Or perhaps she had prepared the fried bread, baked trout, and corn stew to prove that she already knew how to prepare food that Indians made in their lodges.

He glanced at her, thinking her head would be bowed as her father spoke words to his God, but instead found her gazing at him.

When she smiled at him, then quickly bowed her head again and closed her eyes, Silver Arrow's heart sang and beat more soundly with his love for her.

Today, after the meal, he hoped for so much, yet he would not rush her into anything. She would have to prove that she wished to be with him sexually as badly as he wished to be with her.

He glanced over his shoulder and smiled when he saw on a counter the big jug of maple syrup that he had brought to this family for their morning meals, to be used with their biscuits or their "flapjacks" that he had heard so much about. The syrup had been made by his people in late winter while gathering maple sap to make sugar.

"Amen," Anthony said, and everyone around the table except Silver Arrow repeated the word after him.

"Now we can finally eat," Jake said, fitting his white linen napkin beneath his chin like a bib. "I'm starved."

"The napkin," Anthony whispered, frowning at Jake. "Son, show your manners. Place the napkin where it belongs. On your lap."

Jake glowered at his father, then at Silver Arrow, then yanked the napkin down and begrudgingly placed it on his lap.

One by one the platters of food were passed around the table.

"I forgot to pour the coffee," Yvonne said, smiling softly at Silver Arrow as she pushed her chair back from the table.

She went to the fireplace where she had left the coffeepot sitting in the coals at the edges, then noticed that the fire had burned too low to keep the coffee hot enough.

Bending over, she lifted a log to place in the coals. She screamed and dropped the log when a snake crawled out from a small hole at the side.

"A snake!" she cried as she watched it wriggle away across the wooden floor.

"Get outta the way," Jake shouted, lunging from his chair. "I'll kill it!"

"No need in doing that," Silver Arrow said, moving more quickly than Jake. As fast as a lightning flash, Silver Arrow had the black garter snake by the neck. He carried it to the door and gently flung it outside, then went to Yvonne, who was still shaken.

Silence fell around them as Silver Arrow took Yvonne's hands. "You are all right," he said thickly. "It was not a poisonous snake. But you must be more careful about the wood you bring into your lodge. The next hidden snake might be poisonous."

"Jake brought the wood inside this morning," Yvonne said, mesmerized by how Silver Arrow held her hand, and by the way he gazed down at her with his beautiful, dark eyes. For the moment she was not aware of anyone else being in the room. There was only this man who had come to her rescue and who now stood over her, her protector.

Jake stared a moment longer at the affectionate scene, then stamped back to the table. "I still say you should've killed it," he said, his voice full of sarcasm.

He sat down and glowered at Silver Arrow as he came back to the table with Yvonne. Jake groaned to himself as Silver Arrow ever so politely, and much too lovingly, assisted Yvonne as she sat back down, the coffee obviously forgotten.

Disgruntled over Yvonne's telling him, not once, but twice now, that she would never share Silver Arrow's gold with him even if she did get her hands on it, Jake dove into his food. His thoughts were spinning in search of other ways to find the hiding place of the gold.

Antelope Skin.

Yes, he seemed to be the only answer.

Perhaps after Antelope Skin's brain was soaked enough with firewater he would get the courage to ask his cousin where he kept his gold, or perhaps even force answers out of him at gunpoint.

Antelope Skin had to know that if he got the gold in his possession, he could flee his village and live a life of luxury elsewhere.

Jake smiled wickedly, knowing that he would share only a very small portion with the drunken savage Ottawa warrior.

"Silver Arrow, tell us more about your family," Anthony said as he delicately picked through the trout on his plate with a fork, to make sure there were no bones in his next bite. "You have said that your parents died during an Indian raid. You said the raiders were Iroquois?"

"Yes, and then my grandfather died shortly thereafter from what I have always thought to be a broken heart," Silver Arrow said, enjoying the food that his White Swan had prepared. From time to time, he sent her quick, appreciative glances, which she received with a shy smile and lowering of eyes.

"I should have invited Rustling Leaves to dinner today also," Anthony said, giving Stanley a quick look. "Little Stanley here thinks a lot of your sister. She is a delight, Silver Arrow. And how does she like school?"

"Each day she accepts it with much more ease," Silver Arrow said, taking a sip of water from a tall-stemmed glass that sparkled beneath the light of the candles.

He looked over at Jake, who occasionally pulled a wind watch from his vest pocket, nervously checking the time as though he had an appointment soon. As Silver Arrow's and Jake's eyes met, Silver Arrow noticed how nervously Jake thrust the watch back into his pocket, then pried his index finger between his tight collar and fleshy neck.

"And you, Jake, what do you do to pass time other than hunting?" Silver Arrow asked. "What about those steel traps I find in the woods, which much too often have snared an innocent animal that suffers as it lies there slowly dying?"

Jake blanched. He gave his father a quick, worried glance as Anthony laid his fork down, shock registering on his face.

"Jake, I told you to quit using those traps," Anthony said, his voice drawn. "Son, I . . ."

Jake glowered at Silver Arrow, then rose so quickly from his chair it slammed over backward on the floor. "I've had enough of this powwow," he said, his teeth clenched. He glared darkly at Silver Arrow. "I don't know what he's even doin' here. He ain't nothin' but a troublemaker."

As he stamped toward the door, he yanked off his coat, his vest, and his tie. He threw them all on the floor, then grabbed his rifle and left the cabin in a huff.

Anthony scrambled to his feet and went to the door. "Son, you get back in here and apologize to Silver Arrow!" he shouted, a fist doubled to his side.

It was obvious that Jake wasn't going to apologize to anyone. The sound of his horse riding away in a hard gallop was the only thing that anyone heard.

His head hanging, Anthony went back to the table and sat down. "I don't know what I'm going to do with him," he said thickly. "He's so way out of hand, I doubt I will ever be able to get a handle on him."

"Never give up on a son," Silver Arrow said, his voice drawn. "It is obvious that he is a troubled man. In time things change. He will change back to someone you will be proud of."

"Since his mother's death he's been someone I don't even know," Anthony said, nodding a thank-you to Yvonne as she poured him a cup of coffee, then set a piece of apple pie before him. "Jake's never accepted his mother's death. A bear clawed her to death right before his eyes. This is why he hunts and kills animals with such a vengeance. He always sees that one murderous bear in every animal he kills."

"That is tragic," Silver Arrow said, his eyes widening at the large piece of pie that Yvonne placed before him. The pies she had brought to him earlier as a peace offering had whetted his appetite for more. He eagerly lifted the fork and dove into the tasty morsel.

"To Jake, Yvonne's mother, when I married her, never did seem to take the place of his own mother," Anthony said between bites. He looked over at Stanley who gobbled up one piece of pie and motioned to Yvonne for another, which she smilingly gave to him. Then she sat down and slowly ate a piece herself.

"So you have had two wives?" Silver Arrow said, forking an eyebrow. "I was not certain if that was a practice of the white man."

"We take one wife at a time," Anthony said, laughing. "And you, Silver Arrow? What is your people's custom about wives?"

"We Ottawa also have one wife at a time," Silver Arrow said, sending a quick smile toward Yvonne. Then he shoved his empty plate away from him and looked more seriously at Anthony.

"The gifts I brought you are only a small portion of what I will bring you as a bride price for your daughter."

Anthony almost choked on his pie, even though he had expected talk of marriage today since the subject had been shoved aside the last time they were together.

"You wish to marry my daughter?" Anthony asked, looking at Yvonne to see her reaction. In her eyes he saw adoration as she gazed at Silver Arrow. And her cheeks were slightly flushed, which was surely caused by her excitement over having been singled out by this proud, handsome chief to be his bride.

"I wish for no other woman than your daughter for a wife, ever," Silver Arrow said. "Will you give your permission?"

Anthony stood up and went to Yvonne. He reached for her hands and pulled her to her feet. "Yvonne, tell me your feelings about this," he said, aware of how her fingers were trembling in his. "Do you wish to marry Silver Arrow?"

"Yes," she murmured. "I do so want to marry him."

"Then you have my blessing," Anthony said, laughing as she wrenched her hands free and flung herself into his arms.

Silver Arrow's heart was pounding like a thousand drums within his chest as he rose from his chair. Stanley rushed to him and hugged him, then stood back as Silver Arrow went and eased Yvonne from her father's arms.

"My woman," he said, his eyes dancing into

hers. "*Wau-e-baw*, soon. We shall marry soon."

She crept into his arms. They embraced.

Then Anthony cleared his throat nervously. "You two go on now," he said, stacking the dirty dishes. "Take that horse ride."

Yvonne turned to him. She stared down at the cluttered table, then again at Anthony. "But mustn't I first do the dishes?"

"No, I don't think so," Anthony said, laughing throatily. He gave Stanley a slow wink. "Stanley and I will do them, won't we, son?"

Stanley nodded and hurried to the table. He began gathering the dirty dishes, glancing and smiling from Yvonne to Silver Arrow.

Yvonne gazed down at her dress, thinking she should change into riding clothes, but, not wanting to delay the time alone with Silver Arrow, cast the thought aside and ran from the cabin with him. She needed no shawl, and she did not want to wear a bonnet. The day was warm. The sun lay like a path of fire across the land.

Laughing, she ran to her gentle mare that she had saddled earlier for the ride with Silver Arrow. Before he could catch up with her to help her into the saddle, she had already mounted her horse.

She waited for him to swing himself into his saddle, then they rode off together along the banks of the river.

Anthony went and stood at the door and watched them until they rode out of sight.

"Father, when Yvonne and Silver Arrow are married, will they have Indian babies or white?" Stanley suddenly asked.

Taken by surprise by the question, not only because he had not thought that far ahead himself, but because it was a small child asking it, Anthony turned to his son, whose wide, wondering eyes were lifted to his.

"Stanley, I think we've dishes to do, don't you?" he said, patting his far too inquisitive son on the shoulder. "That's all you should bother yourself with now, my son. Not such things as babies. That sort of talk is for adults only."

Stanley blushed and followed his father to the table, but in his mind he was thinking of someone else besides Silver Arrow and Yvonne.

When Stanley married Rustling Leaves, he could not help but wonder if their children would be white skinned, or red.

Chapter Seventeen

Yvonne was only partially aware of the beauty of the land as she rode beside Silver Arrow. Her pulse raced at the thought of being alone with him again, yet she could not help but wonder where he was taking her. After riding a short distance, he had taken the lead with his pinto stallion.

At first they had ridden in a slow trot along the riverbank, sharing small talk about the weather, the meal they had just eaten, and then had laughed and talked of their brother's and sister's obvious caring for one another.

They had even laughingly teased about Stanley and Rustling Leaves marrying once they reached adulthood.

Yvonne had become more relaxed in Silver Arrow's presence while sharing the light conversation, yet deep inside herself, where her desires were formed, she wondered if he was leading her to an isolated place where they could once again embrace. It dizzied her to recall how his embrace and kisses had affected her the day before.

And now that they had agreed to marry, would it be so wrong to give her all to him?

Shame flooded Yvonne's senses to realize where her thoughts had taken her. Never in her life had she been this wickedly sinful in her thoughts and desires.

But never before had she met a man whose very presence made her knees feel wobbly as jelly!

A shudder ran up and down her spine to realize that her life had changed so much this quickly, and that she had agreed to marry a man with whom she had spent only a few moments alone.

Would having children happen as quickly once they were married? she wondered. It seemed hard to imagine a child at her breast, suckling.

Yet the realization that it would be Silver Arrow's child made her smile and accept the possibility of becoming with child perhaps even the first time they made love.

A love child, she marveled to herself. Surely such a child could add to, and even strengthen, their relationship.

It would be the ultimate sharing!

They were now riding across a wide, spacious meadow. The breeze was so brisk the roses and lilies of the valley fluttered from Yvonne's hair and into the wind, and then her combs blew away, leaving her hair fluttering in wild, long waves down her back.

Occasionally a wisp of hair would flick around her face, stinging her cheeks. Then it would be behind her, flowing across her shoulders.

Yvonne glanced over at Silver Arrow. When she had asked him where he was taking her, he had only given her a soft smile as his answer.

She saw how his copper face shone in the bright sunshine, and how his hair was fluttering as wildly in the wind as hers. His sculpted face made a sensual thrill soar through Yvonne anew. She looked at his hands as they held the reins which controlled his steed. She recalled their strength, and how he could lift her from a horse as though she weighed no more than a feather.

Yet there was such gentleness in the way he always held her, and touched her face when he looked adoringly down at her just before he kissed her.

Swallowing hard, these thoughts making her tremble with desire, she focused her eyes elsewhere. She rode beside Silver Arrow as he rode from the meadow into the fringes of the forest, where wild irises were in full bloom, their purple heads contrasting against the stark white of a patch of lily of the valleys that surrounded them.

The sweet scent of the flowers wafted toward Yvonne. She closed her eyes and deeply inhaled, then opened her eyes wide again when she heard squirrels scampering from limb to limb overhead.

She saw a snowshoe hare rush into a thicket, and a bluejay squawked as though to warn the hare to flee from danger as the horses approached.

The shine of the river came into view through a break in the trees. Along its banks were many more flowering plants—arbutus, wild daisies, lady's slipper, and beautiful purple and white violets.

Silver Arrow looked over at Yvonne. "We will stop beside the river and rest," he said. He tightened his hold on the reins and slowed his horse to a trot.

He frowned at Yvonne when he saw the disarray of her hair and the flush of her cheeks. "Have I waited too long to stop?" he asked, his voice deep with concern. "Has the ride tired you?"

"No to both questions," Yvonne said, laughing. "I'm just fine. The ride did me good. I haven't gone at that clip on a horse for way too long now. I haven't gone horseback riding for such a long time. I've truly enjoyed myself this afternoon, Silver Arrow. You seem to have known what I needed."

"It is not wise for you to ride a horse unescorted," he said, leading his pinto stallion to a thick stand of birch trees. "I have worried about you riding the horse and buggy when you take Stanley to school without your father or older brother there to watch over you. There are many wicked-minded men who wander through this forest to hunt. Do you not know how beautiful you are? How you could become the target of some woman-hungry man?"

Yvonne was stunned by the depth of his concern for her, yet knew she shouldn't be. He had come and asked for her hand in marriage. He had held her and told her how much he cared. He seemed the sort who would go to any length to protect the one he loved. He was the sort of man who, when he loved, loved totally; unconditionally.

She gazed at him as he drew a tight rein and dismounted. Feeling lucky to be the woman of his desire, she smiled. She looked forward to the strengthening of their bond. She was certain that he would surprise her many times over in how he would prove his devotion to her.

After drawing a tight rein herself, Yvonne raked her fingers through her hair to untangle it. She ran a hand down the front of her dress, smoothing its skirt down over her knees.

Silver Arrow flipped his horse's reins over a tree branch, then went to Yvonne. "Come, let us sit by the river," he said, placing his hands around her waist.

Yvonne slid from the saddle to the ground and into his arms. Her heart pounding, an incredible sweetness sweeping through her, she gazed up at him.

His arms locked around her as he held her in a torrid embrace, his body hard against hers.

Passion glazed his eyes.

"How fiercely I want you," he said huskily, his gaze burning. His breath mingled with hers as his mouth closed over hers.

His lips of fire dazzled Yvonne's senses. Feelings of passion overwhelming her, she twined her arms around his neck and returned his kiss with abandon.

When he snaked a hand between them and cupped a breast through the soft fabric of her dress, delicious shivers of desire rode Yvonne's spine, and she only momentarily thought to protest.

Soon she forgot why she had even thought to. All she was aware of was how a delicious languor was stealing her breath and her senses away.

Silver Arrow slid his mouth from her lips. Her throat arched backward as his lips traveled along the delicate, vulnerable line of her neck. She scarcely breathed and her eyes opened wildly when he released his hold on her and his hands crept around to the buttons of her dress and slowly began unbuttoning them.

Her heartbeats were threatening to swallow her whole. She knew that if she did not stop him now, it would be too late.

As he slowly began to slide the dress down from her shoulders, she sighed a guttural sigh of pleasure and closed her eyes, his lips sending feathery kisses across her shoulders.

Yvonne fought to reclaim her sanity when she felt his hot breath on her bared breasts, yet she could not deny him anything now, especially now, when her hunger for him was finally being fed.

She gasped with a sensual shock when his mouth fastened gently on one of her breasts.

She cried out with pleasure when he flicked his tongue around her nipple and his teeth nipped.

Never had she experienced anything as deliciously wonderful as those feelings that were now traveling through her, his mouth and tongue causing silver flames of desire to leap high within her.

She felt a strange tingling between her thighs, a warmth that was spreading as his tongue, his lips and his mouth went from one breast to the other, while his hands now finished disrobing her.

The breeze was warm on Yvonne's naked flesh. Her face grew hot with a blush to know that for the first time in her life someone besides herself was seeing her without clothes.

This thought brought her somewhat back to reality. She stepped away from Silver Arrow, her eyes wide, her heart pounding, as she attempted to cover her breasts with her folded arms.

Silver Arrow gently placed his hands on her wrists and drew them away from her breasts. "Do not feel as though it is wrong to share life to the fullest with this man who will soon be your husband," he said huskily. "Let me show you now the mysteries of lovemaking. You know that you do not want to wait until later. Your eyes, your heartbeat, your flushed cheeks, reveal too much to me."

He eased his hands from her wrists. He took her hand and led it to that part of him that had reacted to her nakedness as he raked his eyes over her, seeing just how right he had been to envision her body as that of perfection.

Her hips were well rounded.

Her waist was tiny.

Her breasts were ripe, their nipples erect.

Down below, at the juncture of her thighs, a cloud of curly hair covered the secrets of her total desire.

His eyes traveled upward again.

Ae, everything about her was flawless.

He led her trembling hand to his heat. "Touch it. Rub it. Familiarize yourself with that part of me that throbs with need of you," he said as he pressed her hand firmly against his manhood, the buckskin of his breeches impeding the true touch of her flesh against his.

"I feel so wicked," Yvonne gasped out as she felt the full outline of his manhood, and even the heat of his flesh through the fabric of his breeches. Never had she imagined a man could be this big; this fascinating. "I feel . . . as though . . . I shouldn't."

"When you are with me, the man who will soon be your husband, there is nothing we cannot share," he said, his heart beating soundly as she slightly squeezed his throbbing member. He closed his eyes and thrust himself even more boldly within her hand. "Stroke it. Stroke my heat."

Yvonne's body turned to liquid fire as he ran his hands slowly down her body, while her fingers ran up and down the full length of his manhood.

When his fingers came to that place where she strangely throbbed, and then his fingers wove their way through her soft tendrils of hair, touching the very core of her womanhood, she closed her eyes and moaned.

She was so ecstatic from the building pleasure that his fingers were arousing in her as he stroked her womanhood, her knees threatened to buckle beneath her.

Then when he thrust a finger up inside her and she became filled with such sudden ecstasy, frightened by it, Yvonne's eyes flew open and she stepped quickly away from him.

"Do not be afraid of your feelings," Silver Arrow said, now slowly undressing as she watched. He tossed his shirt away, and then dropped his breeches to the ground.

When he was totally nude, he moved toward her, his eyes darkening with the depths of his emotion.

"Look at me, naked," Silver Arrow said. "I want you to feel comfortable with my body."

Breathless, mesmerized by how he looked unclothed, Yvonne ceased fighting her feelings. Her senses were spinning as he swept her up into his arms, his lips devouring hers as he carried her to the bank of the river and laid her among a patch of flowers.

She surrendered herself to him and gave herself up to rapture as he lay down over her and, with a knee, gently parted her thighs.

While kissing her, he gently slid himself inside her.

Anchoring her fiercely, he probed more deeply, then stopped when he reached her maidenhead, which lay intact, proving her virginity.

"The pain will be only brief," he whispered

against her lips. "The pain is needed to open up a whole new way of life for you."

He wrapped her gently in his arms, spinning his golden web of magic around her, then came into her suddenly, thrusting deeply.

His mouth seared into hers with intensity, kissing away her cry of pain.

The discomfort had been brief for Yvonne, and now she was swimming in a pool of ecstasy as Silver Arrow's hips moved rhythmically. His each thrust sent a message of wonder to her soaring heart and delicious shivers of desire throughout her.

As though having done this countless times before, feeling so strangely practiced, Yvonne clung and rocked with Silver Arrow.

He made love to her slowly, his tongue leisurely circling one of her nipples and then the other.

Silver Arrow reveled in the sweet, warm press of White Swan's creamy skin against his. He nibbled at her lips as he ran his fingers through the soft glimmer of her hair.

Again he kissed her, his mouth searing into hers.

He felt the nerves in his body tensing.

He held her in a torrid embrace, the heat of his passion spreading . . . rising . . . splashing.

Yvonne's blood quickened when she felt the rapture building, spreading, soon spilling over as his body joined hers in violent, sensual tremors.

When they came down from that place where they had traveled together to the highest realm of pleasure, Silver Arrow cuddled Yvonne close to his side.

"It was as I had thought it would be," he said huskily. "I have never felt as alive as now, while with you."

"I never knew that a man and woman could share such pleasure," Yvonne whispered as she reached an arm around him and stroked his back with her fingertips. "Of course, I have read in novels that it was wonderful to make love. But experiencing it, truly experiencing it, was far beyond anything I could have imagined."

She laughed softly. "I just can't believe that I am here with you like this," she murmured. "That it seems so natural to sit naked with you, to talk with you while I am naked."

"*Ae*, and for me it is as though it is all revisited, as though we have been together like this many times before," Silver Arrow said, pushing a lock of hair back from her eyes. "You see, in my dreams I have lain with you, I have made love with you, I have filled my hands with the soft plushness of your breasts."

"You dreamed of me also?" Yvonne gasped, recalling her own dreams in which she had made such passionate love with him.

"Also?" Silver Arrow asked, arching an eyebrow.

"I dreamed of you many times before we even were introduced to one another," Yvonne said. She laughed softly. "It is as though, now, it is not the first time but perhaps the hundredth!"

He chuckled.

A rustling in a tree overhead drew Yvonne's attention. She eased from Silver Arrow's arms and searched for the source of the sound.

When she saw a crow, she sat up quickly, then sighed when she realized that this wasn't the crow that had kept vigil near her cabin so many times she would never mistake it for another.

"What are you looking at so intensely?" Silver Arrow asked, moving to sit beside her. Following her gaze, his eyes locked on those of a large crow.

Then he looked guardedly at Yvonne. "It is only an *awn-dayg*," he said, his voice strangely drawn.

"A what?" she questioned, not understanding the Ottawa language.

"A crow," he said, watching her expression.

"Oh, I see. Yes, I know that it is only a crow," Yvonne sighed. "I just thought it was . . ."

Realizing that he knew nothing of the crow of which she was thinking, she smiled softly at him. "Yes, it's only a crow," she murmured.

Her smile faded when she again thought about not having seen the crow since that night when it escaped from her bedroom. She could not help but think that it was dead, and the thought saddened her.

Jake! she thought angrily. Damn him for shooting the innocent bird!

Then another thought about Jake came to her, which amused her. She laughed softly. "I'll never forget the look on Jake's face when you grabbed up the snake and let it loose outside," she said. "Jake would have loved to kill it."

"I do not kill or destroy so easily," Silver Arrow said. He nodded toward a rotten log beside the river. "Do you see the log and how it is covered by moss? It suggests the legend of the log demon."

"A log demon?" Yvonne said, forking an eyebrow.

"*Ae*, in everything I see many things," Silver Arrow said, nodding. "Indian corn, and sweet flag in the swamp, are the descendants of beautiful spirits who still live in them. Flowers, beasts, and trees have all loved and talked and sang. They can even now do so, should the magician only come to speak the spell."

"I so wish to learn the lore of your people," Yvonne said, moving to her knees before him. She gazed adoringly into his eyes. "Do you think I will be able to know it all one day?"

"*Ae*, but it will take time," he said, taking her hands, holding them.

"I am so glad you came to dinner," she said, sighing. "I look forward to sharing Christmas and Thanksgiving with you. Those holidays are so special."

Silver Arrow eased his hands from hers and gazed moodily into her eyes. "Thanksgiving Day is the hardest day for the Indians because of what the whites did to us," he said, his voice drawn. "But I will join you on that special day and do the best I can not to spoil it for you."

"You could never spoil anything for me," Yvonne said. She drifted into his arms and pressed her cheek against his chest. "I still can't believe I'm here with you like this." She giggled.

"I would have never thought I could ever sit this casually with a man unclothed. I am so deliciously wicked and proud of it!"

She scooted onto his lap and straddled him with her legs. She twined her arms around his neck.

Her gaze slowly swept over the magnificent broadness of his hairless chest, marveling at the width of his shoulders.

Then her gaze stopped at a puckered wound on Silver Arrow's left shoulder. It seemed fresh, as though perhaps a bullet had grazed his flesh only recently.

She turned quick eyes up to him. She flinched and went cold inside when in his eyes she saw the eyes of the crow that she had grown fond of, yet feared was dead.

Frightened, not understanding why she would see a crow's eyes when she looked into Silver Arrow's, Yvonne rose to her feet.

Her heart pounding, she turned and ran from him.

Silver Arrow ran to her and grabbed her wrist, stopping her. He swung her around to face him. "I see much fear in your eyes," he said solemnly. "I will not question it, but I will say to you not to be afraid of the mysteries of life. One by one these mysteries will be unfolded to you, not by my speaking them, but by you witnessing them."

"I . . . don't . . . understand," Yvonne cried, pleading up at him with her eyes. She glanced at the puckered wound, thinking back to where the crow had been shot, then gazed up at him again, trembling.

"In time you will understand all things about me," Silver Arrow said softly. "But I will tell you this now—that the highest ambition of an Ottawa Indian is to become a *mequomoowessoo*, a mystical being who enjoys all highest privileges of humanity allied to the supernatural. My grandfather has left me, his grandson, his greatest inheritance, his *magic*."

Yvonne suddenly recalled something her father had taught her in Saint Louis when they were learning about the different Indian tribes of this area, to make living among them easier.

Anthony had told her about bearwalkers, known in the Ottawa tongue as *me-coub-moosa*.

A bearwalker was a man or a woman who, with herbs and special words which only they knew, could instantly transform themselves into balls of fire, or assume animal forms. Anthony had explained that once the person was transformed, they were able to travel great distances quickly, and go unrecognized. They had the ability to inflict bad luck, disgrace, poverty, sickness, and even death on their enemies, or on people they believed had wronged them. Then there were bearwalkers who did good for mankind called *obzheech-gun*, good medicine.

Her love for Silver Arrow overpowered her suspicion, and Yvonne moved into his arms. "I love you so much," she said. "I want to know everything about you. Nothing you say would make me love you less."

"In time, White Swan," Silver Arrow said, stroking her bare back. "Just be patient."

"Yes, I shall," Yvonne whispered as his lips pressed onto hers, savagely kissing her.

Silver Arrow spread Yvonne beneath him on the ground and again they made love.

Yvonne clung to him, and when doubts began to swirl inside her consciousness, and she saw the eyes of the crow in her mind's eye, she brushed such thoughts aside. But somehow she knew now that the crow that she had thought was dead, was not dead at all, but very close, so close she could feel its savage passions.

Chapter Eighteen

Antelope Skin lifted the jug of whisky to his lips and took several deep swallows. Jake stood over him, chuckling. River Rat stood close by and spat a stream of chewing tobacco from the corner of his mouth.

"Antelope Skin, you'd best enjoy these last swallows of whisky, for, by damn, River Rat and I are going to cut off your supply if you don't come up with a plan soon to get that gold from your cousin," Jake said, his face somber. "I'm not going to be able to acquire such information from my sister. She's as stubborn as a mule when it comes to cooperating with me about anything. It's all up to you, Antelope Skin. You *must* find a way to get answers from your cousin about the gold."

Antelope Skin set the jug aside. He wiped his

mouth dry with the back of a hand, then drew River Rat and Jake into a tight circle around him. "I have a plan," he said, his dark eyes dancing. "We'll steal Rustling Leaves from the school ground. We'll use her for blackmail. If my cousin wants his sister back, first he will have to tell us where the gold is."

"I won't touch that plan with a ten-foot pole," Jake growled back at Antelope Skin. "It's crazy! You're a lunatic for thinkin' it up. I don't want that cousin of yours breathing down my neck with a rifle, or worse!"

"I like the idea," River Rat said, chuckling wickedly. "I think Antelope Skin's plan is the only way to get our hands on the gold, since Jake's sister has proven to be a dead end." River Rat kneaded his chin. "Yeah, I think it'll work," he said, nodding. "Blackmail always works if the life of a loved one is placed in jeopardy."

"I just don't know," Jake said, sighing deeply.

"It's two against one that we try it," River Rat said sternly.

Jake inhaled a nervous breath, then nodded.

Chapter Nineteen

Princess Pretty Hawk tossed back and forth in her bed as she took an early evening nap. In her dream she was walking outside in a clearing. Suddenly rain began to fall. She turned her eyes heavenward, then cried out in her sleep when the rain turned to gold. She ran back to her village. She stood there in shock as she watched her people being pelted to death by the gold.

Yet as it fell all around her, none fell on her.

Princess Pretty Hawk awakened in a sweat. She rose shakily from her bed. She walked slowly from her bedroom just in time to see Silver Arrow returning from his day with the white woman.

"Grandmother, you look so weary," Silver Arrow said as he went to her and gathered her into his arms. "What has happened while I was gone to make you look so tired . . . so drawn?"

"Another dream, my grandson," Princess Pretty Hawk said, resting her cheek against his powerful chest. "I am afraid of my dreams. Today I dreamed of our people being killed by huge pieces of gold falling from the heavens. They pelted and crushed them to death. Yet the gold did not touch me. I lived while others died. Why, Silver Arrow? Why?"

Silver Arrow stroked her thick back. "Do not let dreams affect you so," he softly counseled.

"I am afraid," Princess Pretty Hawk said, sobbing. "I fear terrible things are in store for our people. I am so tired. I am ready to travel the road to the stars and be with those who have passed on before me. I wish to go soon, Silver Arrow. Why must I stay behind while others are gone before me? They wait for me. I . . . am . . . ready to go to them."

Silver Arrow swayed gently back and forth, rocking his grandmother against him. In his heart, a bitterness was growing against those who wished to have the gold that his grandfather had kept buried.

Those who sought to find the gold were causing the troubled dreams of his grandmother. Only they would cause her to dream of his people being slaughtered by the showers of gold nuggets.

Yet there was no way to stop the rumors about the gold. It was something that grew inside a man's heart like a festering wound. Greed was one of man's worst enemies.

He firmed his jaw. He would stop anyone who tried to invade his people's lives with any more talk of gold.

Chapter Twenty

It was a steamy hot day in June, so hot that Rustling Leaves and Stanley sought the shelter of the outer fringe of the forest as they played outside the school during afternoon recess.

Rustling Leaves sat down on some soft, cool grass and rocked the cornhusk doll that Stanley had made for her. She had named it after the black-eyed Susans that grew wild in the forest.

"Stanley, do you think my Susan doll is also hot?" Rustling Leaves asked as she watched him whittling a stick into the shape of a miniature butterfly.

"Everything and everyone is hot today," Stanley said, flinching when his knife slipped and he scraped off a thin layer of skin from his thumb. He laid his knife and piece of wood aside and sucked on his thumb as blood seeped from the small wound.

"Stanley, Teacher Alice told you not to bring the knife to school anymore," Rustling Leaves said. She scooted closer to him and placed a comforting hand on his knee. "If she catches you with the knife she will switch your legs and make you stand in a corner."

She gazed at him adoringly, remembering how only moments ago he had once again stood up for her against the tormenting teasing from the other boys as they called her a "stupid squaw." She smiled to think that she had stood up for Stanley when those same boys had poked fun at his eyeglasses, calling him a puny sissy.

"I won't let the teacher see it," Stanley said, smiling at Rustling Leaves. He saw her as nothing less than beautiful in her doeskin dress resplendent with colorful beads, and with her wide, dark eyes and glistening black hair that hung in two neat braids down her back. He would never let harm come to her. Never! He loved her and would one day marry her!

Rustling Leaves scrambled to her feet. She pointed to a monarch butterfly as it gently soared past, flying with the wind. "Look, Stanley!" she cried. "You are carving a wooden butterfly for me, but there is a *real* one! Do you think you can catch it?"

Breathless at the sight of seeing not only one butterfly now, but several, Stanley folded up his knife and slipped it into his pocket. He rushed to his feet and scampered after the butterflies. "With so many, surely I can catch one!" he shouted over his shoulder at Rustling Leaves. "Aren't they pretty, Rustling Leaves? Look at the brilliant colors!"

"*Ae*, so pretty!" Rustling Leaves sighed.

She watched Stanley chase the butterflies clear across the schoolyard, then strained her neck to see him when he ran out of sight, past some trees.

Suddenly she felt a presence behind her when a twig snapped.

She turned with a start and raised questioning eyes up at a man whose eyes were gleaming and whose lips were curved in a strange, quivering smile. In his hand he held a cigarette.

"Come closer, little girl," the man said softly as he nervously looked past her. "Come on, Rustling Leaves, I have something to show you."

The warnings of her brother swept through her consciousness, and Rustling Leaves clutched her doll to her bosom. Silver Arrow had warned her that all strangers were possible enemies. He had told her never to trust strangers, nor even to speak to them.

"Don't be afraid," River Rat said, beckoning her with the hand that held the cigarette.

Rustling Leaves watched the glowing red tip of the cigarette that was tracing a semicircle in the darkness of the thick forest in which the man stood.

Again her brother's warnings troubled her. She started to take a slow step away from the stranger but stopped when he dropped his cigarette and stamped it out with the heel of his boot, for just as quickly, in a quick, fluid movement, he slid one of his hands inside his coat pocket and took out a handful of colored glass beads and shiny little shells.

Rustling Leaves' eyes lit up at the sight. She could not help but stare at the glittering objects. "These are yours if you will follow me into the forest," River Rat taunted. He hunched down low as she took a slow step toward him, her eyes never leaving what he was holding in his hand.

"They are so pretty," Rustling Leaves said, unaware that she was following the man as he took slow, backward steps into the darker depths of the forest.

"Come on now," River Rat said, his eyes gleaming. "Just a little farther."

Suddenly Rustling Leaves realized what was happening. She turned to run away, but then a familiar voice behind her made her stop. She made a slow turn and gazed up at Antelope Skin as he came and bent low, close to her, beside the other man.

"Rustling Leaves, your brother needs you back home," Antelope Skin said. "Princess Pretty Hawk, your grandmother, is ill. Silver Arrow was too concerned to leave your grandmother's bedside. He sent me to get you."

"Grandmother is ill?" Rustling Leaves said, tears filling her eyes. "She is old. Will she die?"

"Perhaps," Antelope Skin said, his eyes squinting into hers. "Come now. I will take you home."

Rustling Leaves looked over at River Rat, then back up at Antelope Skin. "This man offered me pretty beads and shells," she murmured. "Antelope Skin, is he your friend?"

"Yes, he is my friend, and those beads and shells are yours," Antelope Skin said, nodding. "I asked him to offer them to you. I thought it might be an easier, less traumatic way to get you from the schoolyard, instead of suddenly blurting out to you about your grandmother. I know how much you love her."

"Yes, I love her so much," Rustling Leaves said, squeezing her corn husk Susan doll to her tiny bosom. She gazed at the beads and shells again. "I want them, but I do not have a way to carry them. There are no pockets in my dress."

"I will carry them for you, then give them to you once we get to your village," River Rat said, sliding the beautiful tokens back inside his pocket.

"Where are your horses?" Rustling Leaves asked as she peered past the men.

"They are drinking from the river," Antelope Skin said, placing a hand behind Rustling Leaves' head, guiding her deeper into the forest. "We will go to them. Then we will go the rest of the way on horseback to our village, Rustling Leaves."

"My brother is wrong about you," Rustling Leaves said, looking trustingly up at Antelope Skin.

"Wrong?" Antelope Skin asked, arching an eyebrow. "What do you mean?"

"He calls you many names that are not pleasant," Rustling Leaves said. "He will not call you those things again, not when he sees that you have brought me home to be with Grandmother."

River Rat chuckled beneath his breath as Antelope Skin glanced over at him.

Antelope Skin then led the way, his head thrust forward.

Rustling Leaves stepped lightly upon the fallen leaves of late autumn, her heart aching for her ailing grandmother. She heard a soft whinnying sound and knew she had only a short way to go to get to the horses. Soon she would be with her brother and grandmother.

She glanced from Antelope Skin to the other man when they reached the horses, suddenly feeling apprehensive about them, especially Antelope Skin who took a jug of whisky from the parfleche bag at the side of his horse and drank it in fast, deep gulps. Her brother had always spoken harshly against firewater. It was bad! That meant that Antelope Skin was bad!

She started to run away, but gasped with alarm when River Rat grabbed her and yanked her up in his arms.

"Let me go!" Rustling Leaves screamed, kicking and flailing her arms.

Antelope Skin and River Rat exchanged glances, then laughed boisterously.

Antelope Skin's laughter faded as he glared into Rustling Leaves' fearful eyes. "Scream and fuss all you want, but no one will hear," he hissed out. "You are now far from the schoolyard, and even farther from our village."

Rustling Leaves went limp in River Rat's arms. "Where . . . are . . . you taking me?" Rustling Leaves sobbed, tears pooling in her eyes.

"Never you mind about that," Antelope Skin said, chuckling. "You'd just better hope that your brother cares enough to cooperate."

"What does the word cooperate mean?" Rustling Leaves stammered out.

No one responded to her question.

She hung her head and cried.

Chapter Twenty-one

The butterflies had been too elusive for Stanley. Winded, he had stopped giving chase.

Panic had grabbed the pit of his stomach when he turned to go back to Rustling Leaves and had caught sight of her just as she stepped into the forest with a white man. There had also been an Indian, surely Ottawa.

Stanley at first had thought that something must have happened at her village, that her brother had sent for her. But now, after he had more time to think about it, something didn't seem right. The Indian he had seen walk away with Rustling Leaves did not seem the sort of warrior that Silver Arrow would send for his sister. He was shifty-eyed. He had stumbled somewhat as he had walked, as though he had been drinking whisky.

And who was this white man with the Indian? He had looked familiar, but Stanley could not remember where he had seen him, or when. But even *he* did not look like a trustworthy type, one with whom Silver Arrow would place his trust, especially when it concerned his beloved sister.

His heart thumping wildly in his chest, Stanley ran into the schoolroom. His teacher's back was to him as she wrote tall letters of the alphabet on the blackboard with a piece of chalk.

"Ma'am?" Stanley said, shuffling his feet on the wood-plank flooring. He clasped his hands behind him when Alice ignored him.

"Ma'am, I need to tell you something," Stanley persisted, fear entering his heart over having to disturb the schoolmarm. She was a stiff-lipped, square-jawed, large woman who was strict with her rules. Stanley was breaking one of them now by entering the schoolroom when he was supposed to be outside for recess.

"Ma'am, *please*, I *must* tell you something," Stanley said, his voice breaking with fear when Alice turned and glared down at him.

She placed her hands on her hips, making her muscled shoulders look even more threatening. Her hair was in a tight bun atop her head. Her plain, dark, floor-length dress had a high, white collar that fit snugly around her long, thick neck. Her eyes and nose flared angrily as she pursed her lips before speaking.

Then she took a hard stomp toward Stanley,

stopping to tower over him as she glared at him. "You are supposed to be outside with the others," she said firmly. "But of course you think you can bend the rules since your father is in charge of the school. But, young man, let me tell you, that makes no difference to me. He hired me to set the rules and carry them out."

Alice pointed toward the door. "Out with you now, Stanley, scat, or be punished severely for disobeying," she said in a loud threatening boom.

"But, ma'am, please *listen*," Stanley begged, wringing his tiny hands before him. "Rustling Leaves! She was taken away from the schoolyard! I'm afraid she's been abducted."

"Harumph, and so let her be gone," Alice said, her eyes narrowing. "One less Indian brat in this classroom would suit me just fine."

Stanley's eyes widened. He took an unsteady step away from her. "You don't care what happens to Rustling Leaves?" he gasped, paling.

"Who did you see take her?" Alice said, sighing heavily.

"An Indian warrior," Stanley stammered.

"You are wrong to suspect foul play," Alice said, smiling slowly. "If she is being escorted by an Indian, surely Silver Arrow is aware of it. Now, Stanley, get on outside with the others or I will have to carry out the punishment I warned you about."

"But, ma'am, there was a white man with the Indian," Stanley said in a rush. "Both men looked evil. Please do something about it. Please?"

"I have warned you for the last time," Alice said,

grabbing him by his suspenders, dragging him closer to her. "Leave now and stop bothering me or I will stand you in the corner for everyone to see. You will be an example for the others who wish to go against my rules."

"No!" Stanley cried. He wriggled away from her and ran from the room, panting.

"Come back here!" Alice screamed. She rushed to the door and looked out just as Stanley disappeared inside the church next door.

Stanley wiped tears from his eyes as he ran through the chapel, back to the study where his father prepared his sermons.

When he opened the door and found the room empty, his heart sank.

His only hope now was his sister Yvonne. *She* would care about what happened to Rustling Leaves!

Stanley ran outside and stared at the long road that lay ahead of him.

Six miles.

Six long miles, he thought with despair. Could he run that far without collapsing?

His jaw tight, his fear for Rustling Leaves' safety urging him on, he broke into a hard run down the dirt road. He watched over his shoulder for approaching horsemen or buggies, hoping he might find a ride to his cabin.

But today the road was empty. All that he heard around him were the forest noises. He jumped with alarm when a chipmunk scampered across the road in front of him.

A rustling in the thicket at his right side drew

his quick attention. His eyes locked with the round, dark eyes of a deer as it paused in its wandering through the woods.

Stanley ran onward, flinching with alarm again when a bluejay let out its startled cry in a tree overhead.

He wiped perspiration from his brow, but continued to run onward. He groaned with pain. His side ached. The muscles in his legs hurt. His throat was dry.

Seeing the shine of the river through a break in the trees, he was tempted to stop and get a drink.

But the memory of Rustling Leaves as she had trustingly walked with the two men into the forest caused him to run steadily onward. The thought of Rustling Leaves at the mercy of the two men sent a sick feeling through him.

Still he ran onward, so tired now he stumbled more than he ran. He left the road and took a short cut through the forest. Panting, his heart pounding, tears of relief flooded his eyes when he finally saw his cabin a short distance away.

"Please, legs, carry me just a little farther," Stanley cried, so bone-tired he feared he might collapse before he made it to the cabin.

Then his heart leapt with gladness when he spied Yvonne outside, hanging clothes on the line.

"Yvonne!" he cried, his throat so dry he feared his words would not carry far enough for her to hear. "Sister, please! Help! Rustling Leaves! She's in trouble!"

Yvonne turned with a start when she heard her

brother shouting at her. Fear gripped her when she saw him stumbling toward her, his hands reaching out for her, his face beet red and sweaty, his eyes frantic.

"Lord," she whispered, dropping the blouse she held back down in the basket.

She lifted the hem of her skirt and ran hard to meet Stanley. When she reached him, she knelt before him and took his hands.

"Stanley, why are you not in school?" Yvonne asked. "What's happened? Tell me."

Stanley finally got his breath. "Rustling Leaves," he said, swallowing hard. "I'm sure she was abducted."

He told her quickly what he had observed, and also how the teacher had ignored him when he had gone to her with his story.

"I can't believe Alice would ignore you like that," Yvonne said.

"Let's tell Father about Rustling Leaves," Stanley said, looking past Yvonne at the cabin. "We must all go and look for her. We must save her!"

"Father is at the trading post," Yvonne said, rushing to her feet. She held Stanley's hand as they walked hurriedly toward the cabin. "It's up to me, Stanley, to go and tell Silver Arrow what's happened."

"I want to go with you," Stanley said, his voice breaking.

"It is best that I go alone," Yvonne said as they entered the cabin. "You stay behind, and when Father returns home, tell him where I am, and what has happened."

She grabbed a rifle and turned to Stanley. "You say it was a white man and an Indian that took her away?" she asked.

"Yes," Stanley said, nodding.

"You don't know them?" Yvonne asked.

"The white man looked familiar, but, no, I don't know either one of them," Stanley said.

Yvonne bent to a knee and hugged him. "I'll be back as soon as I can," she said. "And I'm sure Rustling Leaves is going to be all right. Perhaps this was all done in innocence. Perhaps she is even now safely at her village."

"I hope so," Stanley sobbed, clinging to her around the neck. "She's my best friend, Yvonne."

Yvonne gave him one last hug, then turned and left the cabin. After saddling her horse and placing the rifle in the gunboot, she swung herself in the saddle.

Her skirt blew up past her knees when she rode off in a hard gallop. Her hair blowing in the hot breeze, Yvonne headed her steed in the direction of Silver Arrow's village. She had anticipated her next meeting with him with a racing heart, but never had she expected their next encounter to be filled with fear and anger!

She lifted her eyes heavenward. "Please let nothing happen to Rustling Leaves," she prayed. "Please keep her safe."

Chapter Twenty-two

When Yvonne entered the Ottawa village she slowed her horse to a trot as the Ottawa people scurried out of her way, staring at her.

Yvonne kept her eyes straight ahead, not offering a smile, her gaze locked on Silver Arrow's longhouse.

Oh, if only she could see Rustling Leaves there, playing outside the longhouse.

Finally at Silver Arrow's longhouse, Yvonne slid from the saddle and secured her horse's reins on the ring of a hitching pole.

Swallowing hard, she hurried to the door. She stopped with a start when Silver Arrow swung it open and stood there eyeing her questioningly.

"Is your sister here?" she blurted out. "Did you

send for her? Did you have her taken from the school today?"

When she saw apprehension enter his eyes, he did not have to speak the answer aloud. She covered her mouth, hiding a gasp, for it was certain that he had not sent for his sister.

Clearly Rustling Leaves was not safely in the longhouse. She had been abducted. Oh, Lord, Yvonne despaired, most certainly the child was in mortal danger!

"*Kau*, no, my sister is not here," Silver Arrow said, his voice cold. "Why would you even ask if not because you suspect she . . . is . . . elsewhere?"

Yvonne breathed out a heavy sigh of regret and slowly shook her head back and forth. "How can I tell you?" she said, her voice breaking.

He gripped her shoulders with his fingers. "Tell me what?" he demanded, his teeth clenched. "Is my sister not safely at the school?"

"No, she's not," Yvonne said, flinching at the mixture of fear and anger in his eyes.

Silver Arrow's heart was thudding hard at the thought of what Yvonne had not yet said. His insides were cold, for he could see fear and despair in her eyes. He had heard it in her voice.

He tried to collect himself. He sucked in a wild breath of air, then let it roll out slowly from inside him. He dropped his hands to his sides, yet could not help but circle his fingers into two tight fists.

"Where is my sister?" he asked, his voice drawn.

"I don't know," Yvonne said, her voice again breaking. "My brother Stanley saw her taken from the schoolyard by an Indian and a white man. He said she seemed to have gone willingly. She had to have known the men, or at least the Indian."

A sick feeling swept through Silver Arrow. He closed his eyes to keep his composure, while inside him rage was building to an inferno.

He gazed at Yvonne. "Who besides your brother saw this happen?" he asked.

"No one that I know of," Yvonne said.

"Where was the schoolmarm?" he growled out. "Is she not supposed to be the children's guardian while they are away from those who usually protect them?"

"She was inside the school building," Yvonne said. She gulped hard. She hated to tell Silver Arrow how negligent the teacher had been.

"Did your brother go and tell the schoolmarm what he had witnessed?" Silver Arrow asked, his voice tight, the anger building.

Again Yvonne swallowed hard. Her eyes lowered, but she lifted them again when Silver Arrow placed a finger beneath her chin and brought her eyes to his.

"She seemed not to care," Yvonne said, flinching when Silver Arrow jerked his hand away and emitted a low growl of rage.

Suddenly Silver Arrow grabbed her by the shoulders. "Your brother Stanley has been at the trading post with your father, and he has been at my village," he said, his voice low, even, and threatening. "Did he recognize the red man who took my sister away? Did he recognize the white man?"

"He did not get a good look at the white man because he stayed hidden in the shadows," Yvonne said. She winced when his fingers dug into her shoulder. "And the red man? No, he said he did not know him."

Silver Arrow stepped quickly away from her. He hung his head in his hands and groaned.

Then he raised his head and reached his hands heavenward and let out a heart-wrenching, shrill wail which made Yvonne pale and take several steps away from him.

She looked nervously around her when the Ottawa people came in a panic and made a wide circle around her and Silver Arrow. Yvonne backed away from them, stopping with a start when she bumped against Silver Arrow.

Her pulse racing, she turned on a heel and gazed up at him. Her heart went out to him when she saw the tears in the eyes of this powerful leader. Tears filled her own.

"I'm so sorry," she said, stifling a sob behind a hand.

He reached a gentle hand to her cheek and smoothed the tears away with his palm. "None of this is your fault," he said huskily. "And thank you for coming to tell me what has happened. You should not have come alone, though. Did you not know the danger you were placing yourself in? Apparently there are maniacs loose in our forest today. They could have taken you, as well as my beloved sister."

He drew her into his arms. She could feel the desperation in the way he held her.

"Should anything happen to you, I would die a million deaths before I truly took my last breaths on this earth," he whispered into her ear.

He held her for a moment longer, then eased her to his side. She stood beside him and listened to him relate to his people what had transpired today.

Then he turned and gazed with somber eyes at his grandmother as she came outside and looked up at him with tear-filled eyes.

"Grandmother, I will find her," he said, then pulled Princess Pretty Hawk into his arms and hugged her reassuringly. "I . . . will . . . find our little Rustling Leaves."

Four Horns came leading Silver Arrow's horse, his own trailing behind.

Silver Arrow took the reins and shouted orders to his warriors about the search that lay before them, the women quietly watching.

Four Horns slipped inside Silver Arrow's lodge and got his rifle for him, then returned and gave it to him.

"We will go first to the Iroquois village to look for my sister!" Silver Arrow shouted, raising the rifle high over his head. "Chief Old Elk came with his daughter's bride price! I refused it *and* his daughter! It is perhaps he who has my sister, as a way to make me pay for the humiliation I inflicted on both Old Elk and Searching Heart! We will go there first on our search! If my sister is there, tonight we smear war paint on our bodies and return to the Iroquois camp and leave a slaughter behind!"

Yvonne paled at the thought of a war breaking out between two tribes, for once such warring began, it would not be easily stopped. She could even now envision her own family's cabin going up in smoke, as well as her father's church and schoolhouse.

So many lives would be taken!

But she cast such worries aside, for there was only one person she should be concerned with now—sweet Rustling Leaves.

"I want to go with you," Yvonne blurted out after Silver Arrow's speech was over.

He turned heavy-lidded eyes down to her. "It is not a normal thing for women to travel with Ottawa warriors," he said dryly. But knowing that she was well skilled with a horse, and knowing that her presence would comfort him while he searched for his sister, Silver Arrow changed his mind.

"You can come," he said, nodding. He sighed heavily. "But should we become involved in fighting, you must promise that you will ride away from the danger and return to your cabin."

"I promise," Yvonne murmured, praying to herself that his sister would be found without lives being lost in the process—especially Silver Arrow's and Rustling Leaves'!

Silver Arrow's eyes locked with Yvonne's for a moment, then he again thrust his rifle in the air. "Let us go now!" he shouted. "And pity those who have taken my sister! Death will not come quickly to them!"

A shudder of dread swept through Yvonne. She did fear the next hours, for what if Rustling Leaves were never found?

What if they found her, and she was dead?

Or possibly raped?

Tears filled her eyes again at the thought of all the possibilities.

She quickly mounted her gentle mare, cursing herself for not having taken the time to dress more properly for riding horseback.

Yvonne rode straight-backed beside Silver Arrow across great sweeps of meadow, and then through thick stretches of forest. She ducked and leaned sideways as low tree branches threatened to knock her from the horse as they rode in the cool shade of monstrous elm trees, and then low, squatty maples.

She eyed the river thirstily as they rode beside it, realizing only after seeing its pristine shine just how thirsty she was, but quenching her thirst would come later.

They rode out in the beating heat of the sun again for several miles. Her thirst deepened.

Then the circle of tepees of the Iroquois village a short distance away came into view.

Yvonne's thirst came second then to a gripping fear.

She sent Silver Arrow a questioning look, wondering how he was going to approach the village. Quietly? Slowly? Or without hesitation?

She gulped hard when she discovered it was the latter.

She clung to her horse's reins more tightly as the Ottawa warriors rode in a hard gallop toward the Iroquois village.

She paled when she saw several Iroquois warriors leaving the village, riding hard in the direction of the Ottawa, their rifles drawn threateningly.

Then the Ottawa and Iroquois warriors came to a quick halt as they quietly faced one another.

"You are approaching our village like those who might come for warring," one of the Iroquois warriors said in a language that was plain enough for Yvonne to understand.

"Do you see our weapons drawn?" Silver Arrow asked tightly, smoothing a hand along his horse's neck to calm it.

"Your weapons are not drawn, but your expressions are fierce!" the Iroquois said, his eyes narrowing into Silver Arrow's. "Tell me. What brings you here today?" His eyes slid over to Yvonne. "And with a white woman? Why does she ride with you?"

"Do not concern yourself with White Swan," Silver Arrow said. "It is my sister that I wish to talk about. Is she with your people? Did your chief order her abduction?"

Yvonne could tell by the surprise that leapt into the eyes of the Iroquois warriors that the child was not there.

"Your sister? Rustling Leaves?" one of the Iroquois warriors gasped out. "She is gone?"

"Taken from the white man's school grounds," Silver Arrow said, his voice drawn.

Silver Arrow could tell by the reaction of the Iroquois warriors that they were not pretending alarm. It was there in their eyes, and in the tone of their voices, that they knew nothing of his sister's whereabouts.

The Iroquois warrior who had been the spokesperson frowned at Silver Arrow. "If your sister was not safe at the white man's school, nor would our children have been," he said tersely. "It is good that our chief forbade our children to mix with the whites at the school!"

Having heard all that he had come to hear, and not wanting to be chided by the Iroquois, Silver Arrow wheeled his horse around and rode off.

Stunned by Silver Arrow's quick decision to leave, Yvonne sat for a moment watching him and his warriors ride away. Then she glanced over at the Iroquois warriors, gave them a nervous, clumsy smile, and sank her heels into the flanks of her steed and rode quickly away.

She was relieved when she gained ground and was riding beside Silver Arrow once again. They rode for many miles, then he raised a fist in the air, a message to his men to stop.

Yvonne drew a tight rein beside Silver Arrow. She edged her horse closer to his as he instructed his warriors. They would go in small groups of four, so that much land could be scoured quickly.

"Look for my sister until the sun leaves the sky, then meet me back at our village!" Silver Arrow shouted. "Search every inch of the land in all directions, my warriors. We will leave no stone un-turned until we find my sister!"

Yvonne went with Silver Arrow on the contin-ued search. She became sorely tired, but did not complain, for she knew the importance of not giv-ing up the search before the sun crept behind the horizon. If Rustling Leaves was not found before it became dark, the chances were that she would never be found.

Yvonne's fingers felt frozen to the reins from having clasped them so hard the long day. Her bottom seemed glued to the saddle. She was so stiff she was not sure if she could even dismount once the search came to a halt. Never in her life had she ached so much as now.

And she knew that she must be a sight! The sun had been unmerciful as it had beaten down upon her. She could smell her own sweat and felt ashamed that, under these circumstances, she could smell almost as bad as a man.

And her hair! Oh, Lord, she despaired. It was filled with dust. It was tangled and knotted from the hot winds.

She reached a trembling hand to her cheeks, flinching when she felt the heat, realizing that she was sunburned.

Never was she so glad to see anything as to see Silver Arrow's village as they rode toward it in the deepening shadows of the quickly approaching night.

But Yvonne felt Silver Arrow's disappointment and hopelessness. She glanced over at him, and gulped back the urge to cry when she saw the

235

bend of his shoulders and the defeat in his eyes.

She turned quickly away from him when she saw someone familiar standing at the edge of the village, waiting. It was her father. Stanley was beside him, clutching his hand.

Yvonne rode up to her father and Stanley. Her gaze locked with Stanley's as she slid achingly from the saddle.

She knew that Stanley could tell by everyone's drawn expression that his best friend in the world had not been found.

Stanley flung himself into Yvonne's arms as she bent down to receive him. "Now, now," she murmured, stroking his back as he clutched her hard and cried. "There are others still looking for her. Perhaps they will find her."

"It's my fault," Stanley cried. "I shouldn't have gone to chase the butterflies."

Silver Arrow rode on past them.

Yvonne watched him, then turned to her father. "I'll be a minute longer. I must say good-bye to Silver Arrow," she murmured. She gently shoved Stanley over to her father.

Anthony swept his son into his arms and held him close.

Silver Arrow dismounted in front of his longhouse. He gave the reins of his pinto stallion to a small brave, then with his head hung, went on inside his lodge.

"She is gone from us forever, is she not?" Princess Pretty Hawk asked, stifling a sob behind a hand when she saw the defeat in her grandson's eyes.

"I will go out again tomorrow to search for her," Silver Arrow said. "She will be all right."

He stiffened when Princess Pretty Hawk handed him a small piece of paper. "What is this?" he asked, forking an eyebrow as he took it.

"It was found nailed to a tree in the corral," Princess Pretty Hawk said somberly. "Read it, grandson. *Then* tell me Rustling Leaves will be all right."

She turned and walked to her rocking chair. Her eyes vacant, she sat down and began to rock slowly back and forth.

Yvonne stepped into Silver Arrow's longhouse as he leaned down low over a flickering candle to read. She flinched when he threw the note to the floor and stamped on it, his eyes filled with fire.

"What was that?" Yvonne asked softly. "Darling, what did it say?"

"A ransom note," Silver Arrow said, his voice drawn. "It says that in order to have my sister returned to me, I must give the abductor gold. Further instructions will follow."

"Lord, no," Yvonne gasped. "Someone is blackmailing you . . . for your grandfather's gold."

Silver Arrow turned on a quick heel to face her. "Someone goes this far to get at my grandfather's hidden gold?" he said, his voice breaking. "Who could be so greedy? So heartless? Who?"

Something grabbed at Yvonne's heart as she immediately thought of Jake's interest in the gold. But the white man responsible for taking Rustling Leaves couldn't be Jake. Stanley had seen the man. He would have known his own half brother, even if he had not gotten a good look at him.

"I must go and pray," Silver Arrow said, walking briskly toward the door. He stopped and turned to Yvonne. "White Swan, go home. Leave the sorrow behind you. It is my sorrow, and my people's."

"Darling, it is also *mine*," Yvonne gulped out, then turned cold inside when he went on outside without her.

She turned and stared at Princess Pretty Hawk. The old woman's eyes were downcast. She seemed lost in another world; in another time.

Sobbing, Yvonne fled from the longhouse and went back to her brother and father. "Let's go home," she said solemnly.

Yvonne followed Anthony and Stanley on her horse as they rode in a buggy ahead of her. She was glad when they finally reached their cabin and each had bathed and prepared for bed.

Yvonne went to Stanley, to say his nightly prayer with him. She knelt on the floor beside him, their hands folded before them. "Now I lay me down to sleep," she whispered with Stanley, yet her heart was not on this childlike prayer. Deep in her heart she was praying more intensely, a more adult prayer, that Rustling Leaves was out there somewhere, unharmed, and cuddled in a warm bed with her cornhusk Susan doll.

Suddenly Stanley stopped in the middle of the prayer. He turned to Yvonne. "Why did no one ask me to point the Indian out?" he blurted out, his eyes wide. "Yvonne, I *could*. I *saw* him. I could point him out if I saw him again!"

A faint ray of hope entered Yvonne's heart. Through all of the confusion and fear, no one had thought to ask Stanley to describe the Indian.

Nor had they thought to ask him to search through those at the Ottawa village, to see if any of them were familiar to him.

And surely it could be an Ottawa warrior who did the abducting. Rustling Leaves had gone too willingly, too trustingly, with him for him to have been a total stranger.

"I will never forget the abductor's face!" Stanley cried out. "Nor his shifty eyes! They weren't friendly and gentle eyes like Silver Arrow's!"

Yvonne drew him into her arms and fiercely hugged him.

Chapter Twenty-three

The sun was hidden behind clouds. The air was cool and refreshing. A shawl draped around her shoulders, Yvonne sat stiffly in the buggy. Her fingers tightly clutched the reins as she rode toward Silver Arrow's village.

She glanced over at Stanley who sat stiffly, his tiny hands folded on his lap as he looked straight ahead, his concern over Rustling Leaves making him unusually quiet.

Yvonne looked away from him and watched the road. Her father had allowed Stanley to skip school this morning to go to Silver Arrow's village, hoping that he might be able to point out the warrior who had been involved in Rustling Leaves' abduction.

Yvonne's only hope was that it *was* one of Silver

Arrow's warriors who was guilty of the crime, so that he could be pointed out. Otherwise, they might never find Rustling Leaves.

A smile lifted Yvonne's lips as she thought of one thing to be glad about today. Anthony had not accompanied her and Stanley to the Ottawa village because he had a duty to perform. He was going to give Alice her "walking papers"!

He already had found someone to take Alice's place—a recent widow who had been a teacher in Boston before she had come to Wisconsin to live with her husband.

Anthony had gone to see Delores Edwards after hearing about Alice's disgraceful behavior at the school. Delores had said she could begin her teaching duties immediately.

Yvonne knew Delores well. She was a member of her father's congregation. She was a lovely lady with a soft voice who taught Sunday school at the church on Sunday mornings. She was sweet and gentle with the children.

Delores had been Anthony's first choice to be the teacher at his school, but she had not felt ready to take on such duties at that time, so soon after the death of her husband. Now she seemed eager to get on with her life.

Yvonne's heart beat anxiously as she rode into the edge of the Ottawa village. She closed her eyes and said a silent prayer that Rustling Leaves might have been found.

The prayer said, she opened her eyes, certain that Rustling Leaves was still missing, or surely Silver Arrow would have brought this grand news to her and her family, knowing how distraught they were over his sister.

As she and Stanley rode through the village, it took only one look to see that nothing good was happening there today. Everyone was moving around halfheartedly doing their chores, their expressions solemn. Except for a steady beating of a drum somewhere in the distance, everything seemed strangely quiet.

Yvonne nodded an occasional hello to those who gazed up at her. She was glad when she finally reached Silver Arrow's lodge.

Stanley leapt from the buggy and ran to Silver Arrow's door and knocked even before Yvonne had stepped down from the buggy. As she eased to the ground and tied the reins on the ring of the hitching post, she watched Stanley nervously shuffling his feet as he waited for someone to come to the door. The longer the wait, the more apprehensive Yvonne became. Surely Silver Arrow was gone, or he would have opened the door by now.

That had to mean that only his grandmother was in the cabin. Princess Pretty Hawk's movements were always slow. It would take her a while to get to the door.

Finally the door slowly opened. Yvonne went and stood beside Stanley as Princess Pretty Hawk gazed at them through squinting eyes.

"Have you any news yet of Rustling Leaves?" Yvonne asked, slipping her arm around Stanley's frail shoulders to comfort him as he stood stiffly staring up at Princess Pretty Hawk, tears near.

"*Kau*, no word," Princess Pretty Hawk murmured. "Silver Arrow is gone again with many warriors to search for her."

"Pretty Hawk, do you remember my brother saying that one of Rustling Leaves' abductors was an Indian?" Yvonne asked guardedly.

"*Ae*, I remember, and that saddens me so," Princess Pretty Hawk said, lowering her eyes.

"Stanley remembers what he looked like," Yvonne said softly. "He says that if he is here, he can point him out."

Princess Pretty Hawk looked quickly down at Stanley. "Young man, you remember the face?" she asked.

"Yes, ma'am, I do believe that if I saw him I could point him out," Stanley said, nervously shoving his eyeglasses farther back on his nose.

Princess Pretty Hawk suddenly left them standing there as she went back inside the cabin.

That puzzled Yvonne. For a moment, Princess Pretty Hawk had seemed excited about the possibility that Stanley could point out the abductor.

Yvonne sighed with relief when Princess Pretty Hawk came back to the door. She had three blankets draped over her arms. Keeping one for herself, she handed one to Yvonne and one to Stanley.

"We will sit outside my lodge and watch everyone of my village as they go about their chores," Princess Pretty Hawk said. "If you see the man who you recognize as one of Rustling Leaves' abductors, speak up quickly, young man. We will stop him. But I want to believe that none of my own people could be responsible."

"Do you think you could have all of the men in the village come and stand before us so that Stanley could see them all at once?" Yvonne asked.

"That will arouse suspicions," Princess Pretty Hawk said. "If we just sit outside my lodge, as though we are enjoying the soft breeze, no one will be the wiser."

Yvonne saw the logic in that. She nodded.

They each spread their blankets and sat down on them. As the morning progressed and there was more activity in the village, Stanley's eyes moved quickly from man to man.

But when the sun came from behind the clouds and reached the center point in the sky, the coolness of the day changed to something oppressive and unbearable.

Yvonne looked over at Princess Pretty Hawk. Her cheeks were flushed from the heat. Sweat trickled from her brow.

"Princess Pretty Hawk, I think you should go inside out of the heat," Yvonne murmured. She glanced at Stanley, whose own cheeks were extremely red. She felt the heat on her face, the sunburn she had received yesterday now worsening.

"Yes, we will all go inside and eat and drink," Princess Pretty Hawk said, moaning as she tried to push herself up from the ground.

When a man came to assist her, Stanley gasped and jumped to his feet. "It's him!" he cried. "That's the Indian. I saw him take Rustling Leaves away from the school ground!"

Antelope Skin's movements froze. He paled and

stared dumbfoundedly down at Stanley, then looked quickly at Princess Pretty Hawk, whose fingers were locked around one of his arms.

"You did this evil thing to my beloved granddaughter? You, a blood kin, a cousin?" she cried, her fingernails digging into the flesh of Antelope Skin's arm.

Antelope Skin gulped hard. He was trapped. Now everyone would know that he was guilty of a crime no Ottawa should have ever committed!

"Let me go!" he cried, wrenching his arm free of Princess Pretty Hawk's grip.

Yvonne was so stunned by the suddenness of what was happening, her insides felt frozen. Her knees felt rubbery as she tried to rise from the ground.

Horrified, she watched Antelope Skin run away.

Finally steady on her feet, Yvonne broke into a run after him. Just as she reached him, he turned around and shoved her to the ground.

"No!" she screamed. She looked frantically around her. "Someone! Anyone! Help me! Grab that man!"

But it was all happening too quickly. Everyone was watching, their eyes wide as Yvonne again dashed after one of their own kind.

When Antelope Skin finally reached his tethered horse, he grabbed the reins and started to swing himself into the saddle.

But Yvonne was there again, grabbing him by an arm.

"Get out of my way, you white witch!" Antelope

Skin shouted, giving Yvonne a kick in her abdomen.

Her breath knocked from her, the pain intense, Yvonne stumbled to the ground, doubled up, groaning.

Antelope Skin rode away in a hard gallop, the Ottawa people scrambling out of his way.

"Please stop him!" Yvonne cried, her voice scarcely a whisper since her breath had not yet fully returned. She looked pleadingly around her. "He abducted Rustling Leaves. Please stop him!"

Her voice was still not strong enough to carry.

Pretty Hawk stood as though in a state of shock as she watched Antelope Skin ride from view. She shifted her gaze down at Yvonne, then turned and ambled lifelessly back inside her lodge and shut her door.

Finally Yvonne was able to get to her feet. She looked frantically around her. No one had understood what was happening, that Antelope Skin was responsible for a terrible crime against his own people.

She gasped when she saw Stanley standing outside Silver Arrow's lodge, alone. Then her gaze went to the closed door. Princess Pretty Hawk had gone back inside the longhouse.

But why? Yvonne wondered. Was it because she could no longer stand the despair?

But that should not be Yvonne's main concern. Catching up with Antelope Skin was! And she didn't have time to gather the warriors around to explain what he had done. Antelope Skin already had a head start on her.

She grabbed the reins of the horse closest to her. She swung herself into the saddle and rode away, ignoring Stanley's shouts begging her not to go, that he feared for her life.

Yvonne closed her heart and mind to her brother's pleas. She saw that she had no other choice but to go after this man. She could not help but think that now, since he knew that he had been pointed out as one of the abductors, he might go into hiding. Then no one could ever discover where Rustling Leaves had been taken.

Another thought came to Yvonne that made her smile. Maybe Antelope Skin would lead her to the hiding place where Rustling Leaves was being held hostage.

She reached down and felt the outline of the small derringer that she had slipped into the pocket of her riding skirt before leaving for the Ottawa village. If she had to, she would use it!

Chapter Twenty-four

The sun was high and hot overhead as Silver Arrow rode up to the outer fringe of a cedar swamp, where wild rice plants grew tall and thick, promising a great harvest in the fall.

His eyes narrowing, Silver Arrow slid from his saddle, holding his horse's reins. While his warriors followed close behind him on their steeds, he walked slowly beside the swamp. They had scoured the land, up one side and down the other, over and over again, and still Rustling Leaves had not been found.

Now walking in the shade of overhanging branches, Silver Arrow kept a slow pace beside the swamp. The cedar trees grew so thick in this area of the swamp, it was impenetrable. The stench of rotted timber was almost overpowering.

Something drew Silver Arrow's quick attention. A sick feeling overtook him. He had to lean against his horse to steady himself, his grief was so intense when he saw his sister's cornhusk Susan doll lying on the ground, where the green slime of the swamp lapped in small waves along the embankment.

"No!" he cried, his eyes reaching up to the heavens. "Why? Why?"

Four Horns leapt from his saddle and ran up to Silver Arrow. He gasped when he, too, saw the doll.

He paled as he stared into the thick, spongy mass of the swamp, shuddered, then gazed over at Silver Arrow. "If she was brought here, it would surely only be for . . . one . . . reason," he said, his voice drawn.

"Yes, I fear now that the swamp is her grave," Silver Arrow said, an uncontrollable shudder racing through him.

His jaw tight, Silver Arrow plunged his moccasined feet into the stinking green mass. Slowly he explored with his feet, feeling around in the slimy water, his insides feeling dead as he searched for his sister.

His warriors dismounted and followed Silver Arrow and Four Horns into the green, murky mire. Soon they were all searching the bottom of the swamp, some with long poles, others with the butt ends of their rifles in the more shallow spots.

They searched wherever it was possible, then after a long hour had passed and no other signs of her were found, Silver Arrow moved slowly from the swamp and sat down on the embankment, his head in his hands.

"My friend, let us return home, where you can grieve in private," Four Horns said as he placed a gentle hand on Silver Arrow's shoulder.

"Who could be this coldhearted?" Silver Arrow said, his voice breaking as he stared into the swamp. "She was an innocent, sweet child."

"Perhaps she is not dead," Four Horns tried to reassure him. "Perhaps those who stole her were traveling by the swamp and she dropped her doll as they passed. Perhaps we were wrong to assume that because her Susan doll lay beside the swamp, that had to mean that she is in it."

Silver Arrow nodded as he rose shakily to his feet. The green slime from the swamp clung to his legs and hands as he walked somberly toward his horse. Slowly he eased into the saddle.

Four Horns brought the doll to Silver Arrow and held it out for him. Silver Arrow stared blankly at it, then took it and held it to his heart.

Blank-faced, feeling defeated, he rode off, scarcely aware of his warriors following behind him on their tired steeds.

Chapter Twenty-five

Yvonne continued chasing Antelope Skin until he entered the dark depths of the forest. Afraid to follow him where he could be lurking, waiting, ready to ambush her, Yvonne wheeled her horse to a quivering halt.

Breathing hard, downhearted over not being able to discover where Rustling Leaves was being held, she lowered her face in her hands.

The sound of horses approaching drew her eyes quickly up. She strained her neck to see who was coming, then stiffened and tightened her jaw when she recognized them both.

One was her stepbrother, Jake. The other was River Rat, a man she despised with all her heart.

She had known that Jake and River Rat drank together at the trading post, and that they occasionally went hunting together, so she was not all that surprised to find them together today.

Disliking both men, Yvonne sank her heels into her steed and rode in the opposite direction. But Jake and River Rat gained on her. Soon she was flanked by them, one on each side.

"What do you want?" she asked Jake, sighing heavily. "Please just go on and leave me be."

Jake grabbed Yvonne's reins from her. He tightened them, drawing her steed to a halt as he stopped his own horse beside hers. "What are you doing out here so far from home, alone?" he asked somberly. He gazed down at the horse, then looked at Yvonne again. "And whose horse is this?"

"Jake, it's none of your business what I do, when I do it, or how," Yvonne blurted out, her eyes flashing angrily into his. She yanked on the reins, but he would not give them up to her that easily. "Damn it, Jake, give me my reins. I have things to do."

"Yeah, that's what concerns me," Jake said, his eyes narrowing. He chuckled. "And whew! If only Father could hear the language you're using today. Why, I imagine he'd make you sit and read the scripture for days to make amends."

"Jake, I don't need a lecture from you," Yvonne said, her heart racing angrily. She again yanked on the reins. "Why are you doing this? Why do you even care? Let me be on my way!"

"Not until you tell me what you are doing out here all alone on someone else's horse," Jake said stubbornly.

Yvonne glared over at River Rat, who was sitting much too quietly, his gaze locked on her. She did not even want to guess what he might be thinking as his eyes roamed over her. She shivered uncontrollably as she stared back at the filthy, bearded man.

"Yvonne, tell me," Jake persisted, drawing her eyes back to him.

"If you must know, I was chasing one of the culprits who is responsible for Silver Arrow's sister's abduction," Yvonne blurted out. "I was chasing Antelope Skin. I'm sure you know him. I've seen him often at the trading post. I am sure you have seen him, yourself."

Yvonne noticed a quick change in expression on both men's faces, and how they looked somewhat guardedly at one another.

"Jake?" she murmured.

"I don't understand any of this," Jake said, interrupting her.

Yvonne spoke in a rush of words about her having been at the Ottawa village with Stanley, and why. "While at the Ottawa village, Stanley pointed Antelope Skin out to me and Silver Arrow's grandmother," she said. "He said that Antelope Skin was one of the two men who took Rustling Leaves from the schoolyard. Antelope Skin seemed to know right away what was happening. He fled on his horse. I was in pursuit of him. I only stopped because he went into the deeper, darker forest where I would endanger myself by following him."

Jake kneaded his brow after he thought

through what Yvonne had told him. "Then Stanley is still at the village?" Jake said, his voice drawn.

"Yes," Yvonne murmured. "I'm going now to get him."

"Yvonne, we have had many differences with each other in the past, but that doesn't mean I want you to die while doing some damn noble thing such as single-handedly trying to stop an abductor," Jake said, frowning at her. "I'll escort you back to the village, then see that you two get safely home."

River Rat edged his horse away from Jake's. "I'll see you later, Jake," he said, then wheeled his steed around and rode off at a brisk clip.

"No, thank you, Jake," Yvonne said, stubbornly lifting her chin. "I can look out for myself just fine. But you *can* go on home and tell Father that Stanley and I are all right, and that we will be home soon."

Jake gave her the reins, then edged his horse back from hers as she rode away.

Disappointed that she couldn't return to the Ottawa village with better news, hating that she had been too afraid to enter the forest to follow Antelope Skin, Yvonne rode sadly back toward the Ottawa village.

When she arrived, she met Silver Arrow at the edge of the village, his many warriors following close behind him.

She gasped when she saw the dried green slime on his clothes, feet, and legs, but his expression was what made her heart sink. She could feel his defeat as he gazed at her with wavering, dull eyes. She knew then that the news was not good about his sister, and that she still was out there somewhere, at the mercy of heartless enemies.

Yvonne almost dreaded telling Silver Arrow that Antelope Skin was involved with his precious sister's abduction.

Yvonne paled and gasped when she saw what Silver Arrow was holding. Rustling Leaves' corn-husk Susan doll!

"You did not find Rustling Leaves?" Yvonne asked, her voice breaking. "But . . . you . . . found her doll?"

"I fear the worst now for my sister," he said thickly as they rode onward, side by side.

"Where did you find the doll?" she asked.

"It lay beside the cedar swamp," Silver Arrow said, his voice filled with emotion.

He turned slow eyes to her. "You are on a horse marked with the brand of the Ottawa," he said. His gaze swept over her. "You look as though you have been on a chase. Why? Where?"

She explained the events of the day, then blurted out what she had discovered about Antelope Skin.

"He is, in part, responsible for your sister's abduction," Yvonne said. "I so wish I could have followed him farther. But . . . I . . . feared the forest. It would have been so easy for him to hide, then ambush me."

Silver Arrow drew a tight rein, drawing his pinto stallion to a halt. "Antelope Skin?" he said, anger leaping into his eyes. "My own *witaw-wis-e-maw*?"

"Yes, it seems so," Yvonne said, lowering her eyes.

Silver Arrow sat silently for a moment in an effort to compose himself, then wheeled his horse around and faced his warriors. He shouted to them what he had just found out. He told them where Yvonne had last seen Antelope Skin. He told them to search for him!

Yvonne watched the warriors ride away, then rode on into the village with Silver Arrow.

When she reached his longhouse, she slid from the saddle and bent to her knees, her arms outstretched for Stanley.

He flung himself into her arms, sobbing, knowing that Rustling Leaves had not been found without even having been told. Silver Arrow bent to a knee beside Stanley. He placed a hand on his shoulder, drawing Stanley's eyes around to him.

"Young brave, you are a hero for revealing one of the abductors of my sister to me, and for telling me about the abduction in the first place," he said. "Young brave, when all of this is behind us, and we have a semblance of peace in our lives once again, I will see to it that we have a celebration to honor your heroism."

Tears filled Yvonne's eyes. She flicked them away as Stanley started to hug Silver Arrow, but he stopped and paled when he saw the doll in Silver Arrow's hand.

He looked desperately up at Silver Arrow. "Is . . . Rustling Leaves . . . dead?" he gasped out, a sob lodging in his throat.

"We still do not know," Silver Arrow said, his voice breaking.

Almost meditatingly, he handed Stanley Rustling Leaves' doll. "Young brave, will you keep my sister's doll safe until we find her?" he asked.

Stanley nodded and took the doll, hugging it to him as though it were Rustling Leaves.

Silver Arrow nodded toward the door of his longhouse. "Let us go inside," he said. He looked over at Yvonne. "You must rest before you leave for your home."

Yvonne nodded, flicking more tears from her eyes when she heard the despair; the utter grief in her beloved's voice.

Chapter Twenty-six

As he stepped inside his longhouse, Silver Arrow looked slowly around him, searching for his grandmother. He dreaded giving her the news that Rustling Leaves had not been found.

And having to tell her that his sister's doll *had* been found made an ache circle his heart. Princess Pretty Hawk had been feeling poorly of late, both physically and mentally. He was not sure how much more pain she could bear.

"Grandmother?" Silver Arrow said. "It is I, Silver Arrow. I have returned home."

Expecting to find her in her bed, resting, Silver Arrow went to her bedroom. He gazed down at the bed. Her blankets lay neatly across it.

But she was not there.

Then his gaze shifted elsewhere. A cold panic

filled him when he discovered his grandmother's favorite personal belongings stacked neatly on a wicker trunk at the foot of her bed. He recognized these as things that she had often told him that she wished to be buried with, when her day came to join those who had passed on before.

Until today, he had only seen these special belongings of his grandmother one other time. That was when she had taken them from the trunk to show them to him. She had then placed them back in the trunk and had told him that they should only be removed one more time—on the day of her death. She wished to be buried with these things.

Silver Arrow stifled a sob behind a hand, knowing that when the elderly Ottawa decided that it was time to die, they placed their belongings together in such a way, then would wander off into the forest to die.

He recalled Princess Pretty Hawk recently saying that she was ready to join those who had already passed on to the other side. That should have given him a fair enough warning that she was soon to die!

Yvonne jumped when she heard Silver Arrow's loud wail of despair coming from Princess Pretty Hawk's room. Fearing the worst, that Princess Pretty Hawk was dead, Yvonne scurried into the room.

She stopped suddenly when she found Silver Arrow on his knees before a trunk, his face buried in a beautiful doeskin dress, whispering his grandmother's name over and over again.

Yvonne looked slowly around the room. She was puzzled when she realized that Princess Pretty Hawk was not there.

Forking an eyebrow, she looked at Silver Arrow again. He was still too distraught for her to disturb him, yet she had to wonder why he was behaving as though his grandmother had died when there were no signs of her anywhere.

Stanley came quietly into the room and stood beside Yvonne. She felt his presence and looked down at him. She could see the questioning in his eyes, for she could tell that he was as puzzled by Silver Arrow's behavior as she.

Gently, Silver Arrow laid his grandmother's dress among her other things and rose slowly to his feet. When he turned and found Yvonne and Stanley there, he swallowed hard.

"I don't understand," Yvonne murmured. "What has happened? You . . . act . . . as though your grandmother is dead."

"I fear that she is," Silver Arrow said, inhaling a deep, quavering breath. His gaze shifted to Stanley. "You were here. Did you see my grandmother leave?"

"Yes, while Yvonne was gone," Stanley stammered out. "Why, Silver Arrow? Why do you ask?"

"She is gone, her burial clothes are laid out for the ceremony, and only a short while ago she talked of how ready she was to join her ancestors in the sky," Silver Arrow murmured.

"Silver Arrow, while you were gone, searching for Rustling Leaves, and before I left to chase Antelope Skin on horseback, I noticed how withdrawn and distraught your grandmother was," Yvonne said. "Could her grief have been this deep? So deep that she might kill herself?"

"My grandmother would never kill herself," Silver Arrow said, his spine stiffening. "But her grieving may have hurried her death along. Her heart is old and weak. Her lungs are tired of breathing."

"I noticed how solemn she was at learning that Antelope Skin, one of your own kind, was involved in Rustling Leaves' disappearance," Stanley blurted out. "She looked so downhearted when she went inside your longhouse. It was soon after that she left and entered the forest behind your longhouse. I . . . thought . . . she had gone there to pray."

"I must find her," Silver Arrow said, brushing past Yvonne and Stanley. "Come, Stanley. Point me in the right direction. Come, White Swan, accompany me on the search."

Glad to be able to help, Stanley broke into a run ahead of Silver Arrow and Yvonne as they followed close behind him.

Yvonne wanted to say soft words of encouragement to her beloved, but knew that this was not the time to interfere in Silver Arrow's mounting grief. She knew how he had worshiped his grandmother. Besides his wicked cousin, Antelope Skin, and Rustling Leaves, Princess Pretty Hawk was Silver Arrow's only remaining living relative.

Wars, time, his Iroquois enemies, and most of all the white man, had not been fair to Silver Arrow's family. Only he would be left to carry on their traditions, for she knew that once he caught up with him, Antelope Skin was the same as dead.

And more than likely, Princess Pretty Hawk was dead.

They ran on through the forest. Yvonne was aware that the day was flying past, for the sun now lay halfway from the noon hour to evening. Her stomach growled, and she realized that she had only eaten breakfast today. And so had Stanley. Perhaps even Silver Arrow.

But this was not the time to think of hunger. A moment later they caught sight of Princess Pretty Hawk's lifeless body, slumped beneath a tree, her back resting against it, her head bowed.

Stanley's footsteps faltered as he stared down at Princess Pretty Hawk. Gulping hard, tears filling his eyes, he stopped and turned his eyes away. He hung his head as Silver Arrow ran on past him.

Yvonne stopped and bent down and drew Stanley gently into her arms, her eyes on the man she loved. She sobbed when she saw the depths of Silver Arrow's emotions as he knelt down before his grandmother on his haunches and gazed at her, then lowered his eyes and saw what she held in her hands.

Yvonne gazed at what Silver Arrow took from his grandmother's stiff fingers. When she recognized the tiny moccasin that belonged to Rustling Leaves, she placed a hand to her mouth and gasped. Surely Princess Pretty Hawk had found the moccasin!

Or perhaps she had taken it from Rustling

Leaves' belongings in the cabin to clutch to her breast as she died.

Silver Arrow's insides felt dead as he stared at the tiny moccasin, and then again looked at his precious grandmother. "Grandmother, oh, Grandmother, why must there be such sadness, such losses, in life?" he whispered.

He reached his free hand over to his grandmother's shoulder and gently clasped his fingers on it. "You lost your will to live," he said, almost choking on the words. "Was my love not enough to sustain you?"

He bowed his head and clutched the moccasin to his heart. He began a low chanting, each breath a painful one, in that never again would he feel his grandmother's embrace. Nor would he hear her voice of reassurance when he became despondent over his own secret woes, which she seemed to automatically know just by being near him.

He wiped tears from his eyes and smiled as he recalled how she had reacted that first time she had seen the crow, and then so quickly thereafter, *him*.

He would never forget how her eyes lit up to know that her husband's, Silver Arrow's grandfather's, mystical powers had been passed on to Silver Arrow!

"Now you carry my secret to the grave with you," Silver Arrow whispered. "But when your spirit rises from the grave and you join Grandfather's spirit in the hereafter, you can tell him that I protect my special powers with my life."

"Silver Arrow?" Yvonne said, breaking through his thoughts and sorrows. She went to kneel beside him. "Darling, I'm so sorry. What can I do to help lighten your burden? I know how much you loved your grandmother."

"Just be here for me," Silver Arrow said, turning his bloodshot eyes to her. "I need you, oh, how I need you."

He drew Yvonne into his arms. He hugged her with all his might. "Life is so sad, so wretched at times!" he cried. "But I find such peace and tranquillity in your arms. Thank you for being here for me. Thank you for caring so much."

"I shall always care," Yvonne said, gently stroking his back. "I shall always be here for you. I love you so."

They clung to one another for a moment longer, then Silver Arrow turned away and gently swept his grandmother up into his arms.

His shoulders squared, his jaw tightly set, his eyes straight ahead, he carried her through the forest and into the village. He said nothing to his people as they came in a rush toward him when they saw whom he carried.

Their wails began, long and sorrowful.

Yvonne opened the door of Silver Arrow's longhouse and stepped aside with Stanley as Silver Arrow carried his grandmother on inside.

Yvonne turned and gazed slowly around her at the throng of Ottawa people, whose eyes showed their sorrow, then stepped inside the longhouse with Stanley at her side.

She closed the door behind her and stood in the

shadows with Stanley as Silver Arrow carried his grandmother into her room.

Feeling out of place there, where there was such a show of union among his people, Yvonne took Stanley's hand. When Stanley gazed up at her, she gave him a smile of reassurance, then turned when she heard some commotion outside.

The wails had changed to excitement. Yvonne wondered what was the cause of the Ottawa people's change in attitude, for it seemed less than respectful to the lady who lay dead in the next room who was their chief's grandmother, and their beloved princess.

Hoping not to disturb Silver Arrow and his time alone with his dear departed grandmother, Yvonne slowly opened the door.

Stanley moved to her side, then let out a shout and ran past Yvonne toward the child who was stumbling through the village.

Yvonne's eyes widened with recognition. "Rustling Leaves?" she gasped. She looked more closely. "Lord, it *is* Rustling Leaves! She's alive!"

She stifled a sob of relief behind a hand, then smiled warmly as she watched Stanley go to Rustling Leaves, his comforting arms soon enfolding her within them.

Tears ran from Yvonne's eyes as she watched the children embrace. It was so touching, so moving, to see how deeply they cared for one another.

Her thoughts returned quickly to Silver Arrow. She turned and ran to the bedroom, then stopped and took a shaky step backwards. She was not sure if she should disturb him during his time of speaking soft words to his Great Spirit as he knelt beside his grandmother's bed.

He had laid her there, and had folded her arms across her chest. He had placed her personal belongings beside her. His one hand touched her face gently as he prayed.

But knowing the depths of his despair over having also lost his sister, and knowing how his burden would be quickly lightened should he know that she was alive, Yvonne decided to interrupt Silver Arrow's prayers. Once he knew that his sister was alive and well, he would have some thank-yous to speak to his Great Spirit!

Yvonne walked softly across the floor.

When she came up behind Silver Arrow, she hesitated only a moment, then placed a gentle hand on his shoulder.

"Darling," she whispered. "I've something to tell you."

Silver Arrow turned slow, wavering eyes up at her.

"Silver Arrow, Rustling Leaves is outside," she murmured. "Darling, she is alive! She is well!"

Joyous relief leapt into his eyes. "She . . . is . . . alive?" he said, his voice breaking. He looked past Yvonne at the door, then smiled. "She is here? She has come home to us?"

Tears spilled from Yvonne's eyes. She nodded. "Yes," she said softly. "Your Great Spirit has heard your prayers. He has brought your sister home safely to you."

Silver Arrow rose quickly to his feet. He swept Yvonne into his arms and swung her around, then paled and looked solemnly down at his grandmother.

He took Yvonne by the hand and walked with her quickly from the room. When they stepped outside, and Silver Arrow saw his sister running toward him, Stanley at her side, his eyes lit up.

He knelt down and received her in his arms as she flung herself into them.

Rustling Leaves sobbed and clung to Silver Arrow as he held her tightly to him.

"Antelope Skin and that bad white man were planning to kill me!" Rustling Leaves sobbed. "But Antelope Skin changed his mind!"

Stanley went to Yvonne and took her hand. They exchanged smiles, then listened to Rustling Leaves explain what had happened.

Silver Arrow's insides tightened. The rage was building inside him to heights never before felt by him as Rustling Leaves continued to tell him about Antelope Skin in a rush of words.

"While the evil white man was gone, Antelope Skin set me free!" Rustling Leaves cried. "He told me to come home. He said that Stanley had pointed him out to our people as one of those who abducted me. Now that everyone knew that he was, in part, responsible for my abduction, he feared your wrath too much not to allow me to return home, unharmed."

"I will never understand how our very own flesh and blood could have taken part in such a filthy scheme as this," Silver Arrow said as he gently held Rustling Leaves at arm's length away from him to look at her. "And he set you free? Did he

not have the decency to bring you home? He just
. . . sent . . . you away, to find your own way
through the forest, alone?"

Eyes wide, Rustling Leaves nodded.

Silver Arrow's eyes raked over her. He shivered
at the sight of her torn and soiled clothes, and at
the dirt on her sweet face, and at how her hair
was filled with briars and cockleburs. She wore
only one moccasin, the mate to the one he had
found clutched in his grandmother's hand.

"You are safe, yet what you must have gone
through at the hands of our cousin," Silver Arrow
said, his voice drawn. "The white man. Who is the
white man?"

"They were careful not to speak names in my
presence," Rustling Leaves said solemnly. "But I
would never forget him. He is a vile, dirty-
smelling, whiskered man. He reeks of dead animals. And he is always either smoking nasty
white man's cigarettes, or he is chewing tobacco."
She visibly shuddered. "It sickened me so when
he spit the ugly brown tobacco from his mouth."

Yvonne's heartbeats quickened. The child's description fit River Rat to a T, yet she could not say
for certain that it was he. Many trappers would
fit the same description.

"I will discover who, and pity the man when I
do," Silver Arrow said, his voice tight. "Little do
Antelope Skin and the white man know the grief
they have brought to our family. They did not take
your life, but they *did* take a life—your grandmother's. Rustling Leaves, she is dead because of
her grieving over your absence. She would be

alive now if not for the misery put on her heart by Antelope Skin and the white man's evil abduction."

Rustling Leaves took a shaky step back from Silver Arrow. The color had drained from her face. "Grandmother . . . is . . . dead?" she gasped out, her eyes brimming with tears.

She ran past him, stumbling from being so blinded with tears.

Yvonne glanced at Silver Arrow, then at the open door of the longhouse. Shivers ran up and down her spine when she heard the shrill cry of despair from Rustling Leaves. Yvonne knew then that Rustling Leaves was at her grandmother's bedside.

Yvonne went to Silver Arrow. "Stanley and I will go on home," she said, her voice trembling.

Scarcely aware that his people were watching his show of intense affection for Yvonne, Silver Arrow took Yvonne in his arms. "Come for my grandmother's wake," he whispered into her ear. "The first day of the four-day burial rites will begin tomorrow. Come on the fourth and final day. Be with me. I will need you."

"Yes, I will be here for you," Yvonne whispered back, clinging. "Darling, I am so sorry for all that has happened."

"Life is never easy," Silver Arrow said thickly.

He eased from her arms and knelt down before Stanley. He placed a gentle hand on his shoulder. "Young brave, soon you will be repaid for your act of courage," he said. "You are a hero in my people's eyes. You will be treated thusly."

Stanley hugged Silver Arrow. "I am so proud to know you," he said. "And I am so lucky to have met Rustling Leaves. I prayed that she would be alive. I feel blessed that my prayers were answered."

He gave Silver Arrow one last hug, then stepped beside his sister.

"I will send warriors to escort you home," Silver Arrow said, motioning for two of his warriors to come to him. "There is no safe place in this world, not as long as such men as Antelope Skin and his white-skinned partner in crime are roaming free."

"I will see you soon," Yvonne said, placing a gentle hand on Silver Arrow's cheek. "May my God and your Great Spirit comfort you at this time of sadness in your life."

When Rustling Leaves began to wail softly, Silver Arrow turned on a heel and went to her. When he entered the bedroom, his heart cried out to the heavens. He found his sister lying on the bed beside Princess Pretty Hawk, cuddled next to her, as though Princess Pretty Hawk were still alive to lend his sister the warmth and comfort of a grandmother.

Silver Arrow went to Rustling Leaves and lifted her into his arms. He held her close as she clung around his neck. He rocked her back and forth.

"Grandmother is in a better place now," he tried to reassure her. "She will know no more sorrow. She will know no more pain. And can you not feel her smiling down at us, to know that you are safe? Carry that smile with you forever, little sister, and never will you be lonely for our grand-mother again."

"Yes, I feel her presence," Rustling Leaves said softly. "And I felt it as I walked toward home. I just did not know why. Now I do. Her spirit left her body and came and led me safely home, did it not, Silver Arrow?"

Silver Arrow swallowed hard. "*Ae*, she led you safely home," he said.

He smiled down at Princess Pretty Hawk, his grief suddenly lifted.

Chapter Twenty-seven

It was the fourth day of the wake being held in honor of Princess Pretty Hawk. Her body had been placed on a scaffold in the center of the village near a great, roaring fire. Pretty Hawk's relations were sitting together on a low platform near the fire, the other Ottawa people sitting on blankets on the ground in a wide circle around it.

Yvonne and Stanley sat on the platform with Silver Arrow and Rustling Leaves. Antelope Skin, Silver Arrow's only other living relative, had disappeared. Without success, these past four days some of Silver Arrow's warriors had scoured the countryside looking for him.

For lack of time, no one had gone as far as Chief Old Elk's Iroquois village to search for Antelope Skin. Silver Arrow had sarcastically said to his warriors that the Iroquois village did seem to be a likely place to look for his cousin, since he was now an enemy of his own people.

They would go there. They would search the village. If they found him there, pity him!

Hands folded on her lap, Yvonne wore a black dress that she had quickly sewn for the wake. She occasionally glanced over at Silver Arrow as he sat so sorrowfully quiet while the wake progressed into the late afternoon.

He wore only a breechclout, without any sort of decorative beads or arm bands. And his hair was not held back with a band. It was left loose to flutter in the wind around his broad, muscled shoulders.

His legs were crossed and he rested a hand on each knee, his eyes turned forward. He was watching many male dancers as they whirled round and round the fire, their bare feet keeping time with the music from handmade wooden flutes and several drums. The dancers, dressed only in breechclouts, sang songs as they danced.

Yvonne had admired the colorful drums earlier in the day, and Silver Arrow had explained to her that every beat of the drum had a meaning.

He had also told her that at midnight there would be a feast for all of his people. Then they would continue the ceremony until the night turned to dawn.

Then would come the burial of his grandmother, after which she would go to the "Happy Hunting Grounds," to be at peace forever.

Yvonne gazed at Silver Arrow again. He had

said hardly a word to her since earlier in the morning after she and Stanley had arrived. He seemed lost in another world, another time. His eyes seemed blank today, as though he had no emotion left in him after mourning so deeply for his grandmother these past four days.

Stanley and Rustling Leaves sat at Silver Arrow's right side, so close to one another that not even a straw from a broom could pass between them. Their shoulders were touching, as were their hands occasionally.

Getting more concerned about Silver Arrow's state of mind, Yvonne scooted closer to him. "Silver Arrow, are you all right?" she whispered, placing a gentle hand on his.

He turned his eyes on her. His lips quivered into a slow, soft smile. "I did not mean to worry you," he whispered back. He laid his hand atop hers. "It is only that I am consumed with sadness over the passing of my grandmother. The remembering of my past with her will always be with me."

"I'm so sorry," Yvonne said, her eyes wavering into his. "I feel so helpless. I wish I could do something to lessen your burden."

Suddenly the music stopped. The dancers paused in midstep. Slowly lowering their feet, they turned and gazed at a man on horseback who was arriving at a hard gallop at the edge of the village.

Silver Arrow glared at the intruder.

Yvonne looked at the horseman, paling when she recognized Jake. A quick panic filled her, for she knew that he would not be there unless there was a dire emergency. And the only emergency she could think of that might warrant Jake's arrival at the Ottawa village would involve her father!

"Jake?" Stanley said, raising an eyebrow as he watched him approaching at breakneck speed through the village. He looked around Rustling Leaves and Silver Arrow at Yvonne. "Sis, why do you think Jake is here?"

Yvonne gave Stanley a troubled glance. "I don't know, but I believe we are soon to find out," she murmured.

She looked at Silver Arrow questioningly.

As though reading her thoughts and understanding that she seemed to believe she needed his approval to leave the platform, he rose and offered her a hand.

"I will go with you to see what brings your older brother to my village," Silver Arrow said, folding his fingers around Yvonne's hand.

"I'm afraid the news won't be good," Yvonne said as she stepped down from the platform with Silver Arrow. "Jake wouldn't be here unless he had something important to tell me."

"No, Jake has never cast even a shadow on my village," Silver Arrow said. He placed a hand on Yvonne's elbow and guided her away from the circle of people.

She felt all of his people's eyes on her as they turned and stared, watching first her, then Jake, and then her again.

She momentarily closed her eyes and said a little prayer that nothing had happened to Anthony. He was a man of goodness. He was a man of God. He was loved by so many, including the Ottawa.

He had not attended the services today because he had not been feeling well. He had said that he needed bed rest.

Oh, surely, she thought, he had not worsened. He had not even had a temperature when she left him. Nor had there been any signs of a cough or a cold.

She feared that he had worn himself out by doing too much. He was a preacher whose heart was in his work. He put himself and his needs second to everyone else's.

Jake wheeled his horse to a shuddering halt a few feet from Yvonne. "Jake, why are you here?" she blurted out. She looked uneasily over her shoulder at all of the eyes that were still on her and Jake. She looked up at him again. "Why would you come at such a time as this, unless you—"

"It's Father," he said, swallowing hard. "He's been injured. The doctor has been there and has seen to his wound, but you are needed, Yvonne. He is suddenly feverish."

"Injured?" Yvonne gasped out. "Wound? What sort of wound, Jake?"

Jake lowered his eyes, then looked at her again. "Father and I, well, we, uh, had a fuss," he said awkwardly.

"What about?" Yvonne said, doubling a fist at her side. "Jake, when I left him, he was feeling poorly. He said that he was going to rest. Did you disturb his rest?"

"Sort of," Jake said, again lowering his eyes.

"Tell me what happened," Yvonne said, placing her hands on her hips. "Everything, Jake. I want to know everything."

"He caught me taking a trap into the barn," Jake mumbled. "He *was* resting. He saw me from his bed, through his bedroom window. He came out and ordered me to show him the rest of my traps. When I refused, he went inside the barn and searched through the piles of straw where I keep them hidden, and . . . and . . . as he kicked through the straw, one of the traps that I thought was disarmed, wasn't. It got him in the ankle."

"Lord, no," Yvonne said, suddenly feeling sick to her stomach. She leaned into Silver Arrow's embrace as he moved closer to her. "How bad, Jake? Will he lose a leg? Or a foot?"

"No, the wound isn't that critical," Jake said, sighing heavily. "It only grabbed his ankle. Mostly it's a flesh wound."

"Thank God," Yvonne said, releasing a relieved sigh.

"He's asking for you, Yvonne," Jake mumbled, raking his fingers through his tousled, thick hair. "You've got to go to him. Do you hear?"

"Yes, I hear," Yvonne said quietly. She turned to Silver Arrow. "I must. He's always been there for me when I needed him. I must be there for him. He's such a sweet, gentle, and caring man."

"Go to him," Silver Arrow said. He placed a gentle hand to her cheek. She trembled as she leaned into it, savoring the comforting feel of his flesh against hers.

Then she straightened her back and stepped away from Silver Arrow. "I wish I could stay for the duration of the burial ritual," she murmured, her eyes locking with Silver Arrow's. "I feel as though I am letting you down."

"You have family that needs you," Silver Arrow said, nodding at a young brave. "Get White Swan's horse and buggy."

The young brave nodded and soon brought the horse and buggy. Silver Arrow helped Yvonne into the buggy.

Rustling Leaves gave Stanley a hug before he climbed in beside Yvonne.

Yvonne's and Silver Arrow's eyes locked with a mutual, sweet understanding, then she slapped the reins and rode quickly out of the village.

Jake rode beside her.

She could hardly stand to look at him. Because of him, a wonderful man was in pain. Jake had been warned time and again about the traps and their dangers. She had always feared that it would be Stanley who would unknowingly step into one of the fiendishly sharp traps. Never would she have guessed that her father would be injured by them!

"You just wouldn't listen, would you?" Yvonne finally shouted at Jake, unable to keep quiet any longer. "Feel lucky, Jake, that it is only a flesh wound. If Father had been injured worse, I might have—"

"Shot me?" Jake asked sarcastically.

"Well, I just might have," Yvonne said, glaring at him. "Jake, if this doesn't sober you up, and make you realize the wrong road in life you've taken, nothing will."

"Don't go preaching at me today, Yvonne," Jake said somberly. "I've heard enough preaching to last me a lifetime."

"Yes, and none of it seems to have done you any good," she said, frowning at him.

Feeling as though she was wasting energy on him, knowing that he had never listened to her before about anything, and doubting he ever would, Yvonne grew quiet.

She rode onward. When she reached her cabin she handed the reins to Stanley and jumped from the buggy before it had stopped.

Picking up her dress, Yvonne ran inside the cabin. She hurried to Anthony's bedside and took an unsteady step away from it again when she saw how feverish her father was.

"Yvonne," Anthony said through parched lips. He beckoned toward her with a hand. "Come, darling. Sit beside me."

Yvonne swallowed back a lump that was growing in her throat. She willed herself not to cry, but to smile as she sat down on the bed beside Anthony.

She took his hand and squeezed it affectionately. "Jake told me what happened," she murmured. "Thank God it isn't worse than a flesh wound."

"Is that what he told you?" Anthony asked, his eyes fluttering closed as he groaned with pain.

"Yes. Is it worse than that?" Yvonne gasped out, paling.

"It feels like it," Anthony said, chuckling beneath his breath.

"Let me take a look," Yvonne said, her fingers trembling as she shoved the blanket back from one leg.

She stared down at the bandage, tightening inside when she saw the blood that had seeped through it.

She was relieved when she discovered that only a small portion of his leg had been bandaged. That was proof enough that it wasn't all that bad, after all.

But it was enough to force him to bed, and to give him a temperature. And it was obvious that his wound was quite painful.

She covered Anthony's leg again. She smoothed the blanket up over him, just beneath his armpits.

She leaned lower over him and brushed a soft kiss across his brow. "I'm going to get a basin of cool water," she murmured. "I'm going to bathe your temperature away."

"Sounds good to me," Anthony said, swallowing hard. "If only you could bathe the pain away."

"I'm sorry you have to go through this needless suffering," Yvonne said tightly.

Stanley edged closer. Yvonne stood up and gave her little brother a gentle shove toward the bed. "Stanley is here, Father," she said. "He'll keep you company until I get back."

"Stanley?" Anthony said, looking up through

hazed-over eyes. "Son, come to me and give me a hug."

Stanley leaned down and hugged him.

"Did you learn anything today, son, about how Indians bury their loved ones?" Anthony asked, patting Stanley's arm.

"Yes, and it varies much from our own burial customs," Stanley said, easing down on the bed beside his father. "Can I tell you about it?"

"Yes, please do," Anthony said, closing his eyes.

For a moment, Yvonne watched Stanley telling Anthony about the day's activities, touched by their closeness and love for one another. She then turned and went to the kitchen to get the basin of water and a cloth. She found Jake at the table, sipping a cup of coffee.

When he looked up at her, pale and meek, Yvonne could not refrain from doing what she had wanted to do since she had first heard how their father had been injured.

She slapped him across the face.

With a lifted chin she stood defiantly over him, her hands planted firmly on her hips.

Jake rose quickly to his feet, then glared down at her. "You know better than to do that," he said, his teeth grinding. "I warned you, Yvonne—"

She laughed sarcastically. "Yes, so you did," she said. "I dare you, Jake, to do something about it."

Jake glared at her a moment longer, then sauntered off, his shoulders slouched.

Yvonne exhaled a long, trembling sigh.

Chapter Twenty-eight

The next day, Yvonne had just returned home from taking Stanley to school when she discovered that the doctor had arrived to check on Anthony. When she had first arisen this morning, she had been amazed at how Anthony's fever had diminished so quickly.

She now stood back and watched Doc Rose apply medicine to the wound, then carefully wrap it with a fresh bandage.

After the bandage was tied off, the doctor smiled down at Anthony and patted his hand. "Seems the fever was not caused by the wound, after all," he said. "If that damn wound was infected, you'd not be feeling this good this quickly."

Yvonne gasped softly at the white-haired doctor's use of foul language in the presence of her father. She was glad when Anthony's only reaction was to smile back at Doc Rose.

Stepping up to the doctor, Yvonne gazed down at him. A short, squat man with a fleshy face, he always wore a black suit and shirts that were wrinkled and yellowed with age. His gray hair lay tousled to his shirt collar, and a black tie had been tied crookedly at his throat.

"Then what caused the temperature?" Yvonne asked.

"You said your father was ailing yesterday morning before the accident?" Doc Rose asked in a husky voice.

"Yes, I was quite worried about him," Yvonne said, her eyes wavering as she glanced down at Anthony. She felt guilty for not having been there for him when she knew that he was ailing.

If she had been there, she would have interceded in his and Jake's argument. Anthony wouldn't have gone out to the barn in a huff and got his ankle injured by a trap.

But then, she would have let Silver Arrow down if she had not gone to him.

Suddenly, loving them both, she felt pulled between two men.

When Anthony smiled at her, as though to reassure her that he did not hold her at fault, she relaxed and returned his loving smile.

"Well, then, there's your answer," Doc Rose said, rising to his feet. He closed his black satchel and latched it. "He must have the ailment that is going around. I've made many calls these past days to homes where the entire family is down sick in bed with this same sort of malady."

He smiled down at Anthony. "Feel lucky, Preach, that your fever is gone this quickly," he said solemnly. He glanced over at Yvonne. "*And* that none of your family joined you in your sickbed. If any of your family was going to catch it, they'd show signs of it by now."

"Then what you are saying is that Father should be back on his feet soon, since the wound is not all that bad?" Yvonne asked anxiously.

"Maybe he'll be behind the pulpit preachin' the gospel by this Sunday," Doc Rose said, lifting his satchel from the bed. He looked down at Anthony. "You might not want to put your full weight on that foot for a day or two. But after that, it'd do you good to get back on your feet."

"Thanks, Doc," Anthony said, sitting up in the bed, resting his back against the headboard.

Yvonne bent over him and patted a pillow into place behind him. She hugged him, then walked the doctor from the room.

The doctor took his black, wide-brimmed hat from a table and plopped it on his head.

Yvonne held the front door open for him. "Thank you for coming," she said. "Your attentiveness to our family is always appreciated."

"My pleasure, ma'am," Doc Rose said, tipping his hat to her. He placed the hat back on his head and ambled slowly down the steps.

Doc Rose climbed aboard his horse and buggy. He gave Yvonne an easy smile, then snapped his reins and rode away.

Yvonne started to go inside, but stopped. Her heart leapt with joy when she caught sight of Silver Arrow riding toward her from the opposite direction. Always taken by his handsomeness, she gazed at his broad shoulders that filled out his fringed buckskin shirt, his muscles bulging. His hair was held back today by a beaded band.

The sun sheened Silver Arrow's sculpted copper face, making Yvonne shudder with anticipation of his kiss, his caress, his hard, lean body against hers.

There had been many interferences in their daily lives that had kept them from being together intimately. She had been with him that way only once, and she did not feel ashamed for being anxious to share such moments with him again.

Soon she would be with him forever. Her insides rippled with passion at the thought that a lifetime of his embraces lay before her.

Silver Arrow saw Yvonne standing on the porch. He saw that she had caught sight of him and was gazing at him now as though she were lost in sensual thoughts of him.

Her eyes seemed to sparkle like the stars in the heavens at night. Her face was flushed. Her lips were slightly parted. Her breasts were heaving.

His need for her was so strong this morning, his loins ached. He was determined that nothing more would delay their private moments together. He was going to make love to her this morning. He was going to awaken her to a rapture she had never felt before.

But first came the formalities of seeing how her

father was. This morning, in an effort to get her father well more quickly, he brought him many types of medicinal cures known by his people. They were in small bags tucked within his larger parfleche bag at the side of his horse.

He had brought the white sap of the willow, which contained a drug useful in treating headaches. He had brought pumpkin seeds for fevers, Indian tobacco for asthma, and squaw root for coughs.

"Silver Arrow!" Yvonne said as she ran toward him. "Darling, oh, darling, I'm so glad you came!"

He rode onward and met her approach, sweeping her on the horse with him when he reached her.

Silver Arrow placed Yvonne on his lap, facing him as his muscled arm held her in place. He brought his pinto stallion to a stop in the shadow of a tall oak tree.

Yvonne twined an arm around his neck and snuggled against him. She trembled with wild, exuberant passion when he lowered his hot and hungry mouth to her lips and kissed her.

Her breasts pulsed warmly with the need of his hands on them. She ached unmercifully between her thighs, her need for him so strong this morning, she could hardly bear it.

"Your father?" Silver Arrow whispered against her lips as he glanced toward the cabin.

"He is much better," she whispered back, their lips still touching. "Silver Arrow, he's going to be all right."

"That is good," Silver Arrow said huskily.

Knowing that they were far enough from the cabin not to be seen, Silver Arrow slipped a hand inside Yvonne's blouse.

Her breath caught when he cupped one of her breasts, feeling the tight nub of her nipple.

"I need you," he whispered. "Can . . . we . . . be together soon this morning?"

"Yes, oh, yes," she whispered, a delicious languor stealing over her as he caressed her breast.

Her passion-heavy lashes closed as his eager mouth covered hers again, his tongue seductively forcing her lips apart. It was a kiss of total demand, making her forget everything but what that kiss promised.

The shriek of a bluejay overhead in the trees made Yvonne jump. She became aware again of where she was! Far too close to her cabin, where her father lay trustingly in his bed, believing in her.

She did not feel ashamed of her feelings or of what she was sharing with Silver Arrow. He would soon be her husband. It was just that she felt she should show more respect in where she acted out her feelings for her beloved. Surely not within shouting distance of her home!

She felt Silver Arrow's eyes on her, imploring her. She reached a hand to his cheek and smiled softly at him. "Let's go and see how Father is doing," she murmured. "Then, darling, perhaps we could take a walk by the river . . . where . . . we could be alone?"

"*Ae*, I would like to pay my respects to your father. And *ae*, then I would like to pay mine to you

287

in the way my heart aches to do," Silver Arrow said, taking her hand, kissing its palm. "My White Swan, I so love you."

"As I also love you," Yvonne said, her body turning to liquid as his eyes touched hers in a sensual pleading. "I shall love you forever and ever."

He brushed a soft kiss across her lips, then rode on to the cabin.

Yvonne slid from his arms to the ground. She took his horse's reins and twirled them around the hitching rail.

"I have brought Ottawa medicine for your father," Silver Arrow said, dismounting. He went to his parfleche bag and lifted it from his horse.

"What sort of medicine?" Yvonne asked, gazing at the bag.

"Various herbs and potions my people use," Silver Arrow said, looking guardedly at her when he sensed some apprehension on her part. "Would you rather I did not take them to your father?"

Yvonne paused for a moment, then went to him and took his free hand. "My father will be delighted to see you," she said. She smiled up at him. "*And* your offers of medicine."

"You look like sunshine this morning," Silver Arrow said, his eyes locked with hers. "So radiant. So beautiful."

Yvonne blushed. "Please," she whispered. "If you fill me with any more desire than I am already feeling, my father will be able to see it."

"I can feel it," Silver Arrow said huskily, his fingers locking more intensely with hers. "I feel your heat, your passion, in your every breath. I hear it in your every word."

"*Please*," Yvonne said. "I'm serious. If you see and feel those things, surely my father will, also. I . . . don't . . . want him to be disappointed in me."

"Disappointed?" Silver Arrow said, his eyebrows forking. "In loving a man? Or in loving an *Indian*?"

Yvonne paled.

She turned and faced him. "You know better than that," she said. "I would never be ashamed of my love for you. Once we are married, I will shout it to the world, I am so proud! It is only that my father is a preacher and has his own sets of rules about things."

She paused and swallowed hard, then spoke softly again to Silver Arrow. "Although Anthony is only my stepfather, he has feelings for me as though I were his true daughter. That is why I must be careful in what I reveal to him about our relationship. I never want to lose his respect."

"We must marry soon," Silver Arrow said, his jaw tight. "Then you will not have cause to hide your true feelings for me ever again to your father."

"Then you do understand?" Yvonne asked.

He placed a gentle hand to her cheek. "*Ae*," he murmured. "Now let us go and see your father, then have that time alone that we both so much desire."

Their eyes locked in a silent, mutual understanding, then they went inside the cabin.

"Father, look who's here to see you," Yvonne said as she walked into the bedroom with Silver Arrow. "Silver Arrow has brought something to make you feel better."

"Oh? What have you brought?" Anthony asked, his eyebrows rising as he gazed at the buckskin bag.

When Silver Arrow saw how well Anthony was, he knew there was no need for his Ottawa medicine. He laid the parfleche bag aside and went and stood at the bedside.

"Brother Stockton, there are many herbs and potions that my people use when they are ill, or have been injured," Silver Arrow said. "I have brought some today for you." He bent and placed a gentle hand on Anthony's bare shoulder. "But I see that your white doctor has worked his own magic on you," he said, smiling down at Anthony. "You need none of the Ottawas'."

"It was kind of you to think of me," Anthony said, reaching over to pat Silver Arrow's hand. "But, yes, I do believe that Doc Rose has proven once again to be a skilled doctor. I can always depend on him."

Anthony cleared his throat nervously as he slipped his hand down to his side, while Silver Arrow drew his own hand away.

"I regret not being able to come to your grandmother's wake," Anthony said. "I was feeling quite poorly, even before my accident. I should've never left my sickbed. But Jake. Aw, Jake. He does rile me so sometimes, so much that I almost forget my religion."

"Yes, Jake has a tendency to bring out the temper in even the meekest of people," Yvonne said, thinking back to how she had slapped him last night.

She had not seen him since and wondered where he had gone. He had spent the entire night away from home.

When Anthony had asked for him early this morning, Yvonne had not told him that Jake had not returned home. She had quickly changed the subject.

She had found herself going often to the window and door to watch for Jake, surprised that she was so worried over his absence. But she had seen something different in Jake's eyes after his father's accident . . . a humility of sorts. Perhaps he was having second thoughts. Perhaps he *was* going to change.

The sound of a horse and buggy arriving outside drew Yvonne to the window. Her eyes widened when she saw several women from her father's congregation in the buggy. On their laps were covered dishes, and some held pies.

She smiled, for she knew why they were there. To see how their preacher friend was faring. News spread quickly in this neck of the woods.

"Well, I do believe you have some women callers, Father," Yvonne said, turning around to smile mischievously at him.

"Oh?" he said, looking at the window. "Who?"

"They are from the church, Father," Yvonne said, hurrying from the room.

She smiled at each of the women as they

walked past her into the cabin. Yvonne reassured
them that he was going to be just fine and then
ushered them into his bedroom.

Silver Arrow stepped back and stood with
Yvonne.

Yvonne stifled a giggle behind a hand as she
watched the women huddle around the bed, chat-
tering like magpies, and showing what they had
brought to their beloved minister.

"Cherry pie," she heard Anthony say, then "My,
oh, my, even a peach pie and molasses cookies. I
do believe you women think your preacher needs
fattening up."

Again they giggled.

Yvonne went and stood behind them. She stood
on tiptoe and got Anthony's attention. "I'm going
for a walk," she said, drawing a nod from her father.

She turned on a heel and hurried to Silver Arrow's side.

Hand in hand, they left the cabin and headed
toward the river. When they were out of eye range
of the house, Silver Arrow turned to Yvonne and
swept her up into his arms.

She laid her cheek on his breast as he carried
her into the darker depths of the forest, seeking
total privacy for their time together. Yvonne was
acutely aware of the thundering of Silver Arrow's
heart, over which her cheek lay. It matched the
erratic rhythm of her own heartbeat.

She drew in a ragged breath when one of his
hands slipped up inside her skirt, the feel of his
flesh against hers setting fires along her legs as

his hand traveled higher.

When his fingers came to the sensitive flesh of her thighs, she quivered with a longing that she had never known until Silver Arrow.

She closed her eyes and moaned when his fingers slipped up inside her undergarment and found her hot, moist place. When he plunged a finger into her, withdrew, and plunged again, a passion-heavy dizziness overtook her. She gave herself up to the rapture as he now caressed the center of her desire, awakening her again to feelings that were blissful.

So lost in a reverie of passion, Yvonne was scarcely aware of Silver Arrow laying her among a patch of beautifully scented lilies of the valley that lay along the banks of the Grand River. Her heart pounding, her pulse racing, she was only aware of him now kissing her with a fierce, possessive heat, while his hands eagerly disrobed her.

Soft moans repeatedly surfaced from inside her when Silver Arrow knelt low over her and pleasured her with his tongue, mouth, and fingers. He made love to her slowly in this way, each lazy caress, each sweep of his warm tongue over her warm flesh, making her feel as though she were soaring among the clouds.

Leisurely, his tongue circled first one nipple, and then the next. Then he left a wet trail downward, across her tummy which shimmered with the wonders of how this way of loving her made her feel so deliriously joyous, then on down amidst the curls of her hair that framed her woman's center.

Yvonne's breath caught in her throat when he flicked his tongue over the tight nub of her womanhood, making her sink farther into a chasm of desire. She had never felt as desired, as wanted, as exquisitely wonderful as now.

And although something at the back of her mind tried to cry out to her that this might be forbidden, she refused to listen. This man who was making love to her was the whole world to her. At this moment in time, she knew that he could do anything he desired, and she would allow it.

Closing her eyes, she tossed her head back and forth. She chewed on her lower lip to keep herself from crying out with the pleasure that was being unleashed within her. She never wanted it to stop, yet something was nagging at her consciousness again, telling her that she was being selfish. He was giving her pleasure and she was not giving back!

"Darling?" she whispered, her face flushed from the ecstasy. She twined her fingers through his thick hair and led his lips away from her body. "Silver Arrow, let me undress you. I need to touch you. I want to caress your body. I want you to feel everything that you have just aroused in me. I want our bodies to join, as though they are one. I want you to fill me with your heat."

Smiling at her, reaching a hand to one of her breasts, gently cupping it, Silver Arrow nodded. "Yes, I do hunger for your touch, for your lips, for your mouth on my body," he said huskily. "I wish to experience it all with you. Today, my White Swan. Not tomorrow or the next day. I am glad that you are as impatient for it all as I."

Yvonne moved to her knees.

Silver Arrow moved to his knees before her.

Yvonne's fingers trembled as she shoved his shirt over his head, then went to the waist of his breeches and slowly slid them down.

Silver Arrow stood up long enough to kick his breeches aside, and then his moccasins. Then he moved to his knees again before her.

Yvonne ran her fingers over his sleek, hairless chest, marveling anew at the tightness of his muscles. She leaned low and flicked her tongue around first one of his nipples, and then the other, glad to hear him moan with pleasure.

"Lie down," Yvonne whispered, gently shoving him down on the bed of flowers. "Relax. Close your eyes. I am going to show you just how much I love you."

Silver Arrow's heart thudded like a thousand drums within his chest as he stretched out on the ground. He shivered at the exquisite touch of her hands as they moved slowly over his body.

Then he cried out with pleasure when he felt her hands on his throbbing sex. His whole body tightened with the rapture of the moment. He breathed heavily and his heart leapt, it seemed, into his throat, when he felt not only her hand on his heat, but now also her mouth. The pleasure of her tongue and warm mouth on him was almost too much for him to bear. He clenched and unclenched his fists as she continued to love him in that fashion.

Then feeling that he was too close to the edge, understanding now why she had stopped *his* caresses, he placed his hands on her cheeks and gently urged her away from him.

"It is time for us to come together," he whispered, shifting positions, sliding her beneath him.

"Yes, it is time," Yvonne whispered back, her voice sounding foreign to her in its huskiness. She licked her lips, tasting him on them.

Her eyes drifted closed when he kissed her with fierce abandon and entered her with one deep thrust.

Clinging to his hardness, she rocked with him as his lean, sinewy buttocks moved, his rhythmic strokes within her taking her breath away with the building rapture.

His tongue flicked through her parted lips, then he kissed her again with a lazy warmth that left her even weaker than before.

Her fingers bit into his shoulders as the passion crested. She could feel his breath coming hot against her lips. She could feel his body tightening as his thrusts within her became maddeningly faster. Suddenly her body exploded. She clung fiercely around his neck as his own body trembled into hers.

When their pleasure subsided, Silver Arrow buried his face between her breasts, breathing hard. Yvonne caressed his back.

"Will it always be this beautiful?" she whispered, trembling when he swept a hand down and parted her thighs, again caressing her damp valley.

"Even when we are old and gray," Silver Arrow whispered, his lips brushing her throat.

He leaned away from her for a moment and gazed into her eyes. He smiled.

"Forever and always," Yvonne whispered, tracing the outline of his lips with a forefinger.

He nibbled at her finger, then his mouth closed hard upon her lips in another fiery kiss. Leaving her breathless and shaking, his mouth seared into hers with intensity.

She felt the full length of him against her thigh and knew that he was ready to make love again. She lovingly wrapped his manhood in her fingers and led him inside her.

Again the silent explosion of their love for one another was accompanied by their sighs and groans.

Chapter Twenty-nine

The next morning, Yvonne stood at the door of her father's bedroom, hardly able to believe what she was seeing. Jake had returned home before sunup and had gone immediately to his father's room. He had sat vigil at Anthony's bedside until he had awakened.

They had eaten breakfast and now Anthony was propped up comfortably against the headboard. Jake was still at the bedside, pouring his feelings out to his father.

Yvonne listened, stunned to realize that Jake seemed sincere in all that he was saying. He *did* appear to be speaking from the heart when he told Anthony how sorry he was for having behaved so badly for so long.

"Father, I spent all day yesterday thinking

about life and what I should make of it," Jake said, his voice filled with emotion. "I've decided that I want to contribute something positive to society."

Tears pooled in Anthony's eyes. He reached over and took one of Jake's hands. He gently clutched it. "Son, I seemed to have waited a lifetime to hear you say that," he said thickly.

"I'm so sorry about the traps," Jake said, swallowing hard. "If you had lost a leg because of me, I swear I would have—"

"Jake, don't say it," Anthony said, interrupting him. With his free hand, he patted his injured leg above the knee. "Son, if it took this to bring you back to me, I don't regret it having happened. And I'll be out of this bed by tomorrow, I imagine. Doc Rose said that I might even be preaching behind the pulpit this Sunday. Who could ask for more than that? To have my son back, and to be able to preach again so soon?"

Jake sat down on the edge of the bed and swept his arms around Anthony's neck. "Father, I love you so," he said, a sob catching in his throat. "I never want to disappoint you again."

They hugged for a while longer, then Jake sat back down on the chair, wiping tears from his eyes.

Yvonne moved to the bedside. She wiped her own tears from her cheeks. "I'm so happy for you both," she murmured. She leaned down and gave Jake a warm hug. "Jake, I do want the best for you. I always have. It's just that you have always carried a chip on your shoulder as far as I was concerned."

"Yes, I guess I have been a bit jealous of your relationship with Father," Jake said, gazing up at Yvonne as she sat down on the other side of the bed beside Anthony. "But I promise it won't happen again."

"What are your plans, Jake?" Yvonne asked, feeling strange, yet happy, to be talking this way to her stepbrother when only yesterday she had been given cause to slap him. Miracles did happen.

Jake's and Anthony's eyes met and held.

"I wish to enter the ministry," Jake said, his voice breaking when he saw the joy that leapt into his father's eyes. "That is, Father, if you will be the one to teach me. I don't want to go away to school. No one else could teach me as well as you, Father. Do you have the time?"

"Do I have the time?" Anthony said, laughing excitedly. "Son, if ever I would have time for you, it is now. It would delight me to be the one to teach you the gospel."

Yvonne looked from Anthony to Jake, suddenly no longer feeling needed. She glanced out the window at the clouds building along the horizon. She frowned and cringed when she saw a zigzag of lightning in the sky, then heard the low, drawn-out rumble of thunder.

She had planned to go to Turtle Island, a small island in the middle of the Grand River not far from her cabin. Turtles nested there at this time of year, and she had planned to go there today and gather some turtle eggs, which were a delicacy. She had wanted to surprise her father with several eggs for his noon meal. They were his favorite.

She slipped from the bed and left the room, then turned when Jake came up behind her.

"Sis, you mentioned earlier about going to Turtle Island," he said. He went to the door and peered up at the sky. He turned to Yvonne. "I don't think it's wise. A storm is brewing."

"I can make it over and back before the worst of the storm hits," Yvonne said, slipping her apron off. She hung it on a peg, then flipped the skirt of her cotton dress around as she rushed to the kitchen and picked up a wicker basket. "Jake, I won't be long. Just go and talk with Father. You've so much to say to one another to make up for lost time."

A rumble of thunder shook the floor of the cabin.

"Yvonne, if you insist on going to that island, I'll go with you," Jake said, grabbing a wide-brimmed hat, plopping it on his head.

Yvonne reached up and took off his hat and placed it back on the peg. "I won't hear of it," she said. "Go and spend time with Father. And don't tell him where I've gone. I want the turtle eggs to be a complete surprise."

She marveled anew at Jake's change. His remorse at being responsible for his father's injury seemed to have snapped something back in place in his mind that had gotten dislodged when his mother had died. The change was wonderful.

She just hoped that it lasted far longer than a day.

"Yvonne, I . . ." Jake began, but Yvonne ignored him and rushed outside.

The basket swinging at her side, she ran to the riverbank where a canoe was beached. This canoe had been a gift from Silver Arrow some time ago when he and Anthony had become friends.

Anthony went canoeing alone from time to time as he communed with nature while thinking of sermons. He had said that while gliding down the quiet avenue of the river he could always feel God right there with him in the canoe as the birds sang overhead in the trees.

"God, I hope you will be with *me* today," Yvonne whispered as she placed her basket inside the birchbark canoe. She flinched when a vivid streak of lightning lit up the ever-darkening sky. She trembled inwardly when thunder followed.

Giving the canoe a shove, she ran into the water and climbed aboard, then sat down and drew the paddle through the water. With each stroke, she watched the island. It was a beautiful place with its flowering bushes and its graceful pine and cedar trees. She knew that along the sandy shore she would find dozens of eggs. She had gathered them at this same time last year.

She glanced heavenward, relieved to discover that the low-hanging clouds seemed to have stopped moving so quickly. But the lightning and the loud cracks of thunder did not lessen in their intensity.

After beaching her canoe at the island, Yvonne

began gathering eggs. One by one she laid them gently in the basket, only occasionally looking heavenward.

On the other side of the river, Silver Arrow was looking at the sky, too. He had been riding toward her cabin when he saw Yvonne beach the canoe on the island. He stood now at the riverbank, first watching her, and then the approaching storm.

He looked up the riverbank, his muscles tightening when he saw no more canoes or boats that he could use to get to the other side.

From the way the wind had begun to moan through the thrashing leaves overhead, he knew that the storm was soon to reach its peak and would make traveling back from the island threatening for someone unskilled at manning a canoe. It would be almost impossible to make it without capsizing.

Silver Arrow stepped into the water. He cupped his hands around his mouth and shouted Yvonne's name.

But the howling wind and the splashing waves kept her from hearing him.

He knew that he did not have time to swim across to the island, to bring her back safely in the canoe, himself.

He knew that there was only one other way. . . .

Yvonne's insides froze when the wind began whipping her hair around her face, and the rain began to blow in hard sheets against her. Fear grabbed her heart when the lightning came in constant vivid streaks above her and thunder roared like a giant lion all around her.

She tried to steady herself against the force of the wind. She screamed when the wind tore the basket of eggs from her hand. She watched the eggs toss about like pebbles along the ground, breaking one by one.

She covered her mouth with a hand when she watched the basket fly into the water, soon to be swallowed by the waves.

Panic filled her when she saw that the wind was rocking the canoe back and forth on the sand. If the canoe was forced out into the water, she would be stranded on the island.

She ran to the canoe and grabbed it with both hands and held it there, praying that the storm would soon pass so that she could return safely home. She now realized how foolish she had been to come to the island in the face of a storm. She knew the fierceness of storms in Wisconsin. She had suffered through many of them as she had huddled in the cabin, waiting for the howling winds to pass on by overhead.

Her father had promised to build a storm cellar, to protect his family from such storms. But he had not yet found the time.

She was at the total mercy of the wind, the rain, the thunder, and the lightning.

She had never felt as alone, as vulnerable, as now!

Suddenly she saw a movement above the water a short distance away. She cupped a hand over her eyes to shield them from the stinging rain. She gasped when she saw a crow flying against the wind toward the island. Surely it was the same crow that she had grown fond of! If so, this was the first time she had seen it since it had strangely disappeared from her room.

Why had it chosen a time like this to make an appearance?

"Go back!" she cried, relieved that it was still alive.

But for how long?

Why was it flying toward the island?

It was as though it knew her dilemma; as though it were coming to try to rescue her.

But again she scoffed at herself and her imagination.

It was just a crow! It had no way of knowing that she was in danger.

Yet it had saved her from danger once before, when it frightened River Rat away after he had tried to seduce her!

Perhaps . . . now . . . it also knew.

"You are going to be killed!" she shouted as she continued to watch the crow, the rain beating against its flapping wings.

When she saw that it was not going to turn around and return to safety, Yvonne began cheering it on as it battled the howling wind. "Just a little farther!" she cried. "Come on, sweet crow. You are going to make it!"

A brilliant flash of lightning blinded Yvonne for a moment.

She jumped with alarm and covered her eyes, trembling when thunder boomed all around her.

When she opened her eyes, her heart sank

when she no longer saw the crow.

She wove her fingers through her hair to keep it out of her eyes as she looked along the beach for the crow. When she didn't see it anywhere, she gulped hard.

She then surveyed the water with probing eyes, dreading the moment she might see the bird floating lifelessly on the surface.

But she did not see it.

"White Swan?" Silver Arrow said, stepping up beside her. He lifted her into his arms and placed her in the canoe. "I have come to get you safely to the other side."

Yvonne stared blankly up at him. "How?" she asked in amazement. "Where is your canoe? I didn't see you crossing." She paled. "I saw only . . . the . . . crow."

He gently gripped her shoulders. "As before when I asked you not to question me, do not question now things you may only think you have seen," he said. He looked intensely into her eyes. "There is no crow. There is only you and I. And all that you must think about now is getting to safety."

Yvonne grew light-headed, in wonder at what had transpired.

She believed that surely, in her fright, thinking that she might soon be swallowed whole by the water, her imagination had played tricks on her.

Silver Arrow shoved the canoe out into deeper water, then sat down and began drawing the paddle through the water as he attempted to make his way to the other shore.

When the wind worsened, he groaned with the effort as he fought against the thrashing waves.

In a near state of shock, Yvonne clung to the sides of the canoe, her eyes on Silver Arrow's back, thinking back to the day the crow had been shot, then a short while later finding a wound on Silver Arrow's shoulder.

And where had the crow been these past several days?

And why had Silver Arrow tried to convince her that she had not seen the crow today?

No. None of it made sense.

She was torn now about this man she loved with all of her heart. Was he a sorcerer? Had she seen something today that just couldn't be?

Yet if the man she loved was a sorcerer, he worked for the good of people. Not the bad!

No. She would not allow herself to think that he might possess such magical powers.

"Yvonne! Silver Arrow!"

She heard Jake's voice shouting at them as the canoe came closer to the shore.

The rain was now only a fine mist. Yvonne could see Jake standing on the riverbank, waving at her and Silver Arrow.

Silver Arrow looked over his shoulder at Yvonne. Their eyes locked, as though he was imploring her to remember what he had said about not asking questions about things she may only have thought she had seen.

Loving him so much, and suddenly feeling as though she was the one doing the protecting, she gave him a reassuring smile.

307

His lips tugged into a relieved smile.

"Thank you for rescuing me," Yvonne said softly. "I shall always be indebted to you for risking your life to save me."

"Having you as my bride will be payment enough," Silver Arrow said huskily.

Jake ran into the water and grabbed the canoe. "Yvonne, thank God, you're safe!" he cried.

When Silver Arrow leapt from the canoe and helped Jake drag it farther onto the sandy shore, Jake looked at him with wonder. "Silver Arrow, how on earth did you get over there in that storm?" he asked, his eyebrows forking. "I saw no other canoe. Lord, man, did you swim?"

Yvonne stepped from the canoe. She went to Silver Arrow and took his hand. "No, he *flew*," she said, her eyes twinkling into Silver Arrow's.

Jake threw his head back in a loud laugh. "Yes, and so shall I sprout wings the next time you need rescuing from the island," he said.

Then Jake sobered. "You gave Father quite a fright," he said, frowning down at Yvonne.

"Yes, I'm sure I did," Yvonne said. She combed her fingers through her wet hair and gazed down at her clinging dress. "And I think it best if I go and make a quick change. I don't want to join Father in his sickbed."

She looked up at Silver Arrow. "You are wet too," she said. "Why not come to the cabin? Jake will lend you some dry clothes."

"I must get back to my village," Silver Arrow said, taking her hands. "I had no idea the storm was going to be so fierce. I have to see if any of our lodges were damaged by the wind."

He brushed a kiss across her lips. "I shall return tomorrow," he said softly.

"Yes, please do," Yvonne said, then watched him go to his pinto stallion and ride away in a hard gallop.

"I still don't know how he got across that water to rescue you," Jake said, placing a hand on Yvonne's elbow, ushering her home.

"Yes, it is quite a puzzle, isn't it?" Yvonne said, fighting back any fears that accompanied her wonder at what she may have truly discovered about her beloved today.

She ran on ahead of Jake and hurried into the cabin. Drenching wet, but smiling, she went to her father's bedside.

Her eyes were filled with a soft, mysterious glow as her father stared into them.

Chapter Thirty

Yvonne's and Stanley's Saturday chores had been done more quickly than usual after they had both received an invitation to Silver Arrow's village at the break of dawn. Silver Arrow had asked them to come at the noon hour. Although he knew Anthony's condition, Silver Arrow had invited him anyhow.

"Now you two scurry on off to Silver Arrow's," Anthony said as he limped into the kitchen. He smiled from Yvonne to Stanley. "Give him my regards. Tell him that I will come another day when I am stronger."

"I wonder why he wants us to come particularly today," Stanley said excitedly as he stood still for Yvonne to brush his shoulder-length blond hair. His face shone from a hard scrubbing, the freckles on his nose more prominent since he had been spending more time in the sun during recess at the school.

"I think I know, but I don't want to say," Yvonne said, laughing. "I might spoil whatever surprise Silver Arrow has cooked up for you."

"Me?" Stanley said, his eyes widening behind his thick-lensed eyeglasses. "You think we've been invited to his village because of me?"

"Well, just perhaps," Yvonne said, smiling over at Anthony who understood what she was referring to. She vividly recalled Silver Arrow promising Stanley that he would be honored soon for his heroism. Although Silver Arrow had not mentioned it yesterday after he rescued her from the island, he must have had it planned all along and had decided to approach it in this way.

This way seemed more special.

Surely nothing else could have put such excitement in her small brother's eyes than the anticipation of what might lie ahead of him.

"And don't worry about rushing back home," Anthony said, leaning his weight against the table as he poured himself a cup of coffee. "I can take care of myself. That should not take much effort since I plan to read the scriptures most of the day. I never tire of reading the Psalms."

Suddenly in deep thought, he shifted his eyes toward the ceiling. Then he smiled at Yvonne. "And once I've finished reading the Psalms, I believe I will read a volume of Thoreau for inspiration," he said. He eased down onto a kitchen chair and took a leisurely sip of coffee.

311

Yvonne nodded toward a fresh bouquet of flowers that she had placed on a table beside the plush, thickly cushioned wing-back chair on which her father would sit while reading. She had purposely moved the table and chair by an open window so that he could enjoy the cool breeze that blew in from the forest.

"Father, do you see what I gathered from my garden for you today?" she said, laying the hairbrush aside as Stanley sat down on the floor and slipped on his shoes.

She gazed at the flowers she'd arranged in a glass epergne. The pale pink tulips, English daisies, and tendrils of maidenhair fern created a lovely picture, among which she had placed several fragrant sprigs of her favorite flower, the lily of the valley.

Anthony smiled as he looked over at the vase of flowers. "You have brought Saint Louis with you to Michigan," he said, chuckling. "I am amazed at how many starts of plants you were able to bring here from your Saint Louis garden. They are all so beautiful, Yvonne. And I can't tell you how much I appreciate them, especially now that I am ailing."

Yvonne went to Anthony and bent low to hug him. "I love you," she murmured. "I so enjoy doing things for you that make you happy."

"Having such a daughter as you is happiness, alone," Anthony said, returning the hug.

"Thank you," she whispered, then eased from his arms. Her heart raced at the thought of soon being with Silver Arrow.

She looked down at Stanley. "Sweetie, I won't be long," she said, then rushed to her room and closed the door.

She went to her full-length mirror and gazed at herself, wanting to look her best today for Silver Arrow. When he had last seen her she had been as wet and wilted as flowers after a spring rain.

Early this morning, after a young brave had brought the invitation from Silver Arrow, she had fussed at length with her hair. It now lay in long waves down her back, the sides drawn back with beautiful wooden combs.

Her face was flushed pink from rushing around getting her chores done.

Then she had chosen one of her daintiest dresses to wear, having run an iron over it to remove any wrinkles that may have been crushed into it while it lay amidst the others in the trunk at the foot of her bed.

She turned slowly in front of the mirror, watching her every movement, admiring the yellow silk dress with its tiny sprays of white flowers embroidered on the skirt. Its neck was low-swept, but not so shamefully low that when she wore it to her father's church she would shock the faint of heart. Frothy white lace trimmed the bodice, matching the lacy crinoline slip that she wore beneath the dress.

"Yes, I feel pretty enough," she whispered. She could even admit to herself that she looked pretty.

Her thoughts slipped back to yesterday, at how stunned she had been when she had seen the crow, and then shortly thereafter, Silver Arrow.

Cassie Edwards

"No, I shan't think of it any longer," she said, trembling inside.

If she thought long and hard about the possibilities of what may have happened yesterday, of what she was almost certain *had* happened, she might become frightened of Silver Arrow.

"No, I will not allow anything to spoil what we have found in one another's arms," she said, slipping her small firearm in the pocket of her dress.

She had found nothing less than paradise while with Silver Arrow. She loved him fiercely! She would love him forever!

Contentment warming her through and through, she left her room. "Stanley, let's be on our way," she said, stopping to give Anthony a soft kiss on his brow. She was glad that he was now sitting comfortably in the cushioned chair beside the window.

"Be careful, hon," Anthony said, frowning up at her. "I'm not even certain I should allow you and Stanley to leave without an escort."

"Hogwash," Yvonne scoffed. She patted the pistol through the soft fabric of her dress. "I can take care of anyone who approaches me and Stanley."

"Yes, I'm certain you can," Anthony said, the bulge in her pocket evident.

Holding hands, Yvonne and Stanley left the house.

They laughed and talked as they boarded the buggy that Stanley had brought from the barn earlier. While riding along the narrow path, they continued chatting. It was with gusto that they breathed in June's perfumed air.

Yvonne was reminded of those times in Saint Louis when she and Stanley had pulled on their sturdy walking boots and had set out together on a healthful nature hike through the woods.

One of the most pleasing pastimes for her had always been to spend an afternoon ambling along a woodland path, noting birds, spotting butterflies, collecting odd bits of moss, pausing to just soak it all in, glad to be a part of it.

When the Ottawa village came in sight, Yvonne's heart raced with the anticipation of soon being with Silver Arrow. She glanced over at Stanley. He was straining his neck as he looked at the village.

"I believe you are as anxious to see Rustling Leaves as I am to see Silver Arrow," Yvonne said, reaching over to pat his knee. "I'm so glad that you have made a fast friendship with Silver Arrow's sister. Like you, she is sweet."

"I am teased at school for playing with a girl instead of boys," Stanley said sullenly. He looked over at Yvonne. "But who cares? They call me sissy no matter what I do." He glowered. "I hope that I will one day be able to discard my eyeglasses. But not for wanting to look less like a sissy in the eyes of the boys. I want to look better for Rustling Leaves."

"Stanley, don't you know that she looks past your glasses when she sees you?" Yvonne said softly. "She sees you, the sweet and gentle young man that you are. Not the glasses."

"Do you really think so?" Stanley said, eyes wide.

"I'm certain of it," Yvonne said, nodding.

They both grew quiet as Yvonne led the horse and buggy into the village. She gasped and stared in awe as she and Stanley were met by a rush of Ottawa children as they ran beside the wagon, reaching up for Stanley, shouting his name over and over again.

Stanley blushed. "Why are they doing that?" he asked, giving Yvonne a quick glance. "They seem so happy to see me. Why?"

Yvonne looked past the children and saw the huge fire, men and women dressed in dancing attire, and drums set back from the crowd with the drummers standing over them.

There were other men and women sitting around the fire on blankets. Past them, on platforms near the fire, was an assortment of food stacked on platters.

"It looks like some sort of celebration," Yvonne said, giving Stanley a quick glance, smiling.

Yes, she thought to herself. This was the celebration that had been promised Stanley. The way the children were behaving toward Stanley this morning, and the way everyone else turned and gazed smilingly at his approach, made her know for certain that this was to be his day, his very own special day.

Silver Arrow stepped from his longhouse and waited for Yvonne to draw rein close by.

Yvonne's pulse raced as her eyes locked with his. She was hardly even aware when a young brave took the reins from her hands, while another reached up and assisted her from the buggy.

Rustling Leaves' squeal of delight as she ran up to Stanley when he jumped from the buggy drew Yvonne out of her reverie. She watched Stanley and Rustling Leaves embrace, then run away, hand in hand, to join the other children.

Silver Arrow came to Yvonne. He took her hands and gazed down at her. "White Swan, today your hair and clothes are dry," he said, chuckling.

"Yes, seems so," Yvonne said, her eyes twinkling. Her insides melted as he continued to gaze down at her.

"You are so beautiful," Silver Arrow said huskily as his eyes swept slowly over her. "My heart aches with need of you."

Yvonne's knees went weak with her own needs, but she did not voice them aloud. She looked adoringly up at him as he swept an arm around her waist and led her amidst his people beside the fire.

She stood with him as he reached a hand out for Stanley, who had come, with Rustling Leaves' encouragement, to stand before the Ottawa people.

"Young brave, whose heart is as brave as the most courageous warrior's, today is yours," Silver Arrow said as he placed a hand on Stanley's frail shoulder. "Today we all eat, dance, sing in celebration of your act of heroism toward my sister. Today a feast will be held in your honor. You will be treated as young Ottawa braves are treated on the day they become warriors."

Stanley stood beside Rustling Leaves, his

mouth agape, his eyes wide. He was awestruck over being honored so highly for what he had done. His actions had come naturally to him, since he loved Rustling Leaves so much.

"Thank . . . you" was all that he could utter. He was rendered speechless by the generosity of these Ottawa people toward him.

"Let the drums play, let the rattles shake, and let the food be consumed," Silver Arrow shouted. "Let there be games! Let there be stories told of our ancestors!"

Rustling Leaves gave Stanley's hand a yank. Giggling, she half dragged him away, where several children sat in a wide circle around one of the elders.

"That is our village storyteller," Silver Arrow told Yvonne as he watched the children scoot in closer to the elderly man. "The children will hear many stories as they eat." He looked at the women who brought platters of food to the children and passed them around the circle.

"Come inside," he said, gesturing toward his longhouse. "We will have our own private celebration."

Yvonne's heart skipped an anxious beat as he led her into his lodge. Inside, she stopped and stared around her, in awe of what he had done to his house to prepare for her arrival.

Candles flickered everywhere. Food was piled high on large platters. Flowers were strewn across the floor. Plush pelts lay amidst the flowers.

She turned and smiled warmly at him when she

heard him latch the door, which assured them of total privacy.

"Are you pleased?" Silver Arrow asked, going to her, gently framing her face between his hands.

She trembled sensually when he guided her mouth to his. "Yes, very," she whispered against his lips. "Oh, how I adore you, my wonderful Ottawa chief."

He swept his arms around her and yanked her close to his hard, lean body. He kissed her with total demand.

Their bodies strained hungrily together as their lips and tongues met in frenzied kisses.

The combs fell first from Yvonne's hair. And then her dress tumbled to the floor, followed by her undergarments and shoes.

Her trembling fingers then quickly disrobed Silver Arrow.

Then they clung together, their heated bodies touching, as they melted together down onto the soft, snow white rabbit-fur blanket.

The music and laughter outside was faint, the thundering of Yvonne's and Silver Arrow's heartbeats drowning out everything but their hungry need for one another.

Theirs was only a world of feeling, touching throbbing, and burning.

Kneeling over Yvonne, with quick eagerness Silver Arrow ran his fingers through her hair. He drew her lips to his and pressed a trembling kiss to them, darting his tongue moistly into her mouth.

Yvonne's skin quivered with the warmth of his

kiss. A sudden curling of heat tightened at the pit of her stomach when his hand moved down to curve over a breast, his thumb caressing the nipple.

A cry of sweet agony escaped through Yvonne's fevered lips when Silver Arrow's mouth moved over the nipple, sucking, nipping, licking.

She shivered as his hands moved down over her ribs, across the tender flesh of her abdomen, and then parted the soft fronds of hair at the juncture of her thighs and began a soft caress which drove her mindless with pleasure.

As Silver Arrow spread himself over her, and his knee nudged her thighs apart, Yvonne sighed with rapture to know that what she felt now probing at her woman's center was no longer his hand, but that part of him that would soon magnificently fill her.

One deep thrust and he was inside her.

She gasped with ecstasy when he began his slow, rhythmic strokes.

And when Silver Arrow kissed her again, and he pressed endlessly deeper inside her, she became lethargic with the building pleasure.

Her gasps against his lips became long, soft whispers.

Silver Arrow's spiraling needs were being fulfilled. With the tip of his tongue he traced the curve of her cheek. His hands found the soft swells of her breasts again. His lips fastened on a soft, pink nub, sucking it hard.

Yvonne arched toward him.

With a groan he pulled her hard against his

heat. His hands touched her, turned her, and drew her more closely against the warmth of his body, and all that he had to offer her.

Then wanting to delay the final throes of ecstasy, to prolong their sensual moments together, Silver Arrow stopped all of his movements and caresses.

Their bodies stilled against each other, he gazed into her eyes.

Their breathing ragged, silence vibrated around them as his eyes held hers, transfixed by the smoldering desire they both saw in one another's eyes.

Yvonne was overwhelmed with longing, with sweet, painful longing as she waited for him to continue. When he did not, she placed a gentle hand to his cheek. "What's wrong?" she whispered, her eyes searching his for answers.

"You are both agony and bliss for me," he said huskily. "I needed to stop, to take a few deep breaths before we reach the ultimate of pleasure again in one another's arms."

"I am not sure how long I can wait," Yvonne said, smiling weakly up at him. "If you knew how my insides are trembling, how I so hunger for you, my darling . . ."

"There are other hungers that need to be fed," he said, his eyes twinkling into hers.

"There are?" she asked, laughing softly. "Like what, my love? All I am aware of is that which I feel for you."

"Did you not see the trays of food that I have in my lodge to offer you?" he asked in a teasing fashion. He glanced over at the food. Her eyes followed his. "Do you not see the fry bread? The pumpkin soup? The cherry *wazapi*? The *timsila* soup made out of wild turnips? And the dried corn soup made of dried blue and white corn?"

"Yes, I see them all," Yvonne said, then turned her eyes slowly back to him. "And none of what I see looks as good to me as you. And none of what I see can fill my hungers, my needs, as you can. Kiss me. Fill me deeply with your heat. Take me with you to that place that awaits us, where our pleasure knows no bounds. I want you now, Silver Arrow. Please? Now?"

Silver Arrow laughed huskily, then with a groan pulled her against him and kissed her savagely as he plunged over and over again within her.

Delirious with sensations, Yvonne arched toward him. Her whole universe seemed to be spinning around, and after only a few of his deeper thrusts, she joined him as they both went over the edge into total ecstasy.

Their bodies shook and vibrated together.

They moaned against each other's lips.

And then they drew apart and lay side by side, their breaths coming in short gasps.

Yvonne finally caught her breath. "You were right," she murmured, turning on her side to face him. "We should have delayed it for a while longer, for it is over too soon."

"For now, it is," Silver Arrow said, stroking a hand down the curve of her thigh. "But remember, White Swan, we have forever and ever to share such moments as this."

Yvonne stiffened inside when she again saw the scar on his left shoulder. Watching his eyes, to see if she could read his thoughts, she ran a finger slowly over the scar. She questioned him quietly with her eyes.

Gently he took her hand and slid it down from the scar. "My White Swan, please do not question me about things that I am not ready to reveal to you. Please listen well when I again tell you that it is best not to delve into the mystery of this scar. Let it be. Just accept it."

Yvonne swallowed hard and moved her hand away from his shoulder. "And listen to me when I tell you that I can accept any and all truths about you," she said, her voice filled with emotion. "I love you, totally."

Their eyes locked in silent understanding, then he pulled her next to him and held her in what she felt was a far too desperate embrace.

To change the subject, to draw her thoughts elsewhere, Silver Arrow eased away from her. He stroked her cheeks with his fingertips as she gazed into his eyes. "Do you hear the music of the magic pipe, or what is also called the flute?" he murmured.

"Yes, it is even more prominent today than the drums," Yvonne said, closing her eyes, listening. "It is so beautiful. So peaceful."

"*Ae, ka-ge-ti*, truly so, it is most pleasing to the ear," Silver Arrow said. "It has the power of persuading every animal to follow him who plays."

Yvonne's eyes opened and widened. "Truly?" she asked, forking an eyebrow.

"*Ae*, and at night, when a man is newly in love and he wants to beckon his loved one to come to him, he will play the magic pipe deep within the forest, knowing that his woman will come to him," he said, slowly drawing her into his arms again.

"You need no flute to encourage me into your embrace," Yvonne said, trembling inside when once again he kissed her pretty and delicate mouth, but this time unhurriedly.

Cradling her in his arms, he kissed her with a lazy warmth that left her weak . . . and wanting more.

"*Ki-daw-yo-im* . . ." he whispered against her lips.

Chapter Thirty-one

Yvonne was just clearing the dishes from the table after Sunday dinner when she heard the sound of an approaching horse outside the cabin.

Thinking of Silver Arrow, and knowing that he could come anytime, she felt her cheeks grow heated with an excited blush.

She closed her eyes and thought of yesterday and their private, sensual moments in his cabin, while Stanley was outside in the village being honored by Silver Arrow's people.

Yvonne was shaken from her reverie when Stanley came running into the kitchen, shouting.

"Yvonne, Silver Arrow is here!" he said as he ran toward the door. "And also Rustling Leaves! He brought Rustling Leaves with him this time."

"Yvonne, he can't seem to get enough of you,

can he?" Anthony said as he limped into the room. "And how nice that he brought Rustling Leaves. She's a bundle of joy, that sweet thing."

Beaming, Yvonne yanked her apron off and tossed it over the back of a chair. She wove her trembling fingers through her hair, straightening it over her shoulders.

"You look just fine, hon," Anthony said, chuckling as he stood just inside the kitchen.

"I wish I had time to change back to the pretty dress I wore to church," Yvonne fussed as she looked down at the plain calico dress she had chosen to wear while cooking.

"Do you truly think Silver Arrow will care about what you have on?" Anthony said, again chuckling. "When he looks at you, he sees an angel."

Yvonne laughed softly. She took the time to go and hug Anthony, then rushed outside and stood on the porch just as Silver Arrow tied his horse's reins on the hitching rail.

Rustling Leaves and Stanley were chasing a butterfly, giggling.

Silver Arrow's eyes moved to Yvonne, but she did not see him looking at her. He smiled at the look on her face, how stunned she seemed to be by what he had brought.

Yvonne stared at a travois tied to the back of Silver Arrow's horse on which lay a thick bundle wrapped in the same rabbit-skin blanket on which she had made love with Silver Arrow yesterday.

Silver Arrow saw the wonder in her eyes as she continued to gaze at the bundle he had brought as a bride's price. Knowing that she wasn't aware of what it was, he smiled slowly.

When Anthony stepped onto the porch beside Yvonne, Silver Arrow asked him, "And how are you feeling on this beautiful day?"

"Better, but I did not give the Sunday sermon today as I had hoped to," Anthony said. "But I will be there for my congregation next Sunday. Not even a herd of wild horses could keep me from standing behind my pulpit."

"There were no church services, then, this Sunday?" Silver Arrow asked, bending to one knee to untie the bundle from the travois.

"Yes, I am proud to say there were," Anthony said, smiling over at Yvonne as she looked with a soft smile at him. "Jake read from the Bible."

That made Silver Arrow's eyes turn in a quick jerk back to Anthony. "Jake?" he asked, raising an eyebrow.

"Yes, Jake," Jake said as he stepped from the barn and walked square-shouldered toward Silver Arrow. "I'm no longer a backsliding Christian. I've come to my senses. I'm studying for the ministry."

Silver Arrow rose slowly to his full height and stared at Jake, who seemed to have made not only an inward change, but an outward one, as well. He was clean-shaven. He wore clean clothes. And he had a sort of radiant glow about him.

Silver Arrow stiffened. Distrustful of this man who until now had been brash and nothing but a troublemaker, he hesitated at taking Jake's proffered handshake of friendship.

But when Yvonne came to Silver Arrow's side and smiled up at him, as though encouraging him to befriend this stepbrother of hers, Silver Arrow reconsidered and shook Jake's hand.

"I hope to come often with my father to have council with you and your people," Jake said, slipping his hand from Silver Arrow's.

"You are welcome at my village as often as you wish to come," Silver Arrow said, then resumed what he was doing as he knelt and lifted the large bundle from the travois.

His eyes dancing, he walked to the porch and held the bundle out for Anthony. "I brought gifts earlier," he said. "Today I have brought my *true* bride price for your daughter."

"That wasn't necessary, Silver Arrow," Anthony said. "You know that you and Yvonne already have my blessing."

"All Ottawa marriages are preceded by gifts of *wampum*," Silver Arrow said, allowing Jake to relieve him of his burden since Anthony was not able to put his full weight on one foot.

Except for Stanley and Rustling Leaves, who were still chasing the butterfly, they all went inside the cabin.

Yvonne stood beside Silver Arrow as Jake untied the bundle, his father sitting in a chair at the table on which the bundle lay.

"I have brought more than *wampum* today," Silver Arrow said as Jake handed his father a necklace of shell beads.

"Beautiful," Anthony said, holding the beaded necklace out before him.

"*Wampum* is the most widely known variety of shell beads," Silver Arrow said softly. "The term *wampum* refers to tubular beads made from white and purple marine shells. They provide personal ornamentation for all Ottawa. Even we men wear such necklaces when we wish to. They are valued. That is why this is a part of the bride price I offer you."

Silver Arrow reached inside the bundle and brought out several rich pelts and laid them across Anthony's lap. "These were tanned by me," he said, proud of what he offered. "Tanning is a matter of pride for the hunter, though it is a long procedure. I favor the old Indian tanning method involving the use of deer brains."

He took something else from the bundle. "Even the tiny bones inside the dew claws of the deer are crafted into jewelry," he said, laying more jewelry on the table. "And I put great faith in the potency of the elk-hoof as a good-luck charm. I recently caught an elk. I saved the hooves, scraped them, bored a hole in each, and strung them together for you to wear on special occasions, such as your daughter's marriage ceremony to me."

Then Silver Arrow pulled out a string of sausage. "Brother Stockton, this I made especially for you," he said, holding the sausage out between his hands. "It is made from the entrails of a bear by turning them inside out. The fat, which clings to the outside, fills the skin. Washed, dried, and smoked, it is a delicacy."

Silver Arrow laid the sausage on the table, then

stood back beside Yvonne. "If these are not enough for the bride price, I shall bring you more," he said, his voice drawn.

"No, nothing more," Anthony said, running his fingers over one of the plush pelts. "As I said before, no payment at all for my daughter was needed. But since you felt the need to make such an offering, I humbly thank you for what you have brought. It means even more to me, since I know that these are gifts from your heart."

Relieved and proud, Silver Arrow heaved a sigh of pleasure.

Stanley and Rustling Leaves rushed into the house. Stanley stood over the table, awestruck by the gifts. Rustling Leaves pointed out each thing to him and explained what it was.

Then Silver Arrow went and knelt down before Stanley and rested his hands gently on the young boy's shoulders. "Do you recall my having promised that I would take you out for a special day all your own?" he asked, smiling at him.

"Yes, I remember," Stanley said, his voice showing his excitement.

"Today is that day if your father will allow you to go with me into the forest so that I can show you how to collect yellow jackets for yellow jacket soup."

Yvonne paled. "Yellow . . . jacket . . . soup?" she said, gasping.

"*Ae*, it is one more delicacy that I would like to share with your father," Silver Arrow said, his eyes gleaming into Yvonne's.

"Won't it be dangerous?" she asked anxiously.

"Not if you know what you are doing," Silver Arrow said. "And I know exactly what I am doing. I have seen some of my people who have had violent reactions when stung by bees. I would not wish that on anyone."

"I don't know. . . ." Yvonne said doubtfully. "I would think yellow jacket soup would be horrible."

"Do not criticize it until you have tried it," Silver Arrow said, chuckling at her attitude.

He looked into Stanley's eyes. "Only the bravest dare venture into the preparation of exotic Indian food," he said thickly. "And Stanley has already proven his bravery."

Then he looked over at Anthony again. "Brother Stockton, can I borrow your son for a while for such a hunt?" he asked.

"Most certainly," Anthony said.

"I want to go, too," Rustling Leaves blurted out. "Please, Silver Arrow, can I go?"

"If Stanley doesn't mind having someone else along on our venture," Silver Arrow said. "Would you like for Rustling Leaves to go with us? Or would you rather we go alone?"

"I want Rustling Leaves *and* Yvonne to go with us," Stanley said in a rush. "It will be more fun, don't you think, if they are with us?"

Silver Arrow gave Yvonne a warm glance. "*Ae*, it will be more fun if they are with us," he agreed.

"Then let's go!" Stanley said.

Silver Arrow rose to his full height. "White Swan, it would be good if we could return to your cabin and prepare the soup on your stove so that your father and brother Jake can share in the delicacy," he said as Yvonne plopped a bonnet on her head and tied it beneath her chin.

"Then that's where we shall prepare it," Yvonne said, becoming more comfortable with the idea of what they were going to do.

"Take care not to get stung," Anthony said as they left the house.

Silver Arrow took a parfleche bag from the side of his horse. "Within this bag are all the ingredients needed for the hunt," he said, slinging it over his shoulder.

"I know where there is a nest of hornets," Stanley offered. "I saw them buzzing around over their hole in the ground while I was running home from school the other day to tell Yvonne about Rustling Leaves' abduction." He pointed. "It's over this way."

He broke into a run, Rustling Leaves beside him.

When they approached the ground nest of hornets, some were flying in and out; some were buzzing around it.

"Stand back and let me do this," Silver Arrow said, lowering his bag to the ground.

Yvonne held Stanley's and Rustling Leaves' hands and watched quietly as Silver Arrow built a small fire and circled rocks around it. Then he covered the nest with a thin piece of buckskin, catching a number of hornets in the buckskin. He tied the buckskin around the hornets, capturing them.

Then Silver Arrow lifted the nest from the hole.

It was full of grubs. He placed the nest on the end of a long stick and held it over the fire, heating the grubs until the thin paperlike covering became parched.

He then placed the heated nest on the ground. One by one he picked out the dead yellow jackets and put them in his bag.

"Now we can take them to your home," Silver Arrow said. "But first I must spread the buckskin filled with captured hornets over the hole so they can return to the ground and make a new nest. In time the wind will blow the buckskin away so they will be free to come and go again as they please."

"Catching them was so simply done," Yvonne said, walking beside Silver Arrow as they headed home. "Yet I would not have been as brave as you, to hold that nest over the fire."

"Once the nest was over the fire, the yellow jackets were rendered helpless," Silver Arrow said, chuckling.

Laughing, they hurried onward.

Once inside the cabin, Silver Arrow instructed Yvonne what to do next. "First brown the yellow jackets on the stove, then cook the browned yellow jackets in boiling water to make the soup. You will then season to taste."

Jake even joined in the fun, laughing and carrying on as the soup was made.

It did Yvonne's heart good to see her older brother so changed, and she hoped that he would stay that way. She could not forget how he had hungered to get his hands on Silver Arrow's gold.

How could he have forgotten it so easily?

No, she did not yet totally trust him, and wondered if she ever could.

When the soup was ladled into bowls around the table, and they were sitting down to eat, someone knocked on the door.

"I'll see who it is," Jake said, pushing his chair back.

When he opened the door, he paled at who he saw. Nervously, he glanced over his shoulder, feeling all eyes on him.

Quickly he stepped out on the porch and led River Rat by one arm back to his horse. "Get out of here, River Rat," he grumbled. "I'm a changed man. I don't want anything more to do with you *or* Antelope Skin."

"But you don't know what's happened to—" River Rat stammered, groaning with pain when Jake took hold of his arm and squeezed as he shoved him hard against his horse.

"I don't want to hear it," Jake said stiffly. "Ride out of here, River Rat, and never let me catch you near here again, or I'll forget my religion again long enough to shoot you in the seat of the breeches."

"I should've known not to trust you," River Rat said, seething as he pulled himself into his saddle. He glanced at the cabin, then glowered down at Jake. "Your whole family is crazy, includin' you."

He rode away in a hard gallop.

Visibly shaken, and trying to gain control of his emotions, Jake waited a moment before going back inside the cabin.

When he finally returned, all eyes were on him, questioning him.

"It was nothing more than vermin that occasionally comes out of the forest," Jake said, laughing crookedly as he sat down to the table.

"Who was that, Jake?" Anthony insisted, not taking Jake's jesting as enough of an answer.

"River Rat," Jake said, his head hung.

"What did that vile man want here?" Yvonne asked, her eyes flashing. "I told him never to come near our place again. Why would he, Jake?"

"Sis, I've admitted to making many mistakes these past several years," Jake said thickly. "Well, you know that being friends with River Rat was one of them. You don't have to worry about seeing him again. I just sent him packing."

"That's good, son," Anthony said, nodding. "I only hope he listens."

"If not, I'll tell him again, but not as gently as this time," Jake growled.

"Now, Jake, let's not start thinking about doing something violent, not after you've just found the Lord again," Anthony said softly.

"You're right," Jake said, his voice drawn. "Once you start backsliding, you go all the way to the devil if you ain't . . . I mean, aren't careful."

Anthony chuckled at how Jake corrected his English, proud of him for it.

"Well, now, everyone, what do you think of Silver Arrow's yellow jacket soup?" Yvonne chirped up, to change the subject, to make the mood light and carefree again.

"It's downright delicious," Anthony said, lifting

another big spoonful to his lips.

"I like it, don't you, Rustling Leaves?" Stanley asked, gazing over at her.

"I have had it often and each time I like it less," Rustling Leaves said, visibly shuddering. "Who could ever enjoy eating bugs, especially those that have vicious stingers?"

Everyone broke into a fit of laughter.

Chapter Thirty-two

A purple haze lay over the Grand River as Silver Arrow and Yvonne sat down on a blanket beside it. Silver Arrow plucked a white violet and slipped it into the strands of Yvonne's hair above her ear.

He then placed an arm around her waist and drew her closer to his side. As the sun set in glorious fiery splendor, Yvonne snuggled into Silver Arrow's embrace.

"I don't think I've ever been as content," she murmured, a gentle warmth flowing through her veins. She gazed up at Silver Arrow. "Loving you is what has caused me to feel this way," she said, trembling sensually inside when he gave her a warm smile. "Yes, before I met you, I was happy. After I accepted my mother's death I became the same person that I was before she died. I've never been one who complains about things. I have always taken from life what it has handed me."

She giggled. "Except for Jake," she said. "He brought out the stubborn side of my nature. Sometimes he has riled me so much I could hardly stand it."

"*Ae*, he does seem to have that way about him," Silver Arrow said. "I am glad that it was your father, not your brother, who came for that first council with me. Had it been Jake, I would not have welcomed him among the circle of my warriors. He would have been bad for my people at a time in our lives when we needed someone with a logical mind."

"My stepfather is so special," Yvonne said, sighing. "I didn't have that much time with my true father. He died before I was old enough to truly know him."

"How did he die?" Silver Arrow asked, arching an eyebrow.

"I don't think you want to know," Yvonne said somberly, turning to look at the shadows in the water as day faded quickly into night.

"Yes, I would like to know, for, my woman, I want to know everything about you," Silver Arrow said, placing a hand to her waist, turning her to face him.

Yvonne's eyes locked with his. She swallowed hard. "After we first moved to Saint Louis from Kentucky, my father . . . was . . . ambushed in the forest by Indians," she said, her voice breaking.

"*Ae*, now I see why you hesitated to tell me that," Silver Arrow said. "But yet, even knowing how your father died, you can still love an Indian?"

"Yes, because you are good, kind, and gentle," Yvonne said, placing a hand to his cheek. "Very unlike those who killed my father. You see, a search party went out. The two Indians responsible for my father's death were found. It was discovered that they were Miami renegades whose sole purpose in life, it seems, was to massacre white people. They shamed the whole Miami tribe. I was told that their chief came and tried to make amends, for it was said that he was kind and gentle, as you are."

"*Ae*, there is good and bad in both white and red skins," Silver Arrow grumbled. "My parents were also killed by those who were bad, and whose skin was red."

"I'm so sorry," Yvonne said, easing into his arms. "But we didn't come to sit by the river to talk of such things. We came to be alone. Hold me more tightly, Silver Arrow. Never let me go."

"I will never let harm come to you," Silver Arrow said, holding her against his hard body. He laughed softly. "It was good to see my sister and your brother sitting by the fire before we left to take a walk by the river. They have made such a solid bonding. I see a future for them where they will never be apart."

"I see that also," Yvonne said, leaning away from him, beaming. "And wasn't it wonderful to see them eating popcorn and playing checkers?"

"It might take some time for my sister to learn the art of playing the game you call checkers,"

Silver Arrow said, chuckling. "She seemed more fascinated by the red and black blocks of wood than the game itself."

"Stanley loves the game so, he will not give up on teaching Rustling Leaves how to play it," Yvonne said, her fingers going to the fringed hem of Silver Arrow's shirt, slowly shoving it up past his chest. "I don't believe we came to sit by the river to talk about our sister and brother, either, did we? Darling, didn't you promise me more than that when you whispered the suggestion of this walk while my father and brother were absorbed in watching the children?"

"Promises made by this chief are promises kept," Silver Arrow said huskily. He pulled the shirt the rest of the way off, then reached around and began unbuttoning Yvonne's dress.

After they were both fully unclothed, and the soft breezes of evening caressed their nudity, Silver Arrow spread Yvonne beneath him, blanketing her with his body.

"Everything today led to this moment," he said, brushing a quivering kiss across her parted lips. "It is hard to pretend attentiveness to others when all the while my heart and mind are on you, my beautiful woman."

"I am so happy that you love me," Yvonne said, running her hands slowly over his sleekly muscled chest. "I am, oh, so feverish with desire."

"I shall feed that fever," Silver Arrow whispered against her cheek. "I shall feed that desire."

Yvonne felt the urgency building. He spread her legs apart with a knee, his manhood seeking her wet warmth, searching, probing.

And then in one long thrust he was inside her. He drove in swiftly and surely. He gathered her in his arms, his fingers pressing urgently into her flesh, as he moved rhythmically within her, her hips answering the call, lifting, falling, gyrating.

His lips moved to one of her breasts. Yvonne felt as though she were melting inside as his tongue flicked around the nipple, his teeth now nipping and playing around the soft curve of the full breast.

Her throat arched backward as he moved his tongue along its delicate, vulnerable line.

"My White Swan," he whispered against her neck.

Then he kissed her, long and hard, and probed his tongue between her parted lips. She touched her tongue to his, her hands caressing his tight buttocks, her mind soaring.

Silver Arrow felt the muscles of his body tensing. He held Yvonne in a torrid embrace as a sudden onslaught of passion overwhelmed him. Everything within him seemed filled with a white light as the passion crested. He kissed her as she trembled against him, her own passion sought and found.

They lay together beneath the soft light of a full moon. They clung. They kissed. They laughed.

Then a bright red, wavering light in the heavens brought Silver Arrow quickly to his feet. He doubled his hands into tight fists at his sides.

"What is it?" Yvonne asked, quickly pulling on her dress. She stood up beside him and gasped

341

when she saw the reflection in the sky.

"There is a fire!" he cried. "It comes from the direction of my village!"

"No," Yvonne cried. "Surely not!"

Her fingers were trembling so violently she could hardly button her dress. Her eyes wavered as she watched Silver Arrow, in desperation, scramble into his clothes.

Finally clothed, they ran through the woods until they reached Yvonne's cabin.

"Stay!" Silver Arrow cried, swinging himself into his saddle. "Keep my sister here from harm! Do not come until I send for you!"

"But I wish to go with you," Yvonne cried, beckoning toward him as he rode off.

Frightened, her pleas ignored, Yvonne watched Silver Arrow until she could see him no longer. Shaken, she went inside the cabin and told what she and Silver Arrow had seen.

Wide-eyed, Jake listened, then ran toward the door. "No!" Yvonne cried. She went and grabbed his arm. "This is not the time for you to make amends with the Ottawa. Silver Arrow must be left to do what he must without anyone's interferences."

Rustling Leaves went to Yvonne and clung to her skirt. "I am afraid," she cried, tears rushing from her eyes.

Yvonne reached for her and lifted her into her arms. "Silver Arrow will make all wrongs right," she murmured. She rocked the child in her arms.

Anthony got his Bible. Clutching it to his chest, he prayed.

Chapter Thirty-three

When Silver Arrow arrived at his village, he grimaced to see half of his people's lodges burning. The men and women had formed a bucket brigade from the river, trying their best to keep any more of their homes from catching fire.

Silver Arrow was touched deeply by how they diligently kept his cabin wetted down, not allowing their chief's cabin to burn. He was grateful that his valuables had been spared: his sacred coat, his war shield, everything precious to him and his ancestors.

But his heart went out to those who had lost everything.

His jaw tightened as he rode into the village and quickly dismounted. He joined the others as he grabbed a bucket and threw water onto the cabin next to his. "How did this start?" he shouted at Four Horns who stood beside him.

"Several cabins were set afire, one after another, until too many were burning to go after the scoundrel who started it!" Four Horns shouted over the roar of the fire behind him. "Yours was the last to be set aflame. That was how we were able to save it. The one responsible for this tragedy ran away after throwing a torch on your roof."

"We can spare no one to search for the culprit now," Silver Arrow shouted back to Four Horns. "That means we may never find him!"

"*Ae*, I am sure he left no trace of himself behind," Four Horns said, his voice hoarse from having breathed so much smoke. "But we must remember always the belief of our people, that the eye of our Great Spirit is the sun by day, and by night the moon and stars, and therefore the Great Spirit sees all things everywhere, night and day. It is impossible to hide any action, either good or bad, from the eye of the Great Spirit. When no human eye can observe a criminal's evil-doings, the criminal actions will be revealed at some future time, to his disgrace and shame."

"That is true, but still I should have been here!" Silver Arrow said.

"You are only one man," Four Horns reassured. "You cannot divide yourself up and be everywhere at once. And you need a life of your own. Do not feel guilty for having one!"

Four Horns paused, then said, "Where is Rustling Leaves?"

"When I saw the reflection in the sky, I felt it was best to leave her with White Swan, to keep her out of possible danger," Silver Arrow said, taking another bucket and throwing water on another cabin.

"I fear for her and our other children's futures," Four Horns said, frowning over at Silver Arrow. "If our lives can be destroyed so quickly, who is to say what might happen next?"

"We will take it one day at a time and take from life what the Great Spirit gives us," Silver Arrow grumbled. "Be it good or be it *motchi-manitou*."

Silver Arrow's thoughts went to White Swan. Was he wrong to bring her into his life, a life that was always filled with danger?

He knew that he must, for he could not live without her.

Chapter Thirty-four

Antelope Skin lay on his stomach peering over the edge of a butte. His clothes carried the stench of the fire. His hand had been burned when he had held on to one of the torches for too long before throwing it on the roof of one of the cabins.

"The magical coat is still untouched. I should've set fire to Silver Arrow's lodge first instead of last," he grumbled to himself, angry to see that his cousin's cabin still stood, scarcely touched by the ravages of the fires set by his own hand. "But I had to set fire to the others first to draw attention elsewhere. And those burning lodges so close to Silver Arrow's should have guaranteed that his would burn, also!"

He rose quickly to his feet and rushed to his horse, which he had tethered in the thick shadows of the forest. "As long as he has his grandfather's coat, Silver Arrow's magic is still intact!"

As he rode off, putting many miles between himself and the fire, Antelope Skin leered into the darkness. There was another way to get back at Silver Arrow!

The white woman!

Yes, he would go to Chief Old Elk and tell him his plan. In Chief Old Elk he would find an ally!

Antelope Skin knew that the Iroquois chief's daughter had been recently scorned by Silver Arrow's refusing to accept a bride price for her.

He smiled darkly when he thought of Silver Arrow having gone a second time to Chief Old Elk's village with accusations and questions. After Princess Pretty Hawk's burial, Silver Arrow had gone to see if Rustling Leaves was hidden there.

Antelope Skin laughed to himself, knowing how perfectly this all fit into place for himself. It would definitely be safe for him to go to Chief Old Elk's village now, for surely Silver Arrow would not go there a third time. Silver Arrow would not push his luck by showing up there again for any reason.

"Yes, now is the time for me to get back at Silver Arrow for having the gold, for keeping it to himself, and for having powers stronger than mine!" he cried to the wind, the trees, and the stars.

Chapter Thirty-five

"Unhand me!" Antelope Skin said as two Iroquois warriors held him between them. It seemed to Antelope Skin that the Iroquois sentries had been waiting for him at the edge of the village. At first sight they had jumped out at him from the shadows and manhandled him.

"I have come in friendship to see your chief!" he cried.

"This time of night no one comes for council," Fire Eyes, one of the Iroquois warriors, said in his Iroquois tongue, which Antelope Skin understood well enough. "We saw the great fire in the sky. We went and investigated and discovered that it was Silver Arrow's village. Who is to say those who set that fire might not come and set fire to the Iroquois village? It is surely white men

348

wanting to rid the Michigan forests of redskins!"

"*Kau*! You are wrong!" Antelope Skin said, trying to wrench himself free as he was half dragged toward Chief Old Elk's lodge. He could see Iroquois men, women, and children at the doors of their wigwams, watching. He cringed when, by the light of the moon, he could see distrust and hate in their eyes.

"What do you mean we are wrong?" Fire Eyes asked, releasing his hold on Antelope Skin. He slid a knife from its sheath at his waist and held it to Antelope Skin's throat. "Tell me how you know so much about the fire. Did you see, first-hand, who set it?"

When Antelope Skin felt the sharp edge of the knife break the skin of his neck, and felt a hot trickle of blood flowing from it across his throat, he tensed. "It was I, Antelope Skin, who set the fire," he said, swallowing hard. "Now will you release me? I wish to speak to your chief."

Fire Eyes dropped his knife to his side and leaned his face close to Antelope Skin's. "Why would you set fire to your own people's village?" he hissed.

"Because I am no longer a part of that village," Antelope Skin grumbled. "I was not banished, but I know that if I were to go there again, I would be."

"Why? What have you done to cause your own people to turn on you, and you to turn on them?" Fire Eyes pressed, taking a slow step away from Antelope Skin. He slid his knife back inside its sheath.

"I was a part of a scheme that backfired," Antelope Skin said, wiping the blood from his throat. "Now I must find another way to get what I am after. Chief Old Elk will surely want to hear what I have to say."

"Who is this who disturbs my sleep at this time of night?" Old Elk said, stepping from his lodge with a bearskin robe draped over his shoulders. He wiped sleep from his eyes.

"It is I, Antelope Skin," Antelope Skin said, stepping away from the two warriors. "I am sorry to disturb your sleep but I have something of importance to talk over with you. It would benefit you and your people if, in the end, you and I succeed."

"You . . . and . . . I?" Old Elk said, raising an eyebrow. He laughed sarcastically. "Why would I ever align myself with you, a cousin to the Ottawa chief who only days ago humiliated me and my daughter; who came to my village more than once with a look and voice of suspicion?"

"Let me explain, then if you do not wish to align yourself with me, I will leave in peace and find someone else who will cooperate with me, and who will share my cousin's buried gold with me," Antelope Skin said in a rush of words.

"Gold?" Old Elk said, kneading his chin. "Yes, I have heard tales of the gold that Silver Arrow's grandfather buried. It is said that only Silver Arrow knows where it is buried. How do you plan to get it?" He flung a hand in the air and gestured with it. "Go away. I do not wish to hear anything more. You are a foolish man."

"There are ways to get the gold," Antelope Skin said, wrenching himself free when the two Iroquois sentries again grabbed his arms. "There is a white woman. Silver Arrow plans to marry her." He laughed throatily. "You know that he is foolish to marry a woman who is not nearly so lovely as your own daughter. I have plans that will do away with her, and get us the gold."

Old Elk's eyes squinted as he gazed at Antelope Skin, then turned his eyes heavenward. The moon was occasionally hidden by columns of smoke coming from the Ottawa village. He then looked at Antelope Skin again. "Did I hear you say that you set the fire at Silver Arrow's village?" he asked, his voice guarded.

"Yes, I did this out of vengeance, and to rid my chief of his magical coat," Antelope Skin said through clenched teeth. "I failed. Silver Arrow's lodge still stands. So he still has magical powers."

"Magical powers?" Old Elk said, forking an eyebrow. "I have only heard whispers of such a thing. Antelope Skin, is it true? Is . . . he . . . a sorcerer?"

"He is many things to many people," Antelope Skin grumbled. "But, no, I would not say that he is a sorcerer. But he does have powers that you and I will never completely know about. He guards them well." He grinned devilishly. "But perhaps a *wife* might learn the powers once he is married. It is still possible that your daughter can become his wife. I have a plan. I beg you to listen."

Old Elk gazed thoughtfully at Antelope Skin a moment longer, then grabbed him by the elbow and ushered him inside his large wigwam.

"Sit beside my fire," Old Elk said, gesturing toward the pit in the center of the lodge, where glowing embers sent dancing shadows along the walls and ceiling. "I shall tell my daughter why you are here."

Antelope Skin nodded and sat down on a blanket, his eyes following Old Elk to a screen at the far side of the lodge opposite the entranceway. He leaned in that direction and heard Old Elk talking to his daughter, then smiled when he heard her lilting voice.

"Yes," he whispered to himself. "She will urge her father to do as I wish him to do. She will do anything to be the wife of a powerful Ottawa chief."

His shoulders tightened and he hunched over when Searching Heart came from behind the screen with her father, dressed in a beautiful white doeskin robe. Her midnight black hair hung in long strands across her shoulders and down her back. Antelope Skin's breath was taken away by her sheer beauty.

She nodded a silent hello to him as she took her place opposite the fire from him on a soft pile of pelts. Her father sat down beside her and glared at Antelope Skin.

"Tell me your plan," Old Elk said, folding his legs, placing his hands on his knees.

"River Rat and I, along with Jake, the preacher's son, came up with a plan to get Silver Arrow's gold," Antelope Skin began, his voice slow and guarded. "But the plan fell through. Jake is no longer a part of it, and River Rat is not to be trusted. He knows my love for firewater. He plied me with it until I was mindless. I understand now firewater's evil. I will not touch it while you and I align ourselves to get the gold."

"Firewater is a curse to all Indians!" Old Elk grumbled. "It distorts the views of those who drink it."

"*Ae*, I know, and I will no longer drink it," Antelope Skin reiterated. "I give you my word. I will not touch it while you and I align ourselves to get the gold."

"I will trust you just so far, and if I see that you cannot keep your word, I warn you now that I will not go easy on you," Old Elk said flatly. "I will kill you myself if you bring harm to my people because of your negligence and love of firewater."

Antelope Skin paled. "I made a promise," he said thickly. "I will keep it." He shifted uneasily on the blanket. "Do you wish to hear my proposal?"

"Yes, continue," Old Elk said, glancing over at his daughter, then back at Antelope Skin. "My daughter wishes to hear it, also, since she will be the one who benefits most from it."

"*Ae*, she will benefit greatly," Antelope Skin said, his eyes gleaming as they raked over Searching Heart.

"Do not look at my daughter as though it is you who will marry her," Old Elk spat angrily. "Turn your eyes to me when you talk to me!"

Antelope Skin's gaze shifted quickly. "It is known now that my cousin has chosen the white woman to be his wife," he said dryly. "Silver Arrow has already taken gifts."

"Yes, I know all of that," Old Elk said, his teeth gritting. "Tell me something I do not know, or be gone with you so that my daughter and I can resume our sleep."

"You know as well as I that Searching Heart is far lovelier than the white woman and deserves to be Silver Arrow's wife," Antelope Skin said, smiling slowly. "There is a way to make that possible."

"I no longer wish to be Silver Arrow's wife," Searching Heart interrupted, stunning Antelope Skin with the dreaded news. "He is not the only fish in the sea."

"But he is the wealthiest!" Antelope Skin said.

"Yes, that is true, *if* the gold is real," Old Elk said, reaching over to pat his daughter's hand. "Continue, Antelope Skin. Tell us your plan."

"Kidnap the white woman, do away with her in a way that Silver Arrow will not know that it was your warriors who abducted her. Then who but your daughter will he wish to take as a wife in place of the dead white woman?" Antelope Skin said, leaning forward, anxious to see Old Elk's reaction.

Old Elk kneaded his chin thoughtfully. He gazed over at Searching Heart. When she did not smile or nod in a show of support of the plan, Old Elk frowned at Antelope Skin. "My daughter does not seem eager to agree to such a plan," he said thickly.

"Is your daughter the voice of your people?" Antelope Skin dared to ask. "Think about it, Old Elk.

If she married Silver Arrow, would she not also marry his gold? As beautiful as she is, as enticing as she can surely be, he will eventually tell her where the gold is. She can then tell you and your warriors where the gold is hidden. The gold will be yours, except for the portion that you will share with me because I am the originator of the plan that will get it for you."

"I do not, I *will* not, marry Silver Arrow," Searching Heart said. "I will never be second choice to any woman."

She rushed to her feet and ran behind the screen.

"There. You have your answer," Old Elk said, then smiled slowly. "But, Antelope Skin, because Silver Arrow has humiliated my daughter, I will enjoy helping you stop his marriage to the white woman by stealing away the woman of his desire. It will please me to see Silver Arrow hurt as he has hurt my precious daughter."

Feeling that he had not progressed very far in his plans to have the gold, Antelope Skin became disgruntled. His only hope was that once the white woman was no longer available, Silver Arrow would change his mind about Searching Heart, and she about him. Antelope Skin still believed that once they got together, the gold would eventually be shared between himself and Old Elk.

"Tomorrow?" Antelope Skin asked, chuckling beneath his breath.

"Tomorrow after sunup my warriors will watch for the white woman to be alone," Old Elk said, nodding. "That is when they will abduct her and bring her here as food for my dogs."

Antelope Skin's eyes gleamed with joy. In his mind's eye he was already counting the gold pieces as they fell between his fingers from his outstretched palm.

Chapter Thirty-six

Yvonne tossed and turned in her sleep, then awakened with a start when she heard a tiny voice cry out next to her.

She turned to Rustling Leaves, having brought the child to bed with her for the night to comfort her as they awaited news from Silver Arrow.

Yvonne's heart went out to Rustling Leaves. Although the child was fast asleep, her fears had not been left behind as she slept. It was obvious that she was having a bad dream: tears were flowing down her cheeks, and again she cried out.

Then Rustling Leaves lay quiet. Her breathing slowed and she slept peacefully.

Glancing out the window, Yvonne saw that daybreak was just brushing the darkness away. The sun was rising past the horizon, casting its beautiful orange glow heavenward.

Birds stirred in the trees, the robins' warbles making everything seem normal and wonderful as a fresh new morning offered its blessings to the world.

"But nothing is normal," Yvonne whispered, slipping from the bed. In her cotton nightgown she began pacing the floor, again glancing at the window. Her insides were aquiver from having heard nothing from Silver Arrow the long night through. That had to mean that the news was not good at his village, or he would have at least sent for Rustling Leaves.

"Was there a massacre as well as a fire?" Yvonne whispered to herself, a slow, agonizing fear circling her heart. "Did Silver Arrow even make it back to his village alive?"

Unable to stand the not knowing any longer, Yvonne yanked off her nightgown and tossed it on the floor. Taking no pains with what she wore, or with her hair, she quickly dressed in a riding skirt and white, long-sleeved blouse.

She sat on the floor and pulled on her riding boots, then left the room in a flurry. Before she left the house, she grabbed the rifle that she kept at the side of the door for protection.

Clutching it hard, she ran outside to the barn. She laid the rifle aside and quickly saddled her gentle mare. Determination etched on her face, she shoved the rifle in its gunboot, then took the reins and led the horse from the barn.

Not wanting to awaken anyone who might stop her flight to the Ottawa village, Yvonne walked her horse into the forest, only then swinging into the saddle and riding off in a hard gallop.

Everything was so peaceful and lovely at this time of morning, it seemed almost impossible that anything was wrong. The rays of the slowly rising sun flowed through the treetops on dew-studded spider webs, turning them into jewel-like prisms. The wildflowers were just opening their faces to the light, impatient bees hovering over them, waiting.

Birds flitted overhead and away from her as the horse's hooves broke the silence of the morning.

Then she became aware of something else. Up to now, everything had smelled fresh and sweet. But now, the closer she came to the Ottawa village, the more she was aware of a charred scent wafting along with the breeze.

She knew what was causing this terrible stench . . . the smoldering embers of the fire in Silver Arrow's village.

Suddenly Yvonne was aware of the total silence of the forest on all sides of her, whereas only moments ago there was such commotion overhead. She jumped when a doe leapt away in panic, its eyes wide.

Thinking that she was the cause of the doe's fright, Yvonne sighed with relief. For a moment there she had felt as though she was no longer alone, as though there were many eyes on her, watching her, waiting.

Yvonne screamed and drew a tight rein when she found her earlier instincts were right. Several Iroquois warriors came out of hiding on their mighty steeds, their faces painted threateningly with ocher and ash.

She quickly noticed that even their horses were painted with strange designs, all the more cause for her to be frightened, for these warriors seemed to be on the warpath.

Her heart pounding, Yvonne looked slowly around the circle of warriors, ascertaining that they were Iroquois. They did not wear their hair long and free as did the Ottawa. They had shaved most of their hair off, except for a tall roach that ran narrowly from the brow, back to the nape of the neck.

"What do you want?" Yvonne asked, slowly slipping her right hand toward her sheathed rifle.

She winced when one of the warriors reached over and yanked the rifle from the gunboot.

"Why are you doing this?" Yvonne asked, now cold from fear. "What do you want of me?"

She soon realized that her questions were wasted. It was apparent that none of the Indians spoke English, and if they did, they were determined not to communicate with her.

In their Iroquois tongue, one of the warriors said something to her as he grabbed her reins away. She stiffened as she watched another warrior edge his horse closer to her on the other side. She screamed and leaned low and clung to her horse for dear life when the warrior reached over and grabbed her around the waist, yanking.

"No!" she cried. "Don't take me captive! What have I done to deserve this? My father and I are friends with all Indians, even the Iroquois!"

When the warrior's fingers dug into her waist and grabbed her more solidly, causing her to lose her grip on her mare, Yvonne screamed again.

As the warrior pulled her onto his lap, she pummeled his chest with her fists. She kicked. She scratched.

Then she leaned over and bit the warrior on the arm.

She knew that was a mistake the minute she heard his loud shriek and saw the blood that her bite had inflicted. In one blow to her chin, she was rendered unconscious.

When she awakened, she froze inside when she discovered where she was. In a pen with dogs!

She cringed when she realized that she was sitting amidst large piles of their droppings, the stench overpowering. Repulsed, gulping hard, Yvonne crawled to a corner where she found a patch of crushed, clean grass.

She stiffened as one dog, and then another, came to her, curiously sniffing her. Then they sauntered away and lay down only a few feet from her, watching her.

She did not feel as threatened by them as she did by the men who had placed her there.

Slowly she lifted her eyes and looked upward. The wooden pen was covered to guarantee she would not escape.

Then her eyes shifted and she looked past the pen, cowering when she saw a group of children staring at her, giggling and pointing.

She stared back at them, then looked past them

at the circle of skin lodges, the wigwams large and colorfully painted. The Iroquois people seemed not to notice her sitting there, for they were busy going about their morning chores. There weren't even any sentries standing close by, guarding their prisoner.

But again, she thought despairingly, there was no cause for them to guard her. She was going nowhere. The poles which made this pen were tightly tied together.

There was no escape.

Now she realized just how foolish she had been to travel alone today when only last night there was proof of trouble brewing in the area. The fire at Silver Arrow's village was a warning she should not have ignored.

Yet she had been so driven to know if Silver Arrow was all right! How could she have been expected to wait any longer to find out?

Yvonne's heart skipped a beat when she recognized someone walking toward her.

"You!" she gasped out as Antelope Skin came and knelt just outside the pen, chuckling.

"The fire was not enough to make my cousin's life miserable," Antelope Skin hissed, his eyes narrowing. "Without you, he will finally suffer as I have suffered by having been born only a *witaw-wis-e-maw*, cousin. I had wanted his gold, to give me means to carry me far away from the disgrace of my people. Since I was not able to have that, at least I will get satisfaction by knowing that Silver Arrow now knows pain as even I have never known it."

"You . . . set . . . the fire?" Yvonne stammered, paling. "You are responsible for my abduction? And all because of your hate and jealousy for Silver Arrow? How could you hate one man so much?"

"I have always hated him," Antelope Skin said, his drawn voice revealing his torment. "I have envied his magic, his leadership, *everything* about him. It was not right that he should have it all. But our grandfather saw that he did. Ah, if only I could have gotten hold of the magic coat! Then Silver Arrow's magic would be gone! Alas, it seems it is Silver Arrow's until he hands it down to a son."

"Magic coat?" Yvonne asked, now recalling seeing the beautiful coat in Silver Arrow's lodge. Now she wished that she had asked him about it. She wondered just how much Silver Arrow would have explained to her. There were some things he would not share with anyone, it seemed. His cousin knew, only because he was someone who would pry until he learned everything about the man he despised.

"I have often brought attention to my cousin's strange, mystical powers, but no one of my village would heed my warnings," Antelope Skin said somberly. "Even you will never know the full mystery behind the man you would have married. Silver Arrow guards his magic as much as he guards his gold!"

Her head spinning from everything that Antelope Skin was saying, Yvonne tried to sort through it all. "How did you get Chief Old Elk to align himself with the likes of you?" Yvonne said as she saw the chief walking from his lodge toward the dog pen.

"It was not a hard thing to do when Old Elk's daughter, Searching Heart, was only recently shamed by Silver Arrow," Antelope Skin said, laughing.

"Searching Heart?" Yvonne murmured.

"Yes, Searching Heart," Old Elk said as he came and stood beside Antelope Skin. "You were chosen over my daughter to be Silver Arrow's bride. It was easy to decide to assist in your abduction. Now Silver Arrow will have *no* bride."

"He will come and rescue me," Yvonne said, her eyes flashing into the chief's.

"Chief Silver Arrow has more things on his mind today than a bride," Old Elk said, his eyes showing his smugness. "I hear that his village half burned yesterday. He has many duties as a chief today. By the time he has time for you, you will be gone from sight. There will be no trace of you left anywhere."

"What?" Yvonne said, feeling light-headed in her sudden fear. "You are going to kill me?"

"Not necessarily *I*," Old Elk said, looking slowly over at the penned-up dogs. He laughed, then strolled away again to his wigwam.

Yvonne looked slowly over at the dogs. "I . . . am . . . to be fed . . . to the dogs?" she asked, a sob catching in her throat.

Antelope Skin laughed boisterously and walked away, joining the chief in his lodge for the morning meal.

Trembling, seized by a desperation to get free,

Yvonne crawled around the pen, gripping and shaking the poles. But none even as much as shifted in the ground.

She tried to untie the knots that held the poles together. She only rendered her fingers sore with the effort.

Exhausted, feeling defeated, she crawled back to the corner and huddled there, her knees drawn up to her breast as she watched the dogs. She had always had a rapport with animals, and she felt a glimmer of hope. The only way those dogs would consume her was if she were dead and . . .

She closed her eyes at the terrible, sickening thoughts that assailed her.

But when she heard soft footsteps outside the pen, Yvonne opened her eyes. She found a beautiful woman standing there, looking in at her with sullen, sorry eyes. Surely this was Searching Heart.

"Set me free, Searching Heart," Yvonne begged, crawling to the poles, gripping them until her knuckles whitened. "Please? Oh, Lord, Searching Heart, please don't leave me here like this. What have I ever done to deserve this? I can't help it if Silver Arrow turned down your father's offer of a bride price. Please don't hold it against me."

Sobbing, Searching Heart ran away, disappearing quickly into her father's wigwam.

Downcast and filled with hopelessness, Yvonne crawled back to the corner and huddled, shivering. She flinched when one of the dogs walked slowly toward her. She cowered back against the poles, then sighed with relief when the dog lay down beside her and fell asleep.

365

Chapter Thirty-seven

"She is gone!" Rustling Leaves cried as she shook Anthony awake. "Yvonne is gone! When I did not find her in bed beside me I went outside. I thought she might be at the river washing her hair. That is the habit of the Ottawa women most mornings. But she was not there. I saw her nowhere!"

Fear gripping his heart, Anthony left his bed. "Child, go and get dressed," he said, placing a gentle hand on Rustling Leaves' shoulder.

He limped from his room and shouted up the ladder to the bedroom lofts. "Jake!" he said. "Come down here. Immediately!"

Jake came to the ladder and peered down at his father. "What's wrong?" he asked, wiping sleep from his eyes. "Father, there is such alarm in your

366

voice. What's happened?"

"Yvonne," Anthony said. "Yvonne's gone. I can only think of one place she would be. Jake, she has surely gone to Silver Arrow's village. I should have known nothing would keep her from going. She is not the sort just to stand back and wait for news to come to her. I'm sure she has gone to see for herself what happened at Silver Arrow's village. I shudder at the thought of what may have happened."

"You fear a massacre?" Jake asked, grabbing his breeches and stepping into them.

Stanley scurried from the bed. "What's wrong?" he asked, slipping on his eyeglasses.

"Yes, I fear a massacre," Anthony said, turning on a heel and returning to his room to dress.

"What's wrong?" Stanley asked more loudly, grabbing Jake's arm when he got no response.

Jake turned to him. "We think Yvonne has gone to the Ottawa village," he said thickly. "If she went out on her own, alone, who is to say what might happen to her? Some maniac is out there doing harm to innocent people."

A quick sob lodged in Stanley's throat. He hurried into his clothes and went down the ladder behind Jake.

Rustling Leaves was standing there, pale, afraid, and trembling. Stanley took her hand. They silently waited for Anthony to come from his room.

And when he did, and Jake was armed with a rifle, they all left together for the barn. Anthony quickly prepared the horse and buggy while Jake saddled his horse.

"Come, children," Anthony said, hurrying into the buggy, grabbing the reins. "We must make haste. Who is to say how long Yvonne has been gone?"

"I'll ride on ahead," Jake said, his horse whinnying and snorting as he sank his heels into its flanks and rode off in a hard gallop.

His heart thudding with fear, Anthony slapped the horse's reins and sent the buggy rattling down the lane, toward the Ottawa village.

Chapter Thirty-eight

Silver Arrow awoke from a troubled sleep. He had overslept this morning because he had worked almost until sunup helping his people tear away the burned portions of their lodges so that new ones could be erected today.

He planned to go to the Iroquois village and again demand answers from Chief Old Elk. Though he had been there more often than he liked of late, another trip was necessary.

Silver Arrow would be able to know just from talking with Old Elk whether or not he had sent his warriors on this mission which had wiped away half of Silver Arrow's people's lodges.

Had any of his people died during the fire, Silver Arrow would not have waited to ask questions. He would have sent fiery arrows into the skin lodges at Old Elk's village, and asked questions later!

But the dream, the horrors of it, had changed everything for Silver Arrow. Holding his temples, he staggered from his bed.

Sweat poured from his brow as he relived the dream in his mind's eye. He had seen his White Swan in the dream. She had not been home, safe, waiting for him to come to her and tell her of the tragedy that had befallen his people the prior evening.

Instead, in his dream she had been . . .

"No, it was only a dream!" he cried out as he tried to shake away the memory of it.

But no matter how hard he tried, the dream clung to him like the swamp debris after he had searched in the murky waters for his sister.

In the dream, his White Swan, his beloved, had been imprisoned in a dog's pen. The stench of it had been all around her. Filth covered her clothes and was smeared across her lovely face. Snarling at her, dogs were slowly surrounding her as she cowered against the posts of the pen, trembling with intense fear.

Then Silver Arrow grew hot with anger and his eyes filled with fire as he recalled something else about the dream. "Antelope Skin was a part of it!" he cried, curling his fingers into tight fists at his sides.

His heart pounded harder the more he remembered. "Also Chief Old Elk!" he said, his voice an angry whisper.

He paced back and forth. "My grandmother put

much faith in dreams," he whispered, absently raking his long, lean fingers through his hair. "Should I?"

He hastily pulled his fringed buckskin breeches on, stepped into his moccasins, and shirtless, left his lodge. The morning sun was high enough now to momentarily blind him. Shielding his eyes with a hand, he gazed intensely at the horseman whose presence was bringing the Ottawa people to the doors of those lodges that had not burned.

Silver Arrow's heart leapt with fear when he recognized the rider.

"Jake!" he gasped out, knowing that Jake would have no reason to be there unless he had some bad news to tell the Ottawa.

Silver Arrow first thought of his sister Rustling Leaves. Silver Arrow had left her in the care of Jake's family. Yet, knowing that Anthony would guard Rustling Leaves with his life, he doubted that she would be the cause of Jake's sudden appearance.

That left only one more person who might be in trouble. And the thought of news being brought to him about his White Swan made him feel ill inside.

Jake wheeled his horse to a shimmying halt next to Silver Arrow as Silver Arrow ran and met him.

"Why have you come in such haste to my village?" Silver Arrow asked in a rush. "What news have you brought to me?"

He looked past Jake, knowing that if his White Swan were not in trouble, she would be with Jake even now, for she would not have let Jake leave the house without her if there was news of his sister to relay to him.

When he saw no one else approaching, his heart sank. He dreaded hearing what Jake had to say; yet he was anxious, too. If his woman was in any trouble, he would save her!

"Yvonne!" Jake said, breathless from the hard ride. He looked over his shoulder when he heard his father's horse and buggy rushing into the outer edges of the village.

"What about my White Swan?" Silver Arrow demanded.

"She's gone," Jake said. "She left her bed before anyone else was up this morning. Tell me she's here, Silver Arrow. Is she?"

Jake looked anxiously past Silver Arrow, hoping that Yvonne would step from the longhouse at any moment, proof that she had gone to Silver Arrow and had stayed the night with him.

But he knew quickly by Silver Arrow's reaction that she had not come here. She had disappeared.

Silver Arrow was so stunned, he was momentarily rendered speechless. Again the dream came to him in flashes.

The pen. His woman smeared with dog feces. The dogs snarling as they slowly approached her.

Then Antelope Skin and Chief Old Elk standing there, laughing at Silver Arrow's future wife!

"Silver Arrow, did you hear what I said?" Jake asked as he slid quickly from his saddle. He turned and gazed at his father as he came and drew rein behind Jake's horse. Everyone clambered from the buggy.

Anthony came and stood beside Jake. He reached a hand out for Silver Arrow, seeing that he was obviously in some state of shock over the news.

Silver Arrow came suddenly to his senses when Rustling Leaves wrapped her arms around his legs, sobbing. "She is not here or she would be standing beside you," she cried. Tears streaming from her eyes, she gazed up at Silver Arrow. "Where is she, big brother? Where is White Swan?"

Seeing his sister's distress, Silver Arrow reached down and lifted his sister into his arms. He held her close, comforting her with soft words spoken in Ottawa.

Then he placed her back on the ground and squared his shoulders. He looked from Jake to Anthony, then to the throng of his people who now stood around him, questions in their eyes.

"My warriors, arm yourselves well!" Silver Arrow shouted, raising a fist into the air to show his anger. "My woman! She is gone! I know where! We will go and rescue her! We will kill many if we must to get to her!"

"How do you know where she is?" Anthony asked as he stepped closer to Silver Arrow. "Have you received word of her abduction? If so, why didn't you alert us about it?"

"My knowledge of where she is came to me in a dream," Silver Arrow said, placing a comforting hand on Anthony's shoulder. "Let us hope that my dream did not come too late."

He did not tell Anthony his worst fears, that if they did not get to her soon, there might not be any traces of her left.

That was surely Chief Old Elk's plan, or he would not be foolish enough to steal her away and keep her long enough for Silver Arrow to discover her there.

"There is no time for war paint or a war dance!" Silver Arrow shouted to his warriors, who were now gripping their weapons, awaiting their chief's further commands. "We shall ride now to the Iroquois village!"

There was a rush to get their horses.

Silver Arrow sent a young brave to fetch his pinto stallion, and sent another brave into his lodge to get his rifle.

Then he turned to Anthony and placed a gentle hand on his shoulder. "I know that you are anxious to know the fate of your daughter," he said thickly. "But I urge you to stay here and await my return."

His gaze shifted to Rustling Leaves and Stanley. "I ask you to stay with the children," he said tightly. "And I ask you to pray many prayers to your God that I return with White Swan safely on my horse with me."

"I will say many prayers," Anthony said, swallowing hard. "May God be with you, Silver Arrow. Godspeed."

"Silver Arrow, I'm going with you," Jake said, swinging himself into his saddle. "I want to do what I can to rescue my sister."

"You are welcome to ride at my left side, while Four Horns, my friend in all things, rides at my right," Silver Arrow said. When his horse was brought to him, he grabbed the reins and swiftly mounted.

Sobered by the weight of responsibility, he grabbed his rifle from the young brave who had gone for it, then thrust it into the air.

"Let us ride!" he shouted.

The ground shook with the weight of many horses as they thundered away from the village.

Anthony watched until he could see them no longer, then gently ushered the children inside Silver Arrow's longhouse.

To busy himself, Anthony built a slow fire in the fireplace. He gave a gentle smile to the lovely woman who entered with a platter of food.

"Thank you," Anthony said, taking the platter.

She smiled sympathetically, then turned and left.

Not hungry, Anthony handed the tray to Rustling Leaves, who also was not hungry. She passed it on to Stanley.

Stanley peered down at the food, gulped hard with revulsion at the thought of eating while his stomach was tied up in knots, then took the platter to the table and left it there.

He sat down on a blanket before the fire with Rustling Leaves.

Anthony brought the rocking chair that Princess Pretty Hawk always sat in beside the fire and sat down. As he slowly rocked back and forth, he prayed, the children listening, tears streaming from their eyes.

Chapter Thirty-nine

Hugging herself, Yvonne looked guardedly at the dogs. She was keenly aware that they had not been fed while she had been in the pen with them. Some were so gaunt their bones were visible. That had to mean they had gone for many days without eating. Perhaps even longer, she thought fearfully to herself.

She was also keenly aware that the dogs were showing more interest in her than seemed normal. They would saunter up to her and show their fangs. Others would pace and back and forth as they stared at her.

For certain her charm with animals no longer worked. She trembled at the thought of one of the dogs suddenly deciding that she might make a good meal. If one tore into her, and her blood was

spilled, surely they would all follow its lead and
. . . and . . .

"So you are still here?" Antelope Skin said as
he walked toward her, carrying a large drumstick
of some sort of animal.

Yvonne's mouth watered as she watched him
yank a large bite of the meat away and chew it.

"Where did you expect me to be?" she asked,
lifting her chin defiantly.

"I am sure by now you have figured out why
you are imprisoned with the dogs," Antelope Skin
said, taking a quick step away when the dogs
picked up the scent of the meat, scrambling and
falling over each other as they tried to get through
the poles of the pen to get to it.

"You idiot, get out of here with that food,"
Yvonne cried, fear gripping the pit of her stomach
when the dogs suddenly grew so out of control
that they rolled all over the ground, fighting, yelping, and biting one another.

"Why would I do that?" Antelope Skin chuckled. "It just might hurry things along. Do you not
see the mercy in that? Am I not a kindhearted
man to want to see you out of your misery?"

"You are a horrid fiend," Yvonne hissed. "But
what I am surprised at is that River Rat was not
in on this meanness with you."

"River Rat?" Antelope Skin said. "*Ae*, he was my
partner in crime until he chickened out. Do you
not know that he was the white man who helped
lure Rustling Leaves from the schoolyard? He
wanted my cousin's gold almost more than me."

He frowned at Yvonne. "But it seems now that

the gold will still belong to my cousin," he said sarcastically. "His powers are stronger than mine. He was blessed with our grandfather's magical coat, not I. By right of inheritance, the best of our family's possessions have gone to Silver Arrow. I will just have to accept it and take from life what it hands me."

"I have heard mention of a magical coat more than once," Yvonne said. "How could any coat be magical?"

"Because it belonged to Silver Arrow's grandfather, who was, himself, steeped in magic," Antelope Skin said, then turned with a start when he felt the thundering of approaching horses in the ground beneath his bare feet. He knew those vibrations well. He had been taught to know them, to alert himself to an attack on his people.

Alarm set in, for he knew that he was not among his people. He was with his people's enemy! And he had been wrong to think that Silver Arrow would be too cowardly to come again so soon to the Iroquois village. No one else had cause to storm the Iroquois village with such a multitude of horsemen.

Word had surely reached Silver Arrow of his woman's abduction. He had taken time from his own people's needs to search for the white woman.

Panic filled Antelope Skin. As close as he could tell, the horses were now at the outskirts of the village. He had no time to escape.

"You look as though you've seen a ghost," Yvonne said. She moved to her knees and turned her eyes in the direction of Antelope Skin's, puzzled when she saw nothing out of the ordinary.

Antelope Skin turned toward her, glared, then broke into a run toward Old Elk's lodge.

Searching Heart came from her father's lodge and ran over to Yvonne. She fell to her knees and clutched the poles. "Do not despair," she whispered. "I will set you free tonight." She looked from side to side, then slipped a small knife from beneath her skirt and held it out to Yvonne.

"Watch out for the dogs," Searching Heart whispered in English as Yvonne crawled quickly over to her and took the knife. "The dogs are hungry enough now to eat anything. Even you."

"Yes, I am very aware of that," Yvonne whispered back, wrapping the knife into the folds of her skirt. "And thank you, Searching Heart. I owe you my life."

"I will set you free tonight after Father and everyone else in my village are asleep," Searching Heart said, then rose to her feet and ran back toward her lodge.

She stopped in midstep when her father came from the lodge, red-faced and angry, Antelope Skin beside him. Afraid that they would realize where she had been, she made a sharp left and rushed into the forest at the edge of the village. She hid behind a tree and watched her father shouting at his warriors. She wondered why he was readying them for an attack.

She then saw why. At the other edge of the village many Ottawa warriors appeared on their horses, then fell back when they saw the many

Iroquois braves making a stand to stop their approach.

"I will circle around to the right side of the village!" Silver Arrow shouted. He motioned to Four Horns. "Take the warriors around to the left. When you see that the time is right, attack."

"Should we wait for you before attacking?" Four Horns asked, his hand gripping a rifle.

"No, do not wait for me," Silver Arrow said. "Did you not see the dog pen at the far side of the village? Did you not see my woman with the dogs, as though she were a dog, herself? I will find a way to release her before I join the fight!"

"I'll go with you, Silver Arrow," Jake said. "I wish to help you release my sister."

"*Kau*, it is best that I, in my own way, release her," Silver Arrow said, frowning at Jake. "You can best serve me and your sister by doing as I ask. Go now. Your part in her release will be appreciated."

Jake saw the determination etched on Silver Arrow's face. "All right," he said, his voice drawn. "I will do as you say. But if I see that you need me, nothing will stop me from coming to your assistance, do you understand?"

"You will be kept busy enough fighting off the Iroquois warriors," Silver Arrow said. He swung his horse to the right and rode away, his warriors fanning out to assume their positions.

As Silver Arrow made his way in a wide circle behind the skin lodges, he cringed when he heard the first spattering of gunfire, and then the war cries and screams that ensued.

"I must get to her in time," Silver Arrow whispered to himself. He raised his eyes heavenward. "Great Spirit, keep her safe. If she should die, I will want to join her!"

He rode low beneath the tree limbs, then drew a tight rein when he saw someone hiding behind a tree.

Searching Heart!

Wary of the way she looked at him now as she stepped from behind the tree, Silver Arrow knew that if he must, he would kill the lovely Iroquois maiden.

If she so much as looked as though she was going to shout his name, to alert others that he was there, he would send a knife through her heart. Hoping that it wouldn't be necessary, he yanked his knife from its sheath at his waist.

"No, do not use that on me," Searching Heart softly cried, slowly backing away from him. "I am not responsible for the white woman being held captive. I have told her I will release her tonight." She held a pleading hand out to Silver Arrow. "Please spare me. It is my father and Antelope Skin who plotted against you. Not I."

"Antelope Skin?" Silver Arrow said, remembering his dream in which he had seen Antelope Skin with the Iroquois chief.

"Step aside," Silver Arrow said, slipping the knife back inside its sheath.

Searching Heart nodded. She turned and ran deeper into the forest until Silver Arrow could no longer see her.

He then rode his horse only a few more feet and stopped and dismounted. After tying his reins on a low tree limb, he went to the edge of the village and saw Yvonne. She was crouching, sobbing, in a corner of the pen. The dogs were pacing and howling, the gunfire having frightened them.

He looked around to see how close the Iroquois warriors were to the pen. They were quite a distance, yet Silver Arrow knew that if he ran out into the open he would be detected and downed quickly with a bullet or an arrow.

"My powers again benefit me and my woman," he whispered.

He threw down his rifle and stretched his arms out on each side of him.

Chapter Forty

Yvonne trembled with fright. She sobbed uncontrollably as she watched the devastation all around her. She was glad that Searching Heart had fled into the forest. At least her life would be spared.

She gulped and tensed as she watched arrows flash. She stifled a gasp behind her hand as she listened to the bullets whistle sharply. The Iroquois men were falling everywhere from their wounds, the women being spared as they dragged their children inside their skin lodges.

One by one the Iroquois warriors fell, while only a few Ottawa warriors winced as bullets grazed the flesh of an arm, or entered a shoulder, or an arrow pierced a leg.

It was the blood, the screams, the cries, and

then the sight of her brother fighting among the Ottawa warriors that made Yvonne die a slow death inside.

But no matter how hard she searched for Silver Arrow, he was nowhere in sight.

It seemed that his warriors were fighting without him. His best friend Four Horns was there. Others that she recognized were there.

Then where was Silver Arrow?

Her heart sank with a thought. What if he had been shot when they had first launched their attack?

"No," she cried. "Please don't let it be true!"

There was loud whirring of wings overhead, and then a blur of black as a large crow flew past her.

But as she peered more closely around her, she no longer saw the crow.

Instead . . . instead . . . she saw Silver Arrow outside the dog pen, tearing first one pole out of the ground and then another.

"Silver Arrow?" Yvonne gasped, her knees weak as she tried to stand.

Tears of happiness splashed from his eyes as he pushed inside the pen and grabbed her up into his arms.

"Thank you, oh, thank you for coming," she whispered, clinging to his neck.

The dogs scampered free on both sides of Silver Arrow as he carried Yvonne to safety in the forest.

Searching Heart stepped into view and watched Silver Arrow place Yvonne on his horse and ride away.

By the time Silver Arrow reached the other side of the village, where the attack had been launched, the fight was over.

Jake rode over and drew rein beside Silver Arrow. He reached a hand out to Yvonne's face. "Thank God," he said breathlessly. His gaze swept over her. He frowned darkly. "How could anyone have done this to you? How?"

"Hold her awhile for me," Silver Arrow said, slipping Yvonne into Jake's arms.

Yvonne cuddled close to her brother, gave him a soft kiss on the cheek, then, feeling safe, watched as the dead were accounted for, the old Iroquois chief among them.

Antelope Skin was brought to Silver Arrow, a rope around his neck.

Yvonne's heart went out to Searching Heart when she came and discovered that her father was dead, as well as many of his warriors.

The children and women of the village came from their lodges, wailing and bending over their dearly departed.

Searching Heart, her head hanging, went to Yvonne. "I know that I should hold hate in my heart for the Ottawa for killing my father, and so many of my people, but my father brought this on himself for how he treated you," she murmured, wiping tears from her eyes. "I no longer wish to stay with my people. They will hate me, for they will blame my father for the deaths of their loved ones. Can I go with you? Can I stay with you?"

"It is Silver Arrow's decision," Yvonne said,

slipping from Jake's arms to the ground. She took Searching Heart into her arms and held her. "But I will encourage it, for you see, I will soon be his wife. He will listen to my suggestions."

Searching Heart caught Jake staring at her as she gazed over Yvonne's shoulder. Through her grief she found enough feelings to smile at him.

He smiled back, then watched her as she went with Yvonne to Silver Arrow to plead her case.

Silver Arrow agreed. "*Ae*, Searching Heart, you can stay with my people, but do not bring trouble to my village," he said sternly. "You are a beautiful woman. Do not stir up my men's hearts into feuding among one another over who will have you."

"I promise not to cause problems," she murmured. "I will stay here long enough to see to my father's burial. Then I will come. Thank you. You are so generous to the daughter of a man who wronged you."

"A daughter cannot rule a father's life, nor his heart," Silver Arrow said, then rode away.

When they reached the Ottawa village, Antelope Skin was questioned about Rustling Leaves' abduction and the fire. He admitted to being involved in both, and to planning Yvonne's capture as well. Everyone was in a state of shock to know that someone of their own village would be so evil-hearted.

"It is time for me to hand down your sentencing for the crimes you have admitted to," Silver Arrow said, looking Antelope Skin in the eye. "Normally a man guilty of crimes against his people would be banished from one's tribe. But that is not enough for all that you have done. I sentence you to death."

Panic gripping him, Antelope Skin grabbed the rope from the warrior who held it tightly around his neck. He turned and ran toward the edge of the village.

Silver Arrow lost no time in going inside his lodge to grab the bow that was strung with his grandfather's hair, then also a lone arrow. He stepped outside again and notched the arrow to the bow.

He aimed and shot.

The arrow pierced Antelope Skin's back. He fell forward onto his knees, then crumpled to the ground, dead.

Silver Arrow went and stood over Antelope Skin. "It was only right that the bow strung with my grandfather's hair would be used to kill such a traitor as you," he hissed. "It was as though my grandfather were here, himself, doing the killing, for, Antelope Skin, surely he looks from the heavens and is ashamed to know you have the same blood as his flowing through your veins."

Eyes wide, Yvonne went to Silver Arrow and took his hand in hers. They exchanged warm smiles.

Rustling Leaves and Stanley ran up and stood next to them and stared down at Antelope Skin.

"It is over," Silver Arrow said, giving them a look of reassurance.

Chapter Forty-one

For two weeks Silver Arrow had labored to help put the Ottawa village back together.

Now he felt that he could take time for himself. Shortly after the morning had broken, Yvonne had exchanged vows with him at her father's church. He had proudly stood at his White Swan's side as her father performed the ceremony in the white man's tradition.

Silver Arrow had not resented her wanting to have this sort of wedding, as long as she agreed to also join hands in love and marriage in the ceremony they were at this moment sharing at the Ottawa village.

Standing beside him, in the presence of all his people and her family, Yvonne looked adoringly up at Silver Arrow. She was so proud of him for so many reasons. Besides her father, Silver Arrow was the most gentle, caring man she'd ever known.

Feeling beautiful in the fringed, snow white doeskin dress that Silver Arrow had asked her to wear on their wedding day, Yvonne watched him expectantly as he spoke his vows to her.

It would soon be dusk. Firelight from the huge outdoor fire played fitfully over her dress, leggings, and moccasins, all of which were richly embroidered with dyed porcupine quills in pink and green.

Strands of *wampum*, beads, woven into curious shapes, hung about her neck, matching those that Silver Arrow wore around his. Elaborate beads were wound into one long braid down her back, which also matched those he wore in his hair.

Yvonne could smell the sweet fragrance of the lilies of the valley that she had placed above each ear. She had plucked the flowers from her garden before dawn this morning as she had prepared herself for this glorious, long-yearned-for wedding.

Many more flowers from her garden were strewn around the ground. Clasped in her hands was a special gift from Silver Arrow—a gorgeous fan of white swan feathers.

He had also lavished her with gifts of beaver furs and lovely necklaces and bracelets, but the most beautiful of all was the white rabbit-skin robe and matching blanket that he'd made with his own hands after he had first seen her, already knowing she would be his wife.

She would treasure them for the rest of her life. They were such a dazzling white, and ever so soft, it was almost like stroking the wings of a butterfly when she ran her fingers over them.

"My White Swan, I take you as my wife and will cherish you and protect you for as long as you will live," Silver Arrow said, his appraisal of her giving heat to his stare as he gazed into her eyes.

He was acutely aware of the eyes of his people on him as he took a white woman as his wife. He felt no resentment in their stares. And he knew that the women of the village had prepared well for the ceremony. Delicious aromas came from the many platters of food around the roaring fire.

Fish, wild game, vegetables, fruits, and berries would please the stomachs of his people once the vows had been exchanged. Also much honey drink had been prepared to soothe the thirst that would be brought on by the richness of the meats.

Having come to his woman today barefoot, and dressed in only a breechclout, Silver Arrow continued his vows. He was aware of the moon shifting slowly upward in the sky, the sun now gone from sight.

His heart was like a steady drumbeat inside his chest, the hour drawing nigh when he and his woman would be sharing more than vows on the softest of furs inside his lodge. He could even now envision her lying there, his wife, his lover, as she eagerly reached her arms out for him. He would go to her and love her, as though it were their first time together.

He would leave her breathless with the powers

of his lovemaking tonight. And they would make love until the sun rose again in the sky on the morrow!

Silver Arrow continued speaking his vows. "My woman, my White Swan, I will not only cherish you for as long as you live, but I will be kind to you," he said. "Our hearts will beat as though they are one until a child born of our love sleeps beneath our roof, adding another breath to listen to, adding to our happiness . . . our joy."

He framed her face between his hands, causing tears of joy to leap to Yvonne's eyes as she gazed into his. "My woman," he continued softly. "You are now my wife, oh, so precious to me, forevermore."

Yvonne trembled with excitement as he drew her lips to his. She held the delicate fan away from her with one hand, then crept her free arm around his neck. She had been told that his vows would speak for them both; hers weren't necessary.

Just as simple as that, they were now married twice in one day. Yvonne smiled to think that surely anyone who spoke vows twice could never expect anything but wondrous, thrilling happiness.

Silver Arrow gave her one more lingering kiss, then stepped to her side. He led her down onto a soft pelt beside the fire, near her family who sat on a blanket with Rustling Leaves.

Yvonne leaned around Silver Arrow and slid her gaze over to Jake, who sat with Searching Heart. When Searching Heart had come to live in the Ottawa village, it had not taken long for Jake to find her and become acquainted with her.

It had gone farther than that now. Rumors abounded that soon they also would be sharing marriage vows.

But since Searching Heart had been practically banished from her village, there would be no Iroquois ceremony. Anthony would proudly marry them in his church.

And Anthony knew to expect another wedding in the future, in which he would lose another child to the Indian world. It was apparent to everyone that Rustling Leaves and Stanley would love one another forever. Such devotion as theirs could surely never change.

The drums beat, the wooden flutes played, and the rattles sent off their soft, rhythmic sounds as everyone joined in the celebration.

Some were eating. Some danced and sang.

All in all, it was a day that Yvonne would never forget.

"Skunk?" Yvonne asked, her thoughts wrenched elsewhere. An uncontrollable shudder raced through her. "This is skunk on my platter?"

"Is it a taste you do not like?" Silver Arrow asked, smiling amusedly at her.

"Well, I must admit, it does taste like chicken," Yvonne said, smiling at him. Then she laughed. "Yes, it is good, but, darling, you will soon learn that I am so softhearted about animals that I hate to see any animal killed to be eaten."

"I do not like to kill either, but it is required to keep my people fed and clothed," Silver Arrow said, watching her drink honey water from a cup, loving the way her lips puckered against the rim of the cup. He could hardly contain his impatience to be alone with her.

"I understand," Yvonne said, nodding. "It is the same in the homes of white people. I have always cooked the meat brought to me. I would never want to starve my family because of my personal beliefs."

Having eaten enough, Yvonne shoved the platter aside. "Darling, now that I am your wife and I will live among your people, what will my duties as wife be?" she asked. "I never want to disappoint you."

"Even if you could not cook, clean, or sew, I would not be disappointed in you," Silver Arrow said warmly.

"But there are things I must do," Yvonne said, moving on her knees before him. "Please tell me."

"There are many things that you will learn must be done only as the seasons change," Silver Arrow said, reaching for her hands. "The women are in charge of growing crops for food. They gather maple sap in the early spring, and berries in the summer. The women also are skillful at weaving."

"What else?" Yvonne asked when Silver Arrow paused to hug Rustling Leaves as she came to him, then ran away again with Stanley to play with the other children.

"The women gather cornhusks, cattail leaves, and other reeds," Silver Arrow said. "Those are dyed into bright colors and woven into mats, bags, and baskets. . . ."

Stanley was suddenly there, Rustling Leaves at his side. "Now that you are married, Yvonne, can I live with you and Silver Arrow?" he asked anxiously. "Can I live with you . . . and . . . Rustling Leaves?"

Stunned by the question, Yvonne glanced over at her father, who was talking with a group of Ottawa warriors. Her gaze shifted to the lovely woman standing beside her father . . . Delores Edwards, the new schoolmarm.

Yvonne took Stanley's hands. "Honey, Father would be so lonely without you," she murmured.

"But I would be so lonely without *you*," Stanley said, his eyes imploring her. "Please? Please talk to Father. Let me stay with you."

"Stanley, you know that both Silver Arrow and I would love to have you," Yvonne said, hating to see the disappointment in her brother's eyes.

Again she glanced over at Anthony and Delores. There was soon to be another marriage. Theirs!

"Stanley, Father will soon marry," Yvonne said softly. "You will then finally have a true mother. Don't you see? Father will also finally have a true family. You would disappoint him if you asked to live with me, instead of with him and his new bride."

Stanley thought for a moment, then smiled. "I love Father too much to disappoint him," he said. "Yes, I will stay with him and his new bride."

"You can come as often as you wish to visit me and my family," Yvonne said. "You can spend the night as often as you wish. I do know your feelings for Rustling Leaves. And I know how you enjoy being with the other children."

"Coming for special visits might be more fun, anyhow," Stanley said, grabbing Rustling Leaves' hand. "It will give me and Rustling Leaves something always to look forward to."

"Sweet brother of mine, you are often wise beyond your years," Yvonne said, laughing. She hugged Stanley, then Rustling Leaves. "Tonight Rustling Leaves is staying with you at *your* house, while Silver Arrow and I have our first night of marriage alone."

"We can have a big bowl of popcorn, Rustling Leaves," Stanley said excitedly. "And I will let you beat me in a game of checkers."

"You will let me . . . ?" Rustling Leaves began, hesitated, then laughed with him. "*Ae*, and I would love winning."

They ran off again, soon laughing and dancing with the other children.

"You handled that well," Silver Arrow said, slipping an arm around Yvonne's waist, drawing her closer to his side.

"I'm so happy," she said, looking adoringly into his eyes. "I hope nothing ever spoils it."

"Even circumstances beyond our control cannot destroy our happiness," Silver Arrow said softly.

"Are you as happy as I am?" Yvonne asked, placing a hand on his cheek.

"*Ae*, as happy as the brown thrush that sits daily upon the uppermost branches of a basswood tree which stands nearby upon the hill," Silver Arrow said huskily. "Early in the morning, as the sun peeps from the east, this brown thrush will begin his warbling songs. So often I have listened and seemed to understand some of its utterances."

He laughed, then continued. "It seems to say, 'Good morning, good morning! Arise! Arise! Come along! Come along!'" he said. "It repeats every word twice. It has a language that the Great Spirit has given to it. Every bird of the forest understands what it says. It was appointed to preach to other birds, to tell them to be happy, to be thankful for the blessings they enjoy among the summer green branches of the forest, and the plenty of wild fruits to eat."

"That is so beautiful," Yvonne said, sighing. "You are a special man—my husband!"

Her gaze shifted when Anthony came to her and took her hand, Delores clinging to his arm.

"Sweetheart, I think it's time for me and Delores and the children to leave," he said, glancing up at the bright moon in the heavens. He smiled into her eyes, and then looked at Silver Arrow. "It has been a wonderful day. And as the night wraps its arms around you, I hope that you will be happy together in the bonds of marriage."

"We were happy the moment we looked into each other's eyes that very first time," Silver Arrow offered. He placed a gentle hand on Anthony's shoulder. "Thank you for accepting my bride price. Thank you for sharing your daughter with me for a lifetime."

"The pleasure is mine to have you as a son-in-law," Anthony said, glancing over at Jake as he and Searching Heart went to Jake's horse and buggy and slipped off.

"Come on," Stanley said, tugging at his father's free hand. "If we don't get home soon it will be too late for checkers and popcorn."

Anthony laughed. "Yes, you'd best not miss your checker game tonight," he said. He gave Yvonne a long hug, then Silver Arrow.

Delores then shared in the hugs.

Yvonne watched them go to their horse and buggy.

Stanley and Rustling Leaves took turns hugging Yvonne and Silver Arrow good-bye, then ran to the buggy.

Yvonne watched them until they were gone from sight, then she turned wondering eyes up at Silver Arrow. "I've had enough to eat and drink," she whispered as she leaned closer to his ear. "I've had enough of everything, my love . . . but you. Can we go now to our home? I so yearn for your lips, my darling. Please?"

"My woman, who is now my wife, is tempting in the way she speaks and looks at me," Silver Arrow said, chuckling.

He looked slowly around him. Everyone seemed to be enjoying themselves so much he doubted they would notice that their chief and his bride had left, to have the rest of the night to themselves.

He turned to Yvonne. He took her hands and urged her to her feet as he rose to his full height. "Come," he whispered, whisking her away into the darker shadows of night, where the fire's glow did not reach so brilliantly.

Giggling, Yvonne glanced over her shoulder at

the celebration, where food was still being consumed, and where there were even more dancers than before as they whirled in time with the rhythmic drums, rattles and flutes.

She then stepped inside Silver Arrow's longhouse with him. Silver Arrow kicked the door shut as he lifted Yvonne into his arms. "My wife, my woman, my very soul," he said huskily, then gave her a kiss that made her weak and dizzy.

He held her close as he carried her to the fireplace where a soft fire was burning to ward off the chill of the early September night.

"We have something that must be done before going to our bed," he said, placing Yvonne on her feet.

"What must we do?" Yvonne asked, too anxious to make love not to start undressing even though she knew there was some reason to hesitate. She bent down and took off one moccasin and then the other, watching Silver Arrow pick up a fistful of sweetgrass.

When he spread the sweetgrass on the hearth and touched it with a piece of wood that was aflame at the tip, she knelt down beside him.

"My wife, to purify our bodies tonight before we make love for the first time as man and wife, do as I do," he said. He plucked some of the sweetgrass up and spread it in the palm of his left hand. This he held out toward Yvonne. "My White Swan, touch the sweetgrass with your lips and fingers," he said.

Yvonne questioned him with her eyes for a moment, then did as he told her.

"Raise the skirt of your dress," he said softly. "I will now bless your limbs as I brush them with the sweetgrass."

Not wanting to question him about anything else tonight, Yvonne did as she was told, then sat back and watched him bless himself by doing all that he had told her to do.

Once the ritual was over, Silver Arrow stood over her. He reached a hand out toward her. "Stand before me," he said huskily, the passion in his eyes firing her insides.

Swallowed almost whole by her intense love of him, Yvonne stood slowly before him and waited to see what he would do next.

She sucked in a wild breath of pleasure when he bent low and bunched the hem of her dress into his hands and slowly slid it up her trembling legs.

When he stood up again and drew the dress away from her and tossed it aside, his gaze raked slowly over her nudity, feasting on it.

Yvonne's heart pounded within her chest so hard she was breathless, yet she stood her ground and waited for him to make the next move.

When he locked his thumbs over the waistband of his breechclout and slowly began lowering it past his hips, his man's root springing free, large from arousal, Yvonne gasped and felt the heat of desire rush to her cheeks.

Words were still not exchanged between them. Yvonne closed her eyes and held her head back, her shoulders sensually swaying when Silver Arrow began making love to her body with his tongue, lips, and fingers.

Her knees grew so weak with her building passion, they threatened to buckle beneath her.

She trembled from head to toe as his hot breath raced across her flesh, his lips leaving a trail of fire from her breasts, across her flat tummy, to that wet, hot valley between her thighs where she was pulsing with need of his caresses.

When the tip of his tongue touched her there, she cried out with pleasure.

And when his lips claimed her there, sucking and kissing, his tongue probing, she wove her fingers through his hair and moaned.

Knowing that she was growing dangerously close to the brink of rapture, Silver Arrow rose to his feet before her. He swept her into his arms and carried her to his bed, which she now knew she could call "theirs."

He laid her on the soft pelts that he had spread on the bed this morning. As he knelt over her, he smiled down at her. He kissed her fingertips as she slowly traced the outline of his lips.

His fingers reached up to entwine in her hair as he imprisoned her against him and shoved into her in one deep thrust. Hot and demanding, his mouth bore down on hers. His hands touched her all over, coaxing passion, answering hers with his own wild, sensuous pleasure.

His head began to reel as the pleasure spread within him. As his strokes deepened and his hips moved in maddening speed, he moaned with the spiraling need of fulfillment.

Again he kissed her.

He parted her lips and touched his tongue to hers.

He kissed her urgently . . . eagerly . . . hungrily.

Yvonne was overwhelmed with pleasure as he moved his body sinuously against hers and filled her so deeply. She felt her breath catch and hold.

She could hear how raggedly he breathed.

And by the way his body suddenly grew quiet, his cheek resting on one of her breasts, she knew that their moment was near. He always rested before taking that final plunge that would take them on wings to the heavens.

Oh, but she was so overwhelmed with a sweet, painful longing, a longing to once again be delirious with sensations that only he aroused in her.

Caught in his embrace, her lips now trembling against his, she moved with him as he once again shoved himself deeply inside her.

She rocked with him.

She clung to him.

She felt a sudden desire wash through her as their bodies trembled together, that surge of ecstasy finally claiming them.

Too soon it was over. They lay snuggled in one another's arms, their bodies fused as though one.

Tremors cascaded down Yvonne's back as Silver Arrow turned her beneath him again and worshiped her body with his lips and hands, his tongue sweeping over her, tasting her, teasing her.

"My love," she whispered.

The spinning sensations spread through her again, and she knew that their wedding night had only just begun!

Chapter Forty-two

It was spring. The country was enveloped in a soft opalescent haze. Wildflowers brightened the summer meadows.

Yvonne felt a great sense of peace as she stood with Silver Arrow and watched his people begin a long day of celebration.

Each spring the Ottawa gathered their cast-off garments that had been worn during the winter. They strung them up on a long pole while they held a festival and jubilee to the Great Spirit. The reason for doing this was so that the Great Spirit might look down from heaven and have compassion on his children. The tattered bundles of old garments were a sacrifice to the Creator *Kit-chi-manito*, the Great Spirit.

Having already raised their own discarded

clothes on the pole, Yvonne moved with Silver Arrow among the crowd. Some were dancing around the pole in time with the beating of the holy drum and sacred rattle. The instruments being used were very old and kept for that purpose only. They were accompanied by two musicians who sang the following words: "The Great Spirit will look down upon us. The Great Spirit will have mercy on us. . . ."

The song was repeated many times, and a response was heard from the company of dancers.

Heavy with child, Yvonne eased down on a raised platform placed there for the comfort of herself and her chieftain husband.

"Are you warm enough?" Silver Arrow asked as he drew the rabbit-fur robe more closely around her, hugging it to her thick bosom.

"Through and through," Yvonne said, smiling at him. She then gazed at the children who danced around the pole, Rustling Leaves and Stanley among them. "To think that at this time next year we will have our own child!

"I'm sorry I didn't get pregnant sooner," she said softly. "I know how you want children. I can see the want for them in your eyes when you watch children at play."

"I do love children and, *ae*, I will feel fulfilled when I hold my own child in my arms, but it makes no difference if we have children now or five winters into the future," he said, taking her hand and squeezing it affectionately. "To have you is to have the world. Who could truly want for more?" He leaned closer and whispered into her ear, "You do not know the selfish side of me, do you?"

"Selfish?" Yvonne said, raising an eyebrow. She laughed softly. "No, there is not one inch of you that is selfish. You are generous, sometimes, to a fault."

"Well, this husband *is* selfish," Silver Arrow said, nodding. "It is good to be with you, and only you, when the moon is high in the sky."

"Yes, it is wonderful to be alone at night, but I know how you look forward to hearing the breathing of our child," Yvonne said, snuggling close to him as he drew her near. "You can't fool me into believing that you are not looking forward to having this child."

Her thoughts shifted to the previous day, when she had discovered just how generous the Ottawa people were, as a whole. She was touched deeply to know they cared so much for her father.

Early in the morning, just past sunup, she had seen the Ottawa people loading one canoe after another with pelts, food, and large birchbark containers called *macoks*, which were filled with fifty to one hundred pounds of maple sugar.

She had questioned Silver Arrow about where they were going with such a huge amount of supplies. She had been stunned speechless to learn that they were taking these things to her father. Silver Arrow had told her that it was a way to thank her father for caring so much for their children. The schooling he'd provided had proved to be useful and right for them.

The Ottawa had taken the gifts by canoe to her

father and had told him that he would have the same sorts of gifts each spring that their children would be attending his school.

He had graciously accepted the gifts but had said that he would not keep them for himself. They would be used for the children. He would take everything to Grand Haven on the shores of Lake Michigan and trade them for more school supplies.

Yes, Yvonne thought, she had been blessed with a kind and caring stepfather, and now a husband. "I shall never forget the look on my father's face when your people arrived in the canoes with the gifts," she said, smiling at Silver Arrow. "It was such a surprise. A *wonderful* surprise. And it meant a lot to me. Their being so generous to my father was another way of showing that they accept me."

"Sometimes it is best not to tell you everything, just so I can see a look on your face that touches my very soul when a secret is revealed to you," Silver Arrow said, chuckling. "There is so much innocence about you. I do hope our children inherit your traits, for it is this innocence that makes you special."

"If we have a son, I want him to look and be just like you," Yvonne murmured.

Her thoughts shifted to someone else. She smiled at Silver Arrow. "Isn't it amazing that not only am I pregnant, but also Searching Heart?" she said, giggling. "Jake is walking around on a cloud and *Father*'s wife is also pregnant! Can you imagine his surprise when he discovered that he was going to be a father again at age fifty?"

"A baby will make your father feel like a young man again," Silver Arrow said. "And as for Jake? He has made a remarkable change from the man I knew when your family first moved to our land. I truly thought that we would come to blows. I saw him as a crude, thoughtless man who cared for nothing except himself. It seems your white man's Great Spirit has worked miracles on him."

"Are you and Jake still planning to go pigeon hunting tomorrow?" Yvonne asked, seeing Stanley's glasses fly from his nose as he swirled around in a fast Indian dance. She was relieved when he picked up the glasses and found them unbroken, slipping them back on his nose and laughingly returning to the dance.

For a moment Silver Arrow did not respond to Yvonne's question. Although he did feel that Jake had changed, tomorrow he would test him, to see if that change was true, imagined, or downright false.

Silver Arrow had a way of knowing whether Jake was a true friend or someone who waited for the opportunity to get what he had hungered for for so long—Silver Arrow's gold.

Yes, tomorrow, while Silver Arrow took Jake on the pretense of hunting pigeons, he would, in truth, be taking him elsewhere. Silver Arrow would know by sunset tomorrow what Jake's true feelings toward the Ottawa were.

"Silver Arrow?" Yvonne asked, questioning him with her eyes as he looked quickly over at her. "What were you just thinking about? Didn't you hear me ask you something?"

"Oh, yes, Jake," he said thickly. "You asked me about going pigeon hunting with your brother." He smiled ruefully. "*Ae*, at sunrise tomorrow we will go hunting, and by sunset tomorrow you will have roasted pigeon on our supper table."

Yvonne visibly shuddered. "I like the idea of you and Jake bonding while hunting," she said softly. "But the thought of eating those beautiful pigeons turns my stomach."

"It is no different from eating things like corn, asparagus, and all things found in our gardens," Silver Arrow said. "Everything lives and breathes, even the plants we eat each and every day for the benefit of keeping our bodies and minds strong."

"But . . . pigeons?" she said meekly, again grimacing.

"Yes, pigeons, and I assure you their taste will outdo the taste of skunk." He reached inside her rabbit-fur robe and slid his hand over the large swell of her tummy. "It is for the benefit of our child that you eat the various foods that our land supplies us with."

"Yes, our child," Yvonne said, enjoying the caresses as his fingers moved along the full breadth of her abdomen. She could feel the heat of his hand through the thin fabric of the buckskin dress that was stretched tight across her tummy. She knew that she did not have much longer to go before the child would be born.

"It kicked again," Silver Arrow said, his eyes beaming into Yvonne's. "And I can now feel the curve of either an elbow or a knee."

"It is so strange to feel the child moving around inside my tummy," Yvonne said, giggling when another kick made Silver Arrow start.

"Our son will be skilled at footraces and *Paw-baw-do-way*," Silver Arrow said, drawing his hand away.

"What is *Paw-baw-do-way*?" Yvonne asked, not questioning why he always referred to their unborn child as a son, for she had recently found herself doing the same thing. Surely she was carrying a boy, for how could they both be wrong?

"*Paw-baw-do-way* is the name for a ballgame that the Ottawa boys play," Silver Arrow said. "Today there will be such games, as well as wrestling, and arrow shooting. Other times the young braves will enter the forest and try to beat one another shooting the greatest number of squirrels in a day."

When Yvonne gave him an astonished look, showing her disapproval, Silver Arrow laughed. He placed an arm around her shoulder and drew her close to him. "And yes, our son will do all of those things," he said. "Even the contest of squirrel shooting. And you will be as proud as I am when he comes out the victor."

"Yes, I am sure that I will," she murmured, saying a soft prayer to herself that she would have a daughter first. She wanted more time to get used to the habits of the young braves!

The dancers continued swirling around the great pole that was heavily burdened with the cast-off garments. The instruments still played in cadence with the dancers. Songs lifted into the air again, the words repeated as before:

"The Great Spirit will look down upon us," they sang. "The Great Spirit will have mercy upon us."

The response was heard among another group of dancers, singing, "*We-ho-we-ho*."

"What are they saying?" Yvonne asked.

"*We-ho-we-ho* signifies 'so be it, so be it,' " Silver Arrow said, nodding his head in time with the music. "It is a good day for my people. This is the beginning of the jubilee in the springtime. And as last summer, there will be many dances during the summertime, such as strawberry dance, green corn dance, fire dance, and medicine dance."

"There are so many," Yvonne marveled.

"All these dances are considered as thanksgiving to the Almighty giver of all things," Silver Arrow said, then looked with alarm at Yvonne as she grabbed her abdomen and winced with pain.

"I believe I'd best go and lie down," she said, her face flushed as the pain grabbed her again.

"Is it time for the child?" Silver Arrow asked, glancing over at the group of women who had been assigned to assist Yvonne's birthing.

"I'm not sure, since I have never given birth before," Yvonne said, taking his hand as he helped her up from the platform. "Right now all I wish to do is lie down. We shall see how things progress."

Leaving the merriment behind, Yvonne walked beside Silver Arrow. By the time they reached the longhouse and she had removed the heavy rabbit-fur robe and she was stretched out on the bed on her side, all pains were gone.

"I believe they were false pains," she said as Silver Arrow stretched out beside her, to hold her. "Perhaps we had best return to the ceremony. I don't want to disappoint your people by keeping you with me."

"They know that my place is with you," Silver Arrow said, raising her dress, caressing her tummy. "Relax. Worry about nothing." He eased her eyelids closed with his fingers. "Sleep," he murmured. "I shall be beside you should you need me."

Feeling wonderfully at peace, Yvonne drifted off into a soft sleep.

Silver Arrow's mind shifted again to Jake and what he had planned for him tomorrow.

Yes, tomorrow would tell if Jake was friend . . . or foe!

Chapter Forty-three

Rifle in hand, Silver Arrow walked beside Jake. White Swan had assured him this morning that she was all right. She had encouraged the pigeon hunt with Jake. She saw this as a time when they could grow closer as brothers.

Silver Arrow smiled as he thought back to her expression when she had told him to go ahead and have this special day with Jake. He knew her feelings about killing the pigeons, yet she had accepted the hunt as necessary. She knew that it was not only for the sport of it, but to put food on the table for her family.

Although the Ottawa people all had planted gardens, it was always a daily struggle to make sure there was enough food for everyone.

With the arrival of the white man, and especially the greedy trappers, the animals dwindled yearly. It was a blessing when fresh meat was laid on the table, be it fowl or otherwise.

"I have never seen such a land as this," Jake said. "Yes, Missouri was beautiful, but look around us today."

Jake shifted his rifle to his left hand and used his right hand to gesture around him. "With the spring came such an abundance of wild strawberries, raspberries, and blackberries," he said. He inhaled deeply. "Ah, smell them. The ripe fruit perfumes the air."

"*Ae*, the Great Spirit has blessed us," Silver Arrow said, enjoying the view, the smells, the very presence of such lushness.

The wild pigeons and other birds filled the groves, warbling cheerfully and feasting on the wild fruits of nature.

Jake looked over at the river which wound across the land. "The fish in the Grand River are even more plentiful than I recall them being in the Mississippi or Missouri rivers in Missouri," he said, watching the play of catfish as they swam along the rocky bottom. They were so large, they looked like big stones slipping along in the current at the river bottom.

"They are so plentiful that as you lift up the anchor stone of your net in the morning, your net is loaded with delicious whitefish," Silver Arrow said, recalling the times he had gathered whitefish early in the mornings.

He would make sure that Jake saw the wonders of such a harvest, but only if Jake passed the test that Silver Arrow would put him through a short while from now. "Often as I look toward my nets I have seen the fins of the fish sticking out of the water in every direction," he added.

"I hope that we can soon share a fishing expedition," Jake said, flashing a wide smile over to Silver Arrow. He inhaled again. "Being out here is so invigorating."

"But I know that your heart and soul are back at my longhouse where your wife sits with mine, embroidering," Silver Arrow said, returning Jake's smile. "It is good that you have found a new life with Searching Heart. Unlike her scheming father, she is a good person."

"Yes, and I love her with every fiber of my being," Jake said. "I never want to disappoint my lady. She is the world to me."

"And soon there will be your child to also marvel over," Silver Arrow said, sighting a flock of pigeons overhead.

"Yes, as will you," Jake said. He followed Silver Arrow's gaze and watched the pigeons wheeling overhead. He was stunned to see their wide wingspan, apparently eighteen inches across. Never in his life had he seen such huge pigeons.

Now he understood why Silver Arrow had urged him to go hunting with him for pigeons. Always before, when Jake had seen pigeons in the groves, he had not thought to kill them. They had always reminded him of the pigeons that roosted on the buildings in Saint Louis.

But these were much different. They had surely flown in from some far-off place.

"Lord, Silver Arrow, the size of those pigeons!" he said, his eyes following the course of the birds as they fluttered and settled into the trees overhead. "They will make a good meal."

"They will make many meals," Silver Arrow said, chuckling at Jake's reaction.

At this moment, Silver Arrow found Jake almost as innocent in his behavior as his wife. He was impressed by Jake's change, his attitude in general toward life. He seemed to be a man of peace now, not one driven by dark demons.

But still Silver Arrow felt the need to test him, to see whether or not he was genuine, or all pretense.

"Shall we shoot them now?" Jake asked as he kept his eyes on the roosting pigeons.

"No, the guns were not brought to shoot the pigeons," Silver Arrow said matter-of-factly. "They are only for protection."

Jake turned to Silver Arrow. "Then how will we kill them?" he asked, his eyes wide.

"There are ways," Silver Arrow said, giving him a sidewise glance. "I came yesterday and prepared the place of their capture. Follow me. We will soon be there."

Jake nodded and trudged along beside Silver Arrow beneath low-hanging trees, past razor-sharp briars which he avoided, and on past flowering bushes heavy with blossoms. He was reminded of the flower garden that his sister had planted around the home she shared with Silver Arrow. Everything was in bloom now. Even her pregnancy had not stopped Yvonne from tending to her garden each day. Soon it would be as elaborate as the one she had left behind in Saint Louis, and at his father's cabin here in Michigan.

Jake smiled as he thought of his own cabin, which sat not far from his father's. Yvonne had taught Searching Heart the skills of gardening. There was now a massive flower garden in their yard, which had attracted many butterflies and bees to the flowers' nectar this spring.

"There it is," Silver Arrow said, gesturing with his rifle toward many holes dug in the ground. "Come. I will show you."

Jake went with him. "Why, that looks like corn," he said, staring at what he saw in the holes. He turned questioning eyes to Silver Arrow.

"Anticipating the arrival of the pigeons, I fermented the corn several weeks ago, then came yesterday and dug these holes in the ground," Silver Arrow explained. "Early this morning, while you were still beneath the covers with your wife, I came and scattered the fermented corn at the bottom of the pits."

Jake kneaded his clean-shaven chin thoughtfully as he studied the holes. "And soon the pigeons will be feasting on the corn," he said, nodding. He gave Silver Arrow a quick look. "And then we will shoot them?"

"No, we will not shoot them," Silver Arrow said, laughing softly. He took Jake to a thick stand of bushes and showed him the layer of nets that he had placed there early in the morning. "We will use these to catch them."

"Ah, I see," Jake said, nodding. "We will kill

them as we kill chickens."

"I am not sure how you kill your chickens before they are placed in a cooking pot, but yes, however you wish to ready them for your dinner table is how it will be done," Silver Arrow said, chuckling.

A loud whirring sound lifted their eyes suddenly heavenward. Silver Arrow smiled at the sight. Jake gasped.

"And so the true migration begins," Silver Arrow said, again seeing, as he usually did in early spring, how the birds blackened the sky in large numbers. Like those few earlier arrivals that he and Jake had seen moments ago, these pigeons had wingspans of no less than eighteen inches. Some were even larger.

Yes, there would be many delicious meals eaten from the hunting today!

"Watch now, Jake, as it all begins," Silver Arrow said, placing a hand on Jake's arm to urge him to hunker down as Silver Arrow was doing.

Jake watched the pigeons sweep from the sky and fly low over the ground a short distance, then turn in unison and settle down over the fermented corn.

"Shall we catch them now in the nets?" Jake whispered as he gave Silver Arrow a quick, questioning glance.

"No, it is too soon," Silver Arrow whispered back, smiling at Jake's anxiousness.

"But what if they fly away?" Jake questioned. "We may not get the same opportunity twice."

"They will not fly away," Silver Arrow said, his

eyes again on the pigeons as they fed on the corn. He could almost see their bellies grow as he watched them.

"I have never seen anything so hungry," Jake marveled as he, too, watched the pigeons.

"They have flown a long way," Silver Arrow said. He chuckled low. "They must have known such a feast awaited them here in Michigan."

"There are more than we will need, don't you think?" Jake asked.

Silver Arrow still watched the birds, knowing that the time was drawing nigh for the net to be thrown over them. "Many will be cooked and stored underground for future use," he said, his fingers creeping over to get a net. "Grab a net, Jake. It is almost time."

Jake did as he was instructed. His eyes widened when he saw the pigeons behaving strangely, their stomachs distended with the fermented corn. "Why, they look as though they are drunk," he said, watching them stagger around, bumping into each other.

"This is the only time I approve of anything akin to white man's firewater," Silver Arrow said, chuckling. "The birds are now too drunk and heavy to fly."

Jake threw his head back in a fitful laugh, which at normal times, when the birds were lucid, would startle them into a quick flight. But they only staggered even more fitfully, their wings seeming misplaced on their bodies as they tried to flap them.

"Now!" Silver Arrow shouted.

He dropped his rifle to the ground and rushed out with his net.

While Jake covered a huge number of pigeons with his net, Silver Arrow filled his own net and scooped them up and tied the ends of the net tightly together.

Sweating, his pulse racing from the exhilaration of catching so many pigeons, Jake tied his net securely, then stood back and stared at the many imprisoned pigeons.

"My wife will truly scold me now," Silver Arrow said, chuckling at the thought of how her eyes would widen as she stared at the netted pigeons.

"Yes, my sister truly loves birds and animals," Jake said, taking a handkerchief from his rear pocket and wiping the sweat from his brow. He smiled at Silver Arrow. "But she also loves to eat."

"Jake, for the time being we must tie our nets high in the trees to keep them safe from forest predators," Silver Arrow said as he lifted his filled net of pigeons as high as he could reach.

"Why?" Jake asked, raising an eyebrow. "Aren't we taking them on home to tend to?"

Silver Arrow tied his net into the trees, then turned slow eyes to Jake. "There is something else that I would like to do first," he said, his voice tight.

"What?" Jake asked.

"Tie your net high and come with me," Silver Arrow said, lifting his rifle in his hand. "I will explain as we walk."

Jake questioned him with a lingering stare, then went ahead and secured his net next to Silver

Arrow's. Ignoring the birds' screeches, he turned and lifted his gun into his hand.

For a while, nothing was said between Silver Arrow and Jake, then Silver Arrow slyly brought Jake into a conversation about the hidden gold. The test was near. Silver Arrow hoped that Jake would not disappoint him by making wrong choices.

He also hoped Jake would not do anything to bring disappointment into his sister's life. Yvonne was all trusting now where her brother was concerned.

Silver Arrow had not planned to tell Yvonne about this scheme in which he would finally know whether Jake had put the hunger for gold from his heart. But, not wanting her to think that he was doing things behind her back, especially anything that had to do with her family, he had finally confided in her just before he had left for the pigeon hunt.

She had been stunned to know that he still did not totally trust her brother. But she had not spoken against his idea, for she knew that her husband always did things from the heart. She had told him that if he needed this reassurance, she would not argue against it.

"You seem so mysterious, Silver Arrow," Jake said warily. "What is this all about?"

"You are now my brother, and brothers bring brothers into their confidence," Silver Arrow said thickly.

He gave Jake another guarded glance, then peered straight ahead again. His insides stiffened when he saw rocks laid in a pile a few footsteps away.

There lay the test.

Soon Silver Arrow would know.

"Yes, it would honor me to know that you trusted me enough to share things with me," Jake said, giving Silver Arrow a look of humility. "Thank you for thinking this much of me, Silver Arrow. It means a lot to know that you trust me. In the not so long ago past I gave no one cause to put faith in me."

"But you *have* changed, have you not, Jake?" Silver Arrow said, watching the rocks grow closer, his heart thumping with the need to get this behind him. With any luck he would walk away from those rocks with good thoughts and with a true bonding with his brother-in-law.

"Yes, I truly have," Jake said, nervously raking his fingers through his hair. "My trust in the Lord is the cause. He has led me back to the life that I forsook for too long."

"Does that mean that you no longer have any interest in my grandfather's gold?" Silver Arrow asked. His heart skipped a beat when he saw how quickly the mention of the gold made Jake stiffen.

Jake gazed at Silver Arrow intensely. "Gold?" he said, his voice drawn. "Why would you ask me about the gold?"

"Jake, it is common knowledge that at one time you wished to find my grandfather's gold," Silver Arrow said thickly. "Can you tell me that you have no more interest in it or the life that having it could bring you?"

Jake paled. "I admit, Silver Arrow, that earlier on, I would have done anything to get my hands on that gold," he said. "But my interests now lie in the ministry . . . not in worldly possessions."

"That is good to know," Silver Arrow said, nodding toward the pile of rocks as they came to them. "Jake, beneath those rocks lies my grandfather's chest of gold. No one but me knows what the rocks mean. Now you also know."

Jake's heart almost leapt into his throat.

He dropped his rifle. He gasped. His fingers trembled.

"The gold is here?" he asked, staring down at the rocks, unable to believe that he finally knew where it was buried.

"The very spot that was dug by my grandfather before he died," Silver Arrow said, closely watching Jake. He was surprised when Jake looked at it a moment longer, then picked his rifle up from the ground, and turned and walked away.

"Jake?" Silver Arrow said, falling into step beside him. "Why do you walk away?"

Jake turned somber eyes to Silver Arrow. "I care nothing about the gold or where it is buried," he said. "But I do thank you for trusting me enough to show me." He swallowed hard. "Let's go get our pigeons and go home, Silver Arrow. What awaits me there is worth more to me than any gold on this entire earth."

Silver Arrow smiled widely. "It is good to know where your values lie," he said, nodding.

"I was wrong ever to scheme to get the gold from you," Jake said, turning an apologetic gaze

421

Silver Arrow's way. "I hope you will forget that side of me. I never want to look back to what I was before I came to my senses."

Suddenly River Rat stepped out in front of them, a shotgun leveled at first Silver Arrow, then Jake. "Drop your firearms or get a hole shot clean through your guts," he snarled.

He spat a long stream of chewing tobacco from the corner of his mouth. His whiskers were so thick he was hardly recognizable. "If you try anything, I'll at least get one shot off," he warned. River Rat looked from one to the other, his eyes squinting. "Now which one of you wants to die while the other tries to be a hero?" he asked, cackling.

"I thought you were long gone from here," Jake said, tossing his rifle aside. "Where have you been hiding yourself? In a cave with skunks? You stink worse than a skunk. You surely aren't as intelligent, or you'd know that you can't get away with what you're trying today."

"Shut your mouth," River Rat squeezed out between clenched, yellow teeth. "You're a traitor. You chickened out on first one deal and then another with me."

River Rat ran his gaze slowly over Jake. "Look at you dressed in fine, clean clothes, with your face clean-shaven," he said mockingly. "You're a preacher boy now, huh? What do you give sermons about? About how you'd like to get your hands on your Indian brother-in-law's gold but just don't know how?"

"My religion is true, as are my feelings for Silver

Arrow," Jake said as Silver Arrow stood quietly by, assessing the situation.

River Rat had been too busy berating Jake to notice that Silver Arrow had not yet dropped his rifle.

He was waiting for the perfect moment.

"Now tell the truth, Jake," River Rat said. "You were just stringing the Injun along until you got a chance to find where the gold was hidden."

He looked past Jake's shoulder at the pile of rocks. "Seems your patience worked, my friend," he said, again cackling. "He finally trusted you enough to show you, didn't he?"

River Rat shifted slow eyes to Silver Arrow, then took an unsteady step backwards when he saw that Silver Arrow still held his rifle. "Drop that damn gun, you savage," River Rat said, placing his finger on the trigger of his shotgun. "Do it or die!"

Silver Arrow had waited too long, yet the right moment had not offered itself to shoot the filthy white man. Even while dying, River Rat might be able to get off a spattering of gunfire which could not only reach one of them, but both. Shotguns were lethal in how far out their spray of pellets reached.

His jaw tight, Silver Arrow dropped his rifle to the ground.

"That ain't guarantee enough for me," River Rat snarled. "Both of you kick away your firearms."

After the rifles were kicked aside, River Rat's look of confidence strengthened. "Aw, Jake, how foolish it was of you to double-cross me," he hissed out. "You waited for Silver Arrow to trust you enough to show you the burial place of the gold and planned to come back and get it when he wasn't around. Then what of me? Your partner-in-crime? Weren't you going to share it with me?"

"I don't want the gold," Jake said somberly. "I was wrong ever to want it. It was an even bigger mistake to ever side with the likes of you."

"But you did," River Rat said, spitting over his shoulder again. He glared at Silver Arrow. "I have waited and watched for you to lead me to the damn burial spot of the gold. I knew that you'd have to go and check on it from time to time. I settled in close to your village and I've waited patiently for this day. It looks as though my waiting paid off."

He frowned from Jake to Silver Arrow. "Before I dig up the gold, I've got something more important to do," he said dryly. "I can't afford to leave you two alive or my name would soon be mud. Sorry, gents, but you've got to die."

A voice rang out from the trees behind River Rat. "I don't think so, River Rat."

Silver Arrow turned startled eyes toward the deep shadows of the trees, gasping to have heard the voice of his wife speaking from their depths.

Jake stared as Yvonne stepped from the trees, her rifle leveled at River Rat's back. "Sis, Lord . . . sis . . ." he stammered out, paling at the thought of her being there in the eye of danger, and only a few hours away from delivering her first child.

424

"White Swan," Silver Arrow said. "You shouldn't—"

His words were interrupted when River Rat made a quick turn on his heel and aimed at Yvonne.

Gunfire splintered the air.

Thinking his wife had been shot, Silver Arrow felt his whole lifetime flash before his eyes.

It had all happened so quickly, he had no chance to intervene.

First his woman was not there, then she was, and then River Rat had shot at her!

When River Rat dropped his shotgun and crumpled to the ground, dead, Silver Arrow came out of his frozen state and ran to Yvonne.

He took her firearm and dropped it to the ground, then caught her as her knees buckled beneath her.

"The child!" she cried, grabbing at her stomach, groaning. "It is time! The excitement has brought the pains on as quickly as a sneeze!"

Silver Arrow lifted Yvonne into his arms.

"What can I do?" Jake asked, his pulse racing at the sight of his sister so pale and in excruciating pain as she clutched her abdomen. He only scarcely gave a glance River Rat's way. The rat was dead, and along with him any further threat to him and his family.

All that was important now was to help his sister in her time of childbirthing. He knew that there was not enough time to return to the village to get the aid of the women who had been chosen for this project.

"We will take her to the river," Silver Arrow shouted over his shoulder at Jake. "I can see it through the trees. Go ahead of me, Jake. Make a place comfortable for your sister. She is going to have the child. We have been chosen by the higher power in the heavens to be the ones to assist her!"

Everything happened quickly. Jake found a soft bed of moss not far from the riverbank. He fell to his knees and cleared it of debris.

After Yvonne was comfortably settled on the moss and her legs were widely spread, her dress hiked up past her tummy, in only a matter of moments the child showed its head to the world.

Yvonne groaned and gave one last push, and the rest of the baby shoved its way free and into Silver Arrow's waiting hands.

Her hair wet from perspiration, Yvonne leaned on an elbow and looked at the baby. Tears flowed from her eyes when the child proved the power of its lungs in a lusty cry.

Tears swept down Jake's cheeks as he took the knife from Silver Arrow's sheath and cut the umbilical cord. Then, choked up with emotion, he stood back as Silver Arrow laid the child in Yvonne's waiting arms.

"A son," Yvonne murmured, her eyes discovering the tiny fingers, toes, nose, and perfectly shaped lips. She gave Silver Arrow a smile of joy after seeing the color of her son's skin. It matched his father's. He would grow up to be the image of his chieftain father. He, himself, would one day be a great Ottawa chief!

"He is as handsome as my husband," Yvonne murmured. She closed her eyes in ecstasy as Silver Arrow knelt over her and cradled both her and the baby within his powerful arms.

"Black Crow," she whispered into Silver Arrow's ear. He had now shared all his secrets with her, about his special powers, about *everything*. It seemed appropriate that their child would be named after the crow that had brought so much into her life.

"Can we name our son Black Crow?" she whispered.

"Whatever you wish," Silver Arrow said, leaning away from her. He touched her delicately on the cheek. "My wife who is now a mother, I am ever so proud."

Jake came and knelt beside Yvonne. "He is beautiful," he said, marveling over the child. "How proud I am to be this child's uncle."

Then Silver Arrow frowned down at Yvonne. "I do not wish to spoil the moment by speaking about things that are unpleasant, but, White Swan, why did you follow us? What made you come with your firearm? Why . . . did . . . you come alone?"

Yvonne's eyes lowered. She swallowed hard. How could she tell Jake that she had not trusted him completely? That she feared that a part of him still wanted the gold to be his? That she feared that he might make an unwise choice when he saw the hiding place of the gold, knowing that its value could buy him more things on this earth than he would ever see under his present circumstances?

Preachers made scarcely any money. Yvonne's father had inherited most of his wealth, which had made his life easier. But Jake was starting from scratch.

What he earned was what he would have.

She looked up at Jake. "I'm sorry," she murmured. "I hate to tell you, but I still did not trust you as much as Silver Arrow trusted you. I knew to what lengths you had gone earlier to find ways to have the gold. How was I to know that you had changed so much? When faced with the gold, I feared you would not be able to turn away from it. I . . . feared . . . for my husband's life."

She turned slow eyes to Silver Arrow. "Darling, that's why I came," she murmured. "And I felt that I had no choice but to come alone. I did not want anyone to know my doubts about my brother. I was ashamed to be doubting him. If I was wrong, I could turn back and return to my home, and no one would be the wiser. That was the chance I took by coming while heavy with child."

She turned her eyes in the direction where River Rat lay. "I never even thought about someone else following you," she said, her voice breaking. "Nor did I think about anyone else putting you in danger." She swallowed hard. "Thank the Lord for having led me here today. If not, you both . . ."

Her words faded away. She did not want to speak her thoughts; of her fear that she could have lost her husband. And her brother. It was enough to know that she had been in time to save them both.

Silver Arrow was stunned by her explanation. But he understood, for her doubts had matched his. And he understood that it took a woman of much courage to take off, alone, to protect the honor of one man, and perhaps the life of another.

He would not allow himself to think of the foolish side of his wife, in that she was very pregnant and had put herself and the child in danger the moment she left the village alone.

It had all turned out for the best. She had not only saved two lives, she had also given birth to a beautiful son.

"How did you get here?" Silver Arrow asked, looking around for her means of transportation. She was not able to ride a horse, and he had not heard the sound of a horse and buggy while he had been walking with Jake to the harvest of pigeons.

"I came a ways in my horse and buggy, then I walked the rest of the way," Yvonne said, placing a gentle hand on her husband's cheek. "The walk did me good. It was just the apprehension that was not good for me."

She turned to Jake. "You've been so quiet since you heard about my mistrusting you," she murmured. "What can I say, Jake? Please forgive me for misjudging you."

Jake took her hand and squeezed it fondly. "Sis, I deserved what you did today," he said humbly. "That's what I get for being a scoundrel for so long. Can you forgive *me* for being the cause of placing you in danger today?"

"I am so glad that I came," Yvonne said, swallowing hard when she thought of that moment when she had seen River Rat holding her brother and husband at bay with his shotgun. She would have seen him earlier but she had stopped to rest beneath a tree.

Black Crow began crying. Yvonne turned smiling eyes down at him. "He's hungry, but he is also in dire need of a bath," she said, laughing softly.

Silver Arrow took Black Crow from Yvonne. He walked up the riverbank until he came to a sun-drenched place in the water. He knelt down and held the child with one hand, while with his other he softly splashed him clean.

"Son of mine, you have a very special mother," he said, still in awe of his wife's bravery. He already knew how he was going to thank her for saving his life. He owed her a lifetime of loving!

Silver Arrow smiled when he thought back to earlier in the day when he had carefully chosen stones from the river to falsify the burial place of his grandfather's gold. He had purposely placed them in a circle to make it look like a legitimately marked place, whereas, in truth, nothing lay in the ground beneath them.

Silver Arrow did not know where the gold was buried!

His grandfather had moved the gold often, and before showing Silver Arrow its last burial spot, he had passed away.

His grandfather had taken the whereabouts of

the hiding place to his grave with him.

Silver Arrow had never told anyone he did not know where the gold was buried. People thinking he knew gave him power over them. To remain a great chief, he needed not only his mystical powers, but worldly powers, as well.

Yes, he had led Jake to a false burial place today, and also River Rat, and so he would probably have to falsify such a burial place again in the future when someone else wrongly hungered for the gold.

Sometimes a lie was necessary, especially when dealing with men whose lives and hearts were ruled by greed.

Chapter Forty-four

It's later than either of us think.
Come and take the sweetest drink.
Hold me tight inside your heart . . .
Pray the "Fates" don't keep us apart.
Come, my woman, and cling to me.
I care not what the world may see.
Your heart will be warmed by the sun . . .
My arms will hold you when day is done.
Put your soft hand inside of mine,
Together we'll march forward into time.
Precious love, I give to you,
I promise you skies will be forever blue.
So come to me, woman, in soft moonlight,
Our hearts will beat, as wild birds in flight.
I will hold you to my heart . . .
Whispering my confession for us to never part.

—Harri Lucas Garnett

Thanksgiving day was drawing nigh. Yvonne had preserved apples, potatoes, cabbage, and carrots for the winter. They were stored in pits dug in the ground, the bottom of the hole covered with wood planking, the planking then covered with straw. Fish and meat had been preserved by drying, the meat cleaned and placed over a low heat to remove much of the moisture.

And Yvonne had not neglected her flower garden. Many of her flowers had been dried for use during the long winter months. Some were used for a gentle fragrance in the house. Others were used in her bath, to sweeten her skin.

"I'm so glad to be able to have everyone here Thanksgiving day," Yvonne murmured as she nestled closer to Silver Arrow in their bed. She relished the feel of the rabbit-fur blanket on which they were lying, as well as the one Silver Arrow had made for their cover. The fire sent a golden glow through the bedroom door.

"It will be quite a chore to do so much cooking," Silver Arrow said, stroking her cheek with a thumb. He slipped a long, lean leg over hers as he turned on his side to face her, the feel of her silken nakedness against his flesh making his heart race with passion.

"There will be your father, his wife, your new sister Sandra, your brother Stanley," he said. "Also there will be Jake and Searching Heart and their daughter Flying Star. Also you have invited my friend Four Horns and his wife Dancing Eyes, who is too heavy with child to benefit you much in the kitchen."

"And then there is our *own* family," Yvonne said, snuggling closer to him, shivering with delight as the warmth of his naked flesh blended wonderfully into hers. "Rustling Leaves, Black Crow, you . . . me . . ."

He framed her face between his hands and drew her lips to his and kissed her, then moved his lips away and whispered to her. "Tonight it is only you . . . only I. Baby Black Crow is asleep in his crib out by the fire. Rustling Leaves sleeps soundly overhead in the loft."

He flicked his tongue over the thick nub of her nipple. He could taste a trace of milk that only moments ago his son had fed upon.

"There is no reason why we cannot make love the long night through," he said huskily.

"Well, perhaps there is one reason we may be disturbed a time or two," Yvonne said, sighing as he rolled above her and nudged her thighs apart, his hot and heavy manhood already probing her moist valley. "Although Black Crow seemed content enough, one can never be sure that he won't awaken with hunger pangs again."

"And I will willingly share you and your breasts again tonight with our son," Silver Arrow said, laughing softly. "But for now you are mine. I want you. I hope your need for me is as fierce as mine is for you."

"Always and forever," Yvonne said, desire raging and washing over her as he shoved his throbbing hardness within her. Her hips responded to the hunger of his body as she thrust her pelvis toward him.

Yvonne closed her eyes as he kissed her nose, eyes and every place that his lips could reach. His hands stroked her woman's center, the sureness of his caress leaving her breathless.

His hand moved slowly up her body, making her skin quiver each place he touched anew. When his lips found the generous swell of one of her breasts, they fastened again on the soft, pink nub, sucking it hard.

The pleasure spreading through Yvonne like wildfire, she arched toward him.

Feeling her urgency in how she ground herself against him, Silver Arrow slipped his hands down her body and splayed them beneath her, across her soft buttocks.

With a groan he pulled her against him, his manhood delving more deeply.

In a wild, dizzying rhythm, he plunged over and over again into her pulsing cleft.

He showered her with heated kisses. His mouth brushed her cheeks and ears. He tenderly kissed her eyelids.

Then he kissed her long and deep, first moving slowly and deliberately within her, then powerfully and more hungrily.

Breathless with the building passion, Silver Arrow whispered Yvonne's name against her throat.

Her fingernails raked lightly down his spine. His hands stroked her every vulnerable, sensitive place.

She wove her fingers through his hair and led his mouth again to her breast, sobbing with pleasure as his tongue flicked, licked, and nipped at her soft flesh.

She then pulled his head up and their lips met in a frenzy of kisses, their bodies joined, her legs wrapped around his waist to assure their utter closeness.

She could feel the passion growing, nearing the bursting point. "I adore you," she whispered against his lips. "My love . . . my love . . ."

Again he kissed her with raw passion, his mouth bearing down hard upon her lips, his mouth hot and demanding.

He surrounded her with his strong arms, crushing her against him so hard she gasped.

Her gasps became long, soft whimpers when his hips thrust hard and he pressed endlessly deeper.

And then Silver Arrow paused. He leaned over her with burning eyes, his palms moving soothingly and seductively over her silken body.

With fierceness he held her close again and took her mouth by storm, a savagery in his kiss that she had never felt before.

She sucked in a wild breath of pleasure. She trembled with readiness as he drove into her, more swiftly . . . more surely.

Silver Arrow felt the flames of his passion spreading within him like wildfire. He kissed her hungrily. He groaned against her lips.

Then he sighed and melted inside when he was totally consumed in the flames of their desire, the release filling him with great bursts of energy, his very soul aglow with the golden light of their shared passion.

Yvonne clung to him as the splendid joy of their passion swam through her in wondrous spirals of golden light, filling her very soul with ecstasy.

Her insides were blazing . . . searing.

Her senses were spinning as she gave herself up to the total rapture of their togetherness.

Afterwards, Silver Arrow still anchored her fiercely against him. "My woman, my wife," he said in a thick, husky groan against her lips.

"My wonderful, adorable husband," Yvonne whispered as his hand ran sensually from her thigh, to her hip, to her breast.

She gazed into his passion-heavy eyes. "Do you know just how happy you have made me?" she murmured, brushing locks of his midnight black hair back from his face.

"*Ae*, I knew from the moment I first saw you that you were, even then, *my* happiness," he said, his eyes darkening even more with the depth of his emotion.

Desire gripped Yvonne, and she felt a tremor deep within her when once again he kissed her, her breasts pulsing warmly beneath his fingers.

When he entered her again and began his rhythmic strokes, she floated away into memories of the past, when her love for him was new, and somewhat fearful.

She had quickly learned that Silver Arrow was not only a powerful Ottawa leader of his people. He was also a man of intrigue; a man of mystical powers. She loved both qualities about him, and even more. She loved everything about him.

She smiled when she thought back to the mystery surrounding the large crow that she had grown to equate with Silver Arrow, even before she had become to realize the full strength of her husband's powers.

She only occasionally saw the crow now, and only in her midnight dreams, where reality and imagination fused into something beautiful and right.

Now, while making sweet love, she clung to his rock hardness and let the exquisite pleasure spread through her. She looked forward to a lifetime of sharing savage passions with this wonderful man, her Ottawa chieftain husband!

Dear Reader:

I hope you have enjoyed reading *Savage Passions*. To continue my *Savage Series*, written exclusively for Leisure Books, in which it is my endeavor to write about every major Indian tribe in America, my next book will be *Savage Shadows*, about the Comanche Indians. This book will be filled with much excitement, adventure, romance, and mystery. I hope you will buy *Savage Shadows* and enjoy it. It will be in the stores six months from the release date of *Savage Passions*.

I love to hear from my readers. For my newsletter and information about The Cassie Edwards International Fan Club, please send a legal-size, self-addressed stamped envelope to me at R#3, Box 60, Mattoon, IL 61938.

Warmly,
CASSIE EDWARDS

SAVAGE SPIRIT

CASSIE EDWARDS

**Winner of the *Romantic Times*
Lifetime Achievement Award for Best Indian Series!**

Life in the Arizona Territory has prepared Alicia Cline to expect the unexpected. Brash and reckless, she dares to take on renegades and bandidos. But the warm caresses and soft words of an Apache chieftain threaten her vulnerable heart more than any burning lance.

Chief Cloud Eagle has tamed the wild beasts of his land, yet one glimpse of Alicia makes him a slave to desire. Her snow-white skin makes him tremble with longing; her flame-red hair sets his senses ablaze. Cloud Eagle wants nothing more than to lie with her in his tepee, nothing less than to lose himself in her unending beauty. But to claim Alicia, the mighty warrior will first have to capture her bold savage spirit.

_3639-8 $4.99 US/$5.99 CAN

TWO BESTSELLING AUTHORS— TWO SPELLBINDING CONTEMPORARY ROMANCES!

Island Rapture by Cassie Edwards. Television talk-show host Lynn Stafford cannot forgive Eliot Smith for high-handedly replacing her former partner and longtime friend—nor can she deny the intense physical attraction that springs up between them at their very first meeting. When Lynn and Eliot are sent to a remote tropical island to film some newly discovered ruins, Lynn finds that the heat of the jungle arouses an answering heat in her blood. But will the passion she and Eliot share in their tropical paradise survive their return to civilization?

_51943-7 $4.99 US/$5.99 CAN

Addy Starr by Ruth Ryan Langan. An orphaned country girl, Addy fights her way to the top until she is the owner of the richest casino in Reno, Nevada. But all the wealth and notoriety in the world can't replace the yearning beauty's passion for the men who will change her life forever. Caught up in a world full of danger and deception, Addy has to rely on her determination and wits to choose the one man who will help uncover the secrets of her past—and share a love that will last a lifetime.

_51989-5 $4.99 US/$5.99 CAN

Dorchester Publishing Co., Inc.
65 Commerce Road
Stamford, CT 06902

Please add $1.75 for shipping and handling for the first book and $.50 for each book thereafter. NY, NYC, PA and CT residents, please add appropriate sales tax. No cash, stamps, or C.O.D.s! All orders shipped within 6 weeks via postal service book rate. Canadian orders require $2.00 extra postage and must be paid in U.S. dollars through a U.S. banking facility.

Name _____

Address _____

City _____ State _____ Zip _____

I have enclosed $_____ in payment for the checked book(s).

Payment <u>must</u> accompany all orders.☐ Please send a free catalog.

Sheik's Promise

CAROLE HOWEY

Bestselling Author Of *Sweet Chance*

Allyn Cameron has never been accused of being a Southern belle. Whether running her own saloon or competing in the Rapids City steeplechase, the brazen beauty knows the thrill of victory and banks on winning. No man will take anything she possesses—not her business, not her horse, and especially not her virtue—without the fight of his life.

An expert on horseflesh and women, Joshua Manners desires only the best in both. Sent to buy Allyn's one-of-a-kind colt, he makes it his mission to tame the thoroughbred's owner. But his efforts to win Allyn for his personal stable fail miserably when she ropes, corrals, and brands him with her scorching passion.

_51938-0 $4.99 US/$5.99 CAN

Dorchester Publishing Co., Inc.
65 Commerce Road
Stamford, CT 06902

Please add $1.75 for shipping and handling for the first book and $.50 for each book thereafter. NY, NYC, PA and CT residents, please add appropriate sales tax. No cash, stamps, or C.O.D.s. All orders shipped within 6 weeks via postal service book rate. Canadian orders require $2.00 extra postage and must be paid in U.S. dollars through a U.S. banking facility.

Name _____

Address _____

City _____ State _____ Zip _____

I have enclosed $_____ in payment for the checked book(s).
Payment <u>must</u> accompany all orders. □ Please send a free catalog.

Futuristic Romance

NANCY CANE

FOR LOVE AND HONOR

FLORA SPEER

Bestselling Author Of *Love Just In Time*

Falsely accused of murder, Sir Alain vows to move heaven and earth to clear his name and claim the sweet rose named Joanna. But in a world of deception and intrigue, the virile knight faces enemies who will do anything to thwart his quest of the heart.

From the sceptered isle of England to the sun-drenched shores of Sicily, the star-crossed lovers will weather a winter of discontent. And before they can share a glorious summer of passion, they will have to risk their reputations, their happiness, and their lives for love and honor.

__3816-1 $4.99 US/$5.99 CAN

LAKOTA RENEGADE

MADELINE BAKER

"Madeline Baker's Indian romances should not be missed!"
                                                    —*Romantic Times*

Handy with six-guns and fists, Creed Maddigan likes his women hot and ready. But the rugged half-breed isn't used to innocent girls like Jassy McCloud who curtsy and make ginger snaps. Then Creed is falsely jailed for a crime he didn't commit, and he can think of nothing besides escaping to savor Jassy's sweet love.

Alone on the Colorado frontier, Jassy can either work as a fancy lady or hope to find a husband. But what is she to do when the only man she hopes to marry is a wanted renegade? For Jassy, the decision is simple: She'll take Creed for better or worse, even if she has to spend the rest of her days dodging bounty hunters and bullets.

__3832-3 $5.99 US/$7.99 CAN

Dorchester Publishing Co., Inc.
65 Commerce Road
Stamford, CT 06902

Please add $1.75 for shipping and handling for the first book and $.50 for each book thereafter. NY, NYC, PA and CT residents, please add appropriate sales tax. No cash, stamps, or C.O.D.s. All orders shipped within 6 weeks via postal service book rate. Canadian orders require $2.00 extra postage and must be paid in U.S. dollars through a U.S. banking facility.

Name _____

Address _____

City _____ State _____ Zip _____

I have enclosed $_____in payment for the checked book(s). Payment <u>must</u> accompany all orders.☐ Please send a free catalog.

Hunters of the Ice Age
Theresa Scott — Broken Promise

BESTSELLING AUTHOR OF *DARK RENEGADE*

Among the tribes warring at the dawn of time, the Jaguars are the mightiest, and the hunter called Falcon is feared like no other. Once headman of his clan, he has suffered a great loss that turns him against man and the Great Spirit. But in a world both deadly and treacherous, a mere woman will teach Falcon that he cannot live by brute strength alone.

Her people destroyed, her promised husband enslaved, Star finds herself at Falcon's mercy. And even though she is separated from everything she loves, the tall, proud Badger woman will not give up hope. With courage and cunning, the beautiful maiden will survive in a rugged new land, win the heart of her captor, and make a glorious future from the shell of a broken promise.

__3723-8   **$4.99 US/$5.99 CAN**